# THE SELKIE QUEEN

## A SEAL ISLAND NOVEL, BOOK FOUR

## SOPHIE MOSS

*For my readers*

# CHAPTER ONE

Grace Callahan stood at the end of the pier, waiting to board the passenger ferry that would carry her to Seal Island. Seagulls cried, circling the harbor. The scent of peat smoke and fried fish drifted down from the village, mingling with the salty gusts blowing in from the ocean. Overhead, the clouds shifted. Sunlight broke through, bathing the harbor in a wash of light. Then the clouds shifted again, and everything faded to gray.

It was the same dance of light and dark, of dull and bright, that had captivated her on the four-hour drive up the coast. In Connemara, she'd passed one charming fishing village after another. Herds of sheep had roamed the stretches of farmland between each village. Winding stone walls had threaded the landscape like ancient stitches of patchwork. And glittering lakes had beckoned in the distance.

It had almost been enough to make her forget the real reason she'd come here. But she wasn't here on vacation. She was here to find answers.

She showed her ticket to the teenage crew member.

He gave it a glance and waved her aboard. "It's going to be a choppy crossing."

Grace nodded, scanning the white caps frothing over the surface of the bay. She knew the full force of that wind wouldn't hit them until they left the sheltered inlet. Nearly six miles of open ocean lay between them and their destination—one of Ireland's most isolated islands.

But it wasn't the crossing that worried her. It was what she might find on the other side.

She followed the other two passengers across the thin walkway as the crew members loaded the rest of the provisions on board. Cartons of milk, butter, and eggs. Bags of potatoes. Loaves of bread. She took in their stoic expressions and the quiet efficiency with which they loaded the supplies onto the ferry. The captain, an elderly man with a creased and weathered face, puffed on a cigarette as he readied the lines.

She thought of the man she was meeting on the island later. In his book jacket photo, Liam O'Sullivan looked professional, studious, and clean-cut, a stark contrast to the three men before her. But she knew that appearances could be deceiving. Ten years of working as an investigative reporter had taught her that.

She watched the crew members board. The engine churned as they slid the walkway onto the deck and clicked the gate shut behind them. A moment later, they were pulling away from the pier. She walked to the edge of the deck and rested her hands on the cold metal railing. The wind blew her hair back from her face. When her phone buzzed, she fought the urge to reach for it. It had been buzzing nonstop since she'd stepped off the plane.

It wasn't like her to let a call go to voicemail or to leave a text message unanswered. There'd been eighty-three new emails in her inbox last time she'd checked. It didn't matter that she'd activated her "out of office" auto-response. No one believed her. And how could she blame them? She'd never really been "out of the office" before. In the past, whenever she'd taken time off, she'd continued to respond to messages. She'd stayed in touch in case anyone needed her. She'd agreed, more than once, to cut a vacation short to break a story.

But some things were more important than work.

Like finding your long-lost mother who'd disappeared over twenty years ago.

Lifting her gaze to the rolling hills in the distance, Grace watched a shadow streak across the moss. She knew it was possible that this search would confirm her worst fears—that her mother had abandoned her.

But what if she hadn't? What if there was another explanation?

Grace had been ten when her mother had disappeared. The police had stopped searching for answers long ago, but she'd never given up. And after twenty-three years, she'd finally gotten her first clue.

A clue that had led her here.

She didn't know what it meant or where this search would lead her next. But she wasn't leaving the island until she found some answers.

Sea spray shot up, splashing over the railing. The other two passengers retreated to the warmth of the cabin. She considered joining them, then decided against it. It had been a while since she'd seen the ocean from the deck of a boat. She missed the drama of it, the vastness of it. Turning her face into the wind, she let her legs adjust to the rhythm of the water. The dips and swells grew more erratic as they motored farther away from land.

"You've a steady pair of sea legs," a gravelly voice said from behind her.

She turned, found the captain watching her from the door of the cabin. One of his crew members had taken the wheel. "I grew up on boats. My father's a waterman."

"Is he, now?"

Grace nodded. "He works on the Chesapeake Bay, in Maryland. Have you heard of it?"

"Ah, yes. I've heard of it. He's a crabber, then?"

"Used to be. He and my brother run an oyster farm now."

The captain nodded. "We've a few of those around here."

"I noticed some traps in the back." Grace gestured to a stack of wire cages behind her. "What are you trying to catch with them?"

"Lobsters. Season ended in September, though. You just missed it."

"That's a shame."

"'Tis," the captain said. "They make a lobster pie at the pub that'll bring tears to your eyes."

"Well, now you're just making me feel bad."

The captain laughed.

"I'm Grace." She walked over and held out her hand.

"Finn." He wrapped a leathery hand around hers. "Is this your first time visiting the island?"

Grace nodded. "First time in Ireland, too."

"Is that so?" Finn's pale blue eyes twinkled. "Céad míle fáilte."

Grace smiled, recognizing the Irish phrase for a hundred thousand welcomes. "Thank you."

"What have you seen so far on your travels, Grace?"

"Just parts of the coast on the ride up from the airport."

"You flew in this morning?"

"I did."

Finn regarded her curiously. "Most people take their time making their way up the coast. Book a night in Galway or Clifden, maybe tour a castle or two. I hope you saved time for that on the way back."

"Maybe." Grace said. "We'll see."

"How long will you be with us?"

"A couple of nights, at least. My plans are flexible."

"Are they, now?"

"I might fall in love with the island and never want to leave."

Finn laughed. "You wouldn't be the first person that's happened to."

No, Grace thought, she wouldn't. She'd done her research before coming here. She always did her research. Pressing up on her toes, she peered through the windshield overlooking the bow, not wanting to miss the first glimpse of the island as it rose out of the sea. But there was nothing but water for miles.

"So, tell me, Grace." Finn dipped his hands into his pockets. "It's a bit late in the season for tourists. And you've traveled quite a ways to get here. What brings you to our island?"

Grace reached into her bag and pulled out Liam's book. In the past two weeks, she'd read it three times, cover to cover. The spine was cracked. Half the pages were dog-eared. And the margins were covered in handwritten notes. It looked like she'd owned it for years.

"Ah, our esteemed professor," Finn said proudly.

Grace nodded. "I'm meeting with him this afternoon."

"So, it's the legend, then?"

"Isn't that what most people come for?"

"Most," Finn said, "but not all." He leaned a shoulder against the doorframe. "There're other islands in these parts with legends, ones that are easier to get to."

True, Grace thought, but it was *this* island, *this* legend that interested her the most. According to Liam's book, the seals who lived on this island were enchanted. When the tide was high and the moon was full, these seals—or selkies—could shed their skin and transform into beautiful women.

Two hundred years ago, a selkie had come ashore, and a fisherman had stolen her pelt. He'd forced her to marry him and trapped her in his home. Unable to return to the sea without her pelt, the selkie had gone mad with grief. After years of isolation and abuse, cut off from everything and everyone she'd ever loved, she'd made the tragic decision to end her life.

That decision had cursed her spirit to remain forever trapped on the island. But before she'd committed the act, she'd given her only child to the seals to protect. The seals had carried that child far away from the island to safety. According to the legend, the only way to break the curse was for that child—or a descendant of that child—to come back to the island, reclaim the stolen pelt, and return it to its rightful owner.

That, alone, would have been enough to catch Grace's attention. But rumor had it that this particular curse had actually *been* broken by an American woman who'd traveled to Seal Island eight years ago. That woman, Tara O'Sullivan, still lived on the island. And Grace was as eager to speak with her as she was with Liam.

Not that she believed in curses. Or legends.

Or magic, for that matter.

Regardless, she wanted to speak with them both. Because one of them might hold a clue—the next piece in a puzzle she'd been waiting over twenty years to solve.

Grace slipped the book into her bag, then looked up at Finn. "Were you on the island when it happened?"

"When what happened?" Finn asked innocently.

"When the curse broke."

"Oh, aye." A ghost of a smile played across his cracked lips. "I was there."

"There was a festival that weekend, wasn't there?"

Finn nodded slowly. "That, there was."

From what Grace had read, hundreds of people had been on the island that weekend. Many of them had claimed to have seen something or heard something when the curse broke. She was about to ask Finn if he'd seen anything when a voice crackled over the radio.

Finn tilted an ear back toward the helm.

One of the crew members picked up a wired handset and spoke into it. Moments later, the crackly voice came back on the line.

Finn's smile faded. "I need to take this." He ducked into the cabin and climbed the steps to the helm. He took the handset from the red-headed crew member and spoke into it. Without having to be asked, the crew member stepped back and yielded the wheel to Finn.

Grace felt the ferry pick up speed. Unable to keep her balance any longer, she grabbed hold of the rack securing the provisions to the outer wall of the cabin. The deck pitched and swayed beneath her feet.

The red-headed crew member stepped down from the helm and crossed the cabin to where the other two passengers sat. He spoke briefly to them in a language Grace didn't recognize, then headed her way.

"What's going on?" she asked.

"A woman on the island might be going into labor. We'll pick her up at the pier and head straight back to the mainland."

All thoughts of legends and curses fled Grace's mind. She'd grown up on an island. She knew what it was like to live over an hour away from the nearest hospital. "What can I do?"

The crew member hesitated.

"I can unload supplies or help with the lines."

The crew member nodded toward the other two passengers in the cabin. "The man in the wheelchair had hip surgery a few weeks ago. He's going to need help getting off the boat."

"I'll help him," Grace said, already making her way over to the elderly couple to introduce herself.

Twenty minutes later, she spotted a rocky shoreline in the

distance. Or at least, she thought she did. She couldn't be sure. The windows were hazy, the thick panes of fiberglass crusted with salt from the lashing they'd taken in the choppy seas.

She waited for the ferry to slow, for the winds to calm and the rocking to subside. When she was sure they were safely inside the protective arms of the harbor, she wheeled Evan Connolly out of the cabin. And got her first glimpse of the island.

She stopped walking, and simply stared.

"She's a beauty, isn't she?" Evan asked.

Grace nodded, speechless. The rocky hills were draped in moss, a thick cloak of sparkling green. Sunlight reflected off a scattering of whitewashed cottages overlooking the harbor. A thin road threaded through the village, leading up to a sheer cliff that rose hundreds of feet above the water.

Over the hum of the motor, she could hear the sound of seals barking. She shaded her eyes, looking for them, marveling at the cluster of sleek black bodies huddled together on a sliver of white sand. At the mouth of the harbor, an ancient stone structure clung to a craggy knuckle of land, its ruins crumbling into the sea.

"This is..." Grace trailed off. She'd never seen anything like this before.

"It never gets old," Evan said. "I have a daughter in Cleggan. She wants me to move off island. But I couldn't. I could never leave this place."

Home, Grace thought, as she wheeled Evan toward the gate. She understood the significance of that word. Lately, she'd been thinking about it more and more. At thirty-three, she was beginning to tire of the city. She envied her twin brother, Ryan, who'd recently moved back to Heron Island. He'd managed to build a life for himself there, and so had a few of their closest friends.

But she didn't see how she could make that work for herself.

Not with her current job.

When her phone buzzed again, she tightened her grip on the

handles of Evan's chair to keep herself from peeking at the screen. Instead, she lifted her gaze to the pier, where a pregnant woman was making her way slowly toward them. A man and a woman were on either side of her, supporting her. The woman paused every few steps, took a moment to breathe, then kept walking.

A lone man stood at the end of the pier, leaning on a wooden cane. As soon as the ferry drew close enough, he held up a hand for the bow line. He caught it effortlessly, looping the thick rope around an oversized cleat. Despite an evident limp, he did the same with the stern line.

Finn cut the engine. The crew moved fast, unlatching the gate and setting the walkway in place. Grace helped Evan out of the portable wheelchair and let him lean on her. She waited for Breana Connolly to fold the chair up, then gestured for the elderly woman to go first. The man on the pier set his cane aside and met Breana halfway, using the guardrails for support. He guided her down to the pier, helped her unfold the chair, and locked the wheels in place. Then he helped Grace settle Evan back into the chair.

"Thank you," Grace said, looking up at him.

"No bother," he said.

Finn came down the walkway as the trio made it to the end of the pier. "How is she?" he asked, addressing his question to the woman with black hair holding the pregnant woman's left arm.

"I'm right here," the pregnant woman said. "I can answer for myself. I'm—" She bent over, grimacing.

"Breathe," the black-haired woman said in an American accent. "Deep breaths. In and out."

The man holding her right arm looked shaken. Grace did a double take when she realized it was the same man who'd written the book she was carrying, the man she was supposed to be meeting. The pregnant woman must be Liam O'Sullivan's wife. Not wanting to delay them, she hurried onto the deck to grab her luggage.

"I called ahead," the black-haired woman told Finn. "The hospital's expecting us."

"They're expecting *me*," the pregnant woman said, pulling herself together. "You don't need to come with us, Tara. I'll be fine."

Tara opened her mouth to protest.

"I've got her." Finn cut Tara off with a knowing look. He took the pregnant woman's arm and guided her toward the walkway with Liam's help. "Hang in there, Caitlin. We'll be out to sea in no time."

As soon as Caitlin was out of earshot, Tara pulled one of the crew members aside. "Is the medical kit fully stocked?"

He nodded. "We checked it a few days ago."

"Where is it?"

"I'll show you." He jogged back up to the deck with Tara on his heels.

Grace watched them disappear into the cabin. The woman's name was Tara. And she had an American accent. Could this be Tara O'Sullivan, the woman who'd allegedly broken the curse?

Beside her, the other crew member caught a sack of flour that Finn tossed him. Grace turned to see if the Connollys needed any help getting home. But they were both gone. And so was the man with the cane. Wanting to be useful, she set her luggage down and walked over to help with the provisions.

"You don't have to do that," the crew member said.

She said nothing, just helped.

He didn't protest again.

By the time Tara came out of the cabin, they'd loaded everything onto a wooden pallet on the pier.

Finn motioned for the crew members to ready the lines. On the deck, Tara handed Liam a wool blanket. Liam draped it around Caitlin's shoulders, then wrapped his arms around her and pulled her against him. His worried gaze swept over the pier and landed on Grace. "Wait... You're...?"

"Grace," she said, realizing he'd finally made the connection.

"I'm sorry. I—"

"It's fine."

"I don't know when I'll be back."

"It doesn't matter."

Caitlin sat up and started to dig through her purse. "She's renting the cottage," she told Liam. "I think I have the keys in here somewh—" She squeezed her eyes shut as another pain hit.

"Dominic keeps a spare set at the pub," Liam cut in.

"I like to show people around," Caitlin protested, breathing through the pain. "There are some quirks."

"I'll manage," Grace said.

"Dominic's my brother," Liam explained quickly. "He owns the pub in the village—O'Sullivan's. You can't miss it."

"Tara can take you," Caitlin said.

Tara looked at Caitlin like she'd lost her mind. "I'm coming with you."

"You don't need to come, Tara. We'll be fine."

"I'm coming," Tara insisted.

"There are others who need you here." Caitlin nodded toward the parking lot at the entrance of the pier, where the man with the cane was helping Evan into the passenger seat of a car.

Tara hesitated.

"Quit your fussing." Caitlin shooed her off the boat with her hand. "You said yourself it was just a precaution."

Tara looked at Liam.

At Liam's slight nod, Tara reluctantly turned and crossed the walkway back to the pier.

Grace watched the last crew member board, pull the walkway onto the deck, and latch the gate. The ferry pulled away, leaving the two of them alone on the pier. Tara said nothing for a long time.

"When is she due?" Grace asked finally, breaking the silence.

"Christmas."

It was only the first week of October. Christmas was almost three months away. "That's too soon."

"Yes," Tara said. "It's way too soon."

"Do you think she'll be okay?" Grace asked after the ferry had rounded the ruins and disappeared from sight.

"She'll have to be." Pulling her gaze away from the empty harbor, Tara turned to face Grace. "I mean, yes, of course, she'll be fine." She forced a smile. "I'm Tara. You were coming to meet with Liam?"

Grace nodded.

"Sorry about all this." She turned to face the man with the cane who'd walked back to join them. "Aidan, could you call Sarah and tell her she needs to send someone down to pick up the supplies?"

"Already done," Aidan said.

"Thank you." Tara blew out a breath. "Come on," she said to Grace. "Let's get you settled into your cottage."

Grace picked up her bag and stole a glance at the man beside her, getting a good look at him for the first time. He was tall, well-built, and attractive in a rugged, outdoorsy type of way. The hair that swept back from his face was thick and black, a striking contrast to his pale Irish complexion. He wore a flannel shirt, worn jeans, and scuffed walking boots. A pair of mirrored shades covered his eyes, but she could feel his gaze on her, assessing her the same way she was assessing him.

He opened his hand, motioning for her to go first. She fell into step behind Tara, listening to the hollow thunk of his cane against the wooden boards as he trailed after them. Even with his injury slowing him down, she'd been impressed with how cool and calm he'd been during the emergency, as if he encountered these types of crises every day.

In the small parking area at the edge of the pier, Tara opened the door to Liam's car. "Hang on. Let me see if he left the keys." She rummaged around inside the car for a while, then straightened and shook her head. "He must have taken them with him."

"I don't mind the walk," Grace said.

Tara looked over at Aidan. "How did you get here?"

"I walked."

"You walked?"

He nodded.

"From where?"

"Brennan's."

"But that's over a mile."

"'Tis."

"I thought we agreed…"

"We agreed I'd take it easy. A mile's nothing."

"You're not ready to be walking a mile yet."

Aidan smiled. "And yet, here I am."

"Take off your glasses."

He lifted a brow.

"I need to see your eyes." Tara dug in her bag for a pen light. "Take them off."

Aidan slipped the glasses from his face, revealing a pair of stunning gray-green eyes.

Grace had never seen eyes that color before. They were the palest shade of milky green. His gaze shifted, locked on hers. She felt a sudden rocking sensation, as if she were still on the boat and she couldn't quite catch her balance.

Tara shone the light in his eyes and let out a curse. "You need to sit down."

"I feel fine, love," Aidan said, his eyes still on Grace.

"You're not fine. Your pupils are dilated. There could be swelling." Tara looked back at Grace. "Sorry."

"It's fine," Grace said.

"See?" Aidan's mouth curved into an easy smile. "We're both fine."

Tara pocketed the pen light. "I'll run up to the village and bring a car back. I'm going to drive you home and do a full exam. Stay where you are. Both of you. I'll be right back." She turned and started to jog up the hill toward the village.

As soon as she was out of earshot, Grace looked at Aidan. "Well?"

"Well, what?"

"What happened to you?"

He lifted a shoulder. "Got a little banged up, is all." He made his way over to the driver's side of Liam's car, then nodded toward the passenger side. "Hop in."

Grace's brows rose. "What are you going to do? Hot-wire it?"

"I could, but no." He held up Liam's keys.

Grace laughed. She couldn't help it. "Why didn't you tell her you had them?"

"I was making my way 'round to it." He smiled again. "Hop in."

Grace got in the passenger seat and set her bag on the floor.

Aidan slipped the key into the ignition and started the engine. He shifted into reverse, then put his arm around the back of her seat to look out the rear window. "What part of the States are you from?"

"Maryland," she said as they backed up and spun around. "Ever been?"

He braked and left his arm around her seat for a moment before reaching for the gear shift again. He was close enough so she could smell him—the earthy, masculine scent of him. Her gaze flickered down to his mouth, then back up. Aidan smiled. "Can't say that I have."

He shifted the car into gear. They sped up the hill, arriving at the pub at the same time as Tara.

Tara turned, put her hands on her hips, and glared at Aidan.

Aidan looked at Grace and nodded toward the pub. "Buy you a glass of whiskey?"

Grace bit back a smile. "Maybe another time."

"Get out of the driver's seat," Tara ordered. "Now."

Aidan laughed and stepped out of the car.

"Give me those." Tara snatched the keys from his hand. She slid behind the wheel, then rolled down the window and called out to Grace, "Go inside and ask for Dominic. He'll help you get into the cottage. I'm so sorry about all of this."

"Don't be," Grace said.

Aidan walked past Grace on his way to the passenger seat. "There's only one pub on the island, you know." He slipped his glasses back on. "I'm sure I'll be seeing you around."

# CHAPTER TWO

"Do you *want* to get better?" Tara asked Aidan as they walked into his guest cottage on the far side of the island.

Aidan lowered himself to the first chair he came to. His head was pounding. There were black spots floating into his vision. And he felt slightly nauseous. But he wasn't about to tell her that. "Yes."

Tara set her bag down. She checked his blood pressure, listened to his heart, and examined his eyes again with the pen light. Frowning, she put the instruments away and pulled out a pack of fresh bandages.

Without having to be asked, he started to unbutton his shirt.

"How's your hearing?" She added a few notes to her records. "Any improvement?"

"Not since yesterday." He shrugged out of his shirt and winced when she ripped a bandage off a little harder than necessary.

He deserved that. He was being obnoxious. But he'd never

had a sister before. He'd never had a sibling, or any family for that matter, to mess with. And while he didn't believe he was related to anyone on this island, he was willing to play along. At least for a few more weeks. Then he'd be out of her hair for good. And he'd probably never see her again. Might as well enjoy it while it lasted.

"What's this?" Tara took hold of his right hand and studied the raw skin on his knuckles.

"It's nothing. Just a few scrapes."

"What did you scrape it on?"

"Brennan's tractor." Aidan took his hand back. "I was helping him fix it."

Tara took a deep breath, looked up toward the ceiling, and appeared to be counting to three. "We've been over this."

"I know, but—"

"You don't need to help Brennan."

"He has arthritis."

"I know that," Tara said, frustrated. "I've been treating him for it since I arrived on this island eight years ago. If he's hurting, he can call me or Sam."

"He can, but he won't."

"He won't if you keep offering to do everything for him."

"I don't offer. I just do it. That's the point. He won't ask for help because he doesn't want to depend on other people. He's used to doing it himself. He *wants* to do it himself."

Tara closed her eyes, took another breath, and let it out. "Look, I know you want to help. And I'm sure Brennan appreciates it. But could you please just call one of us next time, instead of trying to do everything yourself?"

"I'll try." Aidan smiled. "But only because you asked so nicely."

Tara shook her head. "You're hopeless."

"Hopeless, but lovable, right?"

She rolled her eyes and turned to search for something in her bag.

Aidan looked out the window. The truth was, he enjoyed helping Brennan. It made him feel useful.

Brennan Lockley was in his eighties, but he ran this farm mostly on his own. Sam Holt came by in the mornings to help with the animals. But Brennan did the rest, the same way his father had, and his grandfather had, and his great-grandfather had before that.

It wasn't just stubbornness. It was a matter of pride.

Aidan understood that. He respected it. Because he felt the same way about his own career. He had no idea what he would do if his work was taken away from him. It was the one thing he could count on in life, the one thing that had always been there for him. Which was why he was having so much trouble sleeping at night.

It wasn't just the headaches, or the broken ribs, or the burn wounds. It wasn't just that he'd gone deaf in one ear or that his vision was so blurred in his left eye that he'd have to relearn how to shoot with his right.

That, he could manage.

It was the bone-crushing panic that hit him every night around 3AM that his knee might never fully heal.

He needed it to heal. He needed to regain *all* his former strength and flexibility. If he couldn't bend his knee, he wouldn't be able to run when the shells exploded. He wouldn't be able to hit the ground when the gunshots went off. He wouldn't be able to get low enough to capture the photographs of the destruction or the expressions on the faces of the innocent people left behind to pick up the pieces.

He couldn't exactly carry a tripod into a war zone.

A gust of cold air slipped through a crack in the window. It smelled of saltwater and wet wool. He could hear the sheep bleating in the pastures, the sound of waves crashing in the distance, and beyond that...nothing.

"Here." Tara held out a small glass jar filled with a pale cream. "Rub this on your hand twice a day. It'll help fight the infection."

"Thanks." He took the jar from her. "Just add it to my tab."

She gave him a withering look. "You know I have other patients, right?"

He feigned shock. "You do?"

"Yes," she said. "I have three more patients to see right after you—patients who are well-behaved, patients who do what I tell them to do, patients who actually *get better* because they follow my advice."

"That must give you a great deal of satisfaction."

"It does." Tara walked around to the back of his chair. "I like making people feel better. I like knowing I can make a difference in people's lives. I..."

"What?" he asked when she trailed off.

"Your stitches are coming loose. Again."

"Oh."

"I'm going to need to re-do them."

Aidan nodded and shifted slightly so she'd have better access to the wound on his lower back where a piece of shrapnel had lodged in the muscle tissue. At the cold swab of antiseptic, he sucked in his teeth.

"Sorry," Tara said. "Did that sting?"

He managed to flash her a smile. "Not a bit."

"Good," she said sweetly, then went back to stitching the wound.

Aidan tried not to whimper when she turned her attention to

the scorched skin covering his left shoulder and most of his upper back. She cleaned out the burn wounds, coated them with an herbal salve, and covered them in fresh bandages. Then she walked around to face him again and held out her hand for the ace bandage that supported his three broken ribs. He unclipped the fasteners, unwound it with his good arm, and passed it over to her. She wrapped a new one around him, not tight enough to restrict his breathing, but close.

Finally, she stepped back and looked down at his knee. "Okay, let's see it."

He hesitated. "It looks worse than it is."

"Nice try."

"Nothing a little ice won't fix," he said hopefully. "I'll put a pack on it as soon as you leave."

He rolled up his jeans.

"Aidan!" Tara's eyes widened. "It's the size of a grapefruit."

"So...two packs of ice?"

Tara walked to the freezer, pulled out an icepack, and handed it to him. "You know the drill. Twenty minutes on, twenty minutes off until the swelling comes down. And don't put *any* weight on it for the rest of the day."

He took the ice from her. "I thought I might take a stroll down to the beach later, collect some shells."

"Haha," she said flatly. "Do you have anything to read? Brennan has a ton of books in his house. Want me to pick out a few for you?"

"No, thanks." Brennan had offered to loan him a book a few weeks ago, when he'd first arrived on the island. He'd already perused the selection. It was mostly fairy tales, not a genre that interested him.

"You need to rest," Tara said. "You're not going to heal without rest."

What he needed, Aidan thought, was to get back to work. No

one was paying him to lie around and take it easy. Over the past fourteen years, he'd turned down offers to join the staff of almost every major publication.

He freelanced by choice. He sold his images to the highest bidder. And they paid good money for them. Because he went where no one else was willing to go—to the ragged, fraying edges of the world.

He went to those places so no one would forget about the people who lived there, the people who'd done nothing wrong. He knew what it felt like to be forgotten, to be one of the people the world had turned its back on.

Someone had to give those people a voice. Someone had to flash their stories in front of the faces of the ones who'd become complacent—the ones who'd forgotten to care.

His images forced people to care.

He'd taken photographs that had compelled leaders to provide military support, opened doors for relief agencies to deliver aid, and inspired philanthropists to donate huge sums of money. And he would continue to do that, as long as he could heal and get back to work.

Sure, he might be pushing himself too hard. But he needed to get better. And he needed to get better soon. Lying around wasn't going to get him anywhere.

Unless...of course, he had someone with him. Then the idea of staying in bed all day might not be so bad. A vision of a tall, leggy blonde with gray eyes and a killer smile came to mind.

He looked up at Tara, who was gathering her things and getting ready to leave. "Tell me about the woman who arrived today."

"What woman?" Tara asked, distracted.

"The one who came in on the ferry. Grace."

"Oh." Tara closed her notebook and tucked it in the bag. "She came to talk to Liam."

"About what?"

"I don't know."

"How long is she staying?"

"A couple of nights, I think. Why?"

"Just curious."

Tara glanced up, her expression suddenly wary. "No."

"No, what?"

"No to whatever you're thinking. It's a bad idea."

"I thought she might need a friend. Don't you want me to be friendly to the tourists?"

"What I *want* is for you to stay here and rest. And I know it's not friendship you're after."

Aidan smiled.

"You know what you should do?" Tara said, brightening. "You should call your mother. I bet she'd love to spend the evening with you. Here." She pulled out her phone and clicked on a name in her contacts. "Let's call her together."

Aidan took the phone from her hand and ended the call. "Let's not."

Tara sighed. "You can't keep pushing her away."

He could, Aidan thought. And he would.

"It's been three weeks," Tara said. "Can't you spend a little time with her?"

No, Aidan thought. He had zero interest in spending time with the woman who claimed to be his mother.

"She would like to be able to help you, to take care of you," Tara said.

"I can take care of myself."

Tara gave him a look.

"Okay," he relented. "Maybe I need a little help. But only from you."

Tara took her phone back, slipped it in her pocket. "Don't

you want to at least *try* to get to know her? She's your mother, Aidan."

No, Aidan thought. He knew everything he needed to know about Brigid O'Sullivan from the letter she'd written to him. As far as he was concerned, the woman was certifiably insane. She'd actually admitted, in writing, that she thought she was half-seal. She'd even claimed to have spent the first sixteen years of her life underwater. And that was only the beginning of her crazy tale.

He'd only replied because he'd been too doped up on painkillers in the hospital where he'd woken up six weeks ago to know better. When the fog had finally cleared and he'd realized what he'd done, it had been too late. He'd already promised to visit.

And he never broke a promise.

Tara zipped up her bag. "Tell me you'll think about it."

"I'll think about it," he said, but only to appease her. He had no intention of spending the evening, or any evening for that matter, with Brigid.

As a parting gift, she handed him a bottle of pills. "Take two of these with your next meal."

"For what?"

"For the headache."

"What headache?"

"The one you're not telling me about." Tara rolled her eyes. "I'll see you tomorrow."

"Or tonight."

"Aidan," she warned.

He laughed.

"Look," Tara said. "To be honest, it would be better for all of us if you'd steer clear of the pub tonight."

"Why?"

"Because Grace will be there. And with Liam gone, the rest of us will have to handle her."

"Handle her?"

Tara nodded. "Most people who come to the island to meet with Liam want to talk about the legend."

"Ah."

"So, if you do run into her again, which I hope you don't, just stick to the usual story."

"You mean...the story about you?"

"Yes." Tara shouldered her bag. "I'm the one who broke the curse."

Aidan watched her walk to the door. "Aren't you tired of it?"

Tara paused, her hand on the knob. "Tired of what?"

"Talking about it. Reliving it."

Tara took a deep breath. "The others have been through enough."

Hadn't *she* been through enough?

From what he'd heard, Tara's ex-husband had physically abused her for years before she'd found a way to escape. With a new identity and a made-up past, she'd come to this island to hide. But her ex-husband, with the help of a private investigator, had tracked her down. And when he'd followed her here to punish her for leaving, she'd barely managed to survive the attack.

The fact that she'd decided to stay here, to build a life here after all that, impressed him. But what he didn't understand was how a doctor—a woman of science—could believe all this nonsense about seals who could shed their skin and transform into women on land. And even go so far as to claim she was descended from one.

Tara opened the door and looked back at him. "So, you'll stay here tonight? You have everything you need?"

"You know," Aidan said as an intriguing idea began to take shape, "if I came by the pub later, I could distract her for you."

"That is the *last* thing we need."

"I'd be happy to do it. Really, it wouldn't be any trouble at all."

"Aidan," Tara said, exasperated. "She'll only be here for three days. Can you please just play along."

"I think I can manage that." He gave her his best smile. "I think I might even enjoy it."

# CHAPTER THREE

Grace stepped out of the shower, feeling refreshed. She dried her hair, slipped into a pair of jeans, and pulled on a sweater. Barefoot, she walked into the bedroom of the guest cottage.

It was nearly dusk.

She hadn't meant to sleep for so long. But the jet lag had caught up with her. And she was glad, now, that she'd given into it. Her mind felt clearer, and she needed to be able to focus tonight.

It was unfortunate that Liam had left the island. But there had to be others who knew about the legend. She figured she'd spend the evening at the pub and try to find out as much as she could from the rest of the locals.

She pulled on a pair of wool socks and the same boots she'd been wearing earlier. Reaching for her jacket, she lifted her gaze to the window overlooking the ocean. The sun had just set, and the clouds were still lit from below—bands of fire against a dusky purple sky. Halfway down the glass, a crystal shimmered from the end of a piece of string.

Remembering the wind chime Taylor had given her, she crossed the room to the dresser, where she'd looped it around a knob earlier. It was small, the whole thing no longer than the length of her hand. Lifting it up, she studied the tiny silver petals the nine-year-old had fastened to the end of each strand of fishing line.

Rose petals, Taylor had said. Made of some sort of metal. At least a dozen of them.

Back on Heron Island, Taylor and her mother, Annie, were known for their beautiful handmade wind chimes. Annie had moved to the island last year to open the Wind Chime Café, and she'd recently married one of Grace's best friends.

Grace had been touched when they'd given her this chime the night before she'd left for Ireland. She'd wanted to leave it at home, where it would be safe. But Taylor had insisted she bring it with her. And she'd made Grace promise to hang it up right away.

It was an odd request, Grace thought. Especially when she might not be staying anywhere for longer than a few nights. But she was very fond of Taylor, so she'd tucked it into her bag and carried it with her across the ocean.

All she needed to do, now, was find a place to hang it up.

Walking out of the bedroom, she passed through the cozy sitting area with its simple furnishings, working fireplace, and sweeping views of the harbor. A collection of oil paintings—mostly seascapes—hung on the walls, each more striking than the last.

Her gaze lingered on a painting of an underwater palace with glittering white towers and soaring marble gates surrounded by oyster shells and roses made of ice. There was so much detail, it was hard to believe someone could have painted that from imagination alone.

Not that anything like that could exist in real life.

She opened the door. A cold wind rushed in, filling the room with the scent of the sea. There were lights on in a few of the homes in the village. A curl of smoke rose from the chimney of O'Sullivan's pub. She could see people inside, already gathering for the night.

She pulled on her jacket and walked outside. Running a hand under the edge of the thatched roof, she searched for something to hang the chime on. When she came across a sturdy piece of wire, she looped the chime's hook around it and let go. The wind caught the petals, sending them into a frantic spin.

Over the crash of the ocean, she heard a faint clinking as the rose petals tapped into each other. The sound reminded her of home. Smiling, she reached for her phone to take a picture to send to Annie and Taylor. She stepped back, angling the lens to include a bit more of the ocean in the shot. A movement outside the frame caught her eye. She paused and lowered the phone back to her side.

In the fading light, she could just make out the shape of a person in the water. She walked closer, her eyes widening. It was a boy, she realized. A teenager.

And he was surrounded by seals.

What the...?

She looked over her shoulder to see if there was anyone else around. The streets were empty. She scanned the edge of the yard for a path down to the beach. When she couldn't find one, she looked back at the boy. He didn't appear to be in any distress. And he was close enough to the beach that he should be able to stand. But it wasn't exactly swimming weather.

What was he doing in the water? And why were those seals so close to him?

She stayed there for another minute or two, keeping a close eye on him as the last of the colors faded from the sky. When she was certain he wasn't in any danger, she turned and headed for the pub. The first person she saw when she walked in the door was Tara.

"Hi," Tara said brightly. "I was hoping I'd run into you tonight. I'm so sorry, again, about earlier."

"Don't be," Grace said. "How's your friend?"

"Much better. Thanks." Tara handed a pint to one of the three musicians setting up in the corner. "The doctors want to keep her overnight, to be safe. Hopefully, she and Liam will be back by tomorrow afternoon."

"That's great," Grace said. "Listen...it's Tara, right?"

"Yes." Tara smiled and held out her hand. "Tara O'Sullivan. This is my husband's place. He's the one who let you into the cottage earlier. What can we get you to drink?"

So, this *was* Tara O'Sullivan, Grace realized as she shook her hand. This was the woman at the center of the legend, the one who'd broken the curse. She wanted to talk to her, to ask her some questions. But first, she needed to make sure that the kid was okay. "Actually, I could use your help. There's a boy in the water out there."

Tara's smile faded. "Out where?"

"In the harbor, below my cottage. He seems okay, or I wouldn't have left him there. But I'd like to find his parents. I mean, the water temperature alone..."

Tara grabbed her coat. "Show me."

Grace led her back outside. The moon was beginning to rise, a glowing ball of burnished bronze. It loomed over the eastern horizon, casting shadows over the jagged stone walls that criss-crossed the island in every direction. When they came to the edge of the yard behind her cottage, Grace pointed to the spot where she'd seen the boy only moments ago.

"I don't see anyone," Tara said.

"Neither do I," Grace said, confused. "He was right there."

Tara continued to scan the surface of the water. "What did he look like?"

"Dark hair. Thin."

"How old?"

"A teenager. Maybe seventeen or eighteen."

"And you're sure he was *in* the water?"

"Yes." Grace squinted to see through the darkness. "There were seals with him."

"Seals?" Tara asked carefully.

Grace nodded. "They were all around him, in a circle. At least a dozen of them."

Tara was quiet for several moments.

"Should we go down there?" Grace asked. "I couldn't find a path earlier, but—"

Tara laid a hand on Grace's arm. "You must be exhausted."

Grace's brows drew together. "What?"

"Dominic said you flew in from the States this morning, and that you've been traveling all day."

"Yes, but—"

Tara gave her a sympathetic smile. "Jet lag can do funny things to us."

Grace took a step back. "It wasn't jet lag."

Tara turned away from the water. "Let's get you back inside where it's warm. I promise you'll feel better after you've had something to eat."

Grace stared at her. What was she saying? That she'd imagined it? "I know what I saw."

"I don't doubt that you saw...something." Tara was already heading back to the pub. "But it's dark out. And the water can play tricks on us, especially when we're tired."

Grace didn't move. "Are there any kids on the island who match the description I gave you?"

Tara paused.

"Are there?"

Tara turned slowly back around to face her. "There might be."

"How many?"

Tara hesitated.

"More than one?" Grace pressed.

"No."

"Okay," Grace said. "Will you tell me who his parents are so I can talk to them myself?"

Tara looked back out at the water. "I would, but they're not here."

"Where are they?"

"In a hospital in Galway."

"Oh," Grace said when she realized who Tara meant.

"Look." Tara walked back to the edge of the yard. "Even if you did see their son, which I highly doubt since he's supposed to be at his grandmother's house right now, he's an excellent swimmer. One of the best on the island. You have nothing to worry about."

Unconvinced, Grace looked down at the beach again. "What about the seals?"

"What about them?"

"Is it normal for them to surround someone like that?"

"Sure," Tara said. "They're perfectly friendly. This is *Seal Island*."

Grace looked back at Tara. "What about the water temperature? Aren't you worried about how cold it is?"

Tara angled her head. "Haven't you heard the rumors?"

"What rumors?"

"That we're all half-seal and the cold doesn't bother us." Tara laughed and waved for Grace to follow her back to the pub. "Come on. We can talk more inside. I imagine you have questions about the legend if you came here to speak with

Liam. Maybe I can answer a few of them before he gets back."

Conflicted, Grace stayed where she was. There was something off here. She could feel it. And her instincts were never wrong. However, she'd seen the way Tara had taken care of both Caitlin and Aidan earlier. She didn't seem like someone who would abandon a person in need.

If Tara wasn't worried about the kid, then Grace shouldn't be either. With one last glance back at the water, she followed Tara across the street to the pub. They stepped inside and closed the door on the roar of the ocean. The friendly swell of laughter and conversation was a welcome contrast.

"Grab a seat wherever you can find one," Tara said. "I'll come find you later."

Grace nodded, watching her disappear into the crowd. Beside her, the musicians were tuning their instruments, getting ready to play their first set. Several families were seated at the dozen or so tables scattered throughout the dining room. At the bar, people were lined up two rows deep, waiting for pints.

She unzipped her coat, shrugged out of it, and felt someone take it from her hands. She turned and looked up into a pair of pale green eyes.

Aidan smiled. "Fancy that glass of whiskey now?"

In the dim lighting, she could just make out the laugh lines that fanned out from the corners of his eyes—lines, which, at his age, indicated a considerable amount of time spent in the sun. "I thought you were supposed to be at home resting."

"Resting's overrated." He draped her coat over his arm. "Table or bar?"

"I don't think there's much room left at the bar."

"Table it is, then." He nodded toward the only empty table left in the room, nestled between the band and the fire.

She started toward it. He trailed after her, leaning heavily on his cane with each step. His limp seemed worse than earlier, so she took the chair farthest away, trying to save him a few steps. When he shook his head and directed her back to the one closest to the band, she gave him a questioning look.

"I won't be able to hear you over the music," he explained.

The band consisted of two guitar players and a fiddler. None of their instruments were hooked up to an amplifier. "Will they be that loud?"

"No." Aidan touched a hand to his left ear. "But I can't hear anything on this side."

Grace switched places with him.

"It's recent," he added. "And temporary."

Temporary deafness didn't seem like a minor issue. "Did you lose your hearing the same time you hurt your leg?"

Aidan turned toward the bar, caught the eye of the man behind it, and held up two fingers. "Yes."

When he left it at that, she took a moment to study him. From this angle, she could see that a patch of skin on his neck seemed discolored, like he'd been burned recently. And she noticed, for the first time, the edge of a bandage peeking out from beneath the collar of his shirt.

How badly *had* he been injured?

"So, tell me, Grace..." Aidan leaned his cane against the hearth, then slowly lowered himself to the chair across from her. "What brings you to Seal Island?"

Interesting, Grace thought. This was the second time he'd deflected attention away from his injuries. There was a story there. No question about it. But it was too soon to press. She'd let it go for now and work her way back around to it later. It was a subtle dance, trying to get information out of people. It was one she enjoyed and one she was good at. She had no doubt she'd find out what happened before the end of the night. "I came here to meet with Liam O'Sullivan."

"About the legend?"

"And selkies, in general. I've always been fascinated by them," she said, stretching the truth a bit. "My mother used to read me stories about them when I was a child."

Aidan sat back. "Is that so?"

Grace nodded. "You must have grown up hearing stories about them as well."

"I've heard my share of fairy stories."

"Do you have a favorite?"

"Not really," he replied. "I've always preferred reality over fantasy."

"Even as a child?" she asked, surprised.

"Even then."

She thought she detected a trace of bitterness in his voice, but before she had a chance to ask him why, a shadow fell across their table. She looked up to find Dominic delivering their drinks.

"Welcome back," he said warmly.

"Thanks," Grace said, wondering why they were getting special treatment when the bar was still surrounded with people. "Is it always this busy in here at night?"

"Only when the Doughertys play." He set down their drinks, nodded a greeting to Aidan.

The two men had the same tall, broad-shouldered frames, thick black hair, and rugged good looks. Grace thought she'd noticed a resemblance earlier when Dominic had let her into the cottage, but now that they were next to each other, there was no mistaking it. "Are you brothers?"

Dominic nodded, his gaze shifting to Aidan. "You look like hell, by the way."

"Thanks," Aidan said dryly.

"I hope you didn't drive here."

"I didn't," he said. "Brennan dropped me off."

"Good," Dominic said, "because Tara's threatening to mix a sedative into whatever you order tonight."

Aidan eyed the glass of whiskey in front of him, feigning concern. He looked up at Grace. "Do you think it's safe?"

Grace picked up her glass. "Only one way to find out."

Aidan smiled and lifted his, touched it to hers. "Sláinte," he said, holding her gaze as they both took a sip.

The whiskey was smooth and smoky, with hints of vanilla. It warmed her all the way down.

Dominic set two menus between them. "I'll leave you to it."

As he walked away, the first notes of the fiddle floated into the room, softening the conversation to a quiet murmur. Beside them, a peat fire snapped and sizzled in the hearth. Grace took another sip, and for the first time since boarding the plane the night before, she began to relax. "So, brothers, huh?"

Aidan lifted a shoulder.

It made sense, now, why they'd gotten special treatment. It also made sense why Aidan had given Tara such a hard time earlier. He'd been messing with her because she was his sister-in-law.

"Where does Liam fit in?"

"Dominic's the oldest. Liam's next."

"So, you're the youngest?"

He gave a slight nod.

"It must have been wild growing up here."

"Same as anywhere, I imagine."

Grace laughed. "I grew up on an island, but it was nowhere near as isolated as this." She was used to being surrounded by water, but the Chesapeake Bay was a calmer, gentler body of water. Here, there was no escaping the raw, untamed power of the ocean—or forgetting how small and vulnerable you were in comparison. "We are *way* off the beaten path."

"Maryland, right?" Aidan asked.

Grace was surprised he'd remembered. "Yes."

"Tell me about it." He settled back in his chair, the light from the fire flickering over the rough planes and sculpted angles of his face.

She told him about how she'd grown up in a village of less than eight hundred people, how the tight-knit community felt like an extended family, and how most of the islanders still made their living off the water, including her father and brother.

"Do you still live there?" Aidan asked.

"No, I live in D.C. now" She picked up the menu and skimmed it. "Do you live here, on Seal Island?"

Aidan shook his head. "I'm just here for a visit."

"Where do you live?"

"I'm between homes at the moment."

"Between homes?"

He nodded. "I have a flat in Istanbul. That's where I've been living for the past few years. But I just rented it out to a friend. I'm not sure where I'm going next."

She was about to ask what he'd been doing in Istanbul when a waitress in her early twenties appeared and set down a basket of brown bread.

"Hello," she said to Grace, somewhat coolly, then turned to Aidan and brightened. "Hi."

Aidan smiled up at her. "You're looking well tonight, Colleen."

Colleen blushed as she pulled a pen out of her apron. "What can I get for you."

Aidan looked at Grace and nodded for her to go first.

"What do you recommend?" Grace asked.

"On a night like this," Aidan said, considering. "I'd say the potato and leek soup or the shepherd's pie. What do you think, Colleen?"

"Oh," she said, suddenly tongue-tied when his gaze met hers

again. "I—" She looked away, scribbled something on her notepad, then realized she was holding the pen upside down. Flustered, she started to flip it over. It slipped from her fingers and landed on the table.

Aidan picked it up and handed it to her.

"Thanks." She blushed again. "Sorry. You...em...can't go wrong with the shepherd's pie."

Grace bit her lip to keep from smiling. "That sounds great. I'll have a cup of soup and the pie."

"I'll have the same." Aidan handed Colleen the menus. "And bring us each a pint of Guinness with dinner."

Colleen nodded and backed away from the table, still blushing.

"Careful," Grace said once she was out of earshot. "You don't want to break the poor girl's heart."

Aidan's smile deepened, the lines around his eyes crinkling. "I have a feeling you've broken your share of hearts."

"Possibly," Grace said. "But I always try to give them a bit of warning in advance."

Aidan laughed. "Consider me warned, then."

"I don't think you have to worry."

"Why not?"

"Because I'll only be here for two nights."

Aidan put a hand over his heart and pretended like it was already breaking.

She laughed and rolled her eyes.

"Then what?" he asked. "Back to the States?"

"No." She lifted her glass, took another sip. "I'm planning to spend the next three months in Ireland, with a possible side trip to the Scottish Hebrides. They have selkie legends there, as well."

Aidan studied her curiously. "What is it about selkies that you find so fascinating?"

Grace took a moment to consider her response. She didn't

like to stray too far from the truth. It went against everything she stood for. But at the same time, she wasn't ready to share the real reason she'd dropped everything to come here. At least, not yet. "I think it's because of the way so many of their stories end," she said, opting for a half-truth. "Most of them end with the selkie leaving her husband and children to return to the sea. Don't you think that's sad?"

"I guess," Aidan said. "I've never given it that much thought."

Grace gave him a funny look. How could he have grown up on this island and never given it that much thought? "I get why the selkie would want to leave if she were being mistreated. Of course, she would want to get back to the sea. But what about the ones who fell in love with their husbands? The ones who were treated well and lived happy lives on land? Why would they want to leave once they found their pelt? Why couldn't they just stay?"

Aidan shrugged. "I wouldn't get too worked up about it. It's only a fairy tale."

Grace's brows rose. "Is it?"

"Of course."

"But...what about the curse?"

"What about it?"

"I've read about what happened here, or at least, what people say happened. Wasn't it Tara, your *sister-in-law*, who allegedly broke the curse?"

"Ah, yes." Aidan looked off into the distance, appearing to be deep in thought. "I think I might have read that somewhere as well."

Grace sighed. So, this was how he was going to play it.

Colleen reappeared. She placed a steaming cup of potato and leek soup in front of each of them and added a few extra pats of butter to Aidan's bread plate. He flashed her a heart-melting smile in return.

Grace dipped her spoon into the soup and gave it a slow stir. If he wasn't going to be forthcoming with information about himself *or* the legend, she might need to take a different approach. She hadn't planned to reveal much about herself on this trip, but sometimes you had to share to receive. This might be one of those times.

"How did you manage to get three months off work?" Aidan asked Grace after Colleen left. "Did you have that much leave saved up? Or will you be working remotely while you're here?"

Grace sampled the soup, taking a moment to savor the comforting flavors as she noted, again, how deftly he'd changed the subject, putting the focus back on her. "I'm taking a leave of absence from my job."

"What do you do?"

She gave the soup another slow stir, inhaling the rich aromas of melted cream and caramelized leeks as she plotted her next move. "I'm a journalist."

Aidan paused, his spoon halfway to his mouth. "Really?"

Grace nodded. "For *The Washington Tribune*. I cover Capitol Hill, mostly. Politics."

Aidan lowered his spoon back to his bowl. "What did you say your last name was?"

"Callahan."

"Grace Callahan," he murmured, studying her more closely, as if trying to place her.

"Do you follow what goes on in the States, politically?"

"Of course." Aidan pulled out his phone. "Who doesn't?" He tapped the screen a few times, then let out a low whistle. He turned his phone around so she could see the screen. "This is you, I take it?"

Grace saw that he'd pulled up her Twitter profile, which had gained its millionth follower a few weeks ago. "That's me."

He flipped his phone back around so he could take a closer look. "I'm impressed."

Grace took another sip of her soup. She didn't care how many followers she had. What mattered was that people trusted her. She never broke a story without triple-checking her facts. Her sources told her things they wouldn't tell anyone else because they knew she'd protect them. She had a reputation for being able to dig up the truth, no matter how deep it was buried. And since she covered politics, the truth was often hidden beneath layers and layers of lies.

It meant something to her, to be able to share that truth with the public. To be able to hold her country's leaders accountable. To be able to support a fundamental pillar of American democracy.

It wasn't something she took for granted.

Aidan's brows shot up as he skimmed through her Twitter feed. "You're the one who broke that story about the Army colonel who assaulted all those women."

"I am."

He looked up at her. "That was a huge story."

"It was."

"He's behind bars now, isn't he?"

Grace nodded. Because of the courage of the fourteen women who'd come forward to share their stories, Bradley Welker had finally gotten what he deserved.

"That story rocked the military community."

Yes, Grace thought. It had.

Aidan tapped on the screen again. A few moments later, his lips curved.

"What?" she asked.

He turned the phone around so she could see the clip of her most recent guest appearance on a popular cable news show. Her eyes were painted, her lips were glossy, and her hair was pulled back from her face so that viewers could see her high cheekbones and wide gray eyes. At least, that's what the network's stylist had said.

"The camera likes you."

"I hate doing those."

"The morning shows?"

"Yes, they're the worst."

Aidan laughed. "Why?"

For starters, Grace thought, she didn't want to have to sexualize herself to deliver the news. The anchors said they wanted her take on what was happening on the Hill, but she knew her appearance was the main reason she was invited on those shows. An executive at one of the networks had even floated the idea of having her host her own show one day. He'd told her she had the look for it, the face for it. He'd told her he could mold her into a star.

But that would take her even farther away from the type of work that had drawn her toward journalism in the first place. She'd gotten a taste of it again, recently, when she'd worked on the story about Bradley Welker—when she'd helped those fourteen women find their voices.

Those were the stories she wanted to tell. The ones that took time to piece together. The ones that got her out on the streets, knocking on doors, talking to people. The last thing she wanted was to be a pretty face parroting the same headlines as every other pretty face on television.

"Because they're not real news," she said. "Those shows are mostly analysis anyway. I'm not interested in the analysis."

"What *are* you interested in?"

"The truth."

Slipping his phone back in his pocket, Aidan regarded her

curiously. "Why would someone who's only interested in the truth take three months off work to chase after a fairy tale?"

That was a good question, Grace thought. And yet, somehow, she knew, deep down, that this path would reveal the most important truth of all. "Let's just say it's something I've always wanted to do."

Aidan continued to study her as Colleen cleared away their empty soup cups and set two plates of shepherd's pie and two pints of Guinness on the table in front of them. Grace lifted her glass. Now that she'd revealed a bit of information about herself, she hoped he'd return the favor. "So," she said, "speaking of fairy tales..."

He smiled.

She took a sip of stout. "Were you here when the curse broke?"

"No."

That was unfortunate, Grace thought. She'd been hoping for a firsthand account. Taking another sip, she savored the malty sweetness, the notes of dark coffee and chocolate, then set the glass down. "How did you find out about it?"

Aidan took his time filling his fork with the perfect bite before lifting it to his mouth and chewing ever so slowly. He washed it down with a sip of Guinness. "I can't recall."

Grace stared at him. "You can't recall?"

"No." He took another bite. "How did *you* find out about it?"

"We're not talking about me."

"Why not?"

"Because we already talked about me."

"Can't we talk about you again?"

"No." It was time for a different approach. "Where *were* you when it happened?"

Aidan took another bite. "Let's see." He looked away,

appeared to be deep in thought. "Eight years ago? In the summer?"

"That's right."

"I would have been in the States."

"The States?"

He nodded. "D.C."

"D.C.?" she asked, surprised. They'd lived in the same city before? "What were you doing there?"

"I was dating an American diplomat. We met overseas. She wanted me to move back to D.C. with her, so I did. We lived together in the city for about a year."

"What happened?"

"I'm not very good at the whole commitment thing."

Neither was she, Grace thought. Her longest relationship had lasted nine months. She had ended it the same way she'd ended all of them, by using her job as an excuse.

The truth was, it was easier to bury herself in work than risk the possibility of falling in love. Falling in love would leave her too open, too exposed—something she tried to avoid at all costs.

She knew what it felt like to lose someone, to be the one who was left behind.

She had no interest in experiencing that feeling again.

Besides, there were plenty of men who preferred casual relationships. As long as she never met anyone she couldn't walk away from, she'd be perfectly safe. "So," she said, shifting the conversation back on track, "if you weren't here when the curse broke, did you notice anything different when you came back?"

"Different...how?"

"I don't know." Grace picked up her fork. "You must have noticed something."

"The only thing I noticed when I came to this island after the curse broke was that the locals knew how to spin a tale for the tourists."

"All the locals except you."

"Like I said earlier, I prefer reality over fantasy."

She pierced the crusty potato topping of the pie, releasing a pocket of steam that smelled of melted butter and roasted garlic. "Why is that?"

Aidan lifted his glass, took a sip. "I think the bigger question is, why don't you?"

"I never said..." Grace paused, checking herself. He'd done it again, she realized. He'd moved the focus off himself and back on her. For the past half an hour, whenever she'd asked him a question about the legend, the island, or his childhood—anything that might help her with her search—he'd deftly switched the subject.

He was good at this. Too good.

She set down her fork. "What do you do for work?"

"I'm a photographer."

A photographer? That didn't make sense. He was clearly adept at controlling a conversation—a skill she'd learned, and honed, as a journalist. It wasn't a skill that came naturally to most people. "What kind of photographs do you take?"

"Oh, you know." He shrugged. "This and that."

Grace narrowed her eyes. Most artists had a particular medium or subject matter they preferred. "Portraits? Landscapes? Abstracts?"

Aidan took another sip of his drink. "It really depends."

"On what?"

"On what I'm covering."

"On what you're...?" Grace trailed off as several pieces of information clicked together at once. His name was Aidan. He was Irish. He was a photographer. And he'd most recently lived in Istanbul, the gateway to the Middle East. "Wait. You're not Aidan O'Malley, are you?"

He smiled.

Grace's eyes widened. "Are you?"

He gave a slight nod of acknowledgement.

She sat back, stunned. Aidan O'Malley wasn't a photographer. He was a photojournalist. And he only covered one thing—war.

She hadn't recognized him because he rarely shared pictures of himself. It was the images he *took* that captivated her anyway. He was always the first on the ground in a crisis. Before the networks could bring in their video equipment and their satellites and their big-name TV reporters, Aidan was already taking photographs and reporting on what had happened.

His images were emotional, heartbreaking, and often hard to look at. They'd been featured on the cover of *The Washington Tribune* more times than she could count.

Beside her, the fire hissed and sparked. She spotted Aidan's cane leaning against the hearth, and suddenly everything made sense. "That's how you got hurt."

He gave another slight nod.

"Where were you?"

His gaze strayed past her to the flames. "Aleppo."

She thought of the most recent images she'd seen of that city. Death. Destruction. Chaos. Anarchy. She understood, now, why he preferred reality over fantasy. There were no fairy tales that could sugarcoat the life he'd chosen to live. Reaching for her glass, she cupped both hands around it. She had questions, so many questions. But where to begin? And would he even be willing to answer any of them? She looked down at the half-empty pint, brushed a thumb over the etching in the glass.

O'Sullivan's.

The name of the pub. The name Tara had taken when she'd married Dominic. The name of the man Grace had originally come here to meet.

It was not, however, the name of the man sitting across from her.

"Aidan?"

"Hmm," he said absently, still staring into the fire, a million miles away.

"Why do you have a different last name than your brothers?"

# CHAPTER FOUR

They had different fathers," Tara said from behind Aidan. He felt a hand land on his shoulder, then a slight squeeze—the gentlest of warnings. Pulling his gaze from the fire, he looked up at her, surprised at how easily the lie had tripped off her tongue.

She smiled down at him. "How was dinner?"

"Terrible." He gestured to his empty plate. "I could hardly finish it."

"Haha." She squeezed his shoulder again, harder, before turning her attention to Grace. "How are you feeling? Any better?"

"I am." Grace watched the two of them closely. "Dinner was wonderful. Just what I needed after a long day of traveling. Will you join us?"

"I'd love to."

As Tara pulled up a chair, Aidan wondered how long she'd been standing there, listening to their conversation. There'd been no need for her to intervene. He could have handled it. He might have let the silence stretch on a bit too long after Grace's last question. But his response, if he'd given one, would have been similar to Tara's. As far as he was concerned, he and his so-called "brothers" did have different fathers. The only one lying here was Tara.

Grace moved a few dishes aside so Tara could set her glass of wine on the table. "Were you able to track down the kid I saw earlier?"

"I was," Tara said. "He's at his grandmother's house, and he's been there all evening, so you have nothing to worry about."

"What kid?" Aidan asked.

"It's nothing," Tara said, brushing him off.

"I saw a kid in the water earlier," Grace said, answering his question.

"Where?" Aidan asked.

"In the harbor, near the beach by my cottage. Tara said it could have been Liam's son from the description I gave her. But apparently, he's been at his grandmother's house all night, so I must have imagined it."

"I see," Aidan said slowly. It was clear from Grace's tone that she did *not* think she'd imagined it.

"I'm relieved to know he's safe, though." Grace looked back to Tara. "That's all that matters."

Tara smiled and reached for her wine. "I agree."

For the first time since offering to participate in this charade, Aidan wondered if Tara knew what she was doing. Did she know who Grace was? Had she even bothered to look her up?

Grace wasn't some starry-eyed tourist on vacation. She was an experienced investigative journalist who'd built a career on exposing the truth. If something seemed off, she wasn't going to let it go.

Grace leaned forward, resting her arms on the table. To anyone else, it might have appeared she'd simply moved closer to hear Tara better over the music. But he could tell from her body language that she was no longer relaxed. He got the distinct impression that she was preparing for battle. "You said, earlier, you might be willing to answer a few questions about the legend."

"I'd be happy to," Tara said. "What would you like to know?"

"I'd like to know how you broke the curse."

"I guess I'd better start at the beginning, then."

As Tara began to tell her story, a story Aidan had heard several times since arriving on the island, his gaze shifted back to Grace. Why was she so interested in this legend? It was too far outside her scope of work professionally, so it must have something to do with her personal life.

But what?

What had compelled her to take an extended leave of absence from her job—a job she clearly took as seriously as he took his?

Sitting back, he watched the firelight play over the different shades of gold in her hair. It fell in loose waves over her shoulders, the warm tones a striking contrast to her cool gray eyes. She wore no makeup, nothing to accentuate the appealing shape of her mouth, but his gaze lingered there all the same. Her skin was pale and smooth, still carrying the faintest glow of summer. And the thin white sweater she wore over a pair of faded jeans hugged her curves and hinted at toned arms and a tight, athletic body.

He'd offered to serve as a distraction, earlier, because he'd liked the way she looked. Now that he'd spent some time with her, it wasn't just her looks that attracted him. He liked the way her mind worked. He liked the subtle way she steered a conversation, finding clever ways to circle back to the questions she wanted to ask. He liked the confident way she carried herself. And he admired her professional success.

There were plenty of journalists nowadays who took the easy road, who cut corners and chose speed over precision. The field was filled with opportunists looking to go viral, more concerned with building their personal brands than cultivating trust with their sources and conducting the research required to carry out an investigation.

A quick scroll through Grace's Twitter feed had revealed exactly what kind of journalist she was. The kind who'd gotten into this field for the same reason he had—a relentless pursuit of the truth.

Unfortunately, that made their current situation more complicated. Especially if Grace already suspected Tara might be hiding something from her.

He considered pulling Tara aside to warn her. But wouldn't that only raise Grace's suspicions? Besides, did he want to get dragged any deeper into this? It was one thing to serve as a distraction, to deflect Grace's attention away from his past, this island, and the legend. It was another thing, altogether, to lie.

Looking over at Tara, he thought about how easily she'd lied when she'd walked up to their table, earlier, and how she'd probably lied about Liam's son not being in the water, too. He hadn't known her for that long, but she hadn't struck him as the type of person for whom lies came easily or who would lie without a strong motivation.

She was at the point in her story when a nurse, who'd worked at the same hospital as her ex-husband, had given her the means to escape. With a fake passport, a plane ticket, and a new name, she had run for her life. And she'd kept running, for months, until she'd arrived on Seal Island.

She had lied then, too, Aidan realized. Even after she'd arrived, she'd kept her new identity intact. She hadn't told anyone the truth about her past, not even Dominic. And she'd been justified in those actions.

The same way he'd been justified in his actions when he'd lied to protect his sources over the years. Or when he'd lied on his visa application about his purpose for entering Afghanistan at the start of the war. Or when he'd lied to a soldier in South Sudan who'd threatened to report him to government officials after he'd photographed evidence of mass atrocities they'd been trying to hide from the rest of the world.

Everyone was capable of lying if they had something precious enough to protect.

But was he willing to lie about this? To protect a truth he didn't even believe in?

Sensing his eyes on her, Tara glanced over. She smiled, like it was the most natural thing in the world to be talking about a two-hundred-year-old curse. But her story, as crazy as it was, didn't hold a candle to what she—and his "mother"—claimed to have happened afterwards.

*That* was the story they didn't want anyone else to know.

Tara offered her story as a cover so that no one would suspect that the islanders were hiding anything. She answered any questions the tourists had for her. And then she sent them on their way.

As long as she gave them something to explain the mysterious events that had happened on the island that day, they wouldn't dig any deeper. And they wouldn't come anywhere near the three people who had the most at stake if the rest of the story were exposed—his "mother," Brigid O'Sullivan, his "nephew," Owen O'Sullivan, and his "cousin," Glenna McClure.

He looked around the crowded dining room. All the tables were full. All the islanders were talking or tapping their feet to the music, oblivious to the potential threat that lay in their midst. He might not believe in any of their crazy stories. But Tara did. And he couldn't fault her for trying to protect the people she loved. Besides, he thought as her voice from earlier floated back to him, it was only for three days.

It wouldn't kill him to play along for three days.

Looking down at his drink, he saw that it was almost empty.

Tara's was, too. Grace, he noted, had stopped drinking as soon as Tara had sat down. Another indication that she didn't trust her.

They were going to have to fix that.

Mulling over a few ideas, he stretched his bad leg out and winced. It was starting to stiffen up again. Maybe a walk up to the bar and back would help. He reached for his cane. Just as he was starting to push to his feet, the front door opened. A swirl of cold air wafted into the room, followed by two teenagers—a sixteen-year-old girl with wispy, blond hair and an eighteen-year-old boy with dark hair that appeared to be wet.

Aidan looked at Grace. She had turned, and her gaze was fixed on the boy. He could tell that she'd seen him before. This must be the boy she'd seen in the water—the one Tara had said she'd imagined, the one who'd supposedly been at his grandmother's house all night.

Doing what? Taking a shower?

Still gripping his cane, Aidan lowered himself back to his chair. Two more people stepped through the door—a man and a woman in their mid-fifties. As soon as the woman spotted him, she lifted her hand in a tentative wave.

He didn't wave back.

Tara shot him a quick look of warning. But it was too late. Grace had already seen the exchange.

Grace turned back around, and Aidan could only imagine what she was thinking as she took in the woman's long black hair, snow-white skin, and striking silver eyes. Her black dress was hand-made from the finest wool in Ireland. A pair of black leather boots clicked against the floorboards with each step. A silver shawl draped over her shoulders like woven netting.

Several men stood to offer her their chairs as she passed. Two of the band members fumbled their chords, unable to take their eyes off her. The women in the room looked at her not with jealousy, but with reverence, as if her very existence gave them a sense of pride.

The couple made their way to the bar, and the crowd parted to receive them. Two young men slid off their stools, refusing to relent when the woman protested. Dominic greeted the couple warmly as they took their seats, setting a pint of ale in front of the man and leaning across the bar to give the woman an affectionate kiss on the cheek.

"Who's that?" Grace asked, her gaze still locked on the woman.

"Who?" Tara asked, as if the couple's entrance had been perfectly normal.

"She's asking about Brigid." Aidan knocked the rest of his drink back. "Brigid *O'Sullivan.*"

"O'Sullivan," Grace mused aloud, her gaze shifting to Aidan. "Another relative?"

When Aidan said nothing, Tara gave him a long look. "That's Aidan's mother."

# CHAPTER FIVE

The next morning, Grace woke to the sound of gulls crying in the harbor. Sunlight streamed through the gauzy curtains covering both windows. Resisting the urge to burrow under the covers, she forced herself out of bed. Her body might be on D.C. time, but she didn't want to lose another moment of daylight. Not after everything that had happened the night before.

After Brigid O'Sullivan had walked into the pub, Aidan had withdrawn, hardly speaking another word for the rest of the night. Tara, on the other hand, had become *more* animated. She'd seemed almost desperate to hold Grace's attention as she'd launched back into her story. And though her story *had* been compelling, it had also felt somewhat scripted. Almost like she'd rehearsed it.

If Brigid's arrival hadn't broken her rhythm, Tara might have been able to pull it off. But her words had lost some of their polish afterwards. And in the choppy pauses between them, Grace had sensed an undercurrent of fear. Which raised another issue—one that had been bothering Grace ever since Tara had sat down at their table the night before. Why would a woman who'd survived such a traumatic experience be willing to share so much of herself with a complete stranger?

There was something off about that. Particularly when, less than an hour before, she'd been unwilling to share anything about the boy Grace had seen in the water. If Tara had wanted to draw her attention *away* from the boy, wouldn't it have made more sense to come up with a reasonable excuse for why he'd been in the water? It wasn't unheard of for people to swim all year long. Unusual, but not unheard of. Instead, Tara had tried to pretend like he hadn't been there at all.

There was definitely something off about that.

She didn't know what Tara was hiding, but there was no question that she was hiding something. And if the locals weren't going to be straight with her, it was time to do some exploring on her own. She changed into jeans and a long-sleeved shirt, grabbed a granola bar from her bag, and headed for the door. The air was crisp and cool when she stepped outside. Over the rush of the ocean, she could hear the tinkling of Taylor's wind chime, a comforting reminder of home.

She closed the door behind her and followed the road leading east, away from the village. She passed the harbor without seeing another soul and lost sight of the village as the road curved inland. Winding through a patchwork of fields lined by stone walls, she saw white ponies and blonde cows. She crested a small hill and marveled at the stunning views in every direction. It was clear enough to see for miles, all the way to the mainland.

After a while, the road narrowed, and the pavement gave way to dirt. She followed a set of rutted tire tracks to the far side of the island, where the walls opened to reveal two whitewashed cottages, a small barn, and a covered shed holding farm equipment. Wondering who would choose to live out here, so far from the village, she scanned the property for signs of life. But all she could see, or hear, were the farm animals.

Behind the smaller cottage, a sandy path, lined by tall grasses, led to a beach. Walking toward it, she noticed that the tips of the grasses were beginning to brown, turning the color of rust. It was the first indication she'd seen of the coming change in seasons. How strange it was to be on an island with no trees and no defense against the elements.

The wind grew stronger, cutting through her jacket. Glad she'd thought to bring a hat, she slipped it on her head, then buried her hands in her pockets. She'd never felt so vulnerable in a place before, so completely exposed.

She stepped onto the beach and stopped short when she saw a woman knee-deep in the surf. The woman wore a long, white nightgown, far too thin for the cold. Her hair fell in a tangled mass of black waves to her waist. She held a large woven basket in the crook of one arm. With her other arm, she reached into the water and pulled up a handful of something. She discarded most of it, added only two items to her basket, then waded deeper into the surf.

Alarmed, Grace started after her. "Hello?" The wind and the waves swallowed her voice. She walked to the edge of the water, dodging the slippery strands of kelp strewn over the sand. "Hello, there?" she called out again, louder this time. "Are you all right?"

The woman paused, the hem of her nightgown floating around her. She turned. There was something so graceful, so fluid about her movements. It was almost as if she were part of the water itself.

It was Aidan's mother, Grace realized with a start. But she looked nothing like the woman who'd walked into the pub the night before, the one who'd carried herself with an air of elegance and nobility. There was a wildness to her and an intensity in her eyes that reminded Grace of herself when she was deep in the weeds of a story, focused to the point of obsession.

"Are you okay?" Grace asked, wondering if she should slip her shoes off and wade in after her.

Without answering, Brigid began to walk slowly toward Grace. The tide moved with her—a flood tide that crept closer with every crashing wave. Her feet were bare, as pale as the white sand beneath them. Thick blades of eelgrass clung to each of her ankles. She paused in front of Grace and searched her face like she was trying to place her. "I don't know you."

"No." The surf licked at Grace's boots. "We haven't met yet. I'm Grace."

"I'm Brigid," she said, but her voice sounded unsure and far away.

"Are you cold?" Grace started to unzip her fleece. "Do you want my jacket?"

"I'm not cold."

Grace's hands stilled. "Are you sure?"

"Yes." Brigid seemed confused by the suggestion.

Grace gestured behind her to the two cottages on the farm. "Do you live here?"

"No."

Grace wanted to reach out, to take the woman's hand and pull her away from the water. But she didn't want to break the fragile thread of connection. "Do you know who does?"

"Yes." Brigid's expression grew sad.

"Can I go get them?" Grace asked. "Let them know you're here?"

"No," Brigid said quickly. The items in her basket clinked together as she turned. She started to walk north, along the edge of the water, away from the farm.

Grace trailed after her. She didn't know what she was going

to do, but she couldn't leave her alone. "What are you collecting?"

"Shells."

Grace tried to peek in the basket. "Any particular kind?"

"Blue ones."

Okay, Grace thought. That was strange. But so was everything else about this woman so far. She wished she'd brought her phone with her. She could have searched for the number of the pub online and called for help. Instead, she was going to have to keep an eye on her until someone else came along. Either that or find a way to convince her to return to the village.

Brigid stopped walking abruptly. Grace stopped, too. The older woman bent down, sifted through the sand, and extracted a small blue shell that had been buried.

She added it to her basket.

Grace looked around, saw a white shell with a blue stripe nearby. She walked over and picked it up. "Here."

Brigid glanced at it, shook her head. "No."

"It has blue in it."

"No," she said again, switching her basket to her other arm to shield it from Grace and the not-blue-enough shell.

"Okay, got it." Grace tossed the shell over her shoulder, and Brigid seemed to relax. Wanting to regain her trust, she searched again, and spotted a dark blue shell a few feet ahead. She picked it up, showed it to Brigid. "What about this one?"

Brigid looked at the shell, hesitated.

"It has a chip in it," Grace said, wondering if she should have waited to find a better one.

"That's okay." Tentatively, Brigid reached for it.

Grace handed it to her.

With great care, Brigid placed it in the basket with the others before resuming her search.

Not wanting to leave the other two cottages, and the possibility of help, too far behind, Grace veered away from the water. She scanned the top of the beach, where the sand met the grass. "I think there are a bunch over here." She waved for Brigid to follow her.

They made their way over to where a sprinkling of blue shells lay at the foot of a small sand drift. Grace knelt and picked through the shells, only handing Brigid the ones that were solid blue.

Brigid added each one to her basket, then gave Grace a small smile.

Intending to lead her back to the farm by following a trail of blue shells, Grace stood, and noticed, for the first time, the six other baskets on the beach—baskets that looked exactly like the one Brigid was carrying.

How many shells was she planning to collect?

Slowly, not wanting to draw too much attention to herself, she walked over to the nearest basket. It was filled to the brim with white shells. Her eyes widened when she saw that the next one was filled with pink shells. And the next one, black.

Each basket contained one color, and only one color.

What the hell?

She looked back at Brigid, still in her nightgown, the hem soaking wet and clinging to her legs. She should be freezing, but she showed no signs of being the slightest bit cold.

Grace didn't know what was wrong with this woman, but she needed to get her home. "Brigid?"

Brigid waited for a wave to recede, then reached down and picked up another shell. "Yes?"

"Is your home...near here?"

Brigid nodded.

"Where?"

Brigid gestured to a small foot trail that cut through a field, heading toward the north side of the island. "That way."

Okay, Grace thought. She could either stay here, close to the farm, where someone might eventually come out and see them. Or she could offer to walk Brigid home, by way of an unknown trail, to a part of the island that looked mostly uninhabited, which was even farther away from the village.

Staying here definitely seemed like the better option.

Maybe if she could get Brigid to talk, to open up a little more, she could find out who lived on the farm. Then maybe she could persuade Brigid to let her knock on the door of the larger cottage. Hopefully, the owner would have a fire going soon, something hot for Brigid to drink, and a vehicle to drive her home in.

But first, she needed to get her to talk.

Grace picked up another blue shell and carried it over to Brigid. "What are you going to do with all these?"

Brigid took the shell from Grace and added it to her basket. "What do you mean?"

"Are you making something?"

"No."

"Then...why are you collecting them."

"I'm putting them in order."

*In order?*

Brigid looked up, her gaze searching the wide stretch of sand until it disappeared around a bend in the land. "There's so many, though," she said quietly. Something shifted in her expression. She wrapped her arms around the basket of shells, clutching them to her chest as she took a step away from Grace. "I can't keep up."

She'd upset her, Grace realized. That was the last thing she'd wanted to do. She scoured the beach for another blue shell, grabbing the first one she found. "It's okay." She wiped the sand off the shell before offering it to her. "I'll help. We can do it together. I like putting things in order, too."

Brigid regarded her warily. "You do?"

Grace nodded. "Yes. That's what I do for work." Well, not exactly. But she could make a connection out of almost anything if she tried. "I look for things that don't make sense, and I figure out how to fit them together."

Brigid's gaze dropped to the shell. It was a beautiful specimen with a shiny surface and rippled edges. Grace could tell she was struggling to decide what to do.

"Here." Grace took a step toward her. "It belongs with the others."

Brigid reached out slowly and took the shell from Grace. After tucking it in the basket, she let her hand linger there for a moment, touching the shells. Her voice grew quiet again, like before, almost as if she were speaking to herself. "I wish I knew where I belonged."

"What do you mean?" Grace asked. "Don't you belong here?"

Brigid looked down at her feet, which had somehow found their way back underwater. Long strands of eelgrass floated around them again, threading around her ankles, tugging her back out to sea. "I don't know."

Grace's brows drew together. "You live here, on the island, though, right?" She gestured to the trail Brigid had pointed out earlier. "You said your home was up that way."

"Yes, I live here." Absently, Brigid rolled the shells around in her fingers. "Do you live here?"

Grace blinked. Had she seriously just asked her that? "No."

"Where do you live?"

"D.C."

Brigid shook her head, indicating that she'd never heard of it.

"The District of Columbia? In the United States?"

"Oh," Brigid said, but it didn't sound like she knew.

The tide rushed in, further this time. Grace took a step back from the water to keep from getting wet. "It's on the other side of the ocean."

Brigid nodded slowly, as if she'd finally said something that made sense.

"Have you lived here your whole life?" Grace asked, wondering if that might explain it—how she could be so cut off from the rest of the world.

"No," Brigid said softly. She let go of the shells and the saddest expression came over her face.

"Where else have you lived?" Grace asked, unable to resist asking the follow-up question.

Brigid looked away, her gaze drifting past the beach to the sea. "Many different places."

"Grace?" A man's voice, sharp and familiar, cut through the wind.

Grace turned and spotted Aidan making his way toward them. He was limping badly, struggling to keep his balance in the sand. He was barefoot. His black hair was a rumpled mess, like he'd just woken up. He was wearing jeans, a half-buttoned flannel shirt, and a coat, open at the front, like he'd thrown it on at the last minute. And he did *not* look happy to see her.

"What are you doing here?" he asked.

"I went for a walk," she said, relieved to see him even if he didn't want to see her. "I followed the road until it ended, and then I ran into your mother."

Aidan looked at Brigid. He seemed even less happy to see her. But he didn't stop when he came to the water's edge. He kept walking, into the waves, his cane sinking into the wet sand as he limped toward her.

"Hello," Brigid said timidly.

Foregoing the pleasantries, Aidan shrugged out of his jacket, not an easy feat as he was still trying to support himself with the cane. "How long have you been out here?"

"I-I don't know," Brigid stammered "I'm fine, though. You don't have to—"

Ignoring her protests, he wrapped his jacket around her. Then he took her hand and led her out of the water. As soon as they were on dry land, he dropped it again. He took a step back, eyeing her knotted hair, her nightgown, the basket of shells in her arms, and the six additional baskets on the beach. "What are you doing with all these shells?"

Interesting, Grace thought. This wasn't normal behavior for Brigid. At least, not as far as Aidan knew.

Brigid looked at the baskets, and she seemed confused, like she didn't know how to answer him.

"We're putting them in order," Grace said.

Aidan's eyes cut to her. "What?"

"We're putting them in order," she repeated, as if it made complete sense and he was the only one who didn't get it.

Aidan looked at her like she was insane.

"We still have a lot of work to do." Grace said matter-of-factly, "but I need to head back to the village soon." She turned to Brigid. "If you need to reach me later—to finish—you can call me at the cottage I'm renting. If you don't have the number, call the pub. I'm sure Dominic has it."

Brigid reached out and took her hand. "Thank you."

Grace squeezed her hand reassuringly. She didn't know what was up with this woman, but whatever it was, it wasn't her fault. She was clearly struggling with something—to make sense of something.

And Grace could relate to that.

A low rumble of tires on dirt drew her eyes up to the road, where a man was driving toward them in a blue truck. As soon as the vehicle rolled to a stop, he jumped out.

Grace recognized him as the same man who'd been with Brigid the night before.

"Brigid!" He ran toward her. "Thank God! I've been looking everywhere for you."

Brigid let go of Grace's hand as the man pulled her into his arms. He was only an inch or two taller than Brigid. His hair was mostly gray, with a few streaks of brown leftover from his youth. And he had a kind, unremarkable face. He looked so normal, so pedestrian beside Brigid's otherworldly beauty.

But he clearly cared for her deeply.

And she for him.

After a long embrace, he pulled back, concern deepening the lines on his face. "What are you doing all the way out here?"

"I..." Her brows drew together as she trailed off. She seemed confused again, unsure of herself.

"We were collecting shells," Grace said.

The man looked at Grace. Froze.

"Hi," she held out her hand. "I'm Grace."

The man's eyes widened. He looked at Aidan, then back at Grace. Slowly, he extended his hand for her to shake. "Neil."

"It's nice to meet you, Neil." Grace added his name to the growing list of people she had questions about.

Neil's eyes found Aidan's again. The two men exchanged a long look. Then Neil held out a hand for the basket of shells Brigid was carrying. "May I?"

Grace noticed that he asked, rather than took. And Brigid handed them over willingly.

"They're beautiful," he said, admiring them.

"Aren't they?" Brigid's lips curved into a smile.

He nodded. "May I carry them home for you?"

"You may," she said softly.

He held out his free hand. She took it, threading their fingers together.

There was trust there, Grace thought. Deep trust. Even in the state she was in, she knew he would take care of the shells—and her.

This was *not* the first time he had seen her like this.

"Come on." Neil started to lead her off the beach. "Let's get you home where it's warm."

"Wait," Brigid said, stopping him. "What about the others?"

"What others?" Neil asked.

"The other baskets," Brigid said, pointing them out.

Neil looked back, spotted them, and his eyes went wide again. "You collected all those...today?"

Brigid nodded.

"I can help you load them into the car," Grace offered.

"That's not necessary," Aidan said. "I'll bring them by later."

Relieved, Neil nodded a quick thanks to Aidan. Clearly, he wanted to get Brigid off the beach and away from Grace as soon as possible.

But Brigid wasn't ready to leave yet. She was staring at Aidan, the smallest flicker of hope in her eyes. "You'll bring them by?"

"Yes."

"When?"

"Soon."

Brigid's gaze dropped to his leg, the one he could barely put weight on. "But...how will you manage?"

"I'll manage."

"Okay." She offered him a small smile—a smile, Grace noted, that Aidan did not return.

"Brigid?" Grace said as the couple turned to leave.

Brigid looked back, over her shoulder.

"It was nice to meet you."

Brigid smiled again, and this time, it reached all the way to her eyes. "It was nice to meet you too, Grace."

Grace stood on the beach with Aidan as Neil helped Brigid into the truck. She waited for the couple to drive away, until it was only the two of them with the wind and the waves and a lone gull circling overhead for company. "So," she said finally, breaking the silence. "That's your mother."

# CHAPTER SIX

o, Aidan thought, that was *not* his mother.

His real mother, the only mother he'd ever known, had died when he was eight years old. Clara O'Malley had been a kind, generous woman. She'd made him feel safe and loved. The only mistake she—and his father—had ever made as parents was being in the wrong place at the wrong time.

In the twenty-four years that had passed since that day, he had seen more death and destruction than most people would see in an entire lifetime. He'd seen wars, refugee crises, famines, and genocides. But none of those events had cut as deep as the senseless act of violence that had stolen his parents from him when he was a child.

Nothing had ever been the same after that.

And he wouldn't let this woman—whoever she was—disgrace his mother's memory by trying to take her place.

He looked at the six baskets on the beach, overflowing with shells. He wished he hadn't offered to bring them by. He didn't want to see her again so soon. And he didn't want her to think that they were going to spend any time *bonding* while he was here.

The sooner he could get this over with, the better.

He took a step toward the first basket, wincing when he put too much weight on his bad leg. His knee hurt like hell today. And he was starting to wonder if Tara had been right—that he'd pushed himself too hard yesterday. Leaning heavily on his cane, he took three more steps before Grace walked past him on her way to a different basket. "I can manage," he said brusquely.

She said nothing, maintaining her pace as if he hadn't spoken at all.

By the time he reached the first basket, she was already walking back with the second. Irritated that her pace was so much faster than his, he picked up his basket too quickly and lost a few shells in the process.

"Careful," Grace said.

"I don't think the world will end if we drop a few."

"No," Grace said. "But she might have counted them."

He stopped, stared at her.

When she smiled, he realized she'd been joking.

"Here." She scooped them up and placed them back in his basket. "Just in case."

He gave her a withering look, but her ability to make light of the situation melted some of the ice that had formed around his heart at the mere sight of Brigid. He turned, taking a moment to admire the way her long strides ate up the sand, the way her faded jeans molded to her legs, and the way her blonde hair fell in messy waves down her back.

The sight of Grace, now that Brigid was gone, had a completely different effect on him. But as he started after her, he couldn't help wondering why she'd decided to stay. Their evening at the pub, while enjoyable, hadn't quite ended the way he'd planned. She'd left as soon as Tara had finished her story. And she'd declined his offer to walk her home.

He'd begun to think it might be for the best. She would only be here for two more days. And he didn't want to get dragged any deeper into the O'Sullivan family drama. As he watched her set the basket of shells on the road and head back in his direction, though, he started to question that rationale.

It had been a while since he'd been this intrigued by a woman. He'd only met her the day before, but he'd already seen several sides of her, and all of them had been appealing. She gave him another smile as she passed by on her way to the next basket, and he decided that she might be worth a little family drama after all.

By the time he made it up to the road with his first basket, she'd added four more. There was only one basket left. He knew Grace could get it in a quarter of the time it would take him, but he was stubborn enough to want to do it himself.

When he turned and started back down the sandy path to the beach, she didn't try to talk him out of it. She fell into step beside him, slowing her pace to match his.

"I take it you're staying in one of those," Grace said, gesturing to the two cottages.

He nodded.

"Which one?"

"The smaller one."

"Who lives in the bigger one?"

"A man named Brennan."

"Another family member?"

"No."

She looked at him curiously, most likely wondering why he wasn't staying with a family member or renting a cottage in the village.

"I like it out here," he said in response to the question she hadn't asked. A sheep bleated. He lifted his gaze to a small flock roaming the mossy hills in the distance. At sunset, Brennan and his dog would round them up and herd them back into one of the pastures for the night. During the day, they were free to explore the island on their own.

Brennan treated his tenants with the same respect and autonomy he gave to his animals. The farmer's cottage was barely a field's-width apart from Aidan's, but he largely left him alone. He never stopped by unexpectedly or asked intrusive questions. He never tried to meddle or offer unsolicited advice.

And most importantly, he never made Aidan feel guilty for not spending enough time with his "mother."

"So," Grace said as they stepped onto the beach. "Do you want to talk about what happened earlier?"

Grace, on the other hand, Aidan remembered, had no qualms about asking intrusive questions. "No."

"Are you sure?"

"Yes."

"Okay." It was clear from her tone that it wasn't okay. She walked a few more steps in silence, looking down at the sand, then lifted her gaze back to his. "May I ask just one question?"

Aidan sighed. He should have known she wouldn't be able to let it go. The whole time they'd been out here, she'd probably been waiting for him to cool down so she could find out what was going on.

He couldn't blame her for wanting to know. It wasn't every day you came across a grown woman collecting shells in her nightgown. But how was he supposed to explain what Brigid had been doing when he didn't even know himself? "I'm probably going to regret this," he said finally, "but, yes."

"What happened between the two of you?"

It wasn't the question he'd been expecting. This one went deeper, cutting right to the heart of the matter. It made sense, though, given how quickly Grace had taken Brigid's side. She was probably wondering why he'd been so cold to the woman who was supposed to be his mother for the second time in the past twenty-four hours. But the answer to that question was even more complicated than the first. "It's just a bit of family drama, is all."

"That's not an answer."

"Then ask me another question."

"That's not how it works."

For the first time since waking up that morning, Aidan smiled. "That's how it works with me, love."

"Fine," she said. "I have another one. But you *have* to answer it."

He smiled again. "I'm not making any promises."

More gulls appeared, their cries piercing the air. "When you went into the water earlier, did it feel cold to you."

Aidan stopped walking. "What?"

"Did it feel cold?"

He searched her face for a sign that she was joking again, but he couldn't find one. "*That's* your question?"

"Yes."

"What kind of question is that?"

"A fairly straightforward one. A simple, yes, or, no, will do."

Why did he get the feeling like he was walking into a trap? "Then...yes."

She seemed surprised. "It did?"

"Of course." Why would she waste a question on something so obvious? He started to walk again. And so did she. But she didn't say anything else. Even though she'd agreed to only ask one question, it seemed out of character. At least from the short time he'd known her. Between steps, he stole a glance at her and saw that she was looking out at the ocean with a puzzled expression on her face. "What is it?"

"Nothing."

"It's not nothing. What is it?"

They were almost to the edge of the water. The waves were gaining strength. With every crash and spray of foam, the sea raced further inland. The last basket was only a few meters away, but it was partially submerged, at risk of being carried away by the incoming tide.

"I thought it might be hereditary."

"You thought *what* might be hereditary?" He took another step toward the basket. When the wind cut through his shirt, blowing it open at the bottom, he remembered he'd only had time to fasten a few of the buttons before coming outside. He reached for the next one, looking back at her for a response.

"Well..." The wind whipped her hair around her face. "I've seen two other people in the water since I arrived. And neither of them seemed to feel the cold. I thought, since you're related to both of them, maybe..."

He'd forgotten about Owen, Aidan thought. Grace had seen the boy swimming in the harbor the night before. And who knew how long she'd been out here this morning, watching his "mother" wade through the surf. Silently cursing Tara for lying about the boy and giving Grace a reason to doubt them before she'd even set foot in the pub the night before, he wondered how he was supposed to explain his way out of this one.

Especially when what she'd seen didn't make any sense to him either.

She was watching him closely, her gaze sharp and assessing. And he knew, now, why he'd felt like he was walking into a trap. He started to turn, to reach for the basket, to buy some time before he had to respond.

"Aidan, watch out." Grace's hand shot out, grabbed his arm.

He barely had time to react before the wave hit him from behind. The force of it would have been enough to knock him over if she hadn't stepped in front of him, catching him with her body so he wouldn't fall.

She sucked in a breath as the water rushed over their legs, as it seeped through their jeans. It was like stepping into an ice bath. She looked up at him in shock. And he could read the question in her eyes.

How could anyone swim in water this cold?

He had no idea.

And frankly, at the moment, he didn't care.

Because her body was still pressed against his. And though the risk of him falling had passed, neither of them had let go. He wasn't sure who was holding onto whom anymore.

She was soft and warm, and he could smell the subtle scent of her hair mingling with the salt in the air. Her eyes were still locked on his, but the shock had subsided. And in its place, was something that looked a lot like desire.

The water swirled around them, thickening as it slowed. His gaze lowered, settled on her mouth. He'd wanted to know what she tasted like from the moment he'd laid eyes on her.

But the water was already beginning to recede. And as it retreated, rushing back out to sea, he could sense her retreating as well.

She stepped back, suddenly, out of his arms. She seemed unsure of herself, as if she were confused about what had just happened. It was the first time he'd seen a crack in the confidence she wore around herself like a shield.

He wanted to reach for her again, to feel her soft body pressed against his. He wanted to lower his mouth to hers and see how much of that shield he could strip away with a single kiss. And he wanted to know who she was hiding beneath all that armor—who she was trying to protect.

Grace looked down, and her expression grew even more confused.

Reluctantly pulling his gaze from her face to see what had caught her attention, he looked down, too.

Between them, lying in the sand, were a dozen lavender rose petals.

"What the...?" he trailed off.

Grace looked up at him, then back down. "Where did those come from?"

"I don't know."

"They weren't here before...were they?"

He shook his head.

Grace took another step back, looked around. "Do you see any others?"

He scanned the beach in both directions, taking in the sweep of white sand peppered with black stones and broken shells. Unless they were hidden beneath a strand of kelp, he didn't see any more petals. "No."

"They're only right here." Grace looked back at the petals. There were no stems. No thorns. No leaves. Only petals—a dozen perfect petals that hadn't been there before. The scent of them, soft and sweet, rose into the air. "I don't understand."

Neither did he, Aidan thought. But there had to be an explanation. Surely, he could come up with something. He glanced over his shoulder, at the shadow of land in the distance. "Maybe they came from the mainland. Lots of strange things wash up with the tide."

"But look at them." Grace knelt and picked one up. The petal didn't have a single tear or blemish. None of them did. "How long could they have been in the water and still look like this?"

She held the petal out to him. It was the palest shade of lavender he'd ever seen, so pale it was almost silver. He took it gently from her hand. It was so small, so delicate, like the slightest breeze could have torn it apart.

Grace reached down, picked up another one. "Do roses grow on the island? I mean...could there be a plant nearby?"

"I don't know," he said, then caught himself. "There must be."

"Maybe the wind tore the petals off " She looked up at him. "Maybe they fell in the water and the tide...carried them here. Like you said."

Aidan nodded slowly. "That must be it."

Overhead, the gulls continued to circle and cry. When neither of them seemed able to move, Aidan turned his hand over and let the petal drop back to the sand. "Come on.' He started to make his way over to the final basket. "Your boots are soaked. I'll give you a ride back to the village."

Grace nodded. With one last look at the petals, she fell into step beside him. But she didn't let go of the one in her hand. She didn't let it fall back to the sand with the others. And she didn't say another word as they walked back up to the road.

# CHAPTER SEVEN

$\mathcal{I}$t had to be a coincidence, Grace thought as they drove away from the beach. She was three thousand miles from Heron Island. The petals couldn't have followed her here.

Gazing out the passenger side window, she scanned the fields for a plant, a bush, a hedge, a vine—*anything* to indicate that roses grew on this island. And that they were still in bloom.

But the only flowers she saw were chickweed, red clover, and yarrow. The rest of the wildflowers had died off, leaving only the hardiest blooms clinging to the scraggly patches of grass along the road. Even the fuchsia vines that coiled over the walls had lost most of their petals. Their leaves were yellow and curling, their stems turning brown as they dried.

As the harbor came into view, the walls began to blur. She could still smell them, even though she only carried a single petal in her hand. Beyond the harbor, the sunlight on the water was so bright it was almost blinding. Her throat felt tight, like the air in the car was growing thick.

She reached for the switch to roll the window down, to get some air, as Aidan pulled to the side of the road to let another car pass. When they came to a stop, she opened the door instead. "I'll walk from here."

Aidan looked over. "You want to walk?"

She nodded, already stepping out of the car. Her waterlogged boots made a squishing sound as she stood. She could feel little bits of sand between her toes.

"Grace?"

She paused before closing the door.

Aidan leaned over so she could see him. "Are you all right?"

Grace looked at him—really looked at him for the first time since she'd stepped out of his arms on the beach. She felt like she was back in the car again. Like she could hardly breathe.

It wasn't just the petals, she realized.

It was Aidan.

His eyes, still locked on hers, seemed darker now, like the color of a sky right before a hurricane hit.

She took a step back, away from the car. "Yes. I just...need some air."

He continued to study her, his expression growing concerned. "I'll see you later, then?"

She nodded and closed the door before he had another chance to speak. She didn't know when she would see him again, but she hoped it wouldn't be until tonight. At the pub. Where they'd be surrounded by people.

Where they wouldn't be able to finish what they'd started.

She waited for him to drive away, waited until she was alone on the road again. Then she took a deep breath. And tried to shake off the memory of what it had felt like to be in his arms. She'd had chemistry with men before. She knew what it felt like to be drawn to someone, to be so attracted you could hardly keep your hands off each other. But she'd never felt *anything* like that before.

And he hadn't even kissed her.

She took a step forward. Then another. Her boots felt heavy, weighted. Like rocks. But she kept going, following the narrow road as it dipped back to sea level. She passed the church and the ferry dock and the few boats that had returned with their catch for the day. She could hear the fishermen's voices echoing over the water.

The sound reminded her of home, of Heron Island. But it didn't bring her any comfort. Not this time.

She opened her fingers, curled loosely around the petal. If it had been any other flower, any other color, she might have been able to shrug it off. She might have simply added it to the long list of bizarre things that had happened since she'd arrived on this island. But lavender rose petals made this personal.

Too personal.

Because every year, on the anniversary of her mother's disappearance, lavender roses bloomed outside her childhood home. They hadn't been there before her mother had left. Her father hadn't planted them. He'd been as surprised to see them as she had. And none of their friends seemed to know where they'd come from either. They'd simply appeared, in a small patch of soil beneath her bedroom window, exactly one year after her mother had vanished.

In time, Grace had begun to accept that her mother wasn't coming back. Shock and denial had shifted to anger, and she'd needed to take that anger out on something. When the flowers had bloomed again, on the same date, the following year, she'd felt like they were mocking her. So she'd decided to get rid of them. She'd dug the whole plant up, roots and all, and thrown it, as far as she could, into the Bay.

But the very next year, the plant had grown back. And when she'd dug it up again, it had grown back again. She'd continued to try to get rid of it, over and over, using several different methods throughout the years. But nothing had ever worked. It had always grown back—year after year after year.

It didn't make sense. She hated things that didn't make sense. Aside from her mother's disappearance, it was the only mystery she couldn't seem to solve. The two had to be connected. If she could solve one, she was sure she could solve the other.

All she needed was a clue.

Climbing the final hill to the village, she looked back down at the petal. Was that what this was—a clue? If so, what did it mean? What did it have to do with her mother? And what did it have to do with Aidan, if anything?

Closing her fingers around the petal, she let her hand fall back to her side. She had some research to do before her meeting with Liam this afternoon. She didn't want to see anyone, or talk to anyone, for the next few hours. Not until she had some answers.

She rounded the corner to her cottage and stopped short when she spotted a woman outside her door.

"Hello," Grace said warily, slipping the petal into her pocket.

"Hello, there." The woman smiled. "I heard the prettiest sound as I was walking by. I had to come see what it was." She reached up and touched a tiny silver petal hanging from the end of a piece of string. "What a lovely wind chime."

Grace's gaze shifted from the woman to the chime. The chime Taylor had insisted she bring. The chime made of rose petals.

Twelve rose petals.

The same number of petals that had been on the beach. Her grip tightened on the one in her pocket. "Thank you."

The woman continued to study the chime. "Where did you find it?"

She wanted to be alone, Grace thought. She needed time,

and space, to think. She took a small step toward the door, hoping the woman would take the hint. "A friend made it for me."

The woman arched a brow. "And you brought it with you on your travels?"

"Yes." Grace tried to think of a polite way to excuse herself. "She asked me to bring it. She said it would make me feel more at home."

"At home?"

Grace nodded.

"Because of the roses?"

"No." Grace took a breath. Apparently, the woman wasn't in any hurry to leave. Pushing her own concerns aside, she focused on the person in front of her for the first time.

The woman, who appeared to be in her late thirties, had long brown hair and caramel-colored eyes—the same shade as the full-length cashmere coat that cinched at her waist with a matching belt. She wore heeled boots, similar to the ones Brigid had worn the night before, and a midnight blue scarf, shot with silver threads. The threads, along with the silver drops that hung from her ears, glinted in the morning light.

When the woman continued to regard her curiously, Grace decided to offer a brief explanation, hoping it might appease her so they could both be on their way. "There's a place in my hometown called the Wind Chime Café. It's sort of like a community center, where everyone gathers in the morning to catch up on gossip. It's probably like O'Sullivan's is here, except it's a café instead of a pub. Anyway, the front porch is covered in wind chimes, and you can hear them all over town. That's why it's supposed to make me feel at home."

"I see." The woman lowered her hand and turned her full attention on Grace. "I don't think we've met. I'm Glenna."

"Grace," she said, noting that the woman's voice was as smooth and cultured as her clothing. On an island where most people wore denim, wool, and fleece, Glenna's outfit should have seemed out of place. But oddly, on her, it seemed right. Maybe it was her outfit, or maybe it was the way she carried herself, but something about this woman reminded Grace of Brigid.

Not the Brigid she'd met on the beach that morning. The Brigid she'd seen at the pub the night before—the one the islanders had treated like royalty.

Glenna's gaze skimmed down the front of Grace, lingered on her wet jeans and walking boots, then drifted back up. "Did you lose your way in a bog this morning?"

"No," Grace said. "I was walking on one of the beaches. The tide came in fast."

Glenna nodded slowly. "The sea can be unpredictable here."

Grace thought of the rose petals that had washed ashore at her feet. Unpredictable was one word for it. "I should probably change," she said as tactfully as possible.

"Of course." Glenna stepped aside, her long coat sweeping around her ankles. "Don't let me keep you."

"Thanks." Grace started to reach for the door, then stopped. Before she began her research, she ought to find out when Liam was coming back. It would help to know how much time she had. "Do you know Liam and Caitlin?"

Glenna nodded.

"Have you heard from either of them today?"

"I spoke with Caitlin this morning."

"How is she?"

"Much better," Glenna said. "They're on their way back to the island now."

"That's a relief."

"It is. She gave us all a fright."

"What time do you think they'll arrive?"

"If they catch the next ferry, they should be here around three o'clock. Why?"

"I'm supposed to meet with Liam later today."

"Right," Glenna said. "Dominic mentioned something about that. I'm glad you reminded me. Caitlin needs to stay off her feet for the next several days, so I'll plan to watch the twins for a while longer after they arrive."

"Twins?"

Glenna nodded. "They've been with me all night. I just dropped them off at their grandmother's house so I could run a few errands."

Grace thought of the boy she'd seen swimming with the seals the night before—the one Tara had said looked like Liam and Caitlin's son. "How many children do they have?"

"Three, with a fourth on the way."

Grace marveled at the age difference between the eighteen-year-old boy and the child they were expecting. Caitlin must have been very young when she'd had her first child. "How old are the twins?"

"They just turned four." When the church bells began to ring, signaling the top of the hour, Glenna glanced down at her watch. "Will you look at that? It's later than I thought. I promised to bring the twins a treat from the market. And they can be a handful when they don't get their way, so I'd better get on."

Grace nodded.

"It was nice to meet you," Glenna said.

"You, too." Grace watched her turn, then frowned as she put two and two together. "Wait."

Glenna glanced over her shoulder.

"Did you say you left them with their grandmother?"

Glenna nodded.

"Do you mean Brigid?"

"Yes."

Grace thought of the woman she'd seen on the beach that

morning and tried to imagine her taking care of two four-year-olds. "Did she seem okay to you?"

Glenna turned around. "Yes. Why?"

"I ran into her on the beach this morning—the one by the farm, on the east side of the island."

Glenna nodded, as if that seemed perfectly normal. "She often walks that beach in the mornings."

Grace thought of the shells. The baskets. "I'm not sure she was walking."

"What was she doing, then?"

"Well..." Grace took a breath. How could she put this? "When I got there, she was gathering shells."

Glenna looked at her strangely. "Haven't you ever gathered shells when you were walking on a beach before?"

"Yes," Grace said. "But she wasn't just gathering them. She was sorting them."

"Sorting them?"

Grace nodded. "Hundreds of them, into color-coded baskets."

"Ah." Glenna seemed amused.

"What?"

"They're for the twins."

"The twins?"

Glenna nodded. "She collects shells so they have something to play with when they come to her house. You should see how many she has in her back garden. Piles and piles of them, from every beach on the island. It's really quite something."

Grace regarded her skeptically. "Why wouldn't she just take the kids to the beach, let them play with the shells there?"

"The twins are too young to be playing near the ocean. Especially at this time of year, when the waves can be rough." She gestured toward Grace's wet jeans. "As you experienced yourself this morning."

Grace couldn't argue with that. Personally, she didn't think anyone should be going in the ocean right now, children *or* adults. But that didn't explain why Brigid had seemed so distressed. "When I asked Brigid why she was collecting the shells, she said she was 'putting them in order.'"

Glenna laughed. "It's a game they play."

"A game?"

Glenna nodded. "Brigid puts the shells in order. Then the twins scatter them all over the garden and make a big mess. Afterwards, they each pick a color and race to see who can fill their basket the fastest. It keeps them entertained for hours."

Grace thought of the woman she'd met on the beach that morning, how particular she'd been about each of the shells being just the right color. Her behavior had been borderline obsessive. "Why would Brigid sort the shells first if the twins are supposed to do that? Why not just mix them up to start with?"

"Why does any grandmother do what they do?" Glenna asked with a laugh. "To be honest, I don't know. Maybe she sorts them first to make sure there's an equal amount of each color. Each of the twins has their favorite. She probably doesn't want either of them to feel slighted if one ends up with more than the other."

She had an answer for everything, Grace thought. A simple answer that made perfect sense. As much as she wanted to accept those answers and move on, because frankly she had enough to worry about, there had to be more to the story than this.

Glenna hadn't been on the beach with them that morning. She hadn't seen Brigid wading through the surf in her nightgown. She hadn't seen how distressed she'd been, or how relieved Neil had been when he'd finally found her.

If Brigid had been collecting shells for her grandchildren, why would Neil have been driving all over the island searching for her? And why wouldn't either of them have just said so?

She had questions, Grace thought. So many questions. But her instincts told her not to ask any more of them—at least, not to Glenna. The best course of action, at this point, she decided, was to play along. "Well, I guess that explains it." Grace smiled. "I'm just glad she's okay."

"Of course," Glenna said. "No trouble at all."

Grace reached for the door to her cottage. "Thanks for letting me know when to expect Liam."

"I'll send him a message to make sure he hasn't forgotten. Should I tell him to look for you here or at the pub?"

"Here." Grace opened the door.

"Oh, and Grace?"

She turned, looked back at Glenna.

"If you're looking for something to do before then, something *away* from the water," she added with another glance down at Grace's waterlogged boots, "feel free to come by my studio and have a look around. It's a five-minute walk from here. Just follow the footpath that leads north from the village."

"You're an artist?"

"I am." Glenna tilted her head toward the cottage. "I did all the paintings inside."

Grace thought of the underwater palace. The beauty of it. The otherworldliness of it. The amount of imagination that must have gone into creating it. "That one above the fireplace—I've never seen anything like it."

"Thank you," Glenna said, clearly taking that as a compliment. "That one's not for sale, but I have plenty of others that are. Prints and postcards, too. If you're looking for a souvenir to take back with you. Perhaps for your friend..."

"Friend?"

"The one who made you the wind chime."

"Right," Grace said. That was how their conversation had started. "I might take you up on that."

Glenna smiled. "I hope you do." With one last look at the chime, she turned and walked away.

Grace stood in the street for a moment, watching her. Then she walked into the cottage and closed the door.

She could still hear the waves, but they were muffled now. And she was relieved to have a break from the ceaseless crashing. She left her boots by the door and started to peel off her wet socks on the way to the shower. But she stopped when she saw the painting over the fireplace.

And noticed, for the first time, the white roses that lined the path leading up to the palace.

She reached into her pocket for the petal and drew it out. It was still perfectly formed, without a single blemish, as if she'd just plucked it from a fresh flower moments ago. How was that possible?

She looked back at the painting. At the glittering roses made of ice.

And decided the shower could wait.

She went into the bedroom, grabbed her laptop, and carried it out to the living room. Not bothering to remove her jacket or her jeans, she sat on the couch, facing away from the harbor. She typed in her password, closed the pop-up box alerting her to the 309 unread messages in her inbox, and pulled up a search engine.

She didn't remember reading anything about roses during her initial research. And she didn't remember Tara mentioning anything about them the night before. But that didn't mean there wasn't a connection. Sometimes all you needed was one word to add to your search and everything would fall into place.

She typed in the words, "Seal Island" and "roses," then waited for the results to load. The first few pages didn't offer anything out of the ordinary: gardening advice, pruning instructions, lists of the best varieties to grow in this climate, links to seed companies and organic pest controls, musings by naturalists, advertisements for wedding planners, and a map featuring nearby florists on the mainland.

She clicked on a few links, to make sure she wasn't missing anything, then reminded herself that it had been eight years since Tara had broken the curse. Whatever she was looking for might be buried pretty deep.

She scrolled through a few more pages of results, until she came across a thumbnail image that caught her eye. An image of a white cottage covered in red roses. She clicked on the link to enlarge it. Then simply stared.

Blood red roses dripped from dark vines that snaked up the walls, stretched over the top of the door, and tangled with the thatch of the roof. The cottage was perched on the edge of a cliff. It looked like it had been swallowed by them—by a web of roses that grew from a single stem in a garden that held no other plants.

Was that here? On Seal Island?

She skimmed the caption beneath the image. It had been taken by a travel blogger, who'd visited the island in the summer, eight years ago, during a festival.

Grace slowly pushed to her feet. She walked to the west-facing window and looked up, past the village, to the lone cottage on the edge of the cliff. Tara might not have mentioned anything about roses in her story the night before. But she had mentioned where she'd stayed when she'd first arrived on the island—in a cottage, on a cliff, hundreds of feet above the sea.

The roses were gone now. And so was the selkie's pelt. The one the fisherman had stolen. The one Tara had needed to find to break the curse.

The one she claimed they *had* found, eight years ago, buried in a garden outside her house.

ncle Aidan!" Maeve O'Sullivan ran toward him, her red curls blowing in the wind. Her twin sister, Freya, was right behind her. "Come see what we made!" Maeve's four-year-old hand grasped his, tugged him out of the car.

"Hang on." Aidan laughed as he cut the engine. "I've got a few things to unload first."

"What kind of things?" Freya pressed up on her toes to peer in the windows.

"Shells," Aidan said, "from the beach by the farm."

Maeve's eyes went wide. "Seashells?"

Aidan nodded.

Freya jumped up and down excitedly.

With the help of his cane, he unfolded himself from the driver's seat and made his way to the back of the car to pop the hatch.

When the twins spotted the number of shells, their mouths fell open.

"Are those for *us*?" Freya asked.

"Of course, they're for you," Brigid said as she walked out of the house.

Maeve looked at her grandmother. "All of them?"

Brigid nodded, smiling.

Freya let out a delighted squeal as she scooped two handfuls of shells from the nearest basket. Her sister did the same thing. They both raced toward the back garden, leaving Aidan and Brigid alone.

As soon as they'd gone, Aidan tensed. His "mother" had managed to change out of her nightgown, into a white turtleneck and gray pants. She'd brushed the knots out of her hair, and her eyes seemed clear again. But he couldn't let go of the image of the woman he'd seen on the beach that morning.

He waited for her to say something, to explain what she'd been doing there.

"I made tea," she said. "Would you like some?"

No, Aidan thought. He did not want tea. He wanted to unload these baskets and be on his way as quickly as possible. "I can't stay."

"Oh." Her face fell.

The twins came running back for more shells. "Uncle Aidan, come play with us!" Maeve reached for his hand and started to tug him toward the back garden. "We want to show you what we made!"

Aidan hesitated. He hadn't counted on the twins being here. He'd spent a fair amount of time with them over the past few weeks, and he'd grown rather fond of them. But if he agreed to stick around, he didn't want Brigid to get the wrong idea. That he was staying for her. Or that he would ever come back again. "I can only stay for a few minutes."

Maeve beamed, knowing she'd won.

"Neil and I will bring the baskets around," Brigid said, her expression brightening.

Aidan nodded and let Maeve lead him around to the back of the house. He'd seen it from a distance before, but never this close. It was one of the few houses on the island that had been built with brand new construction in the past thirty years. Many of the older homes had been renovated, or added onto, but they'd maintained at least part of their original structure. Even the ones that had been damaged in a fire that had broken out several years ago had been restored with painstaking care to preserve as much of the historical integrity as possible.

This one, though, was a masterpiece in modern architecture. Perched on a flat shelf of land nearly seventy meters above sea level, with two walls made entirely of glass, it offered expansive views of the village and the harbor. The first floor consisted of one large room with a minimalist kitchen, a cozy breakfast nook, several seating areas, and a massive stone fireplace that took up most of the far wall.

Filled with natural light and an abundance of native plants, it seemed to exist as an extension of the landscape itself.

Behind the house, there were two more structures—a shed where Neil, a retired builder, kept his tools and a greenhouse where Brigid grew herbs and flowers. But it was the area *between* the three structures that made him pause. He let go of Maeve's hand, and she ran ahead of him. Leaning his cane on a stepping-stone, he gazed in awe at what they had created.

A trail of blue shells led to a sandbox shaped like a mermaid's tail. Beside it, a shallow pool with a sparkly turquoise bottom held an assortment of floating sea creatures. More trails of shells led to two child-sized playhouses, one for each of the twins.

Behind the playhouses were two goal posts made of driftwood with silver netting stretched between them for the teenagers, Owen and Kelsey, to play football with their friends. Judging from the amount of skid marks in the grass, it appeared they came here a lot.

"Uncle Aidan, look!" Freya waved him over. "Come see mine first."

Aidan limped over to Freya's playhouse and gazed down at a pink window box holding a tiny garden made of moss, ferns, and a few hearty herbs. There was a wooden welcome sign, which looked like something Neil would have made, and a ribbon of blue sea glass, most likely added by Brigid, to resemble a river meandering through the moss. In the middle of the garden, a miniature tea set graced a tiny table covered in a pink cloth, surrounded by four tiny wooden chairs.

"It's for the fairies," Freya explained. "Granny said if we made them a garden, they'd come visit us."

"And bring us fairy dust!" Maeve pulled him over to her playhouse so he could see the one she made.

Aidan smiled as he took in the three gnomes with pointy red hats guarding a crop of magic mushrooms. "I'm sure the fairies will love it."

"I can't wait to see them." Freya adjusted one of the tiny chairs in her garden.

Aidan looked up and made a show of scanning the sky while shielding his eyes from the sun. "How soon do you think they'll be here?"

The twins giggled.

"They won't be here until dark," Freya said.

"Oh." Aidan feigned disappointment.

"They don't like to be seen," Maeve explained, "so they only fly at night."

"If they don't like to be seen, how are you going to see them?"

"Granny said their wings glow," Freya answered excitedly. "She said we can see them from inside the house, if all the lights are out."

Ah, Aidan thought. Clever. It wouldn't be that hard for Neil and Brigid to create something that looked like glowing wings from afar. They could even add a timer so the lights would switch on as soon as night fell. The twins would be beside themselves.

Aidan looked back at Maeve's garden. "Where will they leave the fairy dust?"

Maeve plucked a tiny bottle with a cork stopper from beneath the moss. "They'll put it in here."

They'd thought of everything, Aidan realized. It was impressive, really, given the state Brigid had been in that morning. Perhaps this was all Neil's doing. He reached down to straighten a mushroom that had tipped over. "What are you going to do with it?"

"The dust?" Freya asked.

He nodded.

"We're going to give it to you," Maeve said.

"Me?" he asked, surprised.

"For your leg," Maeve said. "Granny said it would make you feel better, that you'd be able to walk on your own again." She tucked the bottle back under the bed of moss and turned to Freya, as if she'd said nothing of particular importance. "We should add some shells to the gardens."

Freya's face lit up. "Do fairies like shells?"

"Of course, they do," Brigid said from behind them. "They especially like the ones you can see through when you hold them up to the light." She held one up to demonstrate. "Like this."

"Can I see?" Maeve held out her hands for the shell.

Brigid smiled and placed the shell in her hands, then looked up at Aidan as the twins ran toward the rest of the baskets to find more. "Neil just pulled a loaf of bread out of the oven. I know you said you couldn't stay." She smoothed a nonexistent wrinkle out of the front of her shirt. "But would you like to have a small piece before you go?"

Neil walked out of the house, setting a loaf of soda bread on the table by the door. It was the first time Aidan had noticed the table, and he felt a tug of guilt when he saw the spread. In addition to the soda bread, there were scones, biscuits, cookies, and little teacakes drizzled with honey. A jar of clotted cream sat between a bowl of strawberry jam and a dish of softened butter. There was a carafe of coffee on one end of the table and a pot of tea on the other.

It appeared they were expecting a visitor—a special visitor. Someone, perhaps, who had never visited them before.

Aidan took a deep breath. It wouldn't kill him to stay for a piece of soda bread. "Thank you. That would be nice."

Neil cut him a piece and set it on a plate.

Brigid started to retrieve it for him. "Butter?"

"I can get it," Aidan said.

Brigid paused halfway to the table, her gaze dropping briefly to his cane. "I don't mind."

"I can get it," he repeated.

Her smile faltered. "Okay."

She stood there awkwardly as he limped past her.

"Do the twins want any?" he asked, trying to smooth out the rough edges in his previous words—the rough edges he couldn't seem to help when he was around her.

She turned, relieved to have a purpose again. "Girls? Would you like some soda bread?"

"No," they both said in unison, still absorbed with finding the perfect shells for their fairy gardens.

Feeling another tug of guilt, Aidan took the plate from Neil. "The gardens—were those your doing or Brigid's?"

"Mostly Brigid's," Neil said.

Aidan glanced over his shoulder at Brigid. "They're charming."

She seemed taken aback by the compliment. "Thank you."

Aidan set the plate down so he could eat with one hand and continue to grip his cane with the other.

"Would you like to sit?" Neil gestured toward one of the chairs.

"No," Aidan said quickly. He didn't want Brigid to think he'd had a change of heart because he'd agreed to stay for a piece of soda bread. "I can't stay long." He took a bite. It was still warm. "This is excellent, though."

Neil cut another piece. "Thanks."

"Do you like to bake?" Brigid asked as she walked over to join them.

"Not really, no," Aidan said.

"What about cooking?"

Aidan shook his head.

"I'm not much help in the kitchen either," Brigid said, offering him a tentative smile. "I guess we have that in common."

Aidan felt the rough edges coming back. He didn't want to know what they had in common.

"I do love to garden, though," she went on. "Do you like to garden?"

"I've never tried it, so I'm not sure."

"I'd be happy to teach you, if you'd like to learn."

That was the last thing he wanted. "I move around a lot. I wouldn't be around to take care of anything I learned to grow."

"Oh," she said. "Right."

Neil handed Brigid a piece of soda bread and gave her an encouraging look.

She looked back at Aidan. "Do you like that—moving around a lot?"

"It doesn't really matter whether or not I like it. It's part of the job."

"And...you like your job?"

That would be putting it mildly. "Yes."

Brigid looked at Neil. He nodded for her to go on. She took a breath, then looked back at Aidan. "Your photographs... I've been wanting to talk to you about them. They're... Well, they're..."

"Heartbreaking?" Aidan offered.

"Yes," Brigid admitted. "They *are* heartbreaking."

"They're supposed to be," Aidan said. Not everyone could spend their days making fairy gardens with their grandchildren. Not everyone had a husband who would build them a home as a wedding present. Not everyone had an entire family who would indulge their delusions that they'd grown up under the sea.

Someone had to do something about the hundreds of millions of people who were suffering, who couldn't afford to spend their whole lives playing make-believe, completely detached from reality.

Remembering that he'd received a message the night before from one of his contacts at *The Guardian*, and that he still needed to respond to it, he was about to excuse himself when Maeve ran over and pressed a shell into his hand.

"Look what I found!"

Aidan looked down at it.

"Hold it up to the light!" Maeve insisted.

He held it up and watched the sun stream through the delicate ridges.

Maeve did a twirl. "Isn't it beautiful?"

"It's perfect," he said, handing it back to her. "The fairies will love it."

She beamed. And he smiled back at her. He could never stay upset for long when he was around children. They were the one consistently bright spot in a world that had gone dark in so many other ways.

There were times, now and then, when he wondered what it would be like to have a child of his own. A son or a daughter to love the same way his parents—his *real* parents—had loved him. But his lifestyle would never allow him to have a family.

He took too many risks. He traveled to places that were too dangerous. He never knew, on any given day, if he was going to make it out alive.

He wouldn't put a wife or a child through that.

Besides, there were so many other children who needed him. Children in orphanages. Children in refugee camps. Children of war whose parents had been stolen from them. The same way his had.

The world needed to know they were out there. So no one would forget about them.

"Will you help me find a place for it?" Maeve asked.

"I'd be glad to." He ruffled her hair. "And then I have to go."

She pouted for a few seconds. Then she took his hand and led him back to her garden. Together, they found the perfect spot for her shell, nestled in a bed of moss between two tiny unicorns.

"Freya." Aidan called her over after he gave Maeve a hug goodbye. "If, for any reason, the fairies don't come tonight, I want you both to know that your gardens are perfect, just as they are."

Freya ran over and wrapped her arms around his legs. "They'll come. I'm sure of it. And tomorrow, we'll give you the dust."

"Then you'll be all better," Maeve said.

Aidan's heart constricted. They were so sure of themselves, so sure that the dust would heal him. How was he going to break it to them when it didn't?

"Here." Brigid walked over with a takeaway container. "I added a few of everything, in case you're hungry later."

"Thanks." Aidan took the container from her. He wished she hadn't done that. He didn't want her to do nice things for him.

"If you change your mind about learning how to garden, you're welcome to come back anytime."

"Thanks," he said again, though he had no intention of

coming back. "I'll keep that in mind." He nodded a quick goodbye to Neil and turned his attention to navigating the steppingstones.

As soon as he rounded the side of the house, he saw that another car had pulled up. Sam Holt cut the ignition and stepped out of the driver's seat. "Brennan said you might be here."

"What's going on?" Aidan asked.

"We need to talk about what happened this morning."

A lot had happened that morning, Aidan thought. "You're going to need to be more specific than that."

"On the beach," Sam clarified, "with your mother."

"Ah," Aidan said. "Yes." He'd been wondering if anyone was ever going to address that.

Sam closed the door. "Neil called as soon as they got home. We came right away."

That was why the twins were here, Aidan realized. Sam and Glenna must have brought them over when they'd come to make sure Brigid was okay.

Sam crossed the yard to where Aidan stood. "Can you tell me what happened earlier—what sort of state you found her in?"

"I can," Aidan said with a quick glance over his shoulder, "but wouldn't you rather go somewhere more private?"

"No," Sam said. "Neil's going to want to hear this, too."

Neil stepped out of the house and shut the door quietly behind him. Aidan braced himself, waiting for the older man to berate him for continuing to push his "mother" away, for not having the decency to stay for a single cup of tea. If the tables were turned, that was what he would do.

But Neil didn't look angry. He looked concerned.

Very concerned.

"How is she?" Sam asked.

"She seems fine, now," Neil said.

"Does she remember what happened?" Sam asked.

"I don't know. I didn't want to push her by asking too many questions. I was afraid it might upset her."

Sam nodded and turned to Aidan. "Did she say anything to you on the beach about why she was there?"

Aidan shook his head. "How often does this sort of thing happen?"

"Not that often," Neil said. "At least...not until recently." He ran a hand through his hair. "In the past few weeks, she's been doing things she hasn't done in a long time. Things she used do to before I met her."

"Like what?" Aidan asked.

Neil took a deep breath. "Like wandering the shoreline at all hours. Or waking up in the middle of the night to go down to the ocean. Some nights, she stays on the beach until dawn, just sitting there, all by herself, staring out at the sea. Like she's...waiting for something."

"Have you spoken with Sister Evelyn?" Sam asked.

"Yes." Neil paused, looking at Aidan for confirmation that he knew who they were talking about.

Aidan nodded for him to go on. He knew the story. Sister Evelyn was the nun who'd taken Brigid in after she'd been institutionalized. Somehow, Brigid had managed to convince her that she wasn't crazy. And somehow, despite her devout Christian faith, Sister Evelyn had come to believe, like everyone else on this island, that Brigid was a selkie.

And not just any selkie—a selkie *queen*.

"She's concerned as well," Neil went on. "She said Brigid used to do things like this all the time."

"Wander the shoreline in her nightgown?" Aidan asked.

"That," Neil said. "And...put things in order."

"Like what she was doing with the shells earlier?" Aidan asked.

Neil nodded. "She's been sorting things in the house as well. Grouping things by color and shape. Putting all the books in alphabetical order."

"When did you say this started?" Sam asked.

"Three weeks ago," Neil said. "Maybe four, at the most."

"What about before that?" Aidan asked.

Neil shook his head. "She's been fine for so long. I don't understand what's happening."

Aidan looked back and forth between the two men. "You're saying she hasn't done any of these things for seven years?"

"Yes," Neil said.

"So...what?" Aidan asked. "She's regressing?"

"I don't know," Neil said, clearly distressed.

Sam put a hand on Neil's shoulder. "Don't worry. We'll figure it out. We always do."

What they needed, Aidan thought, was a psychiatrist. And he hoped they found one soon. In the meantime, they needed to keep her as far away from Grace as possible. "Not to complicate matters, but Neil and I aren't the only ones who saw Brigid on the beach this morning."

"We've already taken care of that," Sam said.

"How?"

"Glenna went to talk to Grace."

Aidan's brows drew together. "To say what, exactly?"

"I don't know." Sam lifted a shoulder. "She said she'd figure something out."

Aidan shook his head. "That's not going to work."

"Why not?"

"Because she's not going to fall for it."

Sam smiled. "You don't know Glenna."

"And you don't know Grace," Aidan said. "She's not some naïve tourist. She's a journalist."

"We've dealt with plenty of journalists before."

"Not one like her."

"All right," Sam said slowly, his smile beginning to fade. "Why don't you tell us who she is?"

# CHAPTER NINE

At the knock on her door, Grace closed her laptop and pushed to her feet. The past few hours had been enlightening. She felt like she had a better grip on the situation. And she was looking forward to finally getting a chance to speak with Liam. Crossing the room, she opened the door. "Welcome back."

"Thanks." He gave her an apologetic smile. "I'm sorry about yesterday."

"Don't be. How's Caitlin?"

"Much better," he said. "She's at home now, resting. The doctor wants her to take it easy for the next few months, stay off her feet as much as possible. Other than that, both she and the baby are fine."

"I'm happy to hear that." Grace took in the circles under his eyes, the thick layer of stubble lining his jaw, and the lingering shadow of concern etched into his features after spending the night in a hospital with his wife. He would probably like to be at home resting, too. "Is this a good time to talk, or would you rather meet up later?"

"Let's talk now." Liam glanced up at the sky. "We've got about two hours of daylight left, and I could use some fresh air. If you don't mind the cold, we could grab an outdoor table at the pub. Or we could take a walk and I could show you the sights."

"A walk would be great." Grace smiled and reached for the boots she'd set outside to dry about an hour ago. They were still damp, but wearable. After lacing them up, she lifted her jacket off the hook behind the door, checked to make sure the rose petal was still in her pocket, and stepped outside to join Liam in the street.

"Which way would you like to go?" he asked.

She nodded west, toward the cliffs. "I haven't been up that way yet."

He smiled and motioned for her to lead the way. "After you."

She zipped up her jacket, and they set off through the village.

"So, tell me, Grace." Liam dipped his hands in his pockets. "What do you think of our island so far?"

"It's stunning."

"Isn't it?" he asked, and she could hear the pride in his voice. "It's always a relief to come home after spending a night in the city."

Grace could relate to that. It was the same way she felt whenever she crossed the drawbridge to Heron Island. Even though she lived in D.C., Heron Island had always felt more like home to her. "Do you still work at the university in Galway?"

"I do. I teach classes on Tuesdays and Thursdays, and I have office hours on Wednesdays, so I only have to be there a few days a week."

"Do you commute all the way from here on those days?" she asked, wondering how he managed to swing that.

"No, I have a place in the city. It's small—hardly more than a room with a bed and a desk—but it's close to the university, and it gives me a place to lay my head."

That made sense, Grace thought. She'd toyed with the idea of creating a similar arrangement for herself over the years. But she didn't have the same flexibility that Liam had as a professor. She needed to be in the city to conduct interviews and meet up with her sources face to face. She needed to be accessible at all times if something came up.

It was something she'd been struggling with a lot lately—how to reconcile her devotion to her job with her dream to move back to the island where she'd grown up. She wanted to be surrounded by a community of people who cared about each other, not acquaintances who mostly used each other as a ladder to get to the top. "Is it hard," she asked, "straddling those two worlds?"

"Sometimes," he said. "But it's worth it." When they reached the edge of the village and began to climb the hill leading up to the cliffs, he looked at her curiously. "I admit that it's been a few weeks since I read your message, but I don't think you traveled all this way to talk about my work-life balance."

She laughed. "No, I didn't."

"What would you like to talk about?"

"Selkies."

"One of my favorite subjects." He smiled as they passed a small structure that served as the island's medical clinic. "Refresh my memory. Is it our legend specifically that you're interested in, or selkies in general?"

"Both."

"And what sparked this interest, if you don't mind me asking?"

"My mother used to read me stories about selkies before bed at night when I was a child."

"Really?" he asked. "Is she Irish?"

Grace shook her head.

"You don't find many selkie stories in the States."

"I know. Most of the ones she read were set in Ireland. One was set in Scotland—in the Hebrides. I might go there next."

"Let me know if you do. I have friends I could put you in touch with up there."

"Thanks," Grace said. "That would be great."

Liam motioned for her to follow him off the road, onto a worn footpath that skirted the edge of the cliffs. "What are you looking for, exactly?"

"I don't know yet. I just want to learn more about them."

He gave her a sidelong glance. "And what are you planning to do with this newfound knowledge?"

"I guess it depends on what I find."

He took a moment to absorb that. "How long do you expect to be traveling?"

"A few months."

"That's quite a journey."

"I needed a break from work. I've never been very good at finding that balance you mentioned earlier."

He laughed. "Fair enough."

"And," she said, knowing it would put him at ease if she gave him a little more of the truth, even if it led him to make an assumption that wasn't entirely accurate, "I'm hoping this trip might bring me closer to my mother."

"Will she be joining you on your travels?"

"No. She's...gone."

"I'm sorry," Liam said.

Grace heard the sympathy in his voice. He'd assumed that her mother had passed away. She didn't bother to correct him. "It was a long time ago."

"So, you're here for her, then? To honor her memory?"

Unless she found out that her mother was still alive, Grace thought. And that her mother had *chosen* to leave them. Then she wouldn't be honoring anything about the woman at all. But

Liam didn't need to know that. No one on this island needed to know that. As far as Grace was concerned, the best way to honor her mother's memory was by finding out what had happened to her. "In a way, yes."

"Well, I'm happy to answer any questions that you have."

"Thank you," she said as they climbed the final stretch of the hill to reach the flat perch of land where the cottage sat at the top of the cliff. The wind blew her hair back from her face. She could hear the waves crashing against the rocks far below. And then there was nothing but a great drop and the vast sea and sky spread out before her. "Wow. This is..."

Liam joined her at the edge. "It takes your breath away, doesn't it?"

Grace nodded, unable to pull her gaze away from that wild open sea. It was like a fortress surrounding the island, protecting it, isolating it from the rest of the world. It should be unnerving to feel this cut off from everyone and everything that was familiar. But there was something oddly comforting about it, like none of her troubles could follow her here.

She thought of Tara, of how safe she must have felt when she'd first arrived. How, for the first time in years, she must have felt that she could breathe again.

"You won't find a better view anywhere on the island," Liam said. "Even so, the cottage sat empty for decades. Nobody wanted it because they thought it was cursed. Well, nobody except for Dominic. He was never much of a believer in all that stuff until Tara arrived." Liam lifted his gaze to a cluster of islands in the distance. "He bought it as an investment property ten years ago and put it on the market to rent. He figured the tourists wouldn't know any better, so it couldn't hurt them." Liam laughed as he stepped back from the edge and started to walk toward the cottage.

Grace turned. "Dominic didn't believe in the legend until Tara arrived?"

Liam shook his head. "He was always more of a pragmatist."

"But he believes, now?"

"Oh, aye." Liam smiled. "He's a believer."

Grace's gaze shifted to the thatch-roofed cottage with its charming purple shutters and matching door, its whitewashed walls glowing brilliantly in the sun. She thought of the picture of the cottage she'd found online. The way the roses had wrapped around it like a corset. "Is this where the selkie lived with the fisherman who stole her pelt?"

Liam nodded, then glanced over his shoulder. "Tara mentioned she had a chance to talk with you last night, to tell you some of the story."

"She did." Grace walked over to join him. "She said she rented a cottage from Dominic when she first arrived. Is this where she stayed?"

"It is." Liam made his way over to the door. "Let me check to see if anyone's home." He knocked on the door, waited a few moments, then stepped back and shook his head. "I didn't think so."

"Who lives here, now?"

"Tara never moved out," Liam said with a laugh. "Dominic moved in after they got married." He gestured to the far side of the house. "They added that part on a few years ago."

Grace took in the recent expansion that had nearly doubled the size of the cottage. Aside from a slight difference in textures in the two outer walls, she could barely distinguish the old construction from the new. "The original structure ended here?" she asked, pointing to an area on the wall where the rougher texture met the smoother one.

He nodded.

Her gaze fell to the ground in front of the oldest part of the cottage, to what was left of an herb garden that had mostly gone to seed. "Tara said the selkie's pelt was buried in the garden."

"That's right."

She continued to search the ground, looking for signs of a rose bush. "Have they ever grown anything besides herbs here?"

"I'm sure they have. But I'm not much of a gardener, so I can't say I ever paid much attention."

Interesting, Grace thought. There was no way Liam could have missed the roses she'd seen in that picture. "Tara said you were the one who found the pelt."

"I had help," he said modestly.

"Who helped you?"

"Caitlin and Kelsey."

She glanced up. "Who's Kelsey?"

"Dominic's daughter from his first marriage."

"Oh," Grace said. Tara had skipped over that part of the story. "How did the three of you know to look for it here?"

"It was Kelsey's idea. She was only eight at the time, but she's always had a sense about these things."

Kelsey had been almost the same age as Taylor was now, Grace thought. How odd... "How did Kelsey know to look for it here?"

Liam smiled. "Unlike me, Tara loves to garden. She uses herbs in her medical practice, as a supplement to the more traditional remedies. Before she was able to tell us the truth about her past—that she was a doctor—she treated a number of people on the island using herbs alone." He reached down, broke off the tip of a dried-out stalk of lemon verbena, and crumbled what was left of the leaves in his hands. "Many selkies are known for having magical healing powers. Since Tara was a healer who used herbs, Kelsey thought there might be a connection between her garden and the selkie's pelt."

Except Tara hadn't been growing herbs, Grace thought. She'd been growing roses. Or at least, *someone* had been.

Reaching into her pocket, she felt for the petal she'd found on the beach that morning. It was still as soft and velvety as it had been when she'd first picked it up. There had to be a connection.

But what was it?

And what did it have to do with her mother?

Liam opened his hand, letting the crumbled leaves fall to the ground. "Do you want to see the beach where the curse was broken?"

What she wanted, Grace thought, was for Liam to be straight with her. To tell her the truth about how Kelsey had known to look for the selkie's pelt under the roses. But she had other questions to ask him. And she didn't want to apply too much pressure before she had a chance to get the rest of the information she needed.

She would work her way back around to the roses later.

Leaving the petal where it was, hidden deep in her pocket, she looked up at Liam. "I'd love to."

Liam nodded for her to follow him. "It's up this way."

They walked a little further, until the earth fell away to reveal a stretch of soft white sand surrounded by shallow turquoise waters. A steep path led down to the beach, which was empty except for a group of seals cuddled up together, napping in the sun. It looked so serene, so peaceful. It was hard to imagine that anything bad had ever happened here.

Pausing at the top of the path, Grace glanced back at the cottage. "Do you think it's hard for Tara to live this close to where it all happened?"

"What do you mean?" Liam asked.

"Isn't this where her husband almost killed her?"

"Yes. But it's also where she finally freed herself from him."

Grace turned to face him. "Were you on the beach when it happened?"

"I was."

"You saw Tara give the selkie back her pelt?"

"No. All I saw was a flash of green light and a splash in the water."

Grace frowned.

"The only two people who ever saw the selkie were Tara and Dominic," Liam explained.

How convenient, Grace thought. "And you just...took them at their word?"

"Yes."

"So, what happened after Tara gave her the pelt?"

"What do you mean?"

"I mean, what happened to the selkie? Did she walk into the water and disappear?"

"Yes," Liam said. "She went home. Tara freed them both."

Grace looked back at the group of seals lying on the beach and tried to imagine one of them shedding its skin and turning into a woman. She had no doubt that Tara had been in an abusive relationship, and that her ex-husband had tracked her here and tried to kill her. It was the rest of the story—the magical part— that she wasn't quite ready to accept.

"Would you like to go down," Liam asked, gesturing to the path, "or keep walking?"

"Let's keep walking," she said, hoping to avoid the same scripted tour Liam gave to every other tourist who visited this island.

As they continued west along the path, leaving the village even further behind, Grace lifted her gaze to the scattering of islands in the distance. During her research this afternoon, she'd discovered that most of the islands in this area had been evacuated years ago. Entire villages had been abandoned. Communities had been torn apart. Homes that had been passed down through families for generations had been left to crumble and rot.

In a world that was becoming increasingly urbanized, many island communities found themselves struggling to hang onto a way of life that was dying.

And yet, Seal Island had managed to thrive.

Glancing back at the beach, she wondered if the legend was nothing more than a tactic to increase tourism to the island. She was familiar with the fragility of island economies. She knew how difficult it was for them to evolve and keep up with the times. Heron Island had been through several challenges itself in the past year, any one of which could have altered the character of the island forever if it had gone the wrong way.

Perhaps the residents of Seal Island had foreseen this, and instead of waiting around for the inevitable decline, they'd decided to do something about it. To save their island before it was too late.

In a country whose tourist trade was already steeped in magic, why not add a broken curse to the mix?

She had to hand it to them. It was a clever idea.

However, she—unlike most tourists—hadn't come here in search of magic. She'd come here to find her mother. And there was one question, in particular, that had been weighing on her ever since she'd started looking to these tales for answers.

She shifted her gaze back at the man walking beside her. "In the two stories—Tara's and the selkie's—the common theme is the man who mistreated them."

Liam nodded.

"Is that something you find in a lot of selkie tales?"

"It is."

"Because of the power the man has over her once he has her pelt?"

Liam nodded again. "Once he has her pelt, she belongs to

him. He can force her to marry him, to bear his children, to stay on land forever, whether she likes it or not."

"But not all men would choose to abuse that power."

"No," Liam said. "Of course, not. But if he hides her pelt from her, he's still trapping her here. The relationships are rooted in coercion. It's not a healthy place to start."

This was the part that troubled Grace the most. If she was looking to these stories for clues, and her mother's disappearance loosely mirrored that of a selkie wife who eventually found her pelt and left her family to return to the sea, what did that mean for her father? Did he take on the role of the abuser, the man who trapped his wife in a loveless marriage, holding her against her will?

Whenever she thought back to her childhood, at least the first ten years of it, her parents had seemed happy together. She remembered them talking and laughing and being affectionate toward each other. She had no memories of raised voices or slamming doors. They had certainly appeared to be in love, which only added to the mystery of her mother's disappearance. "Is it possible for them to fall in love?"

"Yes, it's possible."

"So, she *can* be happy? Even if it doesn't start out that way?"

Liam nodded.

"Then why does she have to leave if she finds her pelt? Why can't she stay?"

"Because all selkies yearn to get back to the sea."

"Even the ones who are in love with their husbands? And have children together?"

"Yes," Liam said.

"But...how can they just abandon their families like that?"

"It's not an entirely selfish decision."

"Isn't it?" Grace asked.

"No," Liam said. "Remember, they were never supposed to be here in the first place. This isn't their home."

"But doesn't it *become* their home after a while? Isn't a home more about being with the people you love?"

They reached the westernmost tip of the island, and the ocean stretched out before them, as far as the eye could see. "I think for some people that's true," Liam said. "But for others the concept of home is inextricably linked to a sense of place. It's a connection with the environment, the culture, and the history of a place, as much as the people we share it with. There are some places that speak to us, that get in our blood, that grab hold of us and never let go. These places become a part of us. And we lose a part of ourselves if we're separated from them for too long."

Grace thought about Heron Island and all the things she loved about it in addition to the people who lived there. Liam had a point. She *did* feel like a part of herself was missing whenever she was away from it for too long.

But she had also never been in love. What if she met someone, someday, and he wanted to live somewhere else?

Would she be able to give up her home for a man she loved?

As they continued north around the loop, they passed an occasional herd of sheep. Other than that, there was nothing but the two of them, the cliffs, and the open sea. "What would happen," Grace asked a few minutes later when their path curved inland and they could hear each other over the wind again, "if a selkie chose not to return to the sea?"

Liam's eyes cut to hers. "What do you mean?"

"Well," Grace said slowly, "you've studied these legends extensively for years. Have you ever come across a story where a selkie chose to stay?"

Liam looked away, and for the first time since they'd started to walk, he didn't seem quite so at ease with himself. "I..." He trailed off and appeared to be choosing his words carefully. "I can't say I've ever come across one that was written down."

That wasn't an answer, Grace thought. Most legends were passed down orally for generations before they ever got written down. And surely, he hadn't captured all the ones he'd heard in writing yet. "So, let me get this straight," she said, opting to play along rather than call him out, "no matter how happy a selkie is with her family, she will never choose to stay on land if she finds her pelt?"

Liam nodded. "That's the general rule, yes."

"But...?"

He took a breath. "But as a researcher, I tend to avoid using absolutes."

"So, it *is* possible?"

"I think," he said, looking back at her, "that anything is possible."

"Okay," Grace said, "let's assume, just for fun, that there *was* an exception to the rule. What would happen if a selkie chose to stay?"

THAT, Liam thought, was a question he didn't know the answer to. And it was one that had been troubling him a lot lately. Because the only exception to that rule, at least that he knew of, was his mother.

And he didn't know the ending to her story yet.

It had been seven years since his mother had made the decision to stay, to relinquish her crown as the selkie queen and remain on land with her family. For much of that time, everything had been fine. Recently, though, things had begun to change.

*She* had begun to change.

Neil had called him a few hours ago to fill him in on what had happened on the beach that morning. His mother had had another incident. The fact that her incidents were becoming more frequent worried him because he didn't know what it meant.

None of them did.

He wanted to believe it was temporary, that these breaks from reality were related to some sort of internal struggle she needed to work through. But another part of him had begun to wonder if it was more than that. What if her decision to stay *hadn't* defied the odds? What if she had simply postponed the inevitable?

What if this *was* one rule that couldn't be broken?

Pushing the thought away, as he did each time it entered his mind, because it was too painful to even consider at this point, he turned his attention back to Grace. "To be honest, I don't know. Why does this matter to you so much?"

Grace looked up at the sky. The sun was behind them now, and their shadows stretched out before them. "All fairy tales have a lesson, right? They're meant to teach us something?"

Liam nodded. For people who didn't believe in magic—who didn't believe fairy tales were real—yes, they were simply a short piece of entertainment meant to teach a lesson. For others, they were much more than that. They were their history. They were their life.

"What are these stories supposed to teach us?" Grace asked when their path dead-ended at the edge of a bog. "That a mother's love isn't that strong after all?"

Liam frowned. "No."

"What, then?"

Taking her on a short-cut that only the locals knew, he motioned for her to follow closely behind him through the bog. "Well, like we talked about earlier, selkie stories are all about home and belonging. If a man steals a selkie's pelt, she may belong to him temporarily, but he can't force her to love him. These tales teach us about the importance of free will and the perils of attempting to control a woman."

"So, the children are just collateral damage?"

"Unfortunately, yes," Liam said. "In many tales, it's actually the children who find their mother's pelt first. It's often by accident, and they have no idea what will happen when they tell her about it."

Grace looked up as a flock of migrating Arctic Terns passed by overhead, their shrill cries piercing the air. "Have you ever seen a selkie?"

Liam glanced back at her. "Any of those seals we saw napping on the beach earlier could have been a selkie."

"Haha," she said. "That's not what I meant."

Liam smiled. "I didn't think so."

"Have you ever seen a seal shed its skin and become a woman?" she clarified.

"No," Liam said, relieved he could answer that question truthfully. He'd seen a child, his own child, shed his sealskin. But he'd never seen a seal transform into a woman on land.

"But you believe they exist?"

"Of course." Liam helped her navigate the final stretch of the bog. "I take it you don't?"

"No."

When their path reappeared, he slowed down so she could catch up. "Did you come here hoping to find some sort of proof?"

"No," she said. "I mean, I don't think so."

They passed the crumbling ruins of an ancient stone cottage before their path curved inland again. They followed it south, heading back toward the village.

Grace reached out and ran a hand over one of the jagged stone walls that partitioned the mid-section of the island into hundreds of tiny pastures. "You said Dominic didn't believe, either, before Tara came here?"

"That's right."

"What changed his mind?"

"Take a guess."

"Was it seeing the selkie?"

"I'm sure that helped, but no."

"Okay, I give up."

Liam smiled. "It was Tara."

"Tara?"

He nodded. "It was his love for her."

Grace stopped walking. "Oh, come on."

"What?"

"You can't be serious."

"Of course, I'm serious. Dominic started to believe in magic when he fell in love with Tara."

"Wow." Grace laughed. "You really know how to lay it on, don't you?" Still laughing, she started to walk again. "Have you thought about pitching this story to Disney? You all could make a fortune together."

No, Liam thought. Magic, to them, had never been about making money. Yes, the attention they'd received after Tara had broken the curse had brought an unexpected windfall to their local economy. But it had also brought its share of stressors. The more people who came to this island, the harder the islanders had to work to hide the truth.

Tara's ancestor's story was the one that Seal Island was known for. But there were other stories—stories of white selkies and selkie queens and changelings who were stolen from their mothers as children and forced to live underwater. Those were the stories the islanders kept to themselves.

Because the people in those stories were still living.

For the past seven years, Liam had served as the first line of defense between the outsiders who came to learn about magic and the islanders who possessed it. As Tara's brother-in-law, he was able to speak with some authority on the subject. His position at the university lent his words even more credibility. And he knew how to spin a tale for the tourists.

The key was to give them a taste of the truth—just enough to satisfy their curiosity—then send them on their way. Which was exactly what he was planning to do with Grace. "Well," he said, looking back at her, "you know what they say?"

"What?" she asked.

"True love is the most powerful magic of all."

Grace laughed again. "And I suppose Caitlin is your true love?"

"Naturally."

"And your children believe this, as well?"

"Of course."

Shaking her head, Grace stopped walking to say hello to a white pony that had stuck its head over one of the stone walls.

Liam stopped, too, grabbed a handful of grass, and offered it to the pony as a treat. Expecting another sarcastic question, he was surprised when Grace grew quiet again. She seemed to be focused rather intently on petting the pony's soft fur. "What?" he asked when her expression grew pensive.

"I was just wondering," she said slowly, "if it's wise to plant that seed so early."

"What do you mean?"

"Well," she said, combing a knot out of the pony's mane, "not everyone's life can be a fairy tale."

Liam's brows drew together. "Go on."

"Maybe we shouldn't get our children's hopes up at such a young age. Maybe it would be better to manage their expectations—introduce them to reality sooner rather than later."

"They're *children*," Liam countered. "They have plenty of

time to experience reality later. I want my children to have as much hope and faith in the future as possible when they're young. Those beliefs can carry them a long way in life, especially when times get tougher down the road."

Her gaze met his. "But it takes more than faith to overcome life's obstacles."

"Sometimes," Liam said. "Sometimes, not. Sometimes faith is the only thing that can get us through our darkest hours."

She looked away and seemed to take a moment to ponder that. "Okay." She gave the pony one last pat before starting to walk again. "I understand the importance of faith. But most people get that from religion or some other sort of spirituality. They don't get that from fairy tales."

"That's all magic is, essentially," Liam said. "It's faith. It's believing in something bigger than ourselves—something we don't always have control over."

"What...like fate?"

"Yes, that's one example, but there are many others. Take, for instance, finding a four-leaf clover. Depending on what you believe, it could be an omen of good luck, or it could be nothing more than a genetic variation of a three-leaf clover. Personally, I prefer to believe it means good luck."

"But what if it doesn't bring you luck?"

"Then you don't have enough faith," Liam said. "I think if you look hard enough at every aspect of your life after you find a four-leaf clover, you'll notice that *something* has changed for the better, even if it's very small." Slipping his hands in his pockets to warm them, his fingers closed around a bit of loose change. "You've heard the saying that you'll find a pot of gold at the end of every rainbow?"

She nodded.

"You might not find a pot of gold, but you might find a few coins on the ground after you see one. Or maybe you'll simply notice the sun breaking through the clouds for the first time in a while and remember how it feels to know that a storm has passed. And maybe *that* will help you believe in something else you've lost faith in recently." He looked up as a single monarch butterfly passed by overhead, its orange wings glowing like fire in the fading light. "The world offers us all kinds of signs. It wants us to believe. But it's up to us to see them."

Grace's gaze followed Liam's. Together, they watched the butterfly glide over the fields until it disappeared from sight. "What if I can see the signs, but I don't know what they mean?"

"Maybe you're trying too hard to find answers where there aren't any. Maybe the signs are simply there to remind you to keep the faith." When their path merged with the paved road across from the harbor, Liam nodded for her to turn right and loop back to the village. "Is that what you came here to ask me?"

"I don't know," she admitted. "I'm still trying to make sense of it all."

They climbed the final hill to her cottage and Liam thought back to what Neil had told him on the phone earlier—that Grace was an accomplished investigative journalist. Apparently, Aidan had expressed some concern that she might pose a threat. As far as he could tell, they had nothing to worry about.

If anything, she seemed a bit lost. "Well, I'll be around all night if you think of anything else you'd like to ask."

At the top of the hill, she turned to face him. "Actually, I do have one more question."

"Sure," he said agreeably. "What's on your mind?"

"It's about the legend."

"Okay." Rocking back on his heels, Liam saw that the sun was close to setting. The homes in the village cast long shadows across the street, and the smell of peat smoke permeated the air.

"Will you tell me about the roses?"

Liam blinked, coming down hard on the flats of his feet. "What?"

"The roses," Grace repeated. "What role did they play in the legend?"

Liam noticed that the woman in front of him didn't look lost anymore. She didn't look lost at all. "I...don't know what you mean."

"I saw a picture of Tara's cottage online from the year the curse broke. It was covered in roses. She said last night—and you confirmed today—that the selkie's pelt was hidden in her garden. So, what role did they play?"

"Oh, *those* roses." Liam took a step toward her cottage, then another, trying to buy some time. All the pictures of Tara's cottage from that year had been buried. Sam had made sure of it. The former private investigator had worked some of his own magic to ensure that no one would be able to find them unless they knew exactly what they were looking for.

How had Grace known what to look for?

"I also read that people could smell them all over the island that weekend," Grace added, watching him closely. "Some people said they were so sweet, it made them sick."

Liam ran a hand through his hair. "You know, now that you mention it, I do remember that year being a particularly good one for growing roses."

"So, you *do* grow roses on the island?"

Liam opened his mouth, closed it.

"Because I haven't seen any anywhere. And I've covered a lot of ground today."

The reason she hadn't seen any roses was because the islanders didn't grow them. They made a point not to. Which was why, when they came to the front of her cottage, and Liam spotted a scattering of lavender rose petals on the ground outside her door, he felt a chill run through him. "Those weren't there when I knocked earlier."

"No," Grace said. "They weren't."

Liam looked up at Grace, then back down at the petals. What the hell was going on? "Maybe it was Caitlin," he said quickly, catching himself. "Maybe she was trying to make up for missing your arrival yesterday. She likes to do nice things for her guests."

"I thought she was supposed to stay off her feet for a few days."

He *had* said that, hadn't he? Liam forced out a laugh. "She's never been very good at taking orders from doctors—or anyone, really."

Grace looked at him doubtfully. "Why would she sprinkle rose petals outside my door? I'm not here on a romantic getaway."

"Maybe she mixed you up with someone else."

"I'm pretty sure I'm the only tourist on the island right now." Grace narrowed her eyes. "Is this some kind of joke?"

"What?" Liam asked, struggling to keep up.

"The rose petals," Grace said. "These aren't the first ones I've seen today."

Liam's brows snapped together. "They're not?"

"No," she said. "I found some on the beach earlier."

"What beach?"

"The one on the east side of the island, by the farm." She pulled something out of her pocket, and when she opened her hand, Liam saw that it was a petal—the same color as the ones outside her door. With her free hand, she reached down, plucked a petal off the ground, and held them both out.

Despite the fact that she'd been carrying one of them around, neither petal had a single fold or tear on it, not even the slightest bit of browning at the edges. They were practically identical. Liam felt a familiar prickling sensation along the back of his neck. "Was anyone else with you when you found them?"

Grace nodded. "Aidan."

Liam held out his hand. "May I?"

She placed one of the petals in his hand and kept the other one for herself.

Liam looked down at it. He'd never seen a rose this color before. "Just petals, though? Not a whole rose?"

"Just petals," Grace confirmed. "Why? What's going on?"

"Nothing," Liam said quickly. "I mean, I'm sure it's nothing." He forced a smile. "Let me talk to Caitlin. I should have this sorted out in no time. Why don't we meet at the pub later, say... around six o'clock?"

Grace nodded slowly.

Before she could ask any more questions, Liam turned. As soon as his back was to her, his smile faded, and his legs felt wooden as he began to walk away. Because roses on this island only meant one thing.

Trouble was coming.

# CHAPTER TEN

$\mathcal{H}$e didn't know what the big deal was, Aidan thought. Those rose petals could have come from anywhere. Yes, it was strange that it had happened twice in one day. But it was probably just some of the island kids having fun at the expense of a tourist.

It must be hard to be a teenager here, especially in the winter when nothing happened and no one from the outside came to visit. The kids had to find ways to entertain themselves. Playing a harmless trick on what would likely be their last tourist in months seemed like a reasonable thing to do.

He was far more concerned with why Grace had reacted so strongly to the petals they'd seen on the beach earlier. She'd withdrawn afterwards, barely saying two words in the car on the way back to the village. And she'd jumped out before they'd gotten halfway there, making some lame excuse about wanting to walk. She hadn't been able to get away from him fast enough.

What was that all about?

Looking up at the spray of stars overhead, he wondered if it was possible that she might have been reacting to more than the petals. He'd been surprised by how vulnerable she'd seemed when she'd stepped out of his arms after their almost-kiss. The intensity of their connection had caught him off guard as well, but nothing about it had made him want to withdraw. And as soon as he made sure she was all right, he was looking forward to finishing what they'd started.

He waved goodbye to Brennan, who'd given him a ride to the village, and crossed the street to Grace's cottage. He could have met her at the pub, but he wanted a moment alone with her first. He slowed as he came to her door, scanning the ground where Liam had said the petals had been when they'd returned from their walk a couple hours ago.

He didn't see any now. Either they'd blown away or Grace had taken them inside. Remembering how she'd pocketed one of the petals that had washed up at their feet earlier, he was fairly confident she'd have kept at least a few. He lifted his hand to knock, just as the door swung open.

"Aidan," Grace said, clearly surprised to find him there. "Hi."

He took in the woman standing in the doorway. Her face was slightly flushed from the heat of a shower. Her body was clothed in a soft green sweater and worn jeans. And her golden hair was lit from behind by a single lamp she'd left burning inside. The strangest sensation washed over him, like he'd just arrived home.

But this wasn't his home. And they hardly knew each other. Maybe all this talk about magic was starting to get to him. "I was just about to knock," he said, shaking off the strange feeling. "You beat me to it."

"What's up?" she asked.

He nodded across the street to the pub. "I came to see if you'd like to join me for dinner."

"Happy to." She stepped outside and closed the door behind her. "I was just heading over there."

He smiled, relieved to see that she wasn't upset anymore.

Whatever had been bothering her, she must have gotten over it. "Perfect timing, then."

She nodded. "How's the leg?"

"It's a little better, thanks," he said as they started to walk. "I spent most of the afternoon off it."

"You finally took Tara's advice and decided to rest?"

"Something like that." He'd spent the afternoon helping Brennan build a new door for the barn. He'd noticed the pile of lumber outside the older man's cottage a few days ago. When Brennan told him what he'd had in mind for it, Aidan had volunteered to sand and stain the wood first—tasks he knew would be difficult for Brennan to complete with his arthritic hands. Fortunately, they were tasks Aidan could do sitting down.

After icing and elevating his knee for the past several hours, the swelling had finally come down. It still hurt to put weight on it, but the pain had subsided considerably. "How was your chat with Liam?"

"It gave me a lot to think about."

"Really?" Aidan smiled again as they came to the door of the pub. "I can't wait to hear about it." He opened the door and motioned for her to go first.

They stepped into the dark, wooded room. A peat fire snapped in the hearth. Candles flickered on the tables. A few people turned to wave, then went back to their pints or their meals.

"Table or bar?" Aidan asked.

"Bar," Grace said.

He followed her to the bar. They snagged two empty stools near the middle. Dominic walked out of the kitchen a few moments later, carrying a plate of short ribs and a bowl of beef stew. He gave them a brief nod of acknowledgement on his way to deliver the dishes. After engaging in some friendly banter with a couple at the end of the bar, he walked back to greet them.

His smile was warm and welcoming. "What can I get for you two on this fine evening?"

"I'll have a Guinness," Grace said.

"Make it two," Aidan said.

Dominic went to work building the pints. In a wool sweater and jeans, with a bar towel draped over his shoulder, he seemed completely at ease in his surroundings. Neither his expression nor his mannerisms suggested that he was concerned about anything.

He'd obviously received the memo.

When Liam had called Aidan an hour ago to find out what had happened on the beach that morning, he'd also filled him in on the plan for the evening. They were supposed to remain calm and act like everything was fine. As soon as Liam figured out why Grace had seen the rose petals, he would come in and explain it to her, and they'd all have a good laugh about it.

Aidan didn't mind playing along because he didn't think anything *was* wrong. As far as he was concerned, the only thing that he and his "family" should be conspiring on was keeping Grace as far away from Brigid as possible. The rest of the islanders might believe some crazy things, but Brigid was the only one who was experiencing actual psychotic episodes.

Grace didn't strike him as the type of journalist who would go after a story simply for the sensationalism of it. But she *had* come here to learn about selkies. What would she do if she discovered there was a woman on this island who claimed to be one?

Wouldn't it be better, for everyone, if they never found out the answer to that question?

Yes, Aidan thought. It would. And the only way to ensure that outcome was to keep the two women apart. Thankfully, Neil had agreed to keep Brigid away from the pub tonight. And Aidan wasn't planning to leave Grace's side until she boarded the ferry tomorrow morning, so everything should be under control.

All he had to do, now, was enjoy the company of the woman beside him.

Shifting his stool slightly to face hers, he saw that she'd finished looking over the dinner menu. "Anything catch your eye?"

"I've never had this fish before." She pointed to the pan-fried plaice with brown butter and almonds, which was one of the day's specials. "What's it like?"

"Plaice is lovely," he said. "It has a mild, sweet taste, similar to flounder."

"Mmm, that sounds good," she said, giving the menu one last skim. "Okay, I'm between that and the beer-battered haddock and chips."

"Both excellent choices. How about I get one, you get the other, and we share?"

"Works for me."

Aidan took her menu, stacked it on top of his, and handed them both back to Dominic. "The plaice and the fish and chips."

Dominic nodded and set the first pint in front of Grace. "How was your day?" he asked her.

"It was great," she said. "I took a long walk with your brother this afternoon. We did the loop that goes around the west side of the island."

"That's a nice walk," Dominic said.

"It was beautiful," Grace said. "I've never seen anything like it. Liam pointed out your cottage on the way up to the cliffs. I can't believe you get to wake up to that view every morning."

Dominic smiled and set the second pint in front of Aidan. "I couldn't imagine living anywhere else."

"That's because you've never been anywhere else," Aidan said, unable to resist the urge to rag on his "oldest brother." He might not believe they were related by blood, but he was starting to enjoy acting like they were.

"I've been plenty of places," Dominic said. "Enough to know I'm happiest right where I am."

"Where was the last place you went?" Aidan asked.

"Kelsey and I went to Dublin last weekend."

"Where was the last place you went *outside* of Ireland?" Aidan clarified.

Dominic thought for a moment. "Tara and I spent a week in Barcelona after we got married."

"That was eight years ago"

Dominic nodded. "Sounds about right."

Aidan laughed. He couldn't imagine staying in one place for that long without at least taking a trip. Of course, that might be because he'd never tried it. He'd been on the move for so long, he wasn't sure he knew how to stay still anymore.

"What about you, Grace," Dominic asked. "Are you a wandering spirit like Aidan, or do you prefer to stay in one place like me?"

"A little of both, I think," she said. "I like to travel, but I'm always happy to come home."

"Coming home is the best part." Dominic smiled, then gave Aidan a pointed look. "I think some people travel because they don't know how to be grateful for what they have."

"And some people stay home because they're too scared to leave what's comfortable and familiar," Aidan countered.

"It's a good thing those of us who are too scared to leave our homes have people like you to keep us informed about what's going on in the rest of the world," Dominic said.

"Haha," Aidan said drily.

"Speaking of which..." Dominic cleared a few empty glasses off the bar. "I haven't seen you with your camera since you've been here. Have you taken any photographs of the island?"

Aidan shook his head. How was he supposed to take pictures when he could barely walk?

"I wouldn't mind having a few new pictures to hang on the walls." Dominic eyed the scattering of black-and-white photographs that had been hanging there for decades.

"Landscapes aren't really my thing," Aidan said.

"Well, some of us"—he shared a knowing look with Grace—"think it's rather pretty here. Maybe you could find *something* to take a picture of."

"I'll keep it in mind," Aidan said, though he had no intention of it.

Dominic set the empty glasses down when another customer waved him over. "I better get on, then. I'll look forward to seeing those pictures."

Aidan rolled his eyes as Dominic walked away.

"You haven't taken a single picture since you've been here?" Grace asked when they were alone again.

"No." He lifted his pint. "Have you written any articles?"

She narrowed her eyes at his blatant pivot. "This isn't a work trip for me."

"It's not a work trip for me either." He touched his glass to hers. "Sláinte."

"Sláinte," she murmured, holding his gaze while they both took a sip.

He smiled and settled back, happy to have her all to himself again. "Tell me about your chat with Liam. I want to know why it gave you a lot to think about."

She set her glass back on the bar. "And I want to know why you haven't taken any photographs since you've been here."

"In case you haven't noticed, I'm having some trouble getting around."

"Couldn't you set up a tripod? Or take some shots sitting down? Just to get back in the swing of things?"

"No."

"It might make you feel better."

The only thing that was going to make him feel better was having her in his arms again, ideally wearing as little as possible. "If you're interested in helping me get back in the swing of things," he said suggestively, "I might be persuaded to take a few shots. I bet you'd look lovely in the moonlight."

"I'm not volunteering to be one of your subjects."

"I thought you wanted to make me feel better," he said, pretending to be hurt. "Maybe all I need is a little inspiration."

"I'm sure you can find another way to get inspired."

Maybe, he thought. But it wouldn't be nearly as much fun.

"Seriously, though," she said. "I have a friend who went through something similar recently."

"Something similar?" Aidan asked. *Similar to what?*

"She was a cook," Grace went on, "an amazing one. But something happened to her in a kitchen—something traumatic. And she wasn't able to cook for a long time afterwards, because whenever she tried, it brought back all the memories of the incident."

Aidan's brows drew together. What exactly did she think he was going through? "I'm not afraid to pick up my camera again."

"Are you sure? Because the longer you put it off, the harder it'll be to—"

"I'm sure. And I'm not traumatized."

"Okay," she said.

Aidan could tell from the tone of her voice that she didn't believe him. Was this what she thought of him? If so, no wonder she'd jumped out of the car so quickly earlier. "This isn't the first time I've been a little banged up."

"I know."

He paused in the middle of raising his glass to his lips. "What do you mean, you know?"

"I looked you up earlier."

Aidan's brows rose. "Earlier...when?"

"Earlier today. Before my walk with Liam," she said. "According to some of the people you've traveled with over the years, it's a miracle you're still alive."

It *was* a miracle he was still alive, Aidan thought. But he didn't want to talk about that. He wanted to know why she'd looked him up.

"You know what surprised me the most about those stories, though?" Grace asked.

"I'm on the edge of my seat," he said, only half-joking.

"They were all secondhand accounts."

Ah, so that's what this was about. Feeling at ease again, he finally took that sip.

"You've never given an interview before," she said.

"Why would I?" He set the glass down. "My photos aren't about me."

"Don't you think people would be interested in hearing about your life?"

"Maybe." He lifted a shoulder. "But like I said, my photos aren't about me."

"People *have* asked to interview you, though, right?"

"They have."

"And you always say no?"

"That's right."

She looked at him curiously.

"What?" he asked.

"Most people would want the attention."

"I don't do what I do for attention." Hoping to leave it at that, he stretched his bad leg out. He could almost fully straighten it now. Maybe he *could* practice shooting tomorrow, try to get some of that flexibility back. He let his heel come to rest on the middle rung of Grace's stool so his leg was at least somewhat elevated, then lifted his gaze back to hers.

She was still watching him. "Why *do* you do what you do?"

And that, right there, was exactly why he didn't do interviews. "I thought this wasn't a work trip for you?"

"I'm just making conversation," she said innocently.

Aidan took in her calm, self-assured expression. With one arm resting casually on the bar and her stool turned to face his, her body language was open, friendly, and relaxed. She seemed perfectly happy to have his foot resting on her stool, even though the slightest movement from either of them would have their legs brushing together.

As relieved as he was that she wasn't upset anymore, he couldn't help wondering what had brought about this transformation. Somehow, between the time she'd jumped out of his car that morning and when she'd opened the door to her cottage tonight, she'd managed to regroup and regain all her confidence.

What, exactly, had she learned in the past several hours? And why, if she'd come here to learn about selkies, had she been researching *him*?

"May I ask what motivated this bit of online stalking you did earlier?"

She smiled. "I figured we'd be having dinner together again tonight. And I always look up any man I'm going to spend time with. That's just common sense."

"So, this little...search was purely for pleasure?"

"Yes," she said. "Though—"

"Why don't we leave it at that?" he suggested, wanting to shift her focus away from his past and onto a more agreeable topic. "Now that we've established that we're both on holiday, maybe we could put all the work-talk away for a while, focus on enjoying ourselves."

"We could…" she said as if she were seriously considering it, "but I do have one last question."

He sighed. "I feel like we've been down this road before."

She smiled. "It's one of my favorite roads."

Unable to resist her when she was smiling at him like that, all warm and friendly, with her leg almost touching his, he gave in. "Fine. One more question, and then we get to talk about something else."

Pleased with his concession, Grace skimmed a thumb down the side of her glass, making a trail in the condensation. "When I looked you up earlier, I came across an article written by a print reporter you used to travel with a lot, a guy named Rob Walker."

Aidan nodded, only half-listening as he studied the play of light and shadows across her face. He could see why all the networks wanted to have her on their shows. He might even be tempted to start watching a few of them himself.

"In the article, he mentioned that you grew up in Belfast," Grace said.

Aidan nodded again slowly, imagining the shot he would take of her if she'd let him. He would find a way to capture the softness of her, to peel back those layers of confidence and tenacity she wore like a second skin to reveal the hidden part—the real part—the part she didn't want the rest of the world to see.

"Why didn't you say something last night, when I asked you what it was like to grow up here?" Grace asked.

"Because I don't talk about my childhood," he said simply. Then, before she had a chance to ask a follow-up question, he reached for her hand. "You know what I *would* like to talk about?"

Taken aback, Grace looked down at their joined hands. His stool had shifted when he'd reached for her so their legs were touching now, too. He wondered if she felt the same restless need, an almost drunken sensation, that seemed to grip him every time they touched.

"What?" she asked after several long moments when she seemed unable to speak.

"I want to know what you do for fun when you're not working. That is," he added, "if you know how to stop."

"I know how to stop."

"Do you?"

She took a breath, and he watched her compose herself. It was fascinating to watch the transformation, as if she were mentally stepping back into that second skin. "I'm on a leave of absence from work right now."

"But it still *feels* like you're working," Aidan said. "When was the last time you took an actual holiday?"

"When was the last time *you* took an actual holiday?"

"We're not talking about me anymore," he said, happy that she hadn't pulled her hand away yet. "So...how long has it been."

"It's been a while," she admitted.

"I bet it has." He smiled. "You know, all that work can take a toll on you. It's not good for your health."

She laughed. "Look who's talking." She lifted their joined hands so he could see them better. "What did you do all afternoon, anyway?"

Aidan looked down at his hand. The back of it was covered in sandpaper scrapes and smudges of paint. A gash ran across his knuckles from trying to fix the tractor the day before. There was a scar on his wrist from when he'd been tied up and beaten, during a kidnapping in Libya several years ago. And he didn't need her to turn his hand over for him to know that his palm was rough and calloused from years of working in deserts climates and war zones. "See," he said lightly, "this is what happens when you never take a break. The last thing you want is to end up like me."

He expected her to laugh. Instead, she slowly lowered their

hands to rest softly on the top of her knees. The look of understanding in her eyes caught him off guard for a moment before he realized that he shouldn't have been surprised. His addiction to work might be worse than hers, but a workaholic was a workaholic. They did have a tendency to recognize each other.

There was a reason neither of them could remember the last time they'd taken a holiday. It was easier to bury yourself in work than face what was waiting for you if you ever stopped long enough to listen.

Earlier, she had suggested that he might be afraid to pick up his camera, but it was actually the other way around. As long as he was working—as long as he was concentrating on something *other* than himself—he could stay one step ahead of the memories that lurked at the edge of his mind. He didn't know what would happen if he stayed still long enough for them to catch up.

And he didn't want to.

Fortunately, Brennan had plenty of chores to keep him busy until he could return to work. And tonight, he had Grace to distract him. "I may be a lost cause," he said, keeping his tone light to mask the truth in his words, "but I think there's still hope for you. To be safe, though, I've decided to make it my personal mission to help you relax, at least for the rest of your stay on the island."

Grace's lips curved. "Oh, really?"

He nodded. "I'm only thinking about what's best for you and your health."

She laughed and let go of his hand. "That's kind of you, but I think I can manage on my own."

Aidan smiled as the door to the kitchen swung open and Dominic walked out with their meals. He was glad they'd decided to share. She wouldn't be able to wall herself off from him as easily when he was feeding her a chip.

Dominic set the first plate in front of Grace. "Good thing you came in early. These'll go fast tonight."

Grace eyed the almond-crusted fillet. "It looks wonderful."

Dominic set the fish and chips in front of Aidan, then nodded to a customer who waved him over from the dining room. "Be back in a bit."

Aidan waited for Grace to pick up her fork and take the first bite.

"Mmm." She closed her eyes for a moment of decadence. "This is amazing. I'm not sure I want to share anymore."

"Too late to back out now, love."

She glanced at his plate, assessing what was on it. "I'll trade you a carrot for a chip."

"You can have as many of my chips as you want." He slid his plate closer to hers. "Vinegar?"

Relenting, she nodded.

Aidan picked up the bottle of malt vinegar. "How much?"

"As much as you want."

Liking where this conversation was going, he shook the bottle of vinegar over the chips a few times to coat them. The tangy scent floated up, making his stomach growl. "You know," he said, breaking off a piece of beer-battered haddock and taking a bite, "you never answered my question earlier."

"What question?"

"What do you do for fun when you're not working?"

Snagging a chip from his plate, she was about to answer when the door to the pub opened. They both turned to see who it was.

Liam walked in, and Aidan felt a twinge of disappointment, knowing that Grace's attention would be focused elsewhere now.

"Look what the cat dragged in," Dominic said, giving Liam a once over when he made it to the bar. "Have you showered since you spent the night in the hospital?"

"No," Liam admitted. His hair was mussed. His clothes were

rumpled. And there were dark circles under his eyes. He looked like a man more in need of a bed than a shower.

Dominic poured him a glass of whiskey and slid it toward him. "Do you want anything from the kitchen?"

"I told Caitlin I'd bring dinner back.'

"I'll ask Gran to put something together for you," Dominic said. "Is Tara still at your place?"

Liam nodded. "Glenna and Sam are there, as well."

"That ought to be enough people to make sure Caitlin stays off her feet."

Liam gave him a knowing look. "Exactly."

"How's she doing?" Aidan asked, wondering if that was why Liam seemed so stressed.

"Fine." Liam picked up his drink. "She's just tired. We both are. It's been a long day." He tipped the glass back, draining most of it in one sip.

Dominic topped it off, then tucked the bottle away. "I'll let Gran know you're here."

As soon as the door to the kitchen swung shut behind Dominic, Liam turned to Grace. "I think I figured out where those petals came from."

"Oh?" she asked.

"Turns out, my mother's been growing lavender roses in her greenhouse. Usually, she only grows herbs. but when Tara came by the house, she reminded me that she'd decided to grow roses this year, too."

"Tara reminded you?" Grace asked.

Liam nodded, and Aidan winced. Bringing Tara into this was a mistake. Grace already thought Tara was hiding something from her. She wasn't going to trust anything Liam said anymore.

"My mother often goes to the beach where you saw her this morning to pay her respects to a friend she lost at sea many years ago," Liam explained. "She tosses little offerings into the waves, hoping the ocean will carry them to the place where his boat went down in a storm not far from there. She must have tossed a few flowers into the water before you got there, and the waves washed the petals back to shore later."

Aidan frowned. Why was he bringing Brigid into this? Shouldn't he be trying to divert attention away from his mother?

"What about the ones outside my cottage?" Grace asked.

Liam smiled. "I have two four-year-old daughters—twins. They're going through a princess phase, and they're obsessed with anything pink, sparkly, or floral. They spent the day with their grandparents, and when they saw that the roses were in bloom, they each wanted to have one. My mother didn't want them to prick their fingers on the thorns, so she gave them some petals to play with instead." He paused, taking a sip of his drink. "Apparently, it was their idea to sprinkle a handful of petals in front of all cottages in the village tonight. Yours wasn't the only one that had petals in front of it. It was just the first one we came to after our walk."

Grace reached for her own drink. "I see."

Aidan could tell that she didn't believe a word Liam was saying. He wasn't sure he believed him either. The explanation seemed pretty far-fetched.

It was a good thing Grace was leaving tomorrow. Because if Liam wasn't telling the truth, he'd just brought the rest of the islanders into it, at least the ones who lived in the village. Glancing over his shoulder, at the dozen or so people seated at the tables in the dining room, Aidan wondered how many of them were prepared to go along with Liam's lie.

Unless...of course, they were *already* in on it.

It was possible that Liam or Dominic had prepped them before Grace had arrived. And while the thought of such a coordinated scheme left a bad taste in his mouth, he wouldn't put it past them. He'd seen the way the islanders treated Brigid—with a respect that bordered on reverence—and the devotion they showed to Glenna and Owen.

He suspected that most, if not all of them, would be willing to protect their friends at any cost.

The only way this scheme might backfire was if Grace were to run into Brigid or one of the twins before she left on the ferry tomorrow. But Neil had promised to keep Brigid away from the pub tonight. And the twins had insisted on spending the night with their grandparents so they could be on the lookout for fairies. It was unlikely that Grace would run into any of them, which could explain why Liam had chosen to use them in his lie.

Maybe he *had* thought this through.

"I admit," Liam said with a smile, "it did seem strange, even to me, but I knew those petals had to have come from somewhere."

"Your mother's greenhouse, apparently," Grace said.

Liam lifted his glass to clink against hers. "Mystery solved."

Grace smiled and touched her glass to his. "Thanks for looking into it. I know you have a lot on your mind."

"No bother at all," Liam said, finishing his drink.

When Grace picked up her fork, as if the matter were settled, Aidan's brows drew together. Why was she letting Liam off the hook so easily?

Liam set his empty glass on the bar. "Have you decided where you're going to go next?"

"Not yet," Grace said.

"After our walk, I remembered that a colleague of mine is doing some research in a village a few hours up the coast. There's a man there who claims that his great-grandmother was a selkie."

"Really?"

Liam nodded. "I think you mentioned earlier that you were thinking of heading north after this. My colleague will be there tomorrow if you want to meet with him."

"I'll take his number if you have it," Grace said.

Liam slipped his phone out of his pocket, looked up the number, and jotted it down on a napkin. "Shall I send him a text, now, to let him know what time to expect you?"

"That's all right," Grace said. "I'll take care of it."

"Are you sure?" Liam asked. "I'd be happy to make an introduction."

Grace took the napkin from him. "I'm sure."

"All right, then," Liam said, looking slightly less stressed than he had when he'd walked in the door earlier. "Now that that's sorted, I should probably head home, or I might be tempted to lay my head down on the bar."

"I hope you get some rest tonight," Grace said. "Thanks again for answering all my questions."

"You're welcome." Liam stood and started to make his way toward the kitchen. "I'll slip out the back after I grab my food." He nodded goodbye to Aidan, then looked at Grace. "If you think of anything else, feel free to give me a call. And if I don't see you again before you leave, have a safe journey."

"I'm sure I'll see you again."

Liam paused, his hand on the door to the kitchen. "The ferry leaves at 8:15."

Grace took a sip of her drink. "I'm not leaving on the ferry tomorrow."

Liam slowly turned back around to face her. "You're not?"

"No." Grace smiled. "I booked the cottage for the rest of the month."

# CHAPTER ELEVEN

What?" Liam asked as all the color drained from his face. "When?"

"Right after our walk," Grace said. "I checked online, and it was available." She snagged another chip from Aidan's plate, not sure what she was enjoying more, the salty chip coated in malt vinegar or the look on Liam's face.

She knew he'd been lying to her. She didn't know why. And she didn't know if it had anything to do with her mother. But she wasn't leaving this island until she figured out what these people were hiding.

Nudging her empty plate aside, she glanced at Aidan. She could tell from the look on his face that she'd surprised him, too. But he didn't seem nearly as upset about it. If anything, he seemed rather pleased. "What should we have for dessert?" she asked casually.

Aidan's lips curved as he pointed to a small chalkboard that held the day's dessert specials.

Grace gave the board a quick skim, then looked back at the

man on the other side of the bar. "What do you think, Liam. Any recommendations?"

Catching himself, Liam ran a hand through his hair. "Ah… sure." He looked up at the board. "You…uh…can't go wrong with a slice of cake and an Irish coffee."

"That sounds perfect." Grace looked at the two cake choices. The chocolate stout cake was tempting, but she'd never had a whiskey walnut spice cake before. "I think I'll try a slice of the spice cake," she said, turning her attention back to Aidan. "Do you want to get something?"

Aidan was still smiling, and it appeared, now, that he was trying not to laugh. "I'll just have a glass of whiskey and a few bites of your cake."

Liam rubbed his eyes, as if his head were pounding. "I'll… uh…let Dominic know and then be on my way." He started to turn when the door to the pub swung open and two four-year-old girls came running into the room.

"Dad!" one of them shouted.

"Uncle Aidan!" the other one shouted.

"They came! The fairies came!" they shouted together. "We saw them!"

Liam froze, and Aidan uttered a curse under his breath as Brigid and Neil walked into the pub behind the twins. The rest of the islanders fell quiet. Grace saw several of them exchange a worried glance.

"What are you two doing here?" Liam managed to find his voice as he walked out to greet his daughters. "I thought you were supposed to be in bed?"

Both girls ran to their father and gave him a hug.

"We *were* in bed," the one wearing a pair of unicorn pajamas said, so excited she could hardly contain herself, "but then the fairies came!"

"And they brought us fairy dust!" the other one said, holding up a tiny bottle filled with what looked like sparkly sand.

"Fairy dust?"

"Granny said the fairies would come if we planted a garden," the first one said. "They brought us dust so we could heal Uncle Aidan!"

"Didn't you just plant those gardens today?" Liam asked.

Both girls nodded.

"Wow," Liam said. "That was fast."

From across the room, Neil caught Liam's eye and mouthed the word, "Sorry."

Clearly, these particular fairies weren't supposed to have come tonight. Grace wondered if the prospect of their arrival had been nothing more than a convenient distraction to keep the twins away from the pub tonight.

When three women who'd been eating dinner at separate tables stood and went to speak with Brigid, forming a protective wall between her and the bar, Grace blinked. Maybe it wasn't the twins they were worried about. Maybe the twins had simply been part of a plan to keep Brigid away from the pub tonight.

And away from *her*.

Remembering how quickly Neil and Aidan had tried to separate the two of them on the beach that morning, she wondered if Brigid had something to do with whatever these people were trying to hide.

Was there something about Brigid, in particular, that they didn't want her to know?

"Uncle Aidan!" The twin carrying the fairy dust ran toward him. "We came to heal you!"

Grace expected him to laugh. Instead, he reached down, lifted the little girl up, and set her on his lap. The fondness in his expression, when he looked at the child, caught Grace off guard.

"They came, did they?" Aidan asked, the affection in his tone unmistakable.

Beaming, the little girl nodded. "I knew they would."

She handed him the tiny bottle of fairy dust, and he took it carefully, cradling it in his wide palm, like it was the most precious thing in the world.

Grace had never seen this side of him before. And she didn't know what to make of it. She'd been trying to play it cool ever since he'd arrived at her cottage to ask her to dinner. She still didn't know what had come over her, earlier, after that wave had thrown them together on the beach. She hadn't even been able to make it all the way back to the village in the same car with him.

And when he'd taken her hand a little while ago, she'd felt the same half-drugged sensation wash over her again.

Thankfully, that time, she'd been able to pull herself together. But it was taking a lot more effort than normal to keep her cool. And seeing him like this wasn't helping matters.

It wasn't helping at all.

"Are you sure you want me to have this?" Aidan asked once the other twin had come over to join them.

"We're sure," they said together.

The twin on the ground shifted her attention to Grace. "Who are you?"

"I'm Grace."

"You're pretty."

Grace smiled. "Thank you. Who are you?"

"I'm Freya. And that's Maeve," she said, pointing to her sister. "We're twins."

"I can see that," Grace said. "Would like to have a seat, Freya?"

"Yes!"

Grace slid off her stool and helped Freya climb up so that Aidan was surrounded by the two girls.

"What do we do with it?" Aidan removed the cork from the tiny bottle. "Just...sprinkle it on and hope for the best?"

"No." Freya pulled something out of the pocket of the pink jacket she wore over her pajamas. "We have a spell."

Aidan's brows rose. "A spell?"

"A healing spell," Maeve clarified as Freya handed him a small scroll of parchment paper, bound with a silver ribbon.

Aidan took the scroll, untied the ribbon, and looked briefly at the words on the page. "Who wrote this?"

"I did," Brigid said, walking up behind Grace. "Magic always works better when you have a spell."

Grace stepped back to make more room for Brigid.

Brigid smiled at her. "Hello, again."

"Hi," Grace said, noting that Brigid's eyes seemed clearer than before and that she'd regained some of her confidence.

"We'll say it together." Freya brought them back to the task at hand. "The three of us."

"But give us the fairy dust first." Maeve cupped her hands together and held them out.

Freya cupped her hands together as well. "After we say the spell, we'll sprinkle it on your leg."

Aidan's lips twitched, but he managed to maintain a serious expression as he poured the fairy dust into the children's hands. "There." He set the empty bottle on the bar. "I think that's all of it."

The twins looked at Brigid, and she nodded for them to begin.

"With this dust," they said together, then waited for Aidan to join them.

"Right," he said, catching on. "I'm ready now."

*With this dust*
*Bring health to us*

*Let the pain fade away*
*By the end of this day*
*And tonight, when we rest*
*We'll feel nothing but blessed*

As soon as they finished saying the spell, the twins tossed the fairy dust into the air so it would rain down on Aidan.

"You're healed!" Maeve said, clapping her hands together.

Freya clapped, too, dissolving into a fit of giggles when she saw that her hands were covered in glitter.

Aidan smiled and shook some of the sparkles out of his hair. "What do we do now?"

"We walk!" Maeve said, already starting to climb back down to the ground.

Liam stepped forward and helped her down. "The spell said it might not work until the end of the day," he cautioned.

Maeve was undeterred. "Granny said he'd start feeling better right away."

Both Liam and Aidan gave their mother a look, and even Grace couldn't help stealing a glance at her. Brigid didn't *actually* think the fairy dust was going to heal him, did she?

Holding onto the bar for support, Aidan stood, then began to put weight on his bad leg. When he tried to lift his other leg to take a step forward, he winced and set it back down. "I don't think it's quite healed yet."

Freya's face fell. "It didn't work?"

Maeve looked at Brigid. "Why didn't it work?"

Brigid seemed troubled and almost as disappointed as the twins. "It should have worked." Looking down at his leg, she frowned. "Are you sure you're not feeling *any* better?"

"Uh..." Aidan looked at Liam, then Dominic, who'd walked out of the kitchen a few minutes ago, clearly hoping that one of them might help him out. "Yes."

"Maybe we should give it some time," Grace said, feeling compelled to step in when neither of his brothers seemed able to. She could tell that Aidan didn't want to disappoint the twins, and his mother wasn't making this easy for him.

"How much time?" Maeve asked.

"I don't know," Grace said. "Maybe we need to be patient and keep the faith. Right, Liam?"

"R-right," Liam stammered.

"I think that's a fine idea," Aidan said, looking at her gratefully. "Maybe we should relax and give it a few days. In the meantime," he said, looking back at the twins, "you know what *would* make me feel better?"

"What?" Maeve asked, still sounding dejected.

"If you'd tell me about the fairies you saw." Aidan held out a hand to her. "I want to know what they looked like."

That seemed to perk her up a little.

When she took his hand, he helped her climb onto the stool to share with her sister. Then he eased back onto his own stool. "Come on, now. Don't keep me waiting." He smiled, trying to cheer them up. "I've never seen a fairy before, and I want to know everything."

The two girls looked at each other, then both began talking at once.

Grace's heart gave a funny little squeeze. Remembering that Brigid was still standing beside her, she turned to ask how the rest of her day had been. Before she could get the words out, Neil took Brigid's hand and led her over to another couple who was waiting to talk to them. Liam came to stand in the spot that his mother had vacated, putting another barrier between them. Even Dominic, who was busy behind the bar—setting a glass of whiskey in front of Aidan and two cups of hot chocolate in front of the twins—kept stealing glances at his mother.

Those glances grew more concerned when Brigid untangled

herself from Neil and the other couple and made her way back to Grace.

"I was hoping I might run into you tonight," Brigid said. "I brought you something to thank you for helping me earlier."

"You didn't need to bring me anything," Grace said, surprised.

"I know." Brigid drew a small sachet out of the pocket of her sweater and held it out to her. "But I wanted to."

Grace took the sachet. It was made of soft silver cloth, cinched together by a thin blue ribbon.

"Open it," Brigid urged.

Grace opened it and peered inside at what looked like a combination of dried herbs and gemstones. She caught a whiff of a familiar, calming scent. "Is that lavender?"

Brigid nodded. "It's lavender, sage, rose quartz, and black tourmaline. The herbs will help you find the answers to the questions you seek. The black tourmaline will protect you on your journey. And the rose quartz will help you open your heart to love."

Grace wasn't sure how she felt about the addition of the rose quartz. But she liked the sound of what the rest of the items could do. And she was touched by the gesture. "This is very thoughtful. Thank you."

"I heard you were leaving us tomorrow, and I wanted you to have it before you left."

Grace closed the sachet and looped the ribbon around her ring finger before lowering her hand back to her side. "I'm actually not leaving tomorrow."

"You're not?" Brigid seemed as pleased as Aidan had been by the news.

Grace shook her head.

Brigid took a moment to study her, and a slow smile spread across her face. "I had a feeling you belonged here."

Grace laughed. "Well, I don't know about that, but I am staying a little while longer."

"Granny." Freya pointed to the sachet in Grace's hand. "What's that?"

"It's a gift for Grace," Brigid said. "To thank her for helping me earlier. Mostly just herbs from the greenhouse."

Freya climbed down from the stool she was sharing with her sister and walked over to Grace. "Can I see?"

Grace handed the sachet to her, then looked back at Brigid. "Liam mentioned you had a greenhouse."

A look of pride washed over Brigid's face. "I grow herbs for Tara's medical practice."

"Really?"

Brigid nodded. "Not everything can be cured with a pill."

"Interesting," Grace said. She didn't have much experience with herbal medicine, but it did make sense, given how cut off they were, that the islanders might try to use whatever remedies they had at their disposal before making the lengthy trip to the hospital. "Do you ever grow any flowers?"

"A few."

"Roses?"

"No." Brigid shook her head. "I never grow roses. Why do you ask?"

"Just curious." Grace looked at Liam.

All the color had drained from his face again.

"I'd be glad to give you a tour of the greenhouse," Brigid said. "Why don't you come by for tea the day after tomorrow? That'll give me enough time to clean up." She smiled. "The house is a mess with the children staying over."

Grace smiled back. "I'd love that."

"Dad," Freya said, losing interest in the sachet. "Can we have ice cream?"

Liam rubbed a hand over his eyes again, his expression pained.

"You just had hot chocolate," Neil said, stepping in.

Maeve climbed down from the stool to join her sister. "But we want ice cream, too."

Neil put a hand on Maeve's shoulder. "It's time for bed, you two."

"Noooo," they both protested.

"Yes," Brigid said gently, taking Freya's hand. "We need to get home so we can put more bottles out. If we're lucky, the fairies might pay us another visit tonight."

Freya's eyes widened. "*Another* visit?"

"It's possible."

"Will they bring us more fairy dust?" Maeve asked hopefully.

Brigid smiled. "We either need that or a stronger spell."

The twins looked at each other, then nodded. "Okay," they both said at the same time.

Liam knelt and opened his arms. "Come here, you two."

They went to him, and he held onto them for a long time, like he was afraid something was going to happen to them if he let go. When they finally wriggled free, they ran over to Aidan to give him a hug, too. Then they blew kisses to Dominic from across the bar.

"Bye Grace," Freya said.

"Bye Grace," Maeve parroted.

"Bye." Grace caught Brigid's eye before she turned and headed for the door. "Thank you, again," she said, holding up the sachet.

"You're welcome," Brigid said. "I'm so glad you're staying."

Grace watched the four of them leave. As soon as the door shut behind them, she turned to Liam. "I guess those petals must have come from somewhere else."

Liam shifted his weight from one foot to the other. "I...uh... must have been mistaken."

"Right," Grace said, then glanced at Aidan. "You know, I think it might be time for me to call it a night, too."

"What about dessert?" Aidan asked.

"I changed my mind."

"I'll walk you home, then." He was already making his way to his feet.

"You don't need to do that."

He reached for his cane. "I'll feel better if I see you to your door."

"It'll take me less than a minute to walk there. I think I can manage without an escort."

Aidan dropped a few notes onto the bar to pay for their dinner. "Rumor has it, there are fairies about. I wouldn't want you to run into a pack of them on your own. I hear they can be a bit mischievous, especially at night."

She gave him a look.

He smiled and gestured for her to go first.

Relenting, she walked to the door. He held it open for her, and she stepped outside. The air was crisp and cool. The village was bathed in a wash of silver moonlight. The surface of the sea gleamed like polished sterling.

"I take it you don't know where the rose petals came from either," Grace said.

"No."

"Does anyone?"

"I don't think so," Aidan admitted. "Not yet anyway."

Grace looked out at the water. She appreciated his honesty. She was starting to think there were only two people on this island who weren't lying to her—Aidan and Brigid. Aidan might have withheld information about his past the night before, but he hadn't lied to her.

At least, not that she knew of.

And Brigid had seemed genuinely happy to hear that Grace had decided to stay for a while. But then, why were the rest of the islanders so intent on keeping them apart? "Why doesn't anyone want me to talk to your mother?"

Aidan was quiet for a moment. He could have played dumb or pretended that Grace was imagining things. Instead, he appeared to be choosing his words carefully, as if he wanted to provide an explanation without giving too much away. "My mother has an active imagination. At times, she can get rather...caught up in it. Sometimes, she'll seem perfectly normal, like tonight. Other times, she won't make any sense at all, like when you saw her on the beach this morning. You never know what version of her you're going to get. And that can be...unsettling for some people."

Grace let that sink in. "Is that why there's so much tension between you?"

"That's one reason."

When Aidan fell silent again, Grace lifted her gaze to the web of walls on the eastern side of the island. What was he trying to say? That his mother struggled with mental illness? Lots of people struggled with mental illness. It wasn't anything to be ashamed of, and in most cases, it could be managed with the right therapy and medication. It wasn't enough of a reason for the islanders to want to keep her and Brigid apart.

There had to be more to it than that.

Aidan didn't seem to want to elaborate, though. And they were almost to the door of her cottage, so she let it drop for now.

She spotted Neil's taillights in the distance, a blur of red beneath a brilliant moon, and she remembered how good Aidan had been with the twins tonight. "Your nieces adore you."

"Naturally."

She laughed.

"It must be fun to have a twin," Aidan said.

"It is."

"You have a twin?"

"I do."

"There's another woman out there who looks like you?"

"No." Grace smiled when they came to her door. "I have a twin brother."

"Fascinating." The lines around Aidan's eyes crinkled in the moonlight. "You can tell me all about him over dinner tomorrow night."

Grace laughed.

"What?" he asked. "If you're staying on the island for the rest of the month, we really ought to have a proper romance."

"That's not why I decided to stay."

"I know," he said. "But you can't tell me you haven't thought about it."

"Oh, I've thought about it."

He smiled. "What's holding you back, then?"

Grace took a moment to consider her response. Under normal circumstances, Aidan would have made an excellent candidate for a fling. She was wildly attracted to him, and there was a firm end date in sight, which meant she'd be safe from forming any real attachment to him. But these weren't normal circumstances. She didn't like the crazed feeling that came over her whenever he touched her. She didn't know where the rose petals had come from. And she didn't know what the rest of the islanders were hiding from her.

She didn't want to complicate an already complicated situation.

"Well, for starters," she said, falling back on the simplest excuse she could think of, "this island is tiny."

He lifted a brow, waiting for her to go on.

She pointed back to O'Sullivan's. "Like you said yesterday, there's only one pub."

"Right," he said slowly.

"We're both going to need to eat there every day," Grace said.

"I happen to like a bit of company when I eat."

He wasn't making this easy for her. "If something goes wrong, we won't be able to avoid each other."

"What could possibly go wrong?"

Grace turned and slipped her key into the lock. "I don't know," she said, glancing back at him over her shoulder. "What if you're not a good kisser?"

Aidan's lips curved, and Grace realized that was probably the last thing she should have said if she'd wanted to un-complicate things between them. She turned around, intending to regain control of the situation.

"How about this?" Aidan suggested lightly, before she had a chance to speak. "If you don't like the way that I kiss, we can go back to being...whatever we are now."

Grace shook her head. "I don't think..." She trailed off when he took a step closer, then another, until he was close enough for her to catch the earthy scent of him, an intoxicating blend of turf smoke and rain-soaked moss.

His gaze dropped to her mouth, lingered. "We can pretend like it never even happened."

No, Grace thought. This was a bad idea. She needed to stop this, now. But when his hand curved around her waist and he drew her into him, fitting every inch of their bodies together except their mouths, a small sound escaped from the back of her throat.

"What do you say, Grace?" His mouth lowered, pausing a breath away from hers. "Shall we give it a try?"

It was just a taste, Grace thought. How much harm could it do?

The moment his mouth met hers, she knew it wasn't going to be enough. He tasted like whiskey and cloves and something darker. Something edgier. Something that made her want to lose control.

She pulled him closer. His lips slanted over hers, deepening the kiss. She could feel the ocean beneath them, pulsing against the cliffs. She could hear the ragged creak of a weathervane in the distance. When he pushed her against the door of the cottage, covering her body with his, the last sane thought she'd been holding onto vanished.

There was no charm in his kiss, no teasing flirtation. It was like being sucked underwater, dragged out to sea. There was nothing she could do but let go, let it consume her. He made a low sound, like a growl, as his teeth scraped over her bottom lip. And she let herself sink, surrendering to the weightlessness of it.

The chaos of it.

She didn't know how long they stayed there, but when they finally surfaced, she felt delirious. Like she'd been lost at sea for days. She leaned back against the door, not trusting her legs to hold her.

"Well," Aidan asked, after several long moments, his eyes dark and unreadable in the moonlight. "What's the verdict, love?"

Grace's lips parted, but no sound came out.

"That bad, huh?" He smiled as he tipped her face back up to his, brushing his lips over hers one last time. "I guess we'll have to try it again tomorrow, just to be sure."

# CHAPTER TWELVE

The next day, Grace pulled herself out of bed. She didn't know what time she'd finally fallen asleep. She'd spent most of the night tossing and turning, reliving the way her whole body had come alive when Aidan had kissed her. If he hadn't walked away afterwards, she might have done something stupid, like invite him in.

What was wrong with her?

She knew better than to get involved with a man who made her feel restless and needy. If he could break through that many of her defenses with one kiss, what would happen if she slept with him? The thought of spending an entire night with Aidan had her walking into the kitchen and downing two glasses of ice water.

Afterwards, she pressed the cold glass to her forehead, closed her eyes, and tried to get a grip.

She didn't want to admit it, even to herself, but the truth was, she'd never been kissed like that before. She'd never felt anything like that before. He hadn't just broken through her defenses. He'd cracked something open inside her, made her come unhinged.

The intensity of their connection scared her. It made her want things, long for things, that she hadn't realized she'd needed until now.

Lowering the glass to the counter, she opened her eyes and walked to the window overlooking the harbor. A thick gray mist had rolled over the island. The surface of the water was eerily calm. In the distance, she could hear the lonesome bark of a solitary seal.

She took a deep breath, steeling herself against the emotions warring inside her. She'd come here to figure out what had happened to her mother. She couldn't afford to get sidetracked. Not now. Not when she was so close to scratching the surface of what these islanders might know.

Turning away from the window, she headed back to the bedroom. Maybe all she needed was some fresh air to clear her head. She took a shower and changed her clothes, then paused when she spotted the rose petal on her nightstand. It was the same one she'd carried around with her the day before.

She walked over to it and picked it up, marveling at how it hadn't changed. It was still as soft and velvety as it had been when she'd first found it. There wasn't a single sign of deterioration or decay. Feeling compelled to bring it with her again, she tucked it in her pocket and walked out to the living area to check on the ones she'd put in the bowl on the windowsill.

They hadn't changed either.

How was that possible?

Backing away from the window, she glanced at the clock on the wall. It was later than she'd thought. Her body must still be adjusting to the time zone. Thinking she'd feel better after she had something to eat, she went to the kitchen to grab a piece of fruit from the basket on the counter. But her gaze kept straying back to the bowl of petals. Where had they come from? Why had Liam felt like he'd needed to lie about them? And how were they connected to the roses that grew outside her childhood home on Heron Island?

Knowing that she wasn't going to find the answers to any of those questions by spending the day inside, she pulled on her jacket, opened the door, and stepped outside. The wind had subsided, and a hush had settled over the village. A few lights shone through the windows of the neighboring cottages, but they appeared softened, blurred by the heavy mists cloaking the island. Even the petals on Taylor's wind chime were barely moving, the strings weighted down by the dampness in the air.

Resisting the urge to turn around, to retreat to the warmth of her cottage and bury herself in research for the rest of the day, she started to walk. She'd spent enough time on her computer the day before. She needed to keep exploring, to keep moving until the next clue presented itself to her. She headed east toward the harbor. The tide was out, and dark strands of kelp covered the stretches of pale sand. A group of seals watched her from the rocks as she made her way down to the water.

She picked her way over the crusty ropes the fishermen had left behind when they'd gone out to sea for the day and lifted her gaze to the crumbling stone fortress on the far side of the harbor.

Magic, she thought as the heavy air swirled around her. It wasn't a word she'd ever given much thought to. But if there were ever a place that could make her believe, it was here. As a journalist, she'd immersed herself in facts and reality. But it was magic that had held the first clue to the one mystery she'd never been able to solve.

Was it possible she'd been looking in the wrong place all along?

Thinking back to the story her brother had told her a few weeks ago—the story that had sparked this trip to Ireland, she wondered if it might be time to revisit that initial clue. Pulling her phone out, she tapped on the screen a few times until she found her brother's name, then initiated the call.

It would be early there, but her brother worked on the water. He was usually up before dawn.

"Hey," Ryan Callahan said, answering after the second ring.

"Hey," she said, always happy to hear her twin brother's voice. "I didn't wake you, did I?"

"No, I just got to the café. What's up?"

"I need you to tell me, again, what you saw that night in the cove."

"Why? What's going on?"

"I think I might be onto something."

"Yeah?"

"Maybe. I'm not sure yet. It could be nothing," she added, not wanting to get his hopes up.

"It's never nothing with you," he said, and she could hear the smile in his voice. "Hang on, let me say hi to Izzy first."

"Of course." Grace said, remembering that Ryan always ate breakfast at the Wind Chime Café now that his girlfriend, Izzy Rivera, worked there.

"I'm back," Ryan said. "Izzy says hi, and so do Annie and Della."

"Tell them all hi back for me." Grace heard the bell chime on the door, then the soft tinkling of wind chimes as Ryan walked outside. She could picture him settling into one of the comfortable chairs on the porch with a steaming cup of coffee and a delicious pastry that Della Dozier had baked that morning.

Della wasn't just an amazing baker. She was also the closest thing Grace and Ryan had had to a mother since their own had disappeared.

"Do you want me to start at the beginning?" Ryan asked.

"Yes," Grace said. "Tell me the whole story as if I've never heard it before."

"Just the part about what I saw in the cove, right? Not the whole legend?"

"Right," Grace said. She didn't need a refresher on the legend. She'd heard it enough times as a child.

It had been their mother's favorite story to tell them before bed.

Yesterday, when Liam had said there weren't many selkie stories in the States, he had been right. There weren't *many*. But there were a few. And Heron Island was home to one of them.

It was an obscure tale—one that had been passed down quietly through generations of fishermen and their wives. Only a handful of people outside Heron Island had even heard of it until recently. This past summer, one of Ryan's employees had convinced him to feature the legend on his website, because it just so happened that Ryan's oysters came from the same cove where the legend originated.

According to the legend, the cove was enchanted—and had been since the early 1900s—when a fisherman who'd lived on its shores had gotten lost in a storm. Unable to find his way home, he'd heard a strange voice in the wind and decided to follow it. The voice belonged to a woman, and she sang to him, guiding him back to his home on Pearl Cove.

When he returned, a mysterious woman wearing a dark leather coat and a long string of pearls was waiting for him on the beach. Captivated by her beauty, he fell in love with her at first sight. In a matter of days, he'd convinced her to marry him.

At that time, there were a few Irish immigrants living on the island. They warned the fisherman that the woman was not a good choice for a wife. She reminded them too much of the selkies they'd heard about in folktales from their homeland. But the fisherman ignored them. He married her anyway. And they even seemed happy for a while.

But as the years passed, as the Irishmen had predicted, the woman grew restless. Not long after she gave birth to their third child, she began to spend more and more time by the water's edge. She would spend her days collecting seashells and her nights wandering the marshes, singing sad songs as she waded deeper and deeper into the cove.

The islanders begged him to make her stop because her songs were breaking their hearts, too. But there was nothing he could do to console her. And then, one day, she disappeared—never to be seen or heard from again.

The fisherman and his children were devastated. They searched everywhere for her. But the only thing she'd left behind was a single strand of pearls, lying on the beach. Eventually, the fisherman realized that the Irishmen had been right. The woman had been a selkie. And she had gone home.

The fisherman never stopped loving her, though. And each year, on the anniversary of her disappearance, he and his children would drop a single pearl from her necklace into the cove, hoping to lure her back. The woman never returned, but the Irishmen claimed that some of her magic remained in the cove.

As the years passed, some said that if you walked into the marshes at midnight, you could still hear her singing. Others said that if you closed your eyes when a storm was coming, you could hear seashells clinking together in the wind. A few even claimed that when the moon was full, its reflection would come apart— each circle of light slowly separating from the others until it resembled a single strand of pearls floating on the surface of the water.

Grace had heard the tale so many times she could recite it in her sleep. But what she hadn't heard, until last month, was that her brother had witnessed everything those Irishmen had described. He'd been a child, only ten years old at the time. On a night when the moon had been full, he'd waited for everyone else to go to sleep, then he'd snuck out of the house, borrowed their father's rowboat, and paddled out to the cove.

He'd heard the woman's voice and the shells clinking together, and he'd seen the moonlight break, scattering across the cove, until it had slowly re-formed into a single strand of pearls. He'd rushed home to wake their mother and tell her what had happened. She had listened intently and had seemed eager to hear every word. Afterwards, she had told him to get some sleep and had assured him that they would talk about it more in the morning.

The next morning, when they'd woken up, she'd been gone.

For over twenty years, Ryan had kept that part of the story a secret. He'd been too ashamed to tell anyone, convinced that their mother had left because of him. It wasn't until recently, when he and his father had grown closer after years of having a strained relationship, that he'd finally confided the truth.

Grace didn't blame Ryan for keeping the secret. And she didn't blame him for their mother's disappearance. She was just relieved to finally have a clue.

When her brother finished telling her the story again—the same story, almost word for word, that he'd told her a few weeks ago—she decided to ask him a question she'd been reluctant to ask the first time. It couldn't have been easy for him to tell her the truth after keeping it a secret for so long, and she hadn't wanted to make him feel any worse than he'd already felt. But she had been wondering about something ever since he'd told her.

"I agree that our mother's disappearance might have something to do with what you told her," Grace said. "I don't know what yet, but I came here to research selkies in case there was a connection between the legends and what happened to her. And I'm going to continue to follow that lead and see where it takes us. But as far as what you saw in the cove that night..." Grace paused and took a breath. "You were ten, Ryan. You were alone in a boat. It could have been anything. You don't actually believe that it was magic, do you?"

Her question was met with a long stretch of silence.

"It's not that I don't believe you," she said, when he continued to say nothing. "I'm sure you saw *something*. But couldn't it have been headlights flashing from a truck on the other side of the marsh or an old lighthouse flickering on and off?"

"No."

The conviction in his tone surprised her. "No?"

"No," Ryan said. "I was ten years old the *first* time I saw it, Grace. I've seen it many times since."

Grace's eyes widened. "You have?"

"Yes."

"How many times?"

"More than I can count."

More than he could count? How had she not known this? "Do you know anyone else who's seen it?"

There was another long pause, and she could hear the creak of his chair shifting beneath him. "The last time we had a full moon, I took Izzy out to the cove. She saw it, too."

"*Izzy* saw it?"

"Yes."

Grace reached into her pocket and drew out the petal. The scent of it drifted up through the mist, adding a touch of sweetness to the air. Tiny drops of moisture formed on the velvety surface, then slid away, dripping like tears onto the slick wooden planks at her feet.

She remembered what Liam had said about magic the day before—that the world would offer us signs if we were open to seeing them. There was only one sign in her life that she hadn't been open to seeing. Year after year, every time lavender roses had grown outside her childhood home, she had tried to get rid of them.

She hadn't *wanted* to see them.

And yet, here they were again, on the other side of the ocean, forcing her to pay attention.

What were they trying to tell her?

"Ryan?"

"Yes?"

"I'm going to ask you something, and you have to promise not to laugh."

"I promise."

Grace took a deep breath. "Do you think our mother was a selkie?"

"I don't know."

"But...you think it's a possibility?"

"I do."

Grace looked out at the water. It was still shrouded in a thick, gray haze. For the first time since coming here, she tried to imagine that the legends were true. That under the surface of that cold, dark sea, there were creatures who could shift between land and water. Who could fall in love and bear children in a world that was not their own. Who could leave that world as quickly as they'd joined it, and never once look back.

As crazy as that notion was, a small part of her wanted to believe it. If their mother had left them to return to the sea, it wasn't because she hadn't loved them. It was because she'd never belonged on land in the first place.

As tempting as it was to adopt that theory, she wasn't quite ready to go there. Not yet anyway. She would keep her mind open to the possibility *after* she'd ruled out everything else. First, she needed to figure out what the petals meant.

"Did Taylor come to work with Annie this morning?" she

asked, remembering the rose petal chime Taylor had made for her —the one she'd insisted Grace bring with her to Ireland.

"I haven't seen her, but she might be upstairs. Why?"

"I need to talk to her."

"Okay. Let me check."

Grace heard the sound of Ryan's chair creak again as he stood, then the jingle of the bell on the door as he walked back into the café. She heard muffled voices, the soft clattering of dishes, and the hiss of an espresso machine in the background, before he came back on the line.

"She's upstairs reading," Ryan said. "I'll go get her."

"Thanks."

"Oh, and Grace?"

"Yes?"

"Della wants you to send her a picture."

"Of the island?"

"Yeah."

Grace looked over her shoulder, at the mists sweeping over the mossy hills. A picture wouldn't do this place justice, at least not the kind she could take on her phone. She had no doubt that Aidan could capture the surreal beauty of this place, but she wasn't going to ask him for any favors. She knew exactly what he'd want in return. And she had no intention of repeating what had happened between them the night before.

A painting, though. That might work.

She thought of the ones hanging on the walls of her cottage. If she could find a smaller version of one of those, maybe she could send one to Della as a surprise. It would take longer than sending a picture through her phone, but it would be worth it.

Besides, it would give her a chance to talk to Glenna. She hadn't had a chance to talk to her about the legends yet. And she wanted to talk to as many islanders as possible.

"Tell her I'll send her something soon," Grace said.

"Will do," he said. "I'm putting Taylor on now."

Taylor came on the line. "Hi, Grace."

"Hey, Taylor. What are you up to?"

"I'm reading."

"About what?"

"Dragons."

"Oh, yeah?"

"Baby dragons," she clarified. "They're learning how to fly."

Grace smiled.

"Did you hang up my wind chime yet?" Taylor asked.

"I did. I found the perfect spot for it. That's actually why I wanted to talk to you."

"Is there something wrong with it?"

"No. It's fine," Grace reassured her. "I'm just curious... Why did you decide to make me a wind chime out of rose petals?"

"Mom didn't tell you?"

"No."

"I had a dream about you."

"A dream?"

"Yes. Right after I heard you were leaving. I dreamed that you were alone in a forest. It was dark. You were lost. And you couldn't find your way home."

Grace's brows drew together. "What does that have to do with rose petals?"

"There was a trail of rose petals on the ground. They could have led you home if you'd followed them, but you couldn't see them. I kept trying to get your attention to tell you to follow the petals, but you couldn't hear me, and you couldn't see the petals either. As soon as I woke up, I asked Mom to help me make you a wind chime. I didn't want you to get lost and not be able to find your way home."

"The rose petals were supposed to help me find my way home?" Grace asked slowly.

"Yes," Taylor said. "You had to follow them."
Grace looked down at the petal in her hand. "Taylor?"
"Yes?"
"Do you remember what color they were?"
"The petals?"
"Yes," Grace said.
"They were lavender."

# CHAPTER THIRTEEN

Glenna McClure hadn't used magic in seven years. Magic had always been something she'd used to protect the people she loved. And she hadn't needed to protect anyone for a long time. But her powers had never left her. And last night, when she'd heard about the rose petals from Liam, she'd been tempted to light a fire in a circle of stones and let the flames show her what was to come.

Instead, she'd followed the worn path through the fields to her studio. And she'd picked up her paintbrush, hoping a message might come out in her art.

Six canvases later, she still didn't know what the petals meant. But she knew that Grace's arrival had set something in motion. And whatever it was, she needed to find a way to stop it.

Stepping back from the final painting, she took in the scene around her—the empty tubes of oil paint scattered across the floor, the discarded brushes and palette knives tossed haphazardly into the sink, the wet paintings perched on every flat surface.

Barefoot, she walked to the counter and righted a jar of

cleaning solution that had tipped over. There were streaks of paint on her hands, on her arms, in her hair. She didn't know what time it was, but it felt like hours since Sam, her husband, had come by to tell her what he'd learned after spending the night digging into Grace's past.

He'd been up all night, too. Searching for answers. Unable to sleep.

Because he knew what had happened the last few times roses had mysteriously appeared on this island. He knew how close they'd come—how close they'd *all* come—to losing everything.

At least, last time, she'd known who they'd been up against. She'd known what the other person had wanted and why. And she'd been prepared to sacrifice herself to protect her friends. But that was before she'd fallen in love with Sam. Before she'd known what it felt like to have a normal life.

All she wanted, now, was to live on this island in peace with Sam. To be a doting aunt to her friends' children. And to make sure that nothing ever came between Brigid and her family again.

At the sound of footsteps on the walkway leading up to the door, she turned. It was time to drive this outsider away.

"I hoped I might find you here." Grace paused in the open doorway. "I wanted to take you up on your offer to look through some of your paintings. Is now a good time?"

"Of course." Glenna smiled. "Come in."

Grace stepped into the one-room cottage and took in the scene. "You've been busy."

"I have."

Grace walked to the closest painting. Its surface was still covered in a wet sheen. "Did you paint all these today?"

"And last night," Glenna said. "It'll take hours for them to dry in this weather."

Grace made her way over to the next one, then the next, taking her time with each one. "They're beautiful."

"Thank you," Glenna said. "Is there anything in particular you're looking for?"

"I'm not sure," Grace said. "I want to find a gift for one of my friends. Maybe a landscape?"

Glenna nodded. "I have more in the gallery."

She led Grace out the back door and across a small stretch of moss to a larger building. She and Sam lived in the village, but she liked having her own space to create and display her art. Her gallery stood in the same spot where her old cottage had been, before it had burned down seven years ago.

It had been Neil's idea to build a gallery from the ruins of her former home. It had made sense from a practical standpoint, but Glenna had appreciated the symbolism of it, too—beauty taking the place of what had once been a stark reminder of all the pain her mother had caused.

Together, she and Neil had breathed new life into this property. And over the years, it had become an attractive destination for the tourists as well. They were often the first to see Glenna's most recent works of art before she shipped them off-island for an official opening at a larger gallery. With this particular tourist season coming to a close, though, no one outside the island had seen her latest collection.

She opened the door and enjoyed the look of astonishment that passed over Grace's face. In contrast to the heavy mists blanketing the island, the air inside pulsed with color and energy. With the flip of a switch, a series of strategically placed accent lights flickered on, filling the room with a luminous glow. On the walls hung one of her most evocative collections yet—nine separate paintings, each featuring a selkie shedding her skin.

In each painting the woman was alone, on a beach, at night. Moonlight poured down, bathing her in a silver glow as she shifted effortlessly from water to land. The strokes were bold, brushed on quickly, with raw textures meant to suggest rather than show. The selkie's expression grew more alluring, more powerful, as she moved through each phase of the transformation. From her first breath of air, to her first step onto the soft white sand, to the final painting, where she stood with her back to the sea, her sealskin forgotten, pooled at her feet.

"Wow." Grace turned slowly, taking them all in. "These are... Wow."

Glenna smiled.

Grace walked closer to the first one, then made her way around the room again, studying each one in more depth. "What are you going to do with them?"

"I haven't decided yet."

"You can't separate them."

"No," Glenna said, pleased that Grace had realized that so quickly.

Grace stopped in front of the final painting, which filled a canvas so large it stretched nearly from the ceiling to the floor. "These need to be in Dublin or Paris or New York. Somewhere everyone can see them."

"They will be...eventually."

Grace looked at Glenna. "What are you waiting for?"

"The right offer," Glenna said simply. It wasn't a matter of interest. She had plenty of that. Owners of some of the most exclusive galleries in the world were clamoring to host an opening for her latest collection. But she was as protective of her art as she was of the people she loved. She didn't want these paintings to go to just anyone. She wanted them to be treated with the same respect that the selkie they depicted deserved.

"How will you know when you've gotten the right offer?" Grace asked.

"I'll just know," Glenna said. There were a few that had risen to the top already. A man in Florence had proposed an eye-popping marketing campaign. A woman in Athens had appealed to her with a hand-written letter. And a woman in Boston had been particularly persuasive.

The woman in Boston had hosted an opening for Glenna eight years ago. She'd thrown a huge party for her, and it had been one of the classiest events Glenna had ever been to. Within the first five minutes, every single one of her paintings had sold. And the owner had personally bought the two most expensive pieces to hang in her home.

Glenna couldn't help feeling a soft spot for an owner who loved her work enough to display it in her own home.

Even so, something was holding her back. She wasn't quite ready to make a final decision. In the meantime, she had a more important matter to deal with. "A landscape, you said, right?"

Grace nodded.

"I have two more rooms in the back."

Glenna led her down a short hallway to the room where she made most of her sales. It was filled with beautiful renderings of the island in various shapes and sizes. Natural light spilled down from above, through a series of skylights, which even on gray days lent a dreamy, mystical feel to the space. There was one long bench in the middle of the room, covered in sage green velvet, and a cozy wine bar with two stools in the far corner.

She still didn't know what time it was, but after spending the entire night painting, she felt like she'd earned herself a drink. She slipped behind the bar, selected an expensive bottle of Cabernet Sauvignon, and poured them each a glass. "Having a glass of wine during the day always feels a bit decadent, don't you think?" she asked as she carried the second glass over to Grace.

"Oh, I shouldn't," Grace said.

"Taste it first, before you decide." Glenna held the glass out to her. "You won't find this, or any of my wines, on the menu at O'Sullivan's."

Grace hesitated, then took the glass from her. "Thanks."

Glenna waited for her to take a sip and enjoyed the look of surprise that crossed over her face.

"This is wonderful," Grace said.

Glenna smiled. "It's one of my favorites."

"Are we celebrating something?" Grace asked.

"I've never felt the need to wait for a celebration to enjoy the finer things in life."

Grace regarded her curiously. "You're not like the rest of the islanders, are you?"

"I can't imagine what you mean," Glenna said, amused.

"Did you grow up here?"

"No."

"Where did you grow up?"

"I lived in Dublin before this," Glenna said, dodging the question. It was true that she'd lived in Dublin for several years before moving to Seal Island, but the answer to where she'd grown up was more complicated. And she wasn't about to tell an outsider that she'd spent the first sixteen years of her life underwater.

"What brought you here?" Grace asked.

She did ask a lot of questions, didn't she, Glenna mused. Just like Liam had said she would. "The same thing that brings anyone here," Glenna said smoothly. "Peace, quiet, the scenery. You can't beat this landscape for inspiration." She nodded toward the art on the walls, bringing Grace's attention back to the original purpose of her visit.

Taking the cue, Grace walked over to a painting of a row of cottages in the village. Their whitewashed walls glowed in the sunlight, contrasting beautifully with the colorful flowers spilling out of their window boxes. There was a similar painting of the pub beside it, a top seller among the tourists who wanted to remember the good times they'd had there.

Glenna moved back to the bar, letting Grace make her way

around the room, giving her the same space that she would give to any potential customer. Not that she thought Grace had actually come here for a painting. Grace might buy one as a cover, but she hadn't come here for art. She'd come here for answers.

Answers that Glenna had no intention of giving her.

Glenna lifted her glass, barely noticing the rich notes of blackberry, vanilla, and cloves as she watched Grace walk to a painting of a mossy cliff bathed in sunlight. Beneath it, a swirling sea in glittering jewel-tones surrounded a pale white beach. It was the same beach where Tara had broken the curse.

She had a feeling Grace knew that, from the amount of time she spent in front of it.

After several moments, Grace moved on. She passed a painting of a stone wall covered in flowering fuchsia vines with barely a second glance and proceeded past a rendering of a crimson-sailed curragh gliding into the harbor. She paused again, though, when she came to a painting of a pair of seals cuddled together on a rocky beach at night. Moonlight glistened on their wet pelts and reflected in their dark, expressive eyes.

Glenna could tell a lot about a person by which paintings captured their interest. And every move Grace made was reinforcing the theory Sam had shared with her that morning. When Grace finally turned away from that painting, her expression was troubled, as if she were wrestling with something internally. There was a childlike vulnerability in her eyes, that, for a moment, tugged at something deep inside Glenna.

But Glenna tamped it down, dousing the flicker of empathy with a long sip of wine. She'd helped enough lost souls. There was too much at stake, now. This woman was on her own.

"Oh." Grace's expression shifted from troubled to charmed as she came to the final painting in the room. "This one. This is it."

"That one?" Glenna asked, surprised. It was a painting of a female sheep with two lambs in a lush spring field filled with wildflowers. The lambs were only a few days old, and their spindly legs were barely holding them up. The ewe stood behind them—comforting, watchful, protective. The sky above them was gray, but sunlight had broken through a gap in the cloud cover to bathe the field in a warm, golden light.

It was the type of painting a daughter would give to her mother. If that were the case, Sam might be losing his touch.

"Are you sure?" Glenna asked. "There's another room at the end of the hall if you'd like to take a look at the rest of the paintings first."

"No," Grace said. "This is perfect. She'll love it."

"Do you want the painting or a print?"

"The painting."

Surprised again, because it was a sizable investment to purchase the original, she wondered if *she* was losing her touch as well. "Who did you say the gift was for?" Glenna asked as she moved to take the painting from the wall.

"A friend."

"Not your mother?" Glenna asked lightly, unhooking the wire from the clamps in the wall.

"No." That troubled expression came back, just for a moment, then disappeared again. "It's for a friend of mine named Della. She's sort of like a mother hen to everyone. She wanted children but wasn't able to have any of her own. So, she looks after everyone else's."

"Did she look after you?" Glenna asked.

"She did."

"I see." Glenna set the painting on the bar. Maybe Sam hadn't lost his touch after all. "I'm sure she'll appreciate this, then."

"I know she will."

Glenna took a moment to study the painting to see if there was anything she wanted to fix before she shipped it to Della—a woman she already felt a connection to, even though they'd never met. Glenna didn't have any children of her own either. She and Sam had tried, in the beginning, right after they'd married. But she'd never gotten pregnant. And after a while, they'd both accepted that children weren't in the cards for them.

Brushing her finger over a wildflower in the grass, she remembered that she'd painted this then, back when she'd been filled with hope at the thought of starting a family of her own. She was surprised it had taken this long to sell. But maybe it had been waiting for the right person to come along.

Maybe it had been waiting for Della.

Not every woman had to have children to lead a fulfilling life, Glenna reminded herself. Some women had no interest in having children. Some women found other children to mother if they couldn't have their own. And some women were biological mothers and nothing more, like her own.

Battling back a wave of emotions, as she did whenever she thought about how much pain her mother had caused, she took another sip of wine and pulled herself together. Right now, the only thing that mattered was getting rid of Grace. And the last thing she needed was to start softening toward her.

"Here." She pulled a piece of paper and a pen out of a box beneath the bar. "Write down the name and address of the woman you want me to send the painting to. I need to complete a few customs forms."

Grace wrote down the information and handed her credit card to Glenna.

Glenna processed the transaction, handed Grace's card back, and nodded toward the hallway, which led to the final room. "Feel free to have a look around while I finish."

"What's in the third room?" Grace asked.

"See for yourself."

Taking her glass of wine, Grace wandered out to the hallway

and turned toward the final room. Glenna listened to her footsteps fade, then stop completely when she came to the end of the hall. A few minutes later, after she'd finished the paperwork, Glenna walked out to join her. Grace was still standing in the doorway of the third room, her gaze fastened on a single painting inside the room. Glenna knew exactly which one it was.

"Not what you expected?" Glenna asked.

"No."

Glenna moved past her, through the doorway, and took in the collection of paintings that hung on the walls. "It's been a long time since I've painted roses."

Outside, the fog shifted, pressing against the glass. Glenna turned her back on it, trying to appear relaxed. The truth was, these paintings made her feel as uneasy as they made Grace.

She'd never intended to paint roses again. A few weeks ago, when the images had first come into her mind, she'd tried her best to ignore them. But they'd kept coming with an insistence she hadn't felt in a long time with her art. She'd finally given in to it and let the images come out of her. But it hadn't made her feel any better.

She walked slowly toward the largest canvas in the room, reliving how quickly she'd shaped each petal with a palette knife, desperate to get the roses out of her mind as fast as possible. It had been the same way when she'd painted them before, decades ago. When she'd been living alone in a seedy neighborhood on the outskirts of Dublin, struggling to figure out who she was in this unfamiliar world.

Painting roses was how she'd gotten her start as an artist, how she'd initially made a name for herself. But that was before she'd known about the curse. Before she'd known what would happen when wild roses began to grow outside every one of her lovers' homes. Before she'd known that every one of those men would die when the petals on those flowers turned black.

Until Sam, of course. He'd been the first man—the *only* man—strong enough to withstand the curse her mother had cast.

"They're...powerful," Grace said, finally taking a step into the room.

Yes, Glenna thought. They were. It was the only word that could describe them. She'd painted them in a similar style to the way Georgia O'Keefe had painted her flowers—magnified, with the petals filling the entire canvas, the center of the flower unfurling, intimate, exposed.

Grace began to make her way across the room, to the painting she'd been staring at from the hallway—the one with the lavender petals. "Each of the colors is supposed to have a meaning, right?" she murmured, as if she were speaking as much to herself as she was to Glenna.

"Yes," Glenna said.

"What does that one mean?" she asked, gesturing toward the fire-colored rose Glenna was standing beside.

"Passion," Glenna said quietly.

"What about this one?" Grace pointed to a painting of a red rose.

"Romance." Glenna took a breath. The meanings of the colors changed when the flowers grew out of season, but Grace didn't need to know that. Turning, Glenna took in the rest of the paintings one by one. "Yellow means friendship," she said, recalling the more conventional meanings. "Peach, appreciation. Pink, joy. And white, new beginnings."

Grace stopped walking when she came to the painting of the lavender rose. "What do lavender roses mean?"

Glenna lifted her gaze to the final painting. Lavender roses—ones with petals so pale they were almost silver—were the most powerful roses of all. And they always meant the same thing, no matter when or where they grew. "True love."

"True love?" Grace asked.

Glenna nodded as she walked over to join Grace beside the painting. "Or soulmates, if you believe in such a thing."

Grace stared at the painting—at the petals that seemed to be opening before her. There was so much energy and passion in the way they'd been sculpted, with thick layers of paint that looked like they'd been scraped on rather than brushed. The lines and shadows had been etched on just as quickly, in darker shades of purple to accentuate the pale, almost metallic, color of the petals.

"Do you believe in soulmates?" Glenna asked.

"I don't know," Grace admitted, unable to tear her eyes away from the image in front of her. "It's not something I've ever given much thought to."

"No?"

"No."

Glenna turned to face her. "Never dreamed of finding your Prince Charming? Living happily ever after?"

"Not really, no," Grace said. Any dreams she might have had about living happily ever after had been shattered the day her mother had disappeared. She had learned, at a young age, that marriage didn't always lead to happily ever after. For some, it led to loss, abandonment, and heartache.

Her mother might have been the one who'd disappeared physically, but Grace had lost her father that day, too. At least, the man he'd been before that. The light in his eyes had gone out. Every smile, from then on, had seemed forced. As the years passed, he'd become gruff and withdrawn, rarely offering praise or showing affection to either her or Ryan.

He'd pushed them away, too, insisting that they leave the island as soon as they'd turned eighteen, forcing them to do more with their lives than he had. She knew, now, that he'd only been trying to protect them. He'd told them, recently, that he'd always blamed himself for their mother's disappearance. He'd assumed that she'd left because he hadn't been able to offer her enough.

That he hadn't *been* enough.

Grace wanted so badly to prove her father wrong. He'd never remarried or found anyone else to be with or ever really gotten over the loss of his wife. And how could he, when they still didn't know what had happened to her?

If she could just find her mother—if she could just figure out what had happened to her—maybe her father would finally be able to move on.

Maybe they all would.

"When did you paint these?" Grace asked, finally pulling her gaze away from the painting and looking at Glenna.

"A few weeks ago."

A few weeks ago? That would have been right around the same time she'd booked her trip. Right after she'd contacted Liam. Wondering, again, if this could all be a big joke that they were playing on her, she took a step back, away from the painting. But if that were the case, why had Liam seemed so upset the night before?

Reaching into her pocket, she drew out the rose petal she'd brought with her. It was still as soft and velvety as ever.

"Is that one of the petals you found yesterday?" Glenna asked.

Grace wasn't surprised that Glenna had heard about them. News would travel fast on an island this small. "Yes."

Glenna held out her hand. "May I?"

Grace turned her hand over to let the petal fall into Glenna's palm. "Who told you about them?"

"Liam."

"Do you know where they came from?"

"No."

"The petals are the same color as the rose that you painted."

"Yes," Glenna said. "I can see that."

These petals worried her, Grace realized when she caught the sudden tightness in Glenna's voice. The same way they worried Liam. Why? "What else did you hear?"

Glenna glanced up. "That you decided to extend your stay."

Grace nodded. "I did."

"What are you hoping to find by staying?" Glenna asked.

"Answers."

"To what questions, exactly?"

"Well, for starters, I'd like to find out what these petals mean."

"I just told you what they mean."

"You told me what lavender *roses* mean. That doesn't explain what these petals mean. Or where they came from. Or why they haven't changed, even though I found them yesterday."

Glenna handed the petal back, as if she'd seen and heard enough. But Grace wasn't done. She'd just gotten started. "Were you on the island when Tara broke the curse?"

Glenna held her gaze for several long moments before answering. "I was."

"Will you tell me what happened? From your perspective?"

"My perspective?"

"I've heard Tara and Liam's stories. I'd like to hear yours."

"My story would be no different from theirs."

Interesting, Grace thought. Maybe that's what she'd been picking up on all along—the coordinated effort, the synching up of stories. Typically, that was something a group of people did when they had something to hide. "If you won't tell me your story, will you tell me what part the roses played in the curse?"

Glenna said nothing as she lifted her glass and took a sip of wine.

Undeterred, Grace pressed on. "I know that Kelsey found the

selkie's pelt under the roses. But why was it there? What did the roses have to do with anything?"

"They were a sign," Glenna said simply.

"A sign?"

"A sign of what was to come."

Grace turned and looked at the painting of the red rose on the far wall. "You said red roses mean romance."

"That's right."

"So...what? They were a sign that Tara and Dominic would eventually get together?"

Glenna smiled. "That's one way of looking at it."

When Glenna turned and headed back towards the hallway, Grace trailed after her. Glenna seemed relieved, smug even, as if she'd discovered that their secret was still safe after all. Grace must have taken a wrong turn somewhere in her questioning. What should she be asking that she hadn't already asked? "The roses outside Tara's cottage are gone now. What happened to them?"

"Kelsey and Liam had to cut the roots to get to the pelt."

"They never grew back?"

"No."

Grace looked at the petal she was still holding in her hand. She'd tried to cut the roots of the lavender roses on Heron Island multiple times. But they'd always grown back. Why? Why couldn't she get rid of them?

Was it because her parents were soulmates, separated by two worlds—land and sea?

When they made it back to the first room in the gallery, Glenna turned to face her again. "Grace," she said, her voice softening.

Grace looked up, surprised to see sympathy in the other woman's eyes. "What?"

"She's not here."

"Who?" Grace asked, confused.

"The woman you're looking for."

Grace blinked, taken aback. "Who told you I was looking for someone?"

"My husband," Glenna said. "He looked you up last night, after we heard you'd decided to stay."

Grace took a step back. Why had her husband felt the need to look her up? And what, exactly, had he found? "Does your husband do a background check on every tourist who decides to extend their stay on the island?"

"No," Glenna said. "But you're not just any tourist, are you?"

Grace wasn't used to losing control of a situation when she was working. But she could feel the tables turning, now, and she couldn't seem to stop them.

"My husband used to work as a private investigator," Glenna went on. "He was quite good at his job, so good he almost got Tara killed because of it."

Grace's heart began to pound.

"Sam was the investigator Tara's husband hired to track her to this island. Fortunately, he decided to switch sides at the last minute and warn us that her husband was coming." Glenna's gaze drifted over Grace's shoulder and lingered on the painting of the selkie fully transformed into a woman. "Sam doesn't like to use his skills much anymore, but from time to time, he'll make an exception."

Grace stared at her. Why did he feel like he'd needed to make an exception this time? How much harm did they think she was going to cause by asking a few questions? "What are you all so afraid of?"

Glenna looked back at her. "Let's just say we've had our share of visitors who've heard the rumors about this island and who've come here looking for more than we're able to give."

Grace shook her head. "I don't understand."

Glenna's expression softened again. "You're not the first person who's come here hoping to find their long-lost mother, Grace."

Grace felt like the wind had been knocked out of her. "How did you—?"

"Like I said, my husband is a skilled investigator. We know your mother disappeared when you were a child. And I *am* sorry about that. But we don't have the answers you're searching for."

"I don't—"

"Let me save you some time and some trouble." Glenna reached out, took Grace's hand, and gently guided her fingers to curl back around the petal so it was hidden from sight. "When a woman runs away from her husband, she doesn't want to be found."

# CHAPTER FOURTEEN

On the eastern side of the island, the sun was beginning to burn through the mists. The wet grass glistened, and steam rose from the fields like smoke. Aidan peered through the lens, watching Brennan guide his sheepdog through the midday ritual of herding the flock from one pasture to another. The shutter clicked once. Twice. Aidan knelt, wanting to capture a slice of the sea in the background, or at least the suggestion of it.

He sucked in a breath at the pain, gave himself a moment to adjust, then pushed through it. He needed to get lower if he was ever going to get back to work.

That was why he'd come out here—to test out his range of motion and start building up his flexibility again. It had nothing to do with the fact that Dominic had asked him to take some shots of the island the night before, or the insinuation that Grace had made that he might be afraid to pick up his camera.

At the thought of Grace, his whole body tightened, the same way it had every time she'd crossed his mind since their kiss the night before. He'd played it off afterwards, like it had been no big deal, but it had taken everything inside him to walk away and leave her there. He'd spent the rest of the night tossing and turning, imagining what might have happened if he'd stayed.

He couldn't remember the last time he'd felt this worked up over a woman. He'd already come up with several reasons for why he might need to drop by her cottage today, just so he could see her again. He wondered if she had any idea how their kiss had affected him—how it had made him feel things he hadn't thought he was capable of feeling in this type of environment.

He was used to meeting women in war zones. Most of his relationships were as intense as they were fleeting. When you were working on the front lines, every emotion felt heightened. Desire was amplified by adrenaline. Lust could be mistaken for love. When you could die at any moment, your attachment to someone could feel like an obsession.

The last thing he'd expected was to feel that same rush here, in the middle of nowhere, with no threats around.

He didn't know what to make of it.

He didn't know what to make of her.

All he knew was that he wanted to touch her again, to taste her again, to feel her whole body soften again in his arms.

In the meantime, he needed to keep his skills sharp so he could hit the ground running as soon as he was cleared to return to work.

He switched lenses quickly, wanting to get a close-up of Brennan and his dog in this light. It wouldn't last long. Soon, the mists would evaporate, and the midday sun would shine down, harsh and unyielding. Right now, though, the sky was tinged with gold. The light was muted. Tiny drops of dew clung to every patch of moss. And the whole scene appeared as if it were wrapped in a soft, ethereal haze.

Lifting the camera, he framed the shot and let the rest of the world fall away.

Across the field, in a faded barn jacket, Brennan stood with his arm draped over an open gate as his dog herded the sheep through the opening. The sound of bleating ewes filled the air, punctuated only by the sharp, commanding bark of the dog and the occasional soft, murmured word from Brennan in Irish. Aidan zoomed in further so he could capture the deep creases etched into the man's face, the cataracts blurring his pale eyes, and the crust of salt on the collar of his work shirt.

When Brennan brushed an arthritic hand over the springy wool coat of one of the animals as it scampered by, Aidan was struck by the affection in the farmer's expression. He took several more shots, then slowly lowered the camera. This wasn't just a job to Brennan. It was a way of life. And it was the only life he'd ever known.

There were others on the island who owned farm animals—sheep, cows, horses, chickens—but they mostly kept them as pets or to save money on milk and eggs. Brennan was the only large-scale farmer left on the island. He was the only one who still sold his wool to other towns and villages in the region. He was the only one who'd managed to hold onto the old ways, while everything around him had changed.

How many changes had Brennan seen in his lifetime?

The farmer had mentioned, once, when they were working together, that Irish used to be the only language spoken on the island. Now, almost everyone spoke English. He'd also mentioned that, when he was younger, most of the jobs on the island had been in farming or fishing. Now, the economy was mainly driven by tourism.

Lifting his gaze to a string of islands in the distance, Aidan remembered that Brennan had said that most of them were abandoned. When the younger generations had moved away in search of a different life, the communities had begun to unravel. What would it have been like to watch the populations of those islands dwindle until they were forced to evacuate?

Knowing, at any time, that your island and your community could be next?

Surprised by the number of questions he wanted to ask, Aidan raised his camera again, adjusted a few settings, and continued to shoot. These were the types of questions that he asked when he was on assignment. These were the types of questions that guided his interviews with people all over the world. These were the types of questions that helped him see beneath the surface of the unfolding crises to the emotions of the people who called those war-torn places their home.

He hadn't expected to be this curious about any of the people, here, on Seal Island.

He hadn't expected to care.

Following Brennan and his dog north along the coast as they guided the flock to a higher pasture, Aidan felt like he was seeing him for the first time. And he couldn't help noticing that, in some ways, he and Brennan were a lot alike, having both devoted their lives to their jobs. In other ways, though, they couldn't be more different. Aidan was constantly moving from place to place, like a junkie searching for his next hit of adrenaline, while Brennan had chosen to stay still, in one place, for over eighty years. And somehow, despite the odds, he had persisted.

There was something admirable in that.

Zooming out, Aidan took a few more shots of the man in his element, doing the same thing he'd done every day since he was a child, like his father and his father's father and his father's grandfather before that.

Slowly, Aidan lowered his camera again. It hadn't occurred to him until now to wonder what would happen to this place when Brennan passed away. What would happen to the farm? To the animals?

As far as he knew, Brennan didn't have any family to inherit this place. It would have to go on the market. But who would buy it? Someone from the mainland? If so, what would they do with it? Tear everything down and build a fancy second home that would sit empty all winter?

The only local who might be able to afford to buy it would be Glenna. She owned most of the land on the island at this point anyway. Every run-down cottage Caitlin had transformed into a holiday home had initially been purchased by Glenna. Caitlin was responsible for renovating and managing the properties, but Glenna was the one who owned them.

Would the two of them decide to invest in this place? Would Caitlin renovate the old barn and the two drafty cottages so tourists could have more options of places to stay when they came here to escape their busy lives in the city? How many years would it take for the fences to come down? For the animal tracks to disappear? For all the memories of Brennan to be wiped from this spot forever?

No matter how much time and attention Caitlin devoted to preserving the history of this place with her renovations, it would never be the same.

Looking down at the camera in his hands, Aidan thought of all the faces he'd captured over the years, all the memories and emotions he'd frozen in time so they wouldn't be lost. He hadn't been planning to keep any of these images. He'd only come out here to practice. But maybe he should save a few of them.

Maybe he'd keep an eye on Caitlin's website, and if—in ten or fifteen years—he saw that she was listing either of the cottages for rent, he would send her the files. That way, she could print them and hang them on the walls so no one would ever forget the man who'd lived here.

The man who had given this farm, and these animals, his whole life.

Glancing up, he saw that Brennan and his flock of sheep had disappeared behind a hill. He started to follow them when a soft breeze blew in from the ocean and a tiny leaf fluttered into his path. It floated gently to the ground, landing in a patch of moss a few meters away. As he made his way closer, though, he realized that it wasn't a leaf.

It was a petal. A rose petal.

Aidan knelt slowly and picked it up. It was the same color as the ones he and Grace had seen on the beach the day before. The same color as the ones she'd found outside her cottage a few hours later.

Where had it come from? Still holding the petal, he lowered his camera until it hung from the strap he wore across his upper body. Shifting the camera and the bag holding his other lens behind him, he pushed back to his feet. He looked around, in every direction. But he didn't see any rose bushes or any other flowers blooming anywhere.

He didn't see anyone else around either.

A second petal fluttered down, landing in the grass several meters ahead. He limped slowly toward it, using the nearest stone wall for support since he'd left his cane at home. When he was close enough, he picked it up. It looked exactly like the first one. He scanned the surrounding area and spotted a third one up ahead, where the trail narrowed and began to curve north. He went to it, picked it up, and continued to hobble along for several more minutes, finding three more, until he came to a rocky beach on the northern coast.

Where a woman stood, all alone, looking out at the water.

*Grace.*

Her back was to him. She hadn't turned, so she must not have heard him walk up. He started to say her name, but his throat felt tight, like he couldn't quite catch his breath. A soft floral scent floated into the air, and he looked down at the petals in his hand. It was almost as if they had led him here.

To her.

But that wasn't possible…was it?

He looked back up, and his heart began to race. The same way it did when he was being shot at. The same way it did when a mortar exploded close enough to knock him off his feet. But he wasn't in any danger, at least not physically. He didn't know what was happening to him emotionally.

He took a step toward her, feeling a sudden, desperate need to close the distance between them. He'd imagined this moment a hundred times since their kiss the night before, wondering how she would react when she saw him again. Now that it was here, though, he didn't know what to say.

He didn't want to say anything at all.

He wanted to pull her into his arms. To bury his hands in her hair. To kiss her until neither of them could think straight.

He took another step toward her, wondering vaguely how he was going to make it across the rocks without falling. But she must have finally heard him. Because she turned then, and her expression stopped him cold. There was pain in her eyes. Deep pain. Any longing he might have felt to touch her again shifted instantly to concern. "What's wrong?"

She looked back at the water, turning away from him.

He waited for her to say something. When she didn't, he slipped the petals into his pocket and picked his way carefully over the rocks. Somehow, he managed to get to her without his knee giving out. "Grace?"

She still wouldn't look at him.

"What is it?" he asked, even more concerned now. "What happened?"

When she finally spoke, her voice sounded hollow. "You don't have to pretend like you don't know."

"Don't know what?"

"Why I'm here."

He searched her face for a clue. "On this beach?"

"No." She pulled her gaze from the water and looked up at him. "On this island."

"I thought you came here to learn about selkies."

She said nothing for several moments. "They haven't told you?"

Aidan shook his head.

She looked away. "I figured everyone on the island would know by now."

"Know *what*?"

"That I came here to find my mother."

Aidan's brows rose. "Your mother?"

Grace nodded. "She disappeared when I was a child. I came here to find her, or at least find out what happened to her."

"Okay," Aidan said slowly. "Why would you think she'd be here?"

Grace let out a breath. "I didn't think she'd be here, exactly. But I thought she might be somewhere in Ireland, and that, if I spent enough time here, I might be able to figure out what happened to her."

So, that was why she'd taken a leave of absence from her job, Aidan realized. She'd come here to find her mother. He'd thought there'd been something off about her original story. But what was the connection to Ireland? And why had she decided to come here now?

Trying to recall if she'd mentioned anything about her mother before, he quickly replayed each of their conversations in his mind. And then he remembered it—what she'd said the first night they'd had dinner together at the pub. "Is this the same woman who read you the selkie stories when you were a child?"

Grace nodded.

"How old were you when she disappeared?"

"Ten."

Aidan let the weight of that sink in. He knew what it felt like to lose a parent. He'd only been two years younger when both his parents had been killed. But at least he knew what had happened to them.

What would it have felt like to lose one of them and not know where they'd gone?

Unable to keep from touching her any longer, he reached for her hand. As much as he'd wanted to strip all those layers of confidence away to see the woman she hid from the rest of the world, he understood, now, why she kept them wrapped so tightly around her. Her confidence was the shield she'd created to protect herself from the pain of that loss. And her professional successes were her way of proving to herself, and everyone around her, that she was worth more than that child who'd been abandoned.

Resisting the urge to pull her into his arms because he knew, somehow, she wouldn't want that type of comfort, he led her, instead, to a large rock that was big enough for both of them to sit on. He kept her hand in his, maintaining that gentle connection, as he lowered himself to the rock beside her. They were both storytellers. It was how they made sense of the world. It was time she told him hers. "Why don't you start at the beginning?"

Grace nodded slowly and began to speak.

Aidan listened, not saying a word as she told him about the morning she'd woken up to find that her mother was gone, about the ensuing inquiries and investigations, about the way her father had changed when the police had eventually stopped looking, about how close she and her twin brother, Ryan, had become because of it, and about the clue Ryan had given her a few weeks ago that had sparked this trip to Ireland.

"I came here to research the legends because I thought I might find another clue hidden in one of them," she said. "I didn't come here because I thought my mother was a selkie. I mean, I didn't even believe in them before."

"But...you do now?"

"I don't know." Grace rubbed a hand over her eyes. "Maybe." When she looked up at him again, she seemed embarrassed to have admitted that out loud. "Am I losing my mind?"

She wouldn't be the first person on this island to experience a break from reality, Aidan thought. But he was pretty sure Grace's sanity was still intact. He was actually impressed with how open-minded she was being. And he couldn't help admiring the fact that she'd decided to drop everything, including her job, to immerse herself in this search the moment she'd gotten her first clue. "No," he said finally. "I don't think you're losing your mind."

Relieved that he wasn't going to judge her, she sat back and watched the last wisps of fog float away. The water lapped at the rocks at their feet. A few gulls rode the soft breezes overhead. "Glenna thinks I should stop searching."

"Why?"

"She said when a woman runs away from her husband, she doesn't want to be found."

That had been true in Tara's case, Aidan thought. But not every woman who ran away from her husband was afraid for her life. And how did Glenna know, for sure, that Grace's mother *had* run away? She could have been taken or killed or any number of other possibilities. "Do you remember your parents fighting a lot when you were a kid?"

"No," Grace said. "That's what's so strange about all this. I never saw them argue. From what I could tell, they seemed happy together. But even if they weren't, why would she run away? Why wouldn't she just ask for a divorce?"

That, Aidan thought, was a question he didn't have an answer to. And he imagined it was one that had haunted Grace for most of her life. "Did the police ever look at your father as a person of interest?"

Grace nodded. "In the weeks after her disappearance, every police officer, detective, and social worker asked my brother and me the same questions whenever they got us alone. Did our parents fight a lot? Did our mother ever seem afraid? Had we ever seen bruises on her? Did our father have a temper? Did he yell at her or at us? Had he ever hit us?"

Aidan pulled her hand into his lap and covered it with both of his. He'd dealt with his share of detectives and social workers after his parents had been killed, but there'd never been a question about *how* they had died or *who* had been responsible. Grace, on the other hand, didn't even know who to blame.

"They never said the words outright," she continued, "but I knew what they were implying. That if he hadn't killed her, he'd probably abused her."

"You don't think that was the case, though?"

"No," she said adamantly.

Then it must not be, Aidan thought. Grace was one of the most perceptive people he'd ever met. If she didn't think her father had anything to do with her mother's disappearance, then something else must have happened. And she would never be able to put this behind her until she found out the truth. Who was Glenna to tell her to stop? "What's your next move?"

She looked up at him. "You think I should keep searching?"

"I do," Aidan said. If someone told him that his mother was alive, he would go to the ends of the earth to find her. Unfortunately, he couldn't tell Grace that, because as far as she knew, his mother *was* alive.

"Well," Grace said, "I still need to figure out what the rest of the people on this island are hiding."

Aidan nodded slowly. He wasn't going to pretend that they weren't hiding something anymore. He'd watched Grace catch Liam in a blatant lie the night before, and he knew she suspected that Tara had been lying as well. But he would need to tread carefully. "You think it has something to do with your mother?"

"I don't know. But right now, it's all I have to go on. And I'm not leaving until I figure it out."

Conflicted, Aidan looked out at the water. He knew what the islanders were hiding, and it had nothing to do with her mother. As much as he wanted to spend the next few weeks with her, he also didn't want to waste her time. He knew how much this trip must be costing her, not just financially, but emotionally. If he told her the truth, she could leave on the next ferry and continue her search.

But he couldn't do that, could he? Not when he'd given Tara his word. Besides, this wasn't his secret to tell.

Looking back at Grace, he wondered if there was a way he could help her without betraying Tara's trust. "You said you came here to research the legends because you thought you might find another clue hidden in one of them?"

Grace nodded.

"The man I'm renting my cottage from has a library full of myths, legends, and fairy tales. I haven't read any of them yet, but he said I could borrow one at any time." Aidan nodded back toward the path that had brought him here. "Want to have a look?"

# CHAPTER FIFTEEN

It was Grace's second time on the farm in two days. She took in the rolling green hills that dipped down to the sea, the winding stone walls that divided the land into pastures, and the curious ponies that glanced up as they passed. A sheepdog stood guard outside a shed where an elderly man was mucking out a stall. She could hear the gentle roll of the ocean all around them, and as they made their way closer, the soft rustle of hay beneath the farmer's pitchfork.

Remembering the strange scene she'd stumbled into the day before, her gaze shifted to the stretch of white sand that bordered the east side of the island. She wondered if Brigid had gone to another beach to gather shells today, or if she'd gotten over whatever had compelled her to gather them in the first place. She had a feeling there was more to Brigid's story than any of the islanders had been letting on. Maybe she'd be able to get to the bottom of that now that she and Aidan were spending the day together.

She stole a glance at the man beside her. This wasn't exactly the day she'd had planned. She'd woken up this morning resolved to avoid him. But how could she decline his offer to help after the kindness he'd shown her earlier? She'd expected him to say she was crazy for trying to find her mother after all these years, even more so for researching fairy tales for clues about what might have happened to her.

Instead, he'd offered to help her with her search.

Was it just an excuse to spend time with her? Or did he genuinely want to help her? Her instincts were telling her that his motives were genuine. But she didn't know if she could trust her instincts around him anymore. Any warning signals that might have been trying to protect her had short-circuited the moment his mouth had met hers the night before. The only thing her body seemed to want when she was anywhere near him was to be fused to his.

And it wasn't just her body that was betraying her. She was struggling to get a grip on her emotions as well. She wasn't used to sharing so much of herself with someone, especially someone she barely knew. She couldn't believe she'd told him as much as she had.

If he hadn't walked up, at that exact moment, she would have had time to pull herself together. She would have had time to figure out her next move. But she'd still been reeling from her interaction with Glenna. And somehow, he'd known exactly what to say and do to get her to talk.

How much more of herself was she going to share with him if they spent the day together? She knew it was a risk to accept his offer, but these books might be her only lead. And at this point, she could use all the help she could get.

"Brennan," Aidan said as they came to a stop in front of the shed. "I'd like you to meet a friend of mine, Grace Callahan. Grace, this is Brennan Lockley."

Brennan paused long enough to touch a finger to the brim of his tweed cap in a wordless greeting, then went back to work.

It was about as much of a greeting as her father would have

given someone who interrupted him in the middle of a job. Comforted by the familiarity of it, she smiled. "It's nice to meet you."

Aidan reached down to pet the sheepdog that came over with its tail wagging at the sound of his voice. "You know those books you told me about, the fairy tales you said I could borrow?"

Brennan nodded.

"Could we take a look at them now?"

"Aye." Brennan scattered a fresh forkful of hay over the ground, then paused, his brow furrowing. "Cá bhfuil do chána?"

Without missing a beat, Aidan responded, "D'fhág mé sa teach é. Ní raibh mé ag pleanáil siúl chomh fada sin."

"Cé mhéad pian atá agat anois?" Brennan asked.

Aidan lifted a shoulder. "D'fhéadfadh sé a bheith níos measa."

Brennan's concerned gaze dropped to Aidan's leg, then shifted to Grace. Taking a closer look this time, his brows slowly un-furrowed and a knowing smile lifted the corners of his mouth. "Measaim go bhféadfadh bean a bhfuil an chuma sin uirthi fear a dhéanamh dearmad go bhfuil sé i bpian."

Aidan smiled back. "Measaim go bhféadfadh sí dearmad a dhéanamh air níos mó ná sin." Giving the dog one last pat on the head, he motioned for Grace to follow him through the open gate that led to the larger of the two cottages.

As soon as they were out of the farmer's earshot, Grace asked, "What language was that?"

"Irish."

"What did he ask you?"

"He asked where my cane was," Aidan explained, using the stone wall beside him for support, as he had for their entire walk back from the beach. "I said I'd left it at home, because I hadn't been planning to walk that far."

"Then what?"

"He asked how much pain I was in. I told him I'd been in worse."

Grace waited for him to go on. When he didn't, she gave him a look. "What did he say after that?"

"Well..." Aidan's pale green eyes met hers. "If you must know, he said that a woman who looked like you could probably make a man forget he was in pain." He stopped walking when they came to the end of the wall. "And I said that I imagined you could make me forget more than that."

When Aidan held out his hand, the same way he had whenever they'd come to a gap between walls on their way back from the beach, Grace hesitated. She knew he needed to hold onto something for support. And she'd been willing to provide that support, until now, by pretending that it didn't mean anything. But how was she supposed to take his hand and pretend that it didn't mean anything after what he'd just said?

She briefly considered offering to run to his cottage to grab his cane for him, but she didn't want to make a big deal about it either. And the longer she hesitated, the more awkward this was going to become. Taking a deep breath, she slipped her hand into his and seized on the first topic she could think of to douse the flames flickering between them again. "I thought you grew up in Belfast."

Aidan let go of the wall and they started to walk. "I did."

"Isn't Belfast part of the UK?"

"Yes."

"Do they teach Irish at schools in the UK?"

"No." Aidan smiled. "I think that's the last language they'd want to teach."

"So, how did you learn it?"

"The same way I learn any language. By talking to people."

"How long does it usually take?"

"Depends on the language."

"How long did it take you to learn this one?"

"I don't know this one that well. I've just been picking up bits and pieces from Brennan over the past few weeks."

"That didn't sound like bits and pieces to me."

"I probably got half the words wrong," he said with a shrug. "But it makes Brennan happy to speak the language he grew up with, so I try to as much as I can when I'm around him."

That must be how he connected with people when he was on assignment, Grace realized. If he learned the native language of the people he wanted to interview, they would open up to him more. They would trust him more. A translator would create too much of a barrier between them. "How many languages do you speak?"

"I can get by in about twelve."

Grace's brows shot up. "Twelve?"

He shrugged again, as if it were no big deal. "When you know that many, picking up a new one isn't that hard."

"You picked up that much in three weeks, just by talking to Brennan?"

"Not *just* by talking to Brennan. Sometimes, at night, I look up words or phrases to fill in the gaps."

"At night?"

He nodded. "When I can't sleep."

"That's what you do when you can't sleep? You study languages?"

"It's not my *first* choice," he said wryly, "but it's generally what I do if I'm alone."

She didn't need to ask him what his first choice was, not when he was looking down at her with the same slightly amused expression that he'd had right before he'd kissed her the night before. Suddenly very aware of how close they were and the fact that she was still holding his hand, she moved to put a little more distance between them. "How often do you have trouble sleeping?" she asked, hoping to steer the conversation back to safer ground.

"Fairly often," he admitted.

"A few times a week?"

Aidan looked away. "Pretty much every night."

"Every night?"

He nodded.

"How long has that been going on?"

When they came to the front door of Brennan's cottage, Aidan stopped walking, but he didn't let go of her hand. "A while."

It was the first time he'd hinted at how his career affected him emotionally. And given what he did for a living, she was willing to bet he'd been having trouble sleeping for years, probably soon after he'd arrived in his first war zone.

She knew veterans back home who struggled with flashbacks and nightmares after only serving in a war zone for a year or two. Aidan had been doing this consistently for almost fifteen years.

What kind of scars would that leave on a person?

Looking down at their joined hands, she wished she knew what to say to make him feel better, but she couldn't seem to find the words. So, she decided to repay the kindness he'd shown her on the beach earlier, and not offer any judgement, even though a part of her wanted to ask how much longer he was going to be able to keep this up.

Physically and emotionally, there was only so much a person could take.

"Couldn't Tara give you something to help with that?" she asked.

"That's a slippery slope."

Surprised by the seriousness in his tone, she lifted her gaze back to his. "Because you're afraid you'd get addicted to whatever she gave you?"

He nodded. "Most of the people who do what I do are addicted to something."

"What are you addicted to?"

"Work."

Of course, Grace thought. He'd alluded to that last night. That was why he studied languages when he couldn't sleep. That was why he went to places no other conflict photographer was willing to go. That was why he kept pushing himself so hard to heal, when all he needed was to rest. Because he wanted to get back out there and get back to work as soon as possible. "What would happen if you stopped?"

"I can't," he said simply.

The honesty in his words and the vulnerability in his expression caught her off guard. It wasn't a joke anymore, as it had been last night, when he'd warned her not to end up like him. Fighting the urge to reach for him, to draw his mouth down to hers and numb his pain temporarily, she needed to find another way to make him see that he didn't have to work so hard. That he didn't have to push himself so hard. That he didn't have to be the best at everything he did. Maybe because she knew, deep down, that that was why *she* couldn't stop.

And if she couldn't stop, then there was no hope for him.

His gaze flickered down to her mouth. Before she knew what was happening, she was leaning into him. And he was leaning into her. She should have been ready for it this time. She should have known what to expect. But when his mouth came down on hers—hard, hot, and demanding—the raw need that whipped through her took her breath away. In one smooth motion, he'd locked their hips together. And then his hands were in her hair. And he was kissing her like he'd thought of nothing else since they'd pulled apart the night before.

If he'd wanted to touch her this badly, why hadn't he tried to come in last night? Why had he left her there all alone?

Didn't he know that she wanted him as much as he wanted her?

Pouring all the frustration from her own sleepless night into the kiss, she felt a flood of emotions sweep through her. The same flood that had caused her to unravel the night before. She didn't know what was happening to her. She didn't understand any of this. All she knew was that she wanted his hands on her. All over her. Everywhere.

She heard the soft hiss of a zipper as the front of her jacket came open. And then his mouth was on her neck. And his hands were beneath her shirt. His strong, calloused palms ran up her bare back, making her body shiver with need. How far away was his cottage? How soon could they get there? "Aidan," she breathed, "I need..."

His lips found hers again, and she felt another wall inside her begin to crumble. She didn't know how many were left, or how she would ever rebuild them after this—or if she even wanted to anymore. Curling her fingers into his shirt, she pulled him closer. She didn't want this to stop. She didn't want it to end.

Except...it had to end.

Because they weren't the only ones here.

At the sound of muffled voices from inside the cottage, she pulled back. Aidan looked down at her, breathing hard. His expression was dazed, like he wasn't sure what had just happened.

She wasn't sure what had just happened either. Taking a long, shaky breath, she uncurled her fingers from his shirt. "I think Brennan's wife has company."

Still holding her, Aidan slowly shook his head. "Brennan doesn't have a wife."

"Then who's in there?"

"I don't know." His voice was thick with emotion. Pulling her closer, he leaned down again. But he didn't kiss her this time. He simply touched his forehead to hers and closed his eyes.

Grace didn't move. She didn't breathe. She wasn't used to having a partner seek comfort from her. The men she dated usually knew better. And if they didn't, they didn't last long. Bracing herself for the familiar urge to run that normally followed a gesture like this, she let several moments pass before she realized, with a start, that it wasn't going to come.

Instead, when she finally allowed herself to breathe, the most incredible sense of peace washed over her. Slowly, tentatively, she reached up and laid a hand on his cheek, surprised at how badly she wanted to offer him the comfort he sought. When his eyes fluttered open, and he looked down at her with the same wonder that must be mirrored in her own, she was lost.

And that, Grace thought, was exactly what she'd wanted to avoid. She couldn't afford to get lost. She needed to stay focused and do what she came here to do—find out what had happened to her mother, not get sidetracked by a man who made her feel things no man had ever made her feel before.

Drawing her hand back quickly, she let it fall to her side. "I think we should see who's in there."

Aidan nodded slowly, but he kept looking at her with that same expression, as if he'd just discovered something rare and precious that he hadn't known existed before. She didn't want him to look at her like that. She wanted him to get a grip.

When he finally eased back and lowered his arms, Grace let out a breath. It was so much easier to think when he wasn't touching her. "Should we knock?" she asked, hoping that whoever was in Brennan's cottage wouldn't leave right away. It would be safer to have a buffer between them, at least until he stopped looking at her like that.

Aidan shook his head. He didn't seem to be able to speak yet, but he managed to reach for the door.

When he held it open and motioned for her to go first, Grace stepped inside. Whoever was in here must not have heard them yet. She could still hear voices, but they were more subdued now. Following the sound through a narrow entranceway lined with rain slickers, rubber boots, and an old work bench, she came to a small living room that looked out over the fields.

In the middle of the room, two teenagers sat on the floor with their backs to her, their heads bent together over a book. More books were spread out around them, some of which were half-read and turned over to mark the page where they'd stopped. Apparently, she and Aidan weren't the only ones who'd decided to do some reading today.

"Brennan," the girl said without turning, "where's that book you told me about last week. The one with the—"

"Kelsey," Aidan said, walking up behind Grace. "Brennan's still outside."

Both teenagers turned at once.

"Uncle Aidan." Kelsey snapped the book shut. "Hi."

Aidan eyed the piles of books on the floor. "What's going on?"

"Nothing," Kelsey said quickly, shoving a few books behind her as she turned to face them. As soon as she spotted Grace, her eyes widened. "Wait... Are you Grace?"

"Yes," Grace said, surprised the girl knew her name.

Kelsey's face lit up. "You're the one who found the rose petals."

Grace nodded slowly.

"We heard you found them on the ground outside the cottage you're staying in," Kelsey said, looking for a confirmation.

"Some of them, yes."

"There were others?"

Grace nodded again.

"Where?" Kelsey asked.

"They washed up on the beach," Grace said, pointing toward the east side of the island, "right out there."

Kelsey looked at Aidan. "Were you with her?"

"I was."

"Was anyone else there?"

Aidan shook his head.

Kelsey exchanged a glance with the boy sitting next to her.

"What did they look like?" the boy asked, speaking for the first time.

Grace reached into her pocket and drew one out. "You can see for yourself."

Both teenagers pushed to their feet and walked over. She could feel Aidan's eyes on her. He was probably wondering why she was carrying the petal around with her. Not wanting to make a big deal about it, she avoided meeting his gaze and concentrated on the teenagers instead.

They were the same two teenagers who'd come into the pub with Brigid that first night. Kelsey, the younger of the two, had blond hair, blue eyes, and delicate, fairy-like features. The boy, on the other hand, was already as tall and lanky as his father, with the same pitch-black hair, ocean blue eyes, and reserved demeanor that made him seem older than eighteen. This was Liam and Caitlin's son, Owen, Grace realized—the boy she'd seen swimming with the seals. The boy Tara had tried to pretend she'd imagined.

"Can I hold it?" Kelsey asked, reaching for the petal.

Grace nodded, remembering that Kelsey was the one who'd found the selkie's pelt under the roses eight years ago. Maybe she'd be able to tell her where the petals were coming from.

Kelsey held the petal up to the light and studied it from every angle, her brows furrowed in concentration. "Have you found any more since last night."

"Yes." Grace reached into the pocket of her jacket and pulled out six more petals. "I found these a couple hours ago, walking north from Glenna's studio."

"Where, exactly?" Owen asked.

"In the grass, scattered on the path leading to the beach on the north side of the island. I was just walking, and they kept appearing on the ground ahead of me. There might have been more, but I only found six." She looked up at Aidan, assuming he'd want to know why she hadn't told him this before. But he wasn't looking at her. He was staring at the petals in her hand, an expression of shock and disbelief on his face.

"It's almost like they were making a trail," Kelsey said, oblivious to Aidan's reaction.

"Do you think Glenna could have put them there?" Grace asked, wondering, again, if this was all some big joke the islanders were playing on her.

Kelsey shook her head, her expression too serious for any of this to be a joke. "She might know what they mean, though."

"I already asked her that," Grace said. "She said lavender roses mean true love."

"Usually, yes." Kelsey picked up another petal and compared it to the one she was holding. "But roses have different meanings when they show up on this island."

"She didn't tell me that."

"That's because she wants you to leave," Kelsey said. "Everyone wants you to leave. Well, everyone except Owen and me. And maybe Uncle Aidan." She glanced up at him. "I don't know where you stand in all this."

"I'm not sure I know where I stand either," Aidan admitted, still staring at the petals in Grace's hand. He couldn't seem to shake whatever was troubling him. Grace wanted to ask him about it. But she didn't want to stray too far from whatever else Kelsey and Owen might be willing to tell her.

If they didn't want her to leave, maybe they'd be willing to tell her what the rest of the islanders were hiding. "Do your parents know you're here?"

Kelsey shook her head. "I overheard them talking about the petals last night. They thought I was asleep, but I wasn't. I told Owen first thing this morning, and we came here to find answers."

Grace lowered her gaze to the floor. "In these books?"

Kelsey nodded.

She wasn't the only one looking for clues inside fairy tales, Grace realized. She lifted her gaze back to the petals, wondering what they were trying to tell her. "Glenna said the roses that grew outside Tara's cottage were a sign of something."

"Yes," Kelsey said, "a sign of trouble."

"Trouble?"

Owen nodded. "They always bring trouble."

Grace looked back and forth between the two teenagers. Both their expressions had grown solemn. "Wait..." she said slowly. "There've been others?"

Neither Kelsey nor Owen said anything for several moments. When Owen gave Kelsey a slight nod, Kelsey took a deep breath.

"Everyone is hoping that things will go back to normal when you leave. That whatever ticking clock your arrival set in motion will stop. But that's not the way this works." Kelsey placed the two petals she was holding back in Grace's hands. "If these rose petals are showing themselves to you, then you're connected to whatever they're trying to tell us. You have a role in it. And we need to figure out what that is, together, so you can help us stop whatever's going to happen."

"What do you think is going to happen?" Grace asked.

"We don't know. That's why we're here." Kelsey gestured to the books.

Grace looked back at the petals. "Tell me about the others."

Kelsey nodded. "When my stepmother—Tara—first arrived

on the island, red roses started growing outside the cottage she was renting from my father. They came out of nowhere. And they grew so fast. Like they were trying to hide her behind a wall of thorns. They couldn't hide her, though. They were only a warning—that the man she used to be married to was coming here. And when he did, he almost killed her." Kelsey looked down, distressed by the memory, even though it had been years since the events had taken place.

"A few months later," Owen said, picking up the story, "a single white rose grew outside a cottage that my mother and father had talked about living in when they were younger. It was a warning that something bad was going to happen to my father. He..." Owen trailed off. "We almost lost him forever."

Grace had no idea what he meant by that, but she didn't want to stop them. Not when they were telling her things no one else had even come close to telling her yet.

"The third time, the roses were orange," Kelsey explained, finding her voice again. "They grew outside Sam's cottage. And when the petals started to turn black, it meant that his time was running out. They were a warning that he was going to die."

"But he didn't die," Grace said. Sam was Glenna's husband. He was the one who'd been up all night investigating her. He was the one who'd found out about her mother.

"No," Kelsey said. "But he came close."

"Too close," Owen said.

Grace could tell they were truly worried about what these petals might mean. Even though, rationally, none of this made any sense, she was starting to worry now, too. "You think these petals mean that something bad is going to happen to someone?"

They nodded.

"Someone's time is running out," Owen said. "We need to figure out who it is so we can save them."

"Okay." Grace glanced up at Aidan, wanting to know how

the only other adult in the room was reacting to this, especially given his lack of faith in magic, but his face gave away nothing. "What can I do?"

"You could tell us about the wind chime you brought with you," Kelsey said.

"The wind chime?" Grace asked, surprised.

"You did bring it with you, didn't you?" Kelsey asked.

"I... Yes."

"I saw it when I walked by your cottage this morning," Kelsey said. "I'd never seen it before. And no one on this island would have made a wind chime like that. So...why did you bring it?"

Grace thought about Taylor's dream—how she'd been lost in a forest and the only way to find her way home had been to follow a trail of lavender rose petals. Figuring it couldn't hurt to tell them about it, she described the dream in as much detail as she could remember.

Kelsey's expression grew thoughtful. "Did you follow the petals?"

"No," Grace said. "Apparently, I couldn't see them."

"But they were making a trail?"

Grace nodded.

Kelsey and Owen exchanged a glance. "Like in Hansel and Gretel?"

"I guess," Grace said. "It was just a dream, though. The forest must be a metaphor for something."

"But you were lost in the woods?" Kelsey asked.

Grace nodded. "In the dream, yes."

"Do you have a brother?"

Grace nodded slowly.

"Was he there?" Kelsey asked.

"Taylor didn't say," Grace responded. "I don't think so."

Kelsey bit her lip. "If you *and* your brother had been lost in the forest, it would have made more sense."

"I'm not sure how *any* of this is making sense," Grace said.

Undeterred, Kelsey walked to the nearest bookshelf and started to scan the titles. Owen immediately went to help her. He found what they were looking for and called her over. Together, they pulled a thick, leather-bound collection of fairy tales from the shelf and flipped through the pages until they found what they were looking for.

"Here it is," Kelsey said. "Hansel and Gretel."

Tucking the rose petals into her pocket, Grace walked over to join them. "It's been a while since I read that."

"Me too." Kelsey skimmed the first few pages, then looked up at Grace. "Do you have a stepmother?"

"No."

"What's your real mother like?"

Grace took a deep breath. There was no point in trying to hide the truth from anyone anymore. "I don't know. She disappeared when I was a child."

"You don't know what happened to her?"

Grace shook her head.

Kelsey looked back at the pages, her expression troubled.

"It's the stepmother who abandons them in the forest, though, isn't it?" Grace asked.

"In this version, yes," Kelsey said. "But in the original version, it was their biological mother."

Aidan made his way over to join them. "Does Brennan have a copy of the original version?"

"He might," Kelsey said. "You two stay here and keep looking. We'll go search the island."

"For what?" Grace asked.

"For the rose bush. The petals had to come from somewhere." Kelsey pushed the book into her hands. "Read this and see if you can find any more connections. We'll look for you tonight, in the pub."

Grace nodded numbly as she watched them leave. As soon as the door shut behind them, she looked at Aidan. He'd barely said two words since they'd walked into the cottage. And he had the strangest expression on his face now, like he wanted to tell her something, but didn't know how.

"What?" she asked.

Reaching into the pocket of his shirt, he drew out six lavender rose petals and held them out to her.

Grace went very still. "Where did those come from?"

"I found them on the ground about an hour ago," he said quietly, "on my way to the beach."

# CHAPTER SIXTEEN

They read until their eyes were blurry, until the light outside began to fade and the first hints of color began to sweep across the sky. Neither of them seemed to know what to do about the petals they'd found leading them to the beach and to each other. So, they did what they did best, bottled up their emotions and buried themselves in work.

Aidan wanted to ask her how she was feeling about all this. But he didn't know where to start. The information Kelsey and Owen had shared about the roses had been news to him as well. Brigid had mentioned some of the underlying stories in the letter she'd written to him, but not the part about the roses. She would have told him if he'd asked. Any of the islanders would have.

But he hadn't asked. He hadn't asked a single question because he hadn't wanted to know. He'd already decided not to believe any of it before he'd set foot on this island. It wasn't like him to be so closed-minded. But opening his mind to the existence of magic would mean he'd also have to consider the possibility that Brigid might not be crazy. That she might be telling the truth. And he wasn't ready to do that.

Glancing at the twelve petals on the table by the window, he noticed that they hadn't changed since Grace had placed them there several hours ago. Not a single one had begun to dry out. If anything, they looked like they'd been plucked from a fresh flower only moments ago. Was that why Liam had seemed so rattled the night before? Did he, like Owen and Kelsey, believe that something bad was going to happen because of them?

How much more rattled was he going to be when he found out that Kelsey and Owen had told Grace that the magical stories on this island hadn't ended with the curse Tara had broken?

Grace wasn't going to stop digging until she uncovered the rest of the truth. It was only a matter of time before she found out what the islanders were hiding. And then what? What would she do with the knowledge that there were three people on this island, right now, who claimed to be selkies?

Aidan had considered stepping outside to call Tara multiple times over the past several hours to warn her. She and the others would want to do damage control as soon as they found out what Kelsey and Owen had revealed. In the end, though, he'd decided against it. He didn't feel comfortable going behind Grace's back to hide the islanders' secret anymore.

The more time he spent with Grace, the more conflicted he felt about hiding anything from her at all.

Setting the book that he'd been reading aside, he nodded toward the darkening sky. "It's getting late. We should head to the pub soon."

Grace glanced at the window, but she made no move to close the book she was holding. "You go. I'll meet you there later."

Aidan shook his head. He wasn't leaving without her. She needed to get out of this room. They both did. "If we were going to find any clues in these books today, we would have found them by now."

Her eyes shifted to meet his. She looked exhausted. Aidan

fought the urge to gently pry the book from her hands. Knowing how he would react if someone tried to take a camera from him when he was working on a story that mattered deeply to him, he waited for her to get there on her own.

After several long moments of silence, Grace closed the book and set it on the pile beside her. "I can't believe we didn't find anything."

"It was a long shot to begin with."

"I know." Grace ran a hand through her hair. "But it was the only lead I had."

"We'll find another one."

She didn't seem so sure. She looked up at the shelves, scanning the titles on the spines of the books that were left. "Maybe we picked the wrong books."

"Maybe," Aidan said. "But I doubt it."

When she kept scanning the titles, he could tell she was reconsidering her decision to stop for the day. He understood her obsession with wanting to stick with it. How many times had he forgotten to eat or sleep because of a story he was working on? He didn't want her to lose herself in this search, though. It was already turning her inside out. She needed to take a step back, come back to it with fresh eyes and a clear head in the morning.

It was time to follow through on the promise he'd made the night before—to help her stop working and relax for the rest of her stay on the island. He hadn't been doing a very good job of that so far. "Let's go get something to eat. We can pick up where we left off tomorrow."

Resigned, Grace looked at the piles of books spread out on the floor around them. "We should put these away."

"I'll do it," Aidan said, not wanting her to see something else and get pulled in again. "Why don't you run to the other cottage and get my cane? You could grab the keys to the car while you're there, too."

Grace nodded and slowly made her way to her feet. "Where are they?"

"Just inside the door," he said. Maybe she'd feel better once she got some fresh air. "The keys are on the table. My cane should be leaning against the wall."

She picked her way through the piles of books, grabbed her jacket from the hook in the entranceway, and walked out the door. By the time Aidan had finished re-shelving the books and made his way to his own feet, she'd returned with his cane and the car keys. She handed them both to him, then crossed the room to the table by the window, where she stared down at the twelve petals for a long time. "Do you want to keep the ones you found?"

"No." He had no interest in keeping the petals. He'd already spent enough time thinking about them today. The only thing he wanted to think about now was helping Grace relax.

She pocketed the petals, then turned back to face him, her expression unreadable. "Ready?"

He nodded and followed her out the door. The air felt cool and refreshing in his lungs. He could hear the steady, soothing beat of the ocean all around them. He could see Brennan still hard at work in one of the upper fields. The sun, only moments away from dipping below the horizon, flooded the landscape with a wash of warm light. Rich autumn hues of gold and bronze contrasted with the dark shadows cast by the stone walls. Instinctively, he reached for his camera before remembering that he'd left it in Brennan's cottage.

He hadn't expected to want to shoot again so soon, especially not something as trivial as a sunset. But it wasn't just the sunset, he realized. It was the picture the sunset painted of an elderly man finishing out a hard day's work. An elderly man who'd spent his entire life on this farm, from sunup to sundown, as the seasons had changed, and the years had passed, and the whole world had evolved around him.

It couldn't last forever. Nothing could. As surely as the vibrant days of autumn would give way to the dark nights of winter, Brennan's time here would end, too. And when Brennan was gone, scenes like this wouldn't exist anymore. It wasn't the sunset that made the picture, Aidan thought. It was the man. And it was the man whose story he wanted to tell.

Wondering if Grace was as moved by the sight as he was, he stole a glance at her. She wasn't looking at Brennan, though, or any of the beauty spread out before them. She was gazing down at the brown-tipped grass at their feet, her fingers worrying over the petals in her pocket.

"Have you heard from Kelsey or Owen?" she asked.

Aidan pulled out his phone and checked the screen. "No."

"Do you think they would have called if they found anything?"

"I don't know. They said they'd meet us at the pub. We'll find out soon enough."

Grace walked to the passenger side of the car. "How are we going to talk to them without any of their parents seeing us?"

"We'll figure something out."

They both got in, and Aidan started the engine.

"Is this going to be awkward for you?" Grace asked. "Keeping it from them?"

Aidan shifted into first gear. "A bit."

Grace turned to face him. "Why are you taking my side in this?"

"It's not just your side. Kelsey and Owen want us to keep it from them, too."

She took a moment to process that. "What if Kelsey and Owen are right? What if I *have* brought some sort of trouble with me? I don't want to drag them into it without their parents knowing."

Neither did he, Aidan thought. But he didn't think they had anything to worry about. Not yet anyway. "Right now, all Kelsey and Owen are doing is looking for a rose bush. How much trouble can they get in by doing that?"

Grace looked away.

He could tell she was still conflicted. "Why don't we see how tonight goes? We can make a decision after we hear what they found."

"Assuming they found anything."

"Right," Aidan said.

Grace grew quiet again, retreating into her own thoughts.

Aidan turned onto the main road leading up to the village. Behind the cluster of whitewashed cottages, the sky was a kaleidoscope of blazing orange, vibrant magenta, and deep purple. It was one of the most striking sunsets he'd ever seen. He glanced at Grace. She was looking at it, too, but her expression was still tense. He needed to find a way to snap her out of this mood. "When was the last time you saw a sunset like this?"

"I've never seen anything like this."

"Not even on Heron Island?"

"No," she said. But he noticed a slight change in the tone of her voice at the mention of her home. He remembered how she'd lit up when she'd talked about it during one of their first conversations together. Maybe Heron Island was the key to helping her break free of the obsessive cycle she was trapped in.

"What's your favorite spot to watch the sunset there?"

"On the water," she said automatically. "In a boat."

When they got to the village, Aidan pulled to the side of the road and cut the engine. "Sounds relaxing."

For the first time in hours, some of the tension released from her expression. "It is."

She loved it there, he thought. He wondered what it would be like to love a place so much that no matter where you were, or how upset you were, just thinking about it could bring you a sense of peace. "Tell me about the house you grew up in."

She told him about it as they walked to the pub. When they made it to the door, he opened it for her, and they stepped inside. Aidan breathed in the comforting scents of rye bread, split pea soup, and malted barley. There was a small crowd at the bar, where Dominic had switched on the television to air a local rugby match. A few people turned to wave, but most of the islanders were too absorbed in the game to pay much attention to them.

"Table or bar?" he asked.

"Table."

He nodded to the near-empty dining room. "Take your pick."

She chose the table by the fire. As soon as they'd taken off their jackets and sat down, she lowered her voice. "I don't see them."

"They'll be here."

Grace started to say something else, then stopped when she spotted Dominic headed toward them.

"Grace," Dominic said with an easy smile once he'd reached their table. "Lovely to see you again."

"You, too."

"What have you been up to all day?"

"Walking." She glanced at Aidan. "And reading."

"Two of my favorite things." Dominic's smile deepened before he shifted his attention to Aidan. "And you? What have you been up to?"

"Same," Aidan said.

Dominic's smile faded a bit. "More reading than walking in your case, I hope." He gave Aidan a once-over, no doubt trying to see how badly he'd reinjured himself. "Do you want me to bring you an icepack?"

"Couldn't hurt."

Dominic shook his head. "I don't suppose you took a camera with you on any of those walks?"

"As a matter of fact, I did."

"You did?"

Aidan nodded.

"What did you take pictures of?"

"Brennan, mostly."

Dominic seemed pleased. "I can't wait to see them." When a cheer rose from the bar, he glanced over his shoulder at the television to see what he'd missed. Someone caught his eye and waved an empty pint glass at him. "I'd better go. What can I get started for you?"

Aidan ordered a bottle of wine for them, and since neither of them had eaten in hours, they put their dinner order in as well.

As soon as they were alone again, Grace looked at him expectantly. "So...?"

"So, what?"

"How did it feel?"

Aidan glanced down at his knee. "Stiff at first. But I'll keep working at it. It'll loosen up eventually."

"I wasn't asking about your knee."

"What were you asking about?"

"How did it feel *emotionally*?"

"Ah."

After a few moments of silence, she asked again, "So...?"

"It felt fine."

"Really?"

"Yes, *really*. As I said last night, that's not an issue for me."

"Okay," she said, backing off, even though it still didn't seem like she believed him. "Do you think you got any good shots?"

"I don't know. Want to come back to my place after dinner and see for yourself?"

Her face broke into a smile, and then she started to laugh.

Dominic returned with their wine, poured them each a glass, and handed an icepack to Aidan.

"Thanks," Aidan said.

Dominic walked away, and Aidan used the hook of his cane to drag a second chair over to prop his foot up. When he found a comfortable position, he laid the icepack on his knee and looked back at Grace. "You'll say, yes, eventually."

She reached for her glass, her eyes still dancing with laugher.

"I can be surprisingly patient, though, so take as much time as you need to come around to the idea." Enjoying himself, Aidan settled back in his chair. "In the meantime, since we're in a photo-sharing mood, why don't you show me some pictures of Heron Island. I bet you have a few on your phone."

"More like a few hundred."

"All right, then." Aidan held out his hand. "Let's see them."

Grace set her glass down and reached for her phone. She tapped the screen a few times before handing it to him. "This whole album is of Heron Island."

Aidan took the phone and thumbed through the photographs. He saw marshes and wildlife, calm waters rubbing against fragile shorelines, marinas filled with workboats, and modest homes on charming, tree-lined streets. From what he could see, Heron Island wasn't as remote as Seal Island, but it had a quiet, tranquil beauty that would make it an ideal place to grow up. If the expressions on the faces of the people in the photographs were any indication, it seemed like an ideal place to live and visit, as well. "It's beautiful. I can see why you love it there."

He swiped through a few more shots, pausing on an image of a large, waterfront farmhouse surrounded by rambling shade trees. He turned the phone around so she could see. "Who lives here?"

Grace leaned forward so she could see the photo. "One of my

best friends from childhood inherited that house from his grand-parents last year. He and his wife and daughter live in one section of the house. They converted the rest into a rehab center for wounded veterans."

Aidan glanced up. "Veterans?"

Grace nodded. "My friend was a Navy SEAL. He and one of his former teammates came up with the idea to open the place earlier this year. They take in about ten or twelve vets at a time. They stay for three months, and they go through a whole program together."

Aidan looked back at the photo, intrigued. "What kind of program?"

"There's an exercise regimen. There's physical therapy and regular therapy, for those who need it. Each of them works at a local business on the island in exchange for room and board. And there's a job placement aspect at the end of it," Grace explained. "Not all of them are wounded physically. Some of them are struggling in different ways. It's basically a place where they can come and stay for a few months to get back on their feet."

"Like a transition center?" Aidan asked.

"Yes, exactly," Grace said. "I think it's the community aspect of it that helps more than anything. From what I hear, that's what people really miss when they leave the military."

Aidan nodded slowly. He would never pretend to understand the bonds that formed between men and women in uniform, people who signed up to risk their lives for their country. But he did understand the trials of transitioning back to normal life. That was the hard part. At least, that was the hard part for him. Trying to find some sense of normalcy after leaving a combat zone.

It was one of the reasons—the reason he was *least* proud of— that he kept going back. When you'd spent that many years on the front lines, it was easier to stay tapped into the adrenaline than to come down from it.

Aidan handed her phone back. "Seems like an ideal place for something like that."

"It is." She set her phone down before giving him a long look. "Kind of like this one."

Aidan was suddenly at a loss for words. Because, in a way, wasn't that exactly what he was doing here? Healing? Rehabilitating? Turning to nature for solace? He looked down at the ice pack on his knee. Except he wasn't transitioning out of his career. And he wasn't a stranger these people had taken in because they cared about the sacrifices he'd made for his country.

These people thought he was family.

He felt a stab of guilt. Then he pushed it away. That, Aidan thought, was not something he was going to dwell on tonight. "How often do you get back there?" he asked, shifting the focus onto her again.

"I drive down for the weekend once or twice a month."

"That often?" Aidan asked. "I figured you'd be the type of person who spent most of your weekends working."

"I am," she admitted. "I usually end up working most of the time when I'm there."

"Then why drive down at all?"

"Because when I do take a break, there's nowhere else I'd rather be."

Where would he want to be, Aidan wondered, if he ever let himself take a break, a *real* break, one where he wasn't recovering from an injury or counting down the days until he could get back to work? He didn't know. "Do you stay with your father when you visit?"

"I used to," she said. "Now, I stay with my brother."

"Your brother lives there, too?"

Grace nodded. "He moved back a couple years ago."

Her brother. Her father. Her best friend from childhood. That was a lot of people, Aidan thought. A lot of people who mattered to her. "Have you ever thought about moving back?"

"To be honest, I've been thinking about it a lot lately."

"Don't you have to be in D.C. to do your job?"

"Yes."

"Then how would you...?" He trailed off. "Wait. You wouldn't *leave* your job to move back there, would you?"

"I don't know." She looked down, twirling the stem of her glass between her fingers. "I was hoping this trip might give me some perspective."

Perspective? Aidan couldn't believe what he was hearing. He might have joked around with her last night about taking an occasional break so she wouldn't become as addicted to work as he was, but she couldn't stop completely. She was too good. The world needed her. "But you love your job."

"I love being a *journalist*," she clarified. "I don't love covering politics."

"Then don't cover politics."

"It's not that easy." She looked up. "I've asked to switch beats for years."

"Ask again. Keep asking until they give you what you want."

"Is that why you freelance? So you don't have to answer to anyone?"

"That's a big part of it, yes." But they weren't talking about him. They were talking about her. And he needed to find a way to convince her that what she did was more important than having a home on Heron Island. "Do you know what I did after we had dinner together that first night?"

She shook her head.

"I sat here, at this table, and I read as many of your articles as I could until Dominic turned the lights off."

Her brows rose.

"And you know what I did when I got home that night?"

She shook her head again, slower this time.

"I read about the changes that have happened because of those articles," he said. "Do you know how many service members have come forward to share their stories since you exposed that colonel who assaulted all those women this past summer?"

Grace held his gaze but said nothing.

He had a feeling she already knew. But he said the number anyway. "Forty-seven. At least, that's as many as I could count. Your article did so much more than lead to one man's conviction. It opened the door for others to feel safe enough to speak out. It gave them a voice. And you know what the U.S. military is doing now, as a result of *that*?"

Grace nodded. "Dismantling the systems that kept those people from being able to speak up in the first place."

"Exactly," he said. "How did writing that story make you feel?"

"Alive."

"Then do more of that." He reached across the table and took her hand. "Do whatever you need to do to make that happen."

# CHAPTER SEVENTEEN

Grace looked down at their joined hands. "Why is this so important to you?"

Aidan started to answer, then stopped, as if he'd just realized how emotional he'd become.

He couldn't be that altruistic, Grace thought. There had to be another reason why this mattered so much to him. Was that why he'd dodged her question the night before when she'd asked him why he'd chosen to be a photojournalist? Had something happened—something he didn't want to talk about? Was that why he'd never let anyone interview him?

She let the silence stretch on, hoping he'd fill it. But he knew this game as well as she did. Silence was a journalist's secret weapon. Most people couldn't stand the awkwardness of it. The longer you let it stretch on, the more likely the other person was to talk.

Aidan wasn't talking, though. And he wasn't going to fall for it. Whatever he was holding back, he wasn't ready to share it with her.

Grace eased her hand out from under his when Dominic arrived with their meals.

Setting the plates down, Dominic glanced at the two of them curiously. He was probably wondering how they'd gone from laughing with each other to not talking at all. She was still trying to figure that out herself.

"Thank you," she said after he'd topped off her wine.

"You're welcome." Dominic smiled, then turned his attention to Aidan. "Kelsey phoned a few minutes ago. She's having trouble with an assignment for her art class. I'm no good at art, and neither is Tara. Glenna usually helps with things like this, but she's not picking up her phone. Any chance you might be able to help her?"

"Sure," he said. "What's she working on?"

"A drawing."

Aidan dipped a piece of bread into the stew he'd ordered. "Did she say what she wants to draw?"

"The harbor."

Aidan took a moment to consider that. "The best view of the harbor is from behind Grace's cottage."

Dominic nodded and looked at Grace. "Is it all right if they set up there? It shouldn't take more than an hour."

"Of course." Grace smiled. "Not a problem at all."

"Tell her we'll be out soon," Aidan said.

"Thanks." Dominic said gratefully, then turned and headed for the bar.

As soon as he was out of earshot, Grace leaned forward. "They must have found something."

"Why do you say that?"

"If they hadn't, they would have come in and said so. Why else would they need to talk to us in secret?"

"Maybe they want to know what *we* found."

Right, Grace thought. She'd forgotten about that. They'd

been looking for something, too. And they had absolutely nothing to show for it.

"I'm not saying they *didn't* find anything," Aidan said. "Just don't get your hopes up too high, okay?"

Grace couldn't help it. She needed to know where those petals were coming from. And she needed to know that they were coming from somewhere on *this* island. Because the alternative— that, somehow, they'd followed her here from Heron Island—was too crazy to consider at this point.

She looked down at her plate. She should probably tell Aidan about the lavender roses that bloomed outside her childhood home every year. Investigations generally worked best when everyone had all the facts. But she didn't know where *those* roses were coming from either. And wouldn't that complicate an already complicated situation?

Yes, she thought. It would. Besides she'd already told Aidan enough about herself today. If he wasn't going to reciprocate and tell her why journalism mattered so much to him, then she wasn't going to reveal any more of herself either. She'd only met him two days ago. She didn't need to tell him everything.

What she needed, Grace thought, were answers. And hopefully Kelsey would have some for them tonight.

Twenty minutes later, when they walked outside, they found both Kelsey and Owen sitting on the bench behind her cottage. Kelsey jumped to her feet as soon as she saw them. "Did you find anything?"

Grace shook her head. "No, did you?"

Kelsey's face fell. "No."

Aidan had been right, Grace realized as her heart sank. How could the four of them have spent all day looking for answers and not found a single clue?

Aidan walked over to where Owen was sitting. The teenager's head was bent over a sketchbook, and he was using a pencil to shade in the background on the page. "I didn't know you could draw."

Owen nodded.

"You've got talent."

"Thanks."

"Did Kelsey do any of that?"

"No." Owen stopped drawing and flipped to a previous page in the sketchbook. "She did this one."

Aidan took in the next drawing. "That's not bad either."

"Owen helped me with it," Kelsey admitted.

"Then why did Dominic think you needed *my* help?" Aidan asked.

"Because I told him I did," Kelsey said.

Aidan looked back at Owen. "But if you were out here anyway—"

"He doesn't know I'm out here," Owen said.

"Where does he think you are?"

Owen shrugged. "At home, I guess."

Grace walked over to join them. "Where do *your* parents think you are?"

"In my room, studying," Owen said.

Grace exchanged a look with Aidan. She'd assumed that Kelsey had used her homework as an excuse to get them out here, but she'd hoped there'd been at least some truth to it. She could tell from the look on Aidan's face that he'd hoped so, too.

It was one thing for Kelsey and Owen to spend the day searching for a rose bush. But lying to their parents? Sneaking out of their houses at night? They might be teenagers, but teenagers were still kids. It was their responsibility, as adults, to look out for them.

"You said, earlier, that the petals were a warning," Grace began, "that something bad was going to happen because of them."

Owen stopped drawing, and Kelsey turned to face her. They both nodded.

"Has anything happened to anyone today?" Grace asked.

"Not that we know of," Kelsey said.

"So, we still don't know *who* these petals are a warning for?"

"Right," Kelsey said. "That's what we're going to work on tomorrow."

"Who's 'we'?" Aidan asked.

"Owen and me."

Aidan shook his head. "Grace and I will do that."

"But you don't know everyone as well as we do," Kelsey protested.

"We'll *get* to know them," Aidan said. "Isn't tomorrow a school day?"

Kelsey and Owen exchanged a glance.

"What?" Aidan asked.

"We don't want to be away from the island if anything's going to happen," Owen said.

"Away?" Grace asked, confused.

"Our school's on the mainland," Kelsey explained.

"And if you don't catch the ferry, you can't get to school," Aidan said, putting two and two together.

Owen dug the toe of his sneaker into the moss beneath the bench. "Finn won't wait for us if we're late."

They were planning to skip school for this? Teenagers were supposed to skip school to have fun. They weren't supposed to skip school because they were afraid of what might happen to someone if they left.

As much as she wanted Kelsey and Owen's help, she wasn't going to hide this from their parents any longer. How would she feel if these were her kids? "I'm not comfortable with this." Before either of them could talk her out of it, Grace turned and started to walk back to the pub.

"Wait." Kelsey trailed after her. "Where are you going?"

"To tell your dad."

"No." Kelsey grabbed her arm. "You can't."

Grace stopped walking. "If someone on this island is in danger, we need to tell your parents."

Kelsey shook her head. "They'll deny it. They don't want you to know that anything's wrong." Her grip on Grace's arm tightened. "They'll make us go to school if you tell them we're thinking of skipping."

"That's the point," Grace said.

Kelsey looked at Owen, her eyes filled with worry. "We can't get on that ferry tomorrow."

Grace turned to face her. "What if nothing happens tomorrow? How many days are you planning to skip?"

Kelsey bit her lip. "We haven't thought that far ahead."

Grace shook her head and started to turn again.

"Don't you understand?" Kelsey refused to let go of her arm. "This is more important than school."

"Actually, I don't."

Owen pushed to his feet. "Wait."

"What?" Grace said impatiently.

"Do you still have the petals with you?"

"Yes."

"Can we see them?"

"I'm not going to change my mind," she warned.

"Please," he said as he started toward her. "We need to see them."

Grace took a deep breath and looked at Aidan. Kelsey and Owen were *his* niece and nephew. Dominic and Liam were *his* brothers. If anyone should be intervening, it should be Aidan.

He said nothing, though, as he walked over to join them. He seemed as conflicted as she was.

Grace reached into her pocket and pulled out a few petals.

Owen took them and held them up to the moonlight, examining each one closely. When he finally spoke, he sounded relieved. "They haven't changed."

"No," Grace said slowly. "They haven't. None of them have."

Kelsey looked relieved as well. "We still have time."

"For what?" Grace asked.

"To figure out how to stop whatever's going to happen," Kelsey said.

Grace looked at Aidan again. Wasn't it time to end this? She waited for him to say something, to step into the role of uncle and take over. Instead, he reached out, took one of the petals from Owen, and held it up to the moonlight.

"They really haven't changed, have they?" he murmured.

Grace shook her head, remembering what Kelsey and Owen had said earlier—that the petals represented some sort of ticking clock. If the fact that they hadn't changed was a good sign, then maybe she could take *some* comfort in that. She still wanted to tell their parents, but maybe that could wait a few more minutes. She turned back to Kelsey. "The clock doesn't start ticking until the petals begin to change?"

Kelsey nodded.

"How soon did they change the first three times?"

"It varied," Kelsey said. "With my mum, it was months. With Uncle Liam, it was..." She trailed off.

"Days," Owen said quietly, finishing the sentence for her.

Aidan lowered the petal and turned to face them. "Days?"

"Three days, to be exact," Owen said.

Grace felt a chill run through her. Three days didn't give them much time to figure out how to stop whatever was going to happen.

"*Now,* do you understand why we need to skip school?" Kelsey asked.

Grace wasn't sure she understood anything anymore.

Owen handed the petals back. "You haven't found any more, have you?"

"No," Grace said, then remembered that Aidan hadn't shown them the ones he'd found. "Aidan did, though."

"What?" Owen asked.

"When?" Kelsey asked.

Grace looked at Aidan. He had a pained expression on his face. He hadn't wanted the kids to know that, she realized. She'd assumed that he'd waited until after they'd left because he'd been too stunned to speak. It hadn't occurred to her that he'd waited on purpose.

"This morning," Aidan said after a long stretch of silence.

"Where?" Kelsey asked.

"I found them on the path that runs from Brennan's farm to the beach on the northeast side of the island."

"How many?" Owen asked.

Aidan looked down at the one in his hand. "Six."

Kelsey and Owen exchanged a glance. "All together, or one at a time?"

"One at a time."

Kelsey's eyes widened. "They were making a trail, like the ones Grace found?"

Aidan nodded slowly.

Kelsey looked at Grace, then back at Aidan. "Did you both end up in the same place?"

He nodded again.

"Why didn't you tell us that earlier?" Kelsey asked.

"I didn't think it was a big deal," Aidan said.

Kelsey's brows shot up. "How could you not have thought it was a big deal after what we told you?"

"I don't know." Aidan let out a breath. "I guess I was still trying to wrap my mind around it."

Kelsey snatched the remaining petal from his hand. "Is there anything else you haven't told us?"

"Not that I can think of," Aidan said. "To be honest, though, the only person I'm worried about keeping in the dark, right now, is your father."

Kelsey's expression shifted from indignant to alarmed. "If you tell him, he'll—"

"Here's what's going to happen," Aidan said, cutting her off. "Grace and I are going to pay a visit to every islander tomorrow to see if anyone is showing signs of distress. You and Owen are going to spend the day at Brennan's to see if we missed anything in our search today. And we're all going to keep looking for the rose bush."

Kelsey looked at him hopefully. "You won't tell on us?"

"Not tonight," Aidan said. "But if we're still no closer to finding any answers by this time tomorrow, I *am* going to tell your parents." He looked at Owen. "Yours, too."

Owen nodded. He looked relieved.

Kelsey opened her mouth to protest, then stopped. "Deal."

Grace had a feeling Kelsey had only agreed because it would buy her enough time to come up with a better excuse tomorrow, but they could cross that bridge when they came to it.

Owen jogged back to the bench to grab his sketchbook.

"Thank you, Uncle Aidan." Kelsey gave him a quick hug, then handed the final petal back to Grace. "We'll see you tomorrow."

Grace nodded, but she couldn't help feeling uneasy as both kids walked away. She waited until their footsteps faded and the only sound was the creak of a weathervane and the crash of the waves below. "Are you sure that was the right decision?"

"No," Aidan admitted, "but it wouldn't be the first time I've trusted a kid and it paid off." When she said nothing, waiting for him to go on, he gestured for her to follow him to the front of the house. "I've spent most of my life working in places where I've had to watch my back. Wherever I go, I make a point of befriending a few kids—not only because I like spending time with them, but because they have a sense about things. Sometimes, they have a better sense of what's going on than the adults."

He looked out at the water, the surface glistening in the moonlight. "Kids are far more observant than most people give them credit for. They see things. They hear things. And they talk to each other rather than keeping secrets like adults do. Most importantly, though, they haven't lived long enough to stop listening to their instincts. They still believe in the truth that lives inside them, rather than what their parents or society wants them to believe."

He stopped walking and turned to face her when they came to her front door. "I don't know if Kelsey and Owen have a better sense of what's going on right now than their parents. But if they're right—if something *is* going to happen—I don't think they should be an hour away on the mainland. I think they should be here, with their family."

Grace couldn't argue with that. And she felt better, knowing the rationale behind the decision he'd made. Besides, Aidan wasn't the only one putting faith in a child's instincts. She looked down at the petals in her hand, remembering Taylor's dream. "Maybe Kelsey and Owen *will* find something at Brennan's tomorrow. If they've done this before, they must know what to look for."

"Grace." Aidan's voice softened. "I didn't ask Kelsey and Owen to spend the day at Brennan's because I thought they'd find something we missed."

She looked up. "You didn't?"

He shook his head. "I'm going to tell Brennan to keep an eye on them. They'll be safe there."

Of course, Grace thought. He'd done that to protect them. He was their uncle, after all. She should have given him more credit. But the small sense of relief that came with that realization did nothing to solve the larger issue—that they were still no closer to finding her mother now than they had been that morning.

They *had* to have missed something. All her instincts were telling her to stay, to keep looking, that there was something here. But what if her instincts had gone rusty? What if coming here had been a mistake? What if this whole trip had been a mistake?

Her gaze fell back to the petals in her hand. "In Taylor's dream," she said, finally putting into words something that had been troubling her all day, "I was lost in a forest, and the rose petals were supposed to lead me home."

Aidan nodded.

"I get the parallel to Hansel and Gretel, and I understand why Kelsey wanted us to start there." Grace opened her palm so he could see the ones she was holding. "But if *these* petals are supposed to lead me home, and Heron Island is my home, what was the point of coming here?"

"Maybe they're leading you to something else."

"Like what?"

Aidan reached out, gently curling her fingers around the petals. "I don't know."

"Aidan," Grace said when he seemed reluctant to let go of her hand. "Why did you wait until we were alone to show me the petals you found this morning?"

He was quiet for a long time, then he slowly released her hand. "Because of what you said they meant."

"You mean...what Glenna said they meant?"

He nodded.

True love, Grace thought as Taylor's wind chime began to sing. Glenna had told her earlier that lavender roses meant true love. "But Kelsey said the colors have different meanings when they show up on Seal Island."

He looked away. "Still..."

She waited for him to go on. When he said nothing, appearing to grow increasingly uncomfortable, she pressed, "I think you're going to have to spell it out for me."

He took a deep breath. "I didn't want Kelsey and Owen to jump to any conclusions."

"About what?"

"About us." Aidan ran a hand over the back of his neck. "That we might be..."

"Oh."

He finally looked back at her, and she went very still. *Soulmates.* He'd waited until they were alone to show her the petals because he hadn't wanted the kids to think they were soulmates. He'd been lying when he'd told Kelsey that he hadn't thought it was a big deal at the time. He *had* thought it was a big deal. He just hadn't wanted Kelsey or Owen to know that. "Wait," she said, her eyes widening. "You don't think that we're..."

"No," he said quickly. "Of course, not."

"Because that would be—"

"Crazy."

"Right."

And yet, why was it that neither of them seemed to be able to speak the word aloud? Taylor's wind chime continued to sing, filling the silence that stretched between them.

Aidan turned slowly and reached up, touching one of the petals on the chime. "You don't believe in true love, do you?"

The question caught her off guard. She hadn't expected him to want to keep talking about this. "I don't know. Do you?"

"I'm not sure I've ever been in love, so I'm probably not the best person to ask."

"What about the woman you lived with in D.C.?"

"I don't think that was love."

"What was it, then?"

"An experiment."

"An experiment…in what?"

"To see if I could live a normal life, I guess," Aidan said with a touch of regret, as if he'd just realized something he wasn't proud of. "I think I wanted to be in love so I could prove to myself that I *could* be normal. That I wasn't too far gone." He shook his head. "I couldn't do it, though. I couldn't make it work."

"Maybe you couldn't make it work because you were with the wrong person."

Her words hung in the air between them.

Aidan looked back at the wind chime, at the twelve tiny petals still dancing in the wind. "Do you think there's only one person for each of us?"

She would have said no before she'd come to this island, Grace thought. She would have laughed at the mere idea of it, the same way she had with Liam the day before. But that was before she'd begun to wonder if her own mother could be a selkie—that the reason no one had been able to find her was because she'd disappeared *into* the water. She was still struggling to come to grips with that, but if she hadn't ruled it out completely, then she had to be at least open to the possibility that magic might exist in this world. And if she could be open to magic, could she be open to true love, too?

"The world is a big place." Aidan continued to think aloud, as if he hadn't noticed her lack of response to his last question. "Doesn't it seem like a cruel joke for two people to have to work that hard to find each other? What if you crossed paths with your soulmate and you didn't recognize each other? What if you never crossed paths at all?"

Grace thought about how adamant Liam had been when he'd told her that Caitlin was his true love, and that Tara was

Dominic's. As far as she knew, both Liam and Caitlin had grown up here, so they hadn't had to work that hard to find each other. But Tara and Dominic had met under highly unusual circumstances. Tara had come to this island to hide. She'd been married to another man at the time, a man she'd been running from. And she'd only planned to stay for a few weeks.

What if she hadn't made the decision to come here? What if she'd chosen a different island? Would she have met Dominic in another place, at another time? Or had she been destined to come here all along?

Grace thought of her own friends who'd found love in the past year—Annie and Will, Becca and Colin, and Izzy and Ryan. Each of those three couples had ended up in the same place at the same time, and that simple twist of fate had changed the course of their lives forever. How many decisions had each of them made to ensure that those connections would happen? What if any of them had taken a step in the wrong direction along the way? Would they have ended up in the same place, regardless?

Was that what Liam had been trying to tell her the day before? That there were forces outside our control, re-routing us over and over, no matter how many times it took, to ensure that we'd be in the same place at the same time with the person we were meant to be with, and all we needed to do was open our eyes?

*'The world offers us all kinds of signs. It wants us to believe. But it's up to us to see them.'*

Uncurling her fingers, Grace looked back at the petals in her hand. She could still hear the ones dangling from the strings of the wind chime clinking together. "I think...if there is such a thing as soulmates," she said finally, still gazing down at the petals, "and we ended up in the same place at the same time, we would recognize each other."

"How?"

She looked up at him. In the moonlight, his face was all hard planes and dark shadows, his eyes as pale as the fog that had rolled in from the sea that morning. She thought about what he'd said about children earlier, that they hadn't lived long enough to stop listening to their instincts, that they still believed in the truth that lived inside them. At what point, as adults, did they stop listening to themselves?

Was there a certain number of mistakes they had to make to determine they couldn't trust themselves anymore? How many times did they have to get hurt, and how badly, before the walls began to form inside them—walls that would both protect them from danger and silence any voices they didn't want to hear.

Were they so scared of getting hurt that they would prefer to keep the walls up than hear the truth?

"I don't know," she said, wondering what her own voices would say if she could hear them. "Instinct, I guess."

Aidan's eyes searched her face. "What are your instincts telling you right now?"

Were they still talking hypothetically? Or was he actually asking her if... No, she thought. He couldn't be asking that. If he was, she needed to end this conversation now. "My instincts," she said, slipping the petals into her pocket, "are telling me to say goodnight so I don't do something stupid like invite you in."

When he took a step toward her, she drew in a breath. She hadn't meant to say the last part of that sentence aloud. She might have been thinking it, but she hadn't meant for the words to come out of her mouth.

She'd been doing such a good job of pretending, all day, that she didn't feel anything for him, that she didn't have this weakness for him.

The truth was, she wanted to touch him again, desperately. So much so, it scared her.

He closed the rest of the distance between them. Her pulse skipped a beat when he tipped her chin up. And her body began to hum as she waited for his mouth to come down on hers—hard and fast and demanding, like it had earlier that day. Instead, he continued to study her, his gaze roaming over every inch of her face until she was sure he could see all the way through her.

"There's nothing I'd love more than to come in tonight. But if you don't want me to, I won't."

It wasn't a matter of wanting. It was a matter of knowing what dangers might lie ahead if she let this go any further. She couldn't seem to form the words, though. She couldn't seem to speak at all anymore.

Leaning his cane against the cottage, he shifted all his weight into his good leg and used both hands to brush the hair back from her face. "I made you a promise last night, and I intend to keep it."

Promise? What promise? How was she supposed to think when he was looking at her like that, when his mouth was only inches away from hers?

"Before you leave this island, I *am* going to come in," he said, still making no move to kiss her, "and I *am* going to help you relax."

Her heart was pounding. She could hardly breathe. Did he think this was relaxing?

"I can assure you, though, that neither of us will be getting much sleep when that happens." Aidan's gaze lowered to her mouth. "And, tonight, you need rest."

Rest? Rest was the last thing she needed. What she *needed* was for him to kiss her. What she *needed* was him. She curled her hands into his shirt and pulled him toward her.

The moment his mouth met hers, all the knots inside her began to unravel. All the ropes she'd used to reinforce the walls he'd broken through earlier fell away. Until there was nothing left to protect her. Until there was nothing standing between her and the voice that should have been telling her to run.

But there was no voice.

There was only sensation. Rivers and rivers of sensation, washing away the fear. She'd been carrying it for so long, she didn't even know who she was without it. Wasn't it time she found out?

As if he could sense something changing inside her, he deepened the kiss. Her lips parted, and she surrendered the last piece of herself she'd been holding back. When his fingers brushed the back of her neck, her breath came out in a shudder. There was no urgency this time. He was touching her like they'd already *become* lovers, like the decision had already been made.

Like it had never been up to either of them in the first place.

Somewhere in the village a door opened and closed. Grace eased back, dazed, as if waking from a dream. "Aidan..."

"I know," he said softly. "I don't understand it either."

This time, when he touched his forehead to hers, she didn't push him away. When he laid a hand on her cheek—almost reverently—she leaned into it, desperate to hold onto the feeling a little longer.

Because she knew, when she stepped back, a new fear would come rushing in. For the first time in her life, she had met a man with the power to break her heart. And if she stayed on this island long enough, she might even be foolish enough to give it to him.

IT SHOULD NEVER HAVE COME to this, Glenna thought. They'd let down their guard, all of them. They'd let an outsider slip through their defenses. For seven years, they'd managed to ward off every threat. No one had even come close to discovering the truth. But in less than three days, Grace had already seen and heard too much.

Glenna stepped onto the sand, barefoot, and made her way to the circle of stones at the edge of the sea. It was after midnight. The rest of the islanders were asleep. She hadn't told anyone what she was planning to do. Not even Sam.

He would have tried to stop her. And she'd already made up her mind.

The wind kicked up as she pulled a black velvet sachet from her pocket. She loosened the strings and poured the contents into the center of the circle, coating a small pile of driftwood with crushed cloves and dried nettle leaves. She added three drops of oil mixed with bloodroot, then stepped back and closed her eyes.

She could feel the power building inside her, feel the rush of it sweeping through her veins. It was like slipping into a second skin, one that fit so well you hardly knew you were wearing it. The ocean surged, spitting sea spray into the air. The wind whipped the hair back from her face as she added the final ingredient—a single sprig of thyme she'd gathered from the garden outside Grace's cottage.

Before she'd even had a chance to light the fire, though, the leaves began to spark and hiss. Black smoke curled into the night like a warning. Glenna took a step back, confused. She'd cast this spell before. She'd cast it multiple times, and she'd never received a warning to stop. What was different this time?

The sparks crackled against the wood, setting pieces of it on fire. She wasn't going to harm anyone. Whenever she cast a banishing spell, she always added a layer of protection at the end, for everyone involved. It was the only way to ensure that Grace would leave the island tomorrow and never come back.

As a test, in case she was misreading the signs, she opened her palms and drew the flames up, into the night. Dark clouds swept in, blotting out the moon. The sea slapped against the sand, each wave breaking harder than the last. When the scent of sulfur drifted up from the earth, she froze.

This spell didn't *want* to be cast.

All four elements were trying to warn her. If she went through with it, she'd be crossing over into black magic. Glenna took another step back. She didn't practice black magic. It went against everything she believed in. Since when did a simple banishing spell qualify as black magic?

Unless...

She felt cold suddenly. Cold all over. She *had* misread the signs. She had misread the biggest sign of all. For the past three days, lavender rose petals had been appearing on this island. She had hoped they might be a sign for her and Sam, and for Tara and Dominic, and for Caitlin and Liam. A sign that their love would be strong enough to withstand any trouble this outsider might bring.

But if the petals *had* been a sign for them, they would have been appearing to them, not to Aidan and Grace.

She should have known better. Deep down, she must have known better. Because lavender roses could only mean one thing.

Grace and Aidan were soulmates.

And separating them would be the cruelest, darkest, blackest magic of all.

The flames snapped higher, like greedy fingers reaching into the shadows. She couldn't do this, Glenna thought as her hands began to shake. She wouldn't be able to live with herself. She'd made mistakes in her life. She'd done plenty of things she wasn't proud of. But she'd never done anything as awful as this.

The wood began to splinter, each shard cracking as it came apart. Wasn't this exactly what her mother had tried to do to her? To separate her from her true love? She could not—*would* not—under any circumstances, turn into her mother. Not tonight. Not ever.

She needed to find another way.

If she wasn't going to banish Grace, she needed to find another way to protect her family. She wasn't worried about anyone finding out the truth about her. She could take care of herself. But Owen was still a child. And Brigid was fragile.

Could they trust Grace with the truth? They'd trusted Aidan, but he was one of them...wasn't he?

How many risks were they willing to take?

She bowed her head and murmured an incantation to slow the spell, to give herself time to think. The wind shifted, changing directions. The scent of sulfur faded. And the moon slipped out from behind the clouds.

As the sea calmed, her mind began to clear. And the answer, when it came, was so obvious.

She needed to look into the future. The flames would tell her everything she needed to know. The only reason she'd held off this long was because she knew she might see something she didn't want to see.

She took a step closer to the fire. And the moment she opened herself to it, the picture began to form. It was hazy at first, a ripple of shapes flickering within the flames. When the image sharpened, though, it didn't make any sense. Because it wasn't the future. It was the past.

*Her* past.

What did her past have to do with any of this?

A collection of paintings she'd done, years ago, hung on the walls of a classy gallery in Boston. The room was filled with people talking, laughing, and drinking champagne. She was surrounded by a circle of men in tailored suits, thousand-dollar cufflinks, and old money surnames like Rockefeller and Montgomery. The women in the room all seemed to know each other. They laughed and gossiped and nibbled on caviar like it was the most natural thing in the world.

And there was one woman in the center of it all. The woman who owned the gallery. The woman who'd sold every one of Glenna's paintings within five minutes of opening the doors. The woman who'd even bought two for herself, to hang in her own home.

In a white silk shift and matching heels, with a single strand of pearls around her neck, she was dressed like the rest of the women in the room—with the understated elegance of someone who'd never had to worry about money. But it wasn't the clothes that had Glenna's breath catching in her throat.

It was her eyes.

They were Grace's eyes.

Glenna staggered back, away from the fire as the image shifted to another time and another place. It was same woman, twenty years younger, without the swarm of friends, without the jewelry and the fancy clothes, without the graceful sweep of long dark hair.

Her hair had been blond, then. She was wearing an oversized sweatshirt and worn jeans. And she was sitting on the floor with two small children, one on either side of her, reading them a book.

A picture book.

A book about a woman who'd left her family, one day, to transform into something—or *someone*—else.

Glenna looked away. She didn't need to see any more. She'd asked the flames to show her the future, but what they'd given her was the truth.

If Grace had come to Ireland to find her mother, she had come to the wrong place.

# CHAPTER EIGHTEEN

An hour before dawn, Brigid stood over the circle of stones. A single log, charred from the fire, rolled back and forth in the shallow waters of the incoming tide. By the time the sun rose, the circle would be fully submerged, and the log would be lifted, carried out to sea.

She couldn't wait that long. The log needed to go. It didn't belong here.

She knelt, reaching for it. Her knees sank into the cold, salty water. The moment her skin met the sea, her breath came out in a rush. The tightness in her chest began to ease. And she closed her eyes briefly to savor the sense of peace that only came, now, when she was touching the ocean.

It was calling to her. It had been calling to her for weeks, each wave whispering her name over and over, like a long-lost friend calling her home.

She had a home, though. Her home was here, on Seal Island, with her family. The sea may have been her home, once, long ago. But she belonged here now.

Didn't she?

The waves swept the log into her outstretched hands, and she rose, lifting it out of the circle. The water swirled around her ankles. The hem of her nightgown, dripping wet, clung to her bare legs. She walked slowly into the water, until the thin white cotton began to float. It moved weightlessly with the waves that ebbed and flowed around her waist.

She held the log away from her, not wanting to touch it for too long. She could still feel the pulse of black magic inside it. The back of her throat still burned from when she'd woken at midnight, panicked, gasping for air. She had sensed it—the moment Glenna had begun to cast the spell.

She couldn't imagine what her niece had been thinking. She would have come straight away if Neil hadn't followed her down the stairs and insisted on making her tell him what was wrong. But then the winds had died. And the sea had calmed. And she'd sensed that Glenna had changed her mind. There'd been no reason to worry him anymore, so she'd told him it was a dream.

It hadn't been a dream.

Her niece had used magic for the first time in seven years. She didn't know what spell Glenna had been planning to cast. But somehow, deep down, she knew that it had involved Aidan. Somehow, she knew—as only a mother could—that her youngest son would have been hurt if Glenna had gone through with it.

Why would Glenna want to hurt Aidan? Couldn't she see how much he was hurting already? Couldn't she see how much he needed his family? She had hoped—hoped more than anything—that he might need *her*. But Aidan had made it clear from the moment he'd set foot on this island that he wanted nothing to do with her.

She took another step. The ends of her hair dipped into the water. The shawl she'd grabbed on her way out the door grew heavy, tightening around her shoulders like a net. She shrugged out of it, pushed it away. Then she pushed the log away and let the ocean swallow them both.

She felt a temporary moment of reprieve. She had done what she came here to do. The salt would wash away whatever toxins were left in the spell. She could go home now. She could go back to sleep and rest easy knowing her son would be safe.

She started to turn. Then realized, suddenly, that she didn't know where home was anymore. She looked back at the ocean. A blade of kelp, soft as silk, snaked around her ankle. She lifted her foot to be free of it, stepping into deeper water. Another blade looped around the back of her knee. The force of the water pulled it forward, making her knee bend with it. She took another step.

Three more steps and the water rose over her chest.

A wave crashed onto the beach behind her. She glanced over her shoulder and blinked. It was that way, wasn't it? It had to be. She searched the sand and spotted a single set of footprints—*her* footprints—leading to the water's edge. It was definitely that way.

Turning all the way around this time, she started to make her way to the beach, just as the ocean sucked the wave back. The water rushed toward her. She had to dig her heels in hard to stay standing. Her arms opened, her palms cupping against the force of the surf to hold her in place.

Why hadn't she thought to tell anyone where she was going? Why had she come here alone?

Because she hadn't wanted to worry them, she remembered as the water receded and a familiar cloak of guilt pressed down on her. She hadn't wanted to worry Neil, in particular. She had worried him so much lately.

She didn't want to be a burden to him—or to anyone.

Her legs felt heavy as she started to walk towards the beach. Mothers weren't supposed to be a burden. They were supposed to be the ones who took care of everyone else. But no one wanted her to take care of them.

No one *needed* her to take care of them.

When her own children had needed her, years ago, she hadn't been there for them.

She pressed a hand to her stomach as the hollow ache deep inside her began to spread. It didn't matter that she hadn't meant to leave them—that she hadn't even known what was happening. She should have tried harder, fought harder. She should have found a way to get back to them.

A mother—a *real* mother—would have found a way.

But she wasn't a real mother, was she? Hadn't the nurses said as much after they'd taken Aidan away? When she'd woken up in the hospital, bruised and bloody—again—from the man who'd stolen her pelt, her baby had already been gone. They had taken him from her while they'd been fixing whatever else had been broken that day.

Hours later, when she'd finally opened her eyes, she'd asked to see him. But they'd refused to bring him to her. Confused, she'd asked again. But still, they'd said no. She'd asked again... and again...and again until she'd grown frantic. She'd tried to climb out of the bed to get to him, but the nurses had forced her back into it. When she'd screamed at them to bring her son to her, they'd fastened her arms to the side of the bed and called for a man in a white coat to sedate her.

The last thing she remembered, before she'd woken up in another bed, in another place—where there'd been no escape for years—was a nurse patting her gently on the arm and saying that it would be better this way.

That her child would be better off with someone else.

Her hands clenched into fists. He hadn't been, though. The couple who'd adopted him had moved to Belfast a year after Aidan had been born to care for an ailing relative. Seven years later, the factory where they'd both worked had exploded, and Aidan had lost them both. He'd spent the rest of his childhood in foster care, moving from one home to the next. No one had ever tried to adopt him again.

She knew because she'd asked Sam to look into Aidan's past, and she'd made him tell her everything. She knew that her youngest son had dropped out of school at seventeen. She knew that he'd run away from his last foster home and lived on the streets for almost a year before he'd aged out of the system. And she knew that he'd been on his own, with no family, for most of his life.

All because of her.

No wonder he could barely look at her.

She wrapped both arms around her mid-section. Neil kept telling her to be patient. He was sure that Aidan would come around eventually. But what if Neil was wrong? What if, by the time Aidan's body healed and he was ready to go back to work, he still couldn't look at her? What if he left before they'd ever had a chance to talk?

If she couldn't get through to him now, she might not get a second chance. And if she couldn't find a way to earn his forgiveness, how could she ever forgive herself?

She stopped walking.

Maybe she didn't deserve to be forgiven.

She turned slowly to face the waves again. Was that why the sea had been calling to her? Was that why she couldn't seem to stay away from it anymore?

Would it be better for everyone if she just slipped away?

Moonlight sparkled on the surface of the water. She could hear the roar of the ocean in her ears. She could fix this, she realized. She could finally do something to make up for all the pain she had caused.

She had seen the way Aidan had been warming to his

brothers lately. They were getting closer. He was beginning to accept them. *She* was the only one he was rejecting. *She* was the only reason he might leave and never come back.

If she left, Aidan would have a family. He would have a home. He wouldn't have to wander forever, searching for something he would never find.

The ocean swelled, swallowing the sand at her feet. She would miss them. She would miss them desperately. But they had lived most of their lives without her already. They didn't need her. Not really.

No one needed her.

Even Neil, as much as he loved her, would probably be better off without her. He wouldn't have to worry about her anymore. He wouldn't have to work so hard to protect her from herself. Maybe, one day, he would even meet someone else. Someone as kind and patient and loving as he was. Someone who deserved him.

She looked up at the moon, at the last moon she would ever see from this place. She needed to find her pelt first. She wouldn't be able to breathe underwater without it. She knew it was somewhere on this island. Liam had told her, once, that they had it. That they were keeping it safe for her.

But she couldn't ask him where it was. If he found out what she was planning to do, he would try to stop her.

There was only one person on this island who might understand why she needed to do this. She looked back at the beach, her gaze settling on the circle of stones. Glenna would know where her pelt was. Glenna knew everything.

SITTING on the floor of her studio, surrounded by crumpled sketchbook pages, discarded canvases, and dried paint stains,

Glenna watched a cold blue dawn break over the island. "I know who she is."

"Who?" Sam asked from beside her.

"Grace's mother," she said quietly. "Her name is Meredith Bradford. She lives in Boston."

Sam shifted slightly to face her. "Boston?"

Glenna nodded. "She owns a gallery in Back Bay. I went there, years ago, for an opening. She invited me."

"You know her personally?"

"I do." Glenna took a breath. "She's been in touch recently. She wants the collection." She gestured toward the building behind them, where her latest collection of selkie paintings hung in the showroom. "She's obsessed with them—with selkies."

"Obsessed with them, but...not one herself?"

"No." Glenna brushed a dusting of sand off her bare feet. "She's not a selkie. There's nothing magical about her."

Sam's eyes searched her face. "How do you know she's Grace's mother?"

"I saw it."

Sam nodded. It was all she had to say. He knew about the visions that had come to Glenna since she was a child. It had been a long time since she'd had one, but he had learned, as she had, to never question them.

"I went to the beach last night to work a spell," Glenna explained. "I tried to banish Grace."

"Tried?"

Glenna ran a hand through her hair. It still smelled like smoke. "I couldn't go through with it."

"Why not?"

For the first time since he'd sat down beside her over an hour ago, waiting patiently for her to speak, Glenna looked at him. "Aidan and Grace are soulmates, Sam. To separate them, I would have had to use black magic."

Sam's expression reflected the same gravity she'd felt, deep in her bones, ever since she'd left the beach. "You can't do that."

"No," she said quietly. "I can't do that."

Sam reached for her hand. They sat there for a long time, listening to the sounds of the island wake up. "What now?"

"I don't know."

"Are you going to tell Grace?"

That, Glenna thought, was a question she'd been struggling with ever since she'd left the beach. "Normally, I'd say everyone deserves to know the truth. But in this case, I wonder if Grace might be better off not knowing."

"Why?"

"Because the truth is going to hurt her."

"You think it'll hurt her more than not knowing?"

Glenna looked out at the fields, where a fine silver mist floated over the moss. She thought of her own mother. She knew what it was like to live with the truth of where you'd come from, to know that you'd never been loved by the woman who'd brought you into this world. Did she want Grace to live with that knowledge? Wouldn't it be better to let her believe in the fairy tale? "There has to be a part of Grace that *wants* to believe her mother is a selkie."

Sam said nothing, waiting for her to go on.

"Selkies *have* to leave their families. They *have* to return to the sea. If Grace's mother left them to return to the sea, she wouldn't have had a choice."

"I get that," Sam said. "But if you don't tell Grace the truth, she'll stay here. She'll keep digging. Eventually, she's going to uncover the truth about us. About *you*."

Glenna squeezed his hand. She could tell he was worried about her. He didn't need to be. "If Grace and Aidan are soulmates, we might be able to trust her with the truth about us."

A sharp intake of breath from across the room had them both

glancing up. Brigid stood in the open doorway, her black hair dripping, her wet nightgown clinging to her body. "Soulmates?"

"Brigid." Glenna shot to her feet. "What are you doing here?" She crossed the room quickly, her pulse picking up at the sight of her aunt looking like she'd just walked out of the sea. "What's wrong?"

"Soulmates?" Brigid repeated, her eyes wide.

Sam appeared by her side with a blanket he'd grabbed from the loveseat. He covered her with it, then wrapped an arm around her waist to help her into the room.

Brigid pushed him away. Her eyes never left Glenna's face. "Is that what happened last night? You tried to separate them?"

Glenna drew in a breath. "You felt it?"

"Of course, I felt it," Brigid said. "Did you think I'd forgotten what black magic felt like?"

No, Glenna thought as a rush of guilt swept through her. She should have thought to check on Brigid as soon as she'd closed the spell. She should have considered the impact it might have had on her.

The only person who'd ever used black magic on this island was Brigid's sister, Moira, who also happened to be Glenna's mother. Moira had been responsible for all the terrible things that had happened in Brigid's life, the first of which had been to separate Brigid from her first love—her *true* love—the man she had risked everything to be with.

No wonder she was so upset.

"It was a mistake," Glenna said quickly. "I didn't know Aidan and Grace were soulmates until I started the spell. It was only supposed to be a simple banishment."

"I don't understand." Brigid took a step back, looking at Glenna like she barely recognized her anymore. "Why would you want to banish Grace?"

"She's a journalist. I wanted to protect us—to protect *you.*"

"I-I don't need you to protect me." Brigid took another step back, shaking her head. "I-I'm the one wh-who's supposed to do the protecting."

Glenna felt a knot form in the pit of her stomach when she heard Brigid's voice begin to break. She'd seen her aunt like this before, but not in a long time. Not in a very long time. "It was a mistake," Glenna repeated as calmly as possible. "I stopped as soon as I realized what was happening."

Brigid shook her head again, like she didn't believe her. When Glenna heard a faint clinking, she saw—for the first time— the shells woven into Brigid's hair. Strands of seagrass clung to the hem of her nightgown, and there was a starfish stuck to one of her legs.

How long had she been in the water?

"Please don't hurt him," Brigid whispered, her fingers tightening around the blanket until her knuckles turned white.

"I won't." Glenna took a step toward her. If she could just get her to come into the room, get her to sit down, maybe she could figure out what was wrong.

Brigid flinched when Glenna reached for her elbow. "If you send her away, it *will* hurt him."

"I know that now," Glenna said, her tone calm and reassuring. Still holding her aunt's elbow, she wrapped an arm around her shoulders and guided her toward the sofa. "I'm not going to send her away. I'm not going to do anything to hurt Aidan."

"You wouldn't, would you?" Brigid's voice sounded small, suddenly, and far off. "You've always looked after them—all of them. You'll still do that after..." She trailed off, her eyes darting around the room.

"After what?" Glenna asked. What was her aunt talking about? What was going on? "After *what*, Brigid?"

"I need to fix it," Brigid murmured, her gaze dropping to a

container of paintbrushes that had fallen on the floor. "I need to make it right."

"Fix *what?*" The knot in Glenna's stomach tightened. "Make *what* right?"

Brigid stopped walking. Her gaze still locked on the paint-brushes, she knelt and began to pick them up, one-by-one.

"Brigid." Glenna struggled to keep the panic out of her voice. "You don't have to do that."

"I have to fix it," she murmured.

Glenna reached for her elbow again.

Brigid shook her off. "I have to make it right."

"Brigid, please." Glenna held out her hand. "Come sit with me on the sofa. I'll make us some tea."

"I don't want tea." Brigid put the paintbrushes in the container. She set it upright on the nearest table, then reached for a plastic container filled with tubes of paint. "I-I don't need tea." She began sorting the paints. The blues in one pile. The greens in another. The reds on a separate table. "I need to fix it."

"*What?*" Glenna asked frantically. "*What* do you need to fix?"

Brigid's gaze lifted, locked on Glenna's. Her eyes searched her niece's face, like she was trying to decide if she could trust her. Drops of water dripped from her eyelashes. A single pearl hung from the end of a silver chain around her neck. When her hand shot out and grabbed Glenna's wrist, Glenna dropped to her knees.

"You *will* look after them, won't you?"

"Who?" Glenna asked.

Brigid's grip tightened around Glenna's wrist. "My boys."

*Her boys?* "Of course," Glenna said. "I'll always look after them. But they don't need me. They need—"

A tube of black paint slipped from Brigid's free hand and dropped to the floor.

"Brigid?"

Brigid released Glenna's wrist. And when Glenna looked down, all the breath whooshed out of her lungs. Her aunt's skin was so pale. She could see the veins on her hands, the blue tracks of them snaking under the skin. Her nails were dry and chipping, the flesh around them beginning to crack.

The next time Brigid opened her mouth to speak, no words came out. All Glenna could hear was a faint wheezing sound, the same sound a fish made when it was pulled from the water, its gills opening and closing, desperate for air.

"Sam," Glenna breathed. "Call Tara."

Aidan woke to the sound of his phone buzzing. Disoriented, he reached for it, almost knocking over a stack of books on the bedside table. When he saw Tara's name on the screen, he answered the call. "Hey," he said, his voice still raspy with sleep.

"Aidan, you need to wake up."

The urgency in her tone had him pushing up to a seated position. Alone in his guest cottage on Brennan's farm, he glanced out the window. The light was still pale and muted. The sun hadn't even risen yet. Clearly this wasn't a check-up call. "Why? What's going on?"

"It's your mother."

"What about her?"

"Something's wrong."

Well, that wasn't news, Aidan thought, rubbing a hand over his eyes. His first thought was that something might have happened to Grace. He didn't feel quite as worried anymore. "More so than usual?"

"Yes."

Aidan frowned. Tara was a doctor. If something was wrong with Brigid, shouldn't she be treating her right now? "Where are you?"

"Glenna's studio."

*Glenna's studio?* That seemed like an odd place to be at this hour. "Is she with you?"

"Yes." Tara lowered her voice. "I need you to come here as soon as you can."

Aidan stood and reached for the clothes he'd worn the night before. "What's wrong with her?"

"I don't know."

"What do you mean, you don't know?" He pulled his jeans on. "Is she having another episode?"

"I don't know," she said again. "Please just get here as soon as you can."

"I'm on my way."

Tara ended the call.

Aidan stared at the screen for a moment, then ran a hand through his hair. He wasn't sure how much help he was going to be, but he'd never heard Tara sound so upset. If she wanted him there, he'd go.

The keys to the car were still in his pocket from the night before, so he grabbed his cane and walked outside. The air was cold and damp. A group of sheep were huddled together in the corner of a nearby field, trying to keep warm. His knee felt stiff as he made his way to the car, and the bandage on his shoulder was coming loose, but he'd deal with both those things later.

He slipped behind the wheel, started the engine, and pulled away from the cottage. The quickest route to Glenna's studio would be to park at Brigid and Neil's house and cut through the fields on foot. If Neil was home, they could walk over together. Maybe he would know what was going on.

When he pulled up in front of their house a few minutes

later, though, it was clear that no one was home. Feeling a tug of apprehension for the first time since Tara had called, Aidan cut the engine and unfolded himself from the car.

Neil had said that Brigid's episodes were becoming more frequent. It had only been two days since her last one. How many more was it going to take until they called a psychiatrist? And what, exactly, were they expecting *him* to do when he got there?

Streaks of red slashed across the sky as he made his way west, on foot, through the fields. The trail was mostly downhill and harder on his knee than he'd anticipated. Wondering if he should have parked in the village and taken the trail with less elevation, it occurred to him that, subconsciously, there might have been another reason why he'd chosen this route.

He knew he wouldn't run into Grace.

As much as it had pained him to leave her the night before, he was glad, now, that he had. She'd already seen Brigid acting crazy once. She didn't need to see it again.

There were only so many crazy things Grace could see before she began to put two and two together—that there were people on this island who believed they were actual fairy tale creatures. He didn't know how she was going to react when she learned that the woman who claimed to be his mother was one of them, but he knew she was *not* going to react well to the fact that he'd kept it from her.

Especially after everything she'd confided in him the day before.

He wanted to tell her the truth—that he wasn't related to any of these people. But if he told her, he'd have to tell all of them. And he wasn't sure how he was going to do that yet.

He kept his eyes on the ground as the slope steepened, searching for safe spots to plant his cane. He was concentrating so hard on putting one foot in front of the other that when he finally looked up and spotted Grace in the path up ahead, he thought he might be imagining it.

Or losing it.

Was insanity contagious?

"Grace?"

Sam appeared beside her, at the edge of the field where Aidan's trail merged with the one that led north from the village. The expressions on both their faces were so tense, Aidan felt a knot form in his stomach.

Grace jogged toward him. Her hair was still mussed from sleep. The laces of one of her boots hadn't been tied. Like him, she was wearing the same clothes she'd been wearing the day before. She must have left her cottage in as much of a rush as he had. But...why? What was she doing here?

As soon as she was close enough, she reached for his hand.

He was starting to have a very bad feeling about all of this. "What's going on?" he asked as they made their way, together, to the intersection in the two paths.

She glanced up, and he caught a flicker of confusion in her eyes. "Something's wrong with your mother."

"I know, but..." Under any other circumstances, he would have been happy to see her, and even happier to be holding her hand, but she shouldn't be here. Not for this. "What are you doing here?"

"She asked to see me."

"Why?" Aidan asked, as confused as she was now.

"I don't know. Sam asked me to come, so I came. He said you'd be here."

A wave of guilt swept through him when she squeezed his hand. He could see the concern in her eyes for him. For *him*. Because something was wrong with his mother.

This was not good.

"Sam came and got you?" he asked, still trying to piece it all together.

She nodded.

They met up with Sam, and Aidan tried to catch the other man's eye as the three of them began walking together to the studio. But Sam's expression gave nothing away. What was Sam thinking, pulling her into this? Weren't they still trying to keep Grace and Brigid apart? If not, why had Sam spent an entire night digging into Grace's past to find a reason for Glenna to get rid of her?

What the hell was going on?

Aidan had kept their secret. He'd done his part. Even when he hadn't wanted to.

Maybe that had been a mistake.

As they closed in on the building, he wondered if he should pull Grace aside now and tell her the truth. Wouldn't it be better if it came from him, even at the last minute, than if she found out on her own?

But then Grace stopped walking. And he stopped with her. They were only a few feet away from the door. When he looked inside, and saw what had made her stop, all his worries about whatever secrets he might have been keeping vanished.

Brigid was on the floor, her knees tucked into her chest, her arms wrapped so tightly around them the knuckles on both her hands had turned white. Her hair fell like wet ropes around her shoulders. Dozens of tiny seashells had fastened themselves to her locks like barnacles. She was in her nightgown again. She was soaking wet. And she was rocking. Back and forth. Back and forth. Back and forth.

Glenna was on one side of her. Neil was on the other. But neither of them seemed to know what to do. Why weren't they helping her up, off the floor?

Aidan let go of Grace's hand and walked into the room. Tara

was huddled in the far corner with Liam. They were on the phone, speaking with someone in hushed tones. A psychiatrist, maybe? He hoped so. But if everyone knew Brigid needed help, why weren't they on their way to the mainland right now?

Sam stepped into the room beside him. Aidan nodded toward Tara and Liam. "Who are they talking to?"

"Sister Evelyn."

"Sister Evelyn?" They were talking to the nun Brigid had lived with for years after she'd been institutionalized? Shouldn't they be talking to a doctor, instead? "Why?"

"Tara wanted to know if it had ever been this bad before."

"And...?"

"It hasn't."

Aidan looked back at Brigid. "Why are her hair and clothes wet?"

"She went into the ocean this morning."

"Where?" Had she come to the beach outside his house again?

"I don't know," Sam said. "She showed up here about an hour ago."

Aidan's gaze cut to Sam's, then shifted back to Brigid. He waited for her to look up, to notice him, but her gaze remained fixed on the tops of her feet, both of which were covered in sand. "Why isn't she on her way to the hospital?"

"Neil's been trying to convince her to go for the past half hour."

Well, he'd be happy to help with that, Aidan thought. But that was all he was going to help with. He took another step closer, addressing his next question to Neil. "Why is she on the floor?"

Neil looked up helplessly. "She won't let anyone touch her."

Come on, Aidan thought. This was getting ridiculous. Why was everyone acting like Brigid was so fragile, they couldn't even convince her to get up, get on the ferry, and get to the hospital. If no one was going to take control of this situation, he would.

He stripped out of his jacket. She had to be freezing if she'd gone into the ocean this morning. He took a few steps closer, then made his way down to one knee so he was eye to eye with her. Her skin was so pale, it was almost translucent. The edges of her lips had turned blue. And he could hear a faint wheezing sound, like she couldn't get enough air into her lungs.

She looked like someone who was about to pass out from a panic attack.

He'd be panicking, too, if he thought he was half-seal.

When she still wouldn't look up at him, he opened the jacket.

"Aidan," Glenna said, a note of warning in her voice.

Ignoring her, he started to put the jacket around Brigid's shoulders. As soon as he lifted it, she shrank back. Her arms came up to cover her face. And she squeezed her eyes shut, bracing herself for a strike.

Aidan froze.

He didn't move. He didn't breathe. He didn't say a single word until her eyes, wild with fear, opened and met his.

This wasn't panic, he realized. This was more than that. This was trauma.

If there was one thing he knew, better than anything, it was trauma. He'd spent the past fourteen years of his life steeped in it, chasing it from place to place. He'd captured it from every angle. Every vantage point.

Every heartbreaking image was seared into his soul.

He would never forget the faces of the people he'd photographed when they'd lost loved ones. When they'd lost their homes. When they'd lost everything that meant anything to them.

There was only so much pain a person could take before they broke.

He knew what a person looked like when they'd been broken. How had he not been able to see it before? Had he been so focused on avoiding her that he hadn't even bothered to look?

For the first time since meeting her, he saw her—really saw her. She was carrying so much pain, she could hardly breathe from the weight of it. What had happened to her? Who had done this to her? Was it the man she'd been married to before, Dominic and Liam's father? Or had something happened before that?

He knew that trauma could make people lose their minds. He had seen it before. At some point along the way, Brigid had begun to believe she was a selkie. And for the first time since reading that crazy letter she'd sent him, he wanted to know her story. Not the one she'd made up to protect herself.

The real one.

Why had she created this fantasy? Why did she need to believe she was a selkie queen? Who had stolen so much of her power that she thought this was the only way she could reclaim it?

He thought of the woman he'd seen on the beach two days ago, the one who'd been gathering seashells in her nightgown. After spending hours reading fairy tales with Grace the day before, he knew that all selkies had to return to the sea. If Brigid truly believed she was a selkie, did she think she was going to have to go back there someday?

What was going to happen if she kept wandering into the ocean alone? What if, one day, she wandered too far, and no one was around to pull her out?

This might all seem crazy to him, but this was *her* reality. And if they weren't careful, if they didn't get her some help soon, she was going to end up drowning herself.

"I'm going to put this around you," he said, his voice as calm as if he were talking to a frightened child "It'll keep you warm."

She didn't say, no, and she didn't shrink back from him again, so he moved ever-so-slowly to cover her with his coat. He settled the heavy material around her shoulders. When she continued to say nothing, to simply look up at him with those wide, broken eyes, he helped each of her arms through the sleeves.

"There," he said after he'd zipped the jacket all the way up. Still kneeling, he offered her a hand. "Let's get you back on your feet."

Her eyes never left his face. And when she finally spoke, her voice was raspy, like she hadn't had a drink in days. "You came."

Aidan nodded slowly.

She was still having some difficulty breathing, but it didn't seem quite as bad as before. Slowly, tentatively, she placed her hand in his. It was the first time they'd touched, he realized. And he felt a strange sensation, a faint tingling of familiarity.

She continued to study him, her gaze roaming over every inch of his face, like she was trying to imprint it into her memory. Like this was one of the most important moments of her life.

If this was what she needed to calm down, he would give it to her. There was no point in trying to wall himself off anymore. He could see, now, that she was just a woman who wanted desperately to reconnect with her son. And for some reason, she thought that son was him.

They could sort that out later.

Right now, all that mattered was getting her to the mainland and into the care of a psychiatrist. Maybe, with the right combination of therapy and medication, she could find a way to let go of the world of make-believe she'd created and learn to live a somewhat normal life.

"Come on." He started to stand. "Let's get you off the floor."

She squeezed his hand, holding him in place. Her grip was surprisingly strong. "Did you bring her with you?"

"Who?"

"Grace."

"Yes." He still didn't know what Grace had to do with any of this. And when he caught the spark of hope in Brigid's eyes, he felt even more confused. Why would Grace's presence make Brigid feel hopeful?

He didn't have long to wonder, because Grace was suddenly at his side, offering to take Brigid's other hand.

Together, they helped her to her feet.

Neil and Glenna stood when Brigid did. Aidan could feel everyone's eyes on them as they led her over to the sofa. As soon as Brigid was seated, she drew Grace down to the seat beside her.

Grace sat hesitantly, no doubt wondering why Brigid had singled her out, especially with so many family members in the room. When Brigid leaned in and whispered something in her ear, Grace's brows drew together. "I don't—"

"Promise me," Brigid breathed, her voice still raspy.

"I'm not sure—"

"Please." Brigid's expression turned desperate.

Grace looked uneasily at Aidan, then back at Brigid. "Okay, I promise."

Brigid took a deep breath. Her skin was still far too pale, and it was starting to flake in places. Her lips were dry. And there were salt stains on her cheeks from the tears she must have shed earlier. But she seemed relieved by whatever Grace had agreed to. When she turned to face Aidan again, he caught another flicker of hope in her eyes.

"I need you to promise me something, too," she said urgently.

Aidan took the cup of tea Neil handed him and tried to offer it to Brigid. "Why don't you have something to drink first?"

She shook her head and shied away from it. Aidan handed it back to Neil. When some of the water sloshed out of the cup onto Aidan's hand, he noticed it was cool. This wasn't the first time they'd tried to get her to drink something, he realized. Neil took the cup, the glimmer of hope in his own expression fading.

Brigid took Aidan's hand again and pulled him toward her. He leaned down so she could whisper in his ear. "Promise me that if Grace leaves, you'll go after her."

Aidan pulled back. He didn't know what he'd expected her to say, but it hadn't been that. "What?"

"Promise me," she repeated, her grip on his hand tightening.

Aidan's gaze cut to Grace. She was watching him, too, her expression troubled. Brigid was still holding her hand. What, exactly, had she said to Grace? How did she even know something was going on between them? And why was it so important to her that he would go after Grace if she left?

He didn't like to make promises that he couldn't keep, but he didn't know how Brigid would react if he said, no. And the only thing that mattered, right now, was keeping her calm. They could revisit this later, he decided, giving her hand a reassuring squeeze. "I promise."

Brigid let out another breath, and the relief that washed over her face was palpable.

Wanting to take advantage of her current mood, knowing it might not last that long, he lowered himself to the arm of the sofa. "How would you like to go to Galway for a few days?"

The relief faded.

"It's a beautiful city," Aidan said, keeping his tone even, "especially at this time of year."

"I could go with you," Neil added, picking up where Aidan left off. "We could stay in Liam's flat."

That seemed to confuse her. "Why would we go to Galway?"

Neil took a step toward her, his voice softening. "To be closer to people who could help you."

Brigid looked back and forth between the two men. "Help me...with what?"

"Help you feel better," Aidan said when Neil seemed unable to find the words.

Brigid let go of Aidan's hand. "What kind of people?"

"Doctors," Aidan said, wanting to be upfront with her. He didn't want her to think they were trying to trick her into anything. He just wanted her to get on the ferry. "There's a hospital there."

Fear flashed in Brigid's eyes. She shifted away from both men and leaned into Grace.

"You wouldn't be going alone," Neil said. "I would go with you. I wouldn't leave your side."

"No." Brigid clung to Grace's hand, her gaze darting around the room. "No. I-I can't go there."

"What if we just went to Galway for the day?" Neil took another tentative step toward her, desperation edging back into his voice. "We could walk along the river...or walk into town and find some presents for the twins. We don't have to do anything you—"

"No." Brigid's breathing grew shallow again. "I don't w-want to go to Galway. I w-want to go home."

Neil looked at Aidan, then Glenna. "Home?"

Brigid nodded. The shells in her hair made a hollow clinking sound.

Neil held out his hand. "I can take you home, if that's what you want."

Glenna looked away, her expression pained.

Aidan sensed that he was missing something. Something crucial. Something everyone but Neil had already realized.

Brigid closed her eyes, shrinking away from Neil when his fingers brushed her arm. "I need to go home," she whispered.

Neil drew his hand back. He looked so hurt, Aidan couldn't stand it anymore. "You *are* home," Aidan said. "This island is your home. Everyone here wants to take care of you. But we need help. We can't do this alone. We need to find out what's wrong so we can fix it. And there are people in Galway who can help us with that."

Brigid pulled her legs off the floor and tucked them under her, making herself as small as possible. When she started to shake, Glenna sank to the floor in front of her. "It's okay," she murmured. "You don't have to go."

"I need to fix it," Brigid said, her voice raspy again.

"You don't have to fix anything," Glenna said softly. "Just breathe."

She was starting to panic again, Aidan realized. Her breathing was labored. He could hear that faint wheezing sound again, and she wouldn't stop shaking. He looked over at Tara. She ended the call, and both she and Liam made their way over to them, their expressions as distraught as Neil's.

"It's okay," Glenna said again. "You don't have to go anywhere. No one's going to make you go anywhere you don't want to go."

"I c-can't go b-back there," she said, struggling to get the words out.

"I know," Glenna said. "I would never make you go back there."

Aidan looked back and forth between the two of them. Back where? What were they talking about? And why was Tara just standing there? Why wasn't she doing anything?

Brigid looked up at Glenna. "I n-need to m-make it right."

"You don't need to do anything," Glenna said calmly. "You don't need to fix anything. All you need to do is breathe."

Brigid tried to breathe, but it only made her body shake harder. The wheezing was getting louder, like her throat was beginning to close.

Aidan stood and pulled out his phone. If no one else was going to call for help, he would.

"Sam," Tara said, her voice as calm as Glenna's. "Do you have a pair of earphones on you?"

Sam reached into the pocket of his coat and pulled out a pair of corded earphones. He handed them to Tara. She plugged them into her phone and started to search for something on the screen.

Aidan stared at her for a split second before beginning his own search—for a psychiatrist who might be able to give them a consult over the phone. Shouldn't Tara be giving Brigid oxygen or some kind of anti-anxiety pill? What the hell was she doing with Sam's earphones?

"I'm sorry," Brigid wheezed, barely managing to get the words out.

Aidan looked up from his screen.

Her gaze was locked on his.

"What?" he asked.

"I'm sorry," she whispered again.

What was she talking about? "There's nothing to be sorry for. You didn't do anything wrong."

Tara handed the earphones to Grace. "See if she'll listen to this."

Grace took them and did as she was told. "Brigid?"

Still clinging to one of Grace's hands, Brigid turned slowly to face her.

"I want you to listen to something." When Brigid started to pull away, Grace put one of the earbuds in her own ear, then held the other one out. "We can listen together."

Brigid stared at the earbud for several seconds before taking it from her. Grace made a gesture, encouraging Brigid to hold it up to her ear.

Brigid lifted it slowly. When it was close enough for her to hear the sound coming out of it, she drew in a breath—her first whole breath since Aidan had tried to convince her to go to the hospital.

"That's it," Tara said from beside them. "Just breathe." She took a deep breath, then let it out slowly. "In and out."

Brigid began to copy Tara, taking long breaths, in and out.

Grace waited until Brigid stopped shaking. "Here," she said gently, offering her the second earbud. "Take this one, too."

Brigid took it from her, and Grace helped her fit them both into place. When all Brigid could hear was the sound playing on Tara's phone, her eyes fluttered closed and her whole demeanor changed. For the first time since Aidan had stepped into the room, she looked at peace.

"What's she listening to?" Aidan asked.

Tara picked the blanket up, off the floor, and walked over to Brigid. She laid it over her mother-in-law's legs, then slowly sat down beside her and ran a hand over her wet hair. "Ocean sounds."

Aidan lowered his phone.

"Grace," Liam said, his voice thick with emotion. "The petals you found yesterday—where are they?"

Grace reached into the pocket of her jeans, the same jeans she'd been wearing the day before, and drew out a handful of petals. Every single one of them had begun to turn brown.

# CHAPTER TWENTY

It took them another hour to get Brigid to calm down. When some of the color began to return to her face, Tara removed the shells from her hair and untangled the seagrass from the hem of her nightgown. Liam washed the dirt and sand off her feet. Sam went to her house to pick up a set of dry clothes, and Glenna helped her into them as soon as he returned. Neil made her a fresh cup of tea. And by the time Brigid finished it, she'd agreed to go home and try to get some rest.

Grace had a feeling that Brigid was the only one who would be resting anytime soon. No one else had said anything about the petals since she'd pulled them out of her pocket. But she could tell from the tense looks Tara, Liam, Glenna, and Sam had exchanged that it was a very bad sign that the petals had begun to wilt.

The only one who didn't seem concerned about them was Brigid. The most wistful expression had come over her face when Grace had opened her hand. Tentatively, she had asked if she could have one, and Grace had let her. The petal was still resting in Brigid's palm, her fingers curled protectively around it.

Clearly, it meant something different to her...but what? And what, if anything, did it have to do with the promise she'd asked Grace to make earlier?

'*Aidan needs you,*' she'd said. '*Promise me you won't leave him.*'

Grace had only met Aidan three days ago. How could he possibly need her? And why would she promise not to leave him? Of course, she was going to leave him. As soon as she found her next clue, she would be leaving Seal Island. In a few weeks, Aidan would be leaving, too, most likely heading back to work somewhere in the Middle East.

They'd probably never see each other again.

The only thing that mattered, right now, was figuring out what was wrong with Brigid. Aidan had said that his mother struggled with mental illness, but this was more than that. This was...something else.

She had questions—so many questions. But she kept them to herself until the others dispersed. Brigid and Neil left first, followed by Sam and Glenna, who promised to spend the rest of the day at Brigid's house and call if there were any changes. Tara said she needed to go back to the village to pick something up, and Liam offered to go with her. Grace suspected that Liam only offered to go with Tara so they could strategize their next move.

She let them go, though. Because the only person she trusted to give her a straight answer was Aidan. And even he had some explaining to do.

As soon as they were alone again, she turned to face him. "We need to talk."

He nodded slowly.

She handed his jacket back. It was still damp, but he slipped it on anyway, and they stepped outside.

"I'll walk you back to the village." He motioned towards the path Liam and Tara had taken rather than the one he'd taken earlier that morning. "I think I'd rather be on even ground for this conversation."

Grace fell into step beside him. Instead of reaching for his hand this time, she dipped both of hers into the pockets of her coat. "What happened in there?"

"I don't know."

She glanced at his profile, looking for a sign that he might be hiding something from her. But he looked as shell-shocked as she did. "Have you ever seen her like that before?"

"No."

"Do you think she's going to be okay?"

"I think I'd have a better answer for that question if she was on her way to the hospital."

"Why won't she go?"

"I don't know."

"You don't know?"

He shook his head.

"How can you not know? Glenna knows. Liam must know, or he would have been trying to convince her to go. Tara clearly knows, and she seems to support Brigid's decision. It's like she doesn't even think medicine can help her anymore, so..." She trailed off, waiting for him to fill in the gaps. When he said nothing, she felt a tug of frustration. "Is it the hospital itself she's afraid of, or is it leaving this island?"

Aidan took a breath. "I don't know."

Grace stopped walking. "How can you know so little about your own mother?"

Aidan stopped walking, too, and turned to face her. The sun was still low in the sky, and dark shadows fell across the grass at their feet. "Because I only met her three weeks ago."

"What?" Grace asked, confused.

"I'm sorry. I wanted to tell you." Aidan's voice was filled with regret. "It's been killing me keeping it from you."

Keeping what from her? What was he talking about? When Aidan ran a hand over the back of his neck, Grace felt something heavy lodge in the pit of her stomach. "But...these people are your family."

"They're not my family."

Grace took a step back. "I don't understand."

"I didn't know any of these people before I came here."

She stared at him. "But...if you're not related to any of them, why does Brigid think you're her son?"

Aidan's expression became pained. "Like I said the other night, she has an active imagination."

"You think she *imagined* giving birth to you?"

"No." Aidan let out a breath. "I'm sure she gave birth to someone. It just wasn't me."

Stunned, because the resemblance was unmistakable, Grace tried to wrap her mind around what he was saying. "Have you taken a DNA test?"

"No."

If he hadn't taken a DNA test, how could he possibly know that she wasn't his mother? "Why not?"

"Because I don't have to. Come on, Grace. You saw her back there. She's...not well."

"What, exactly, do you mean by 'not well'?"

Aidan took another breath. "Look, I don't know what happened to Brigid. Maybe she was born with an imbalance that makes her believe these things. Or maybe—and after what I saw today, I think this is more likely—it's related to some sort of trauma she experienced earlier in life. What I *do* know is that she's been struggling with this for a long time."

"If you only met her three weeks ago, how could you possibly know that?"

"Neil told me after you found her on the beach collecting

shells the other day. He said she used to have episodes like that all the time before he met her."

"According to who?"

"What?"

"According to *who*?" Grace repeated. She could feel herself shifting back into reporter mode. She'd never put much stock in second-hand accounts. And right now, Aidan was seeming less and less like a reliable source.

"According to the woman who took her in after—" Aidan stopped talking. He didn't seem to know if he should go on.

"After *what*?" Grace pressed. Her patience was wearing thin.

Aidan let out a long breath. "After she was institutionalized."

Brigid had been institutionalized? No wonder she hated hospitals. "How long was she...?"

"I don't know." Aidan rubbed a hand over his eyes. "Glenna was there, too, so she would know."

Grace's eyes widened. Glenna had been institutionalized, too? "Why?"

Aidan gave her an odd look, like the answer to that should be obvious. "Why do you think?"

"I don't know. That's why I'm asking. I mean...did they check themselves in, or did someone put them there? And if someone put them there, why? What was their reason? Not everyone who gets locked up deserves to be there."

"Grace—"

"Did you even *bother* to ask? Or did you just assume that, if they'd been institutionalized, they must be crazy?" When Aidan said nothing, she knew the answer to that question was yes. How could he have so much empathy for the suffering of people all over the world but not have any for the people who claimed to be his family? She searched his face, looking for a sign that the man she'd come to know over the past few days was still in there somewhere. "Are there any others?"

"Any others...what?" Aidan asked carefully.

"Any other crazy people?" she asked, tossing the word back at him, as if he were the one who had chosen to use it, not her.

He looked away.

There *were* others, Grace realized. "How many?"

"I think," Aidan said after a long stretch of silence, "that everyone on this island is a little crazy."

"*Everyone?*"

"Yes."

"Why?" Grace asked. "Because...they believe in fairy tales?"

Aidan closed his eyes, his expression growing pained again. "They don't just believe in them. They think they're *living* in one."

"What if they are?" Grace pulled a handful of rose petals from her pocket and opened her palm. "Isn't this what Kelsey and Owen warned us about?"

"Grace—"

"What's going to happen if these petals dry out before we figure out what's wrong with Brigid?"

Aidan closed the distance between them. He took her hand and curled her fingers around the petals without even looking at them. "They're petals. There's nothing magical about them. They're wilting because that's what they do."

Grace's mouth fell open. Was he really going to pretend like none of this was happening?

'*They think they're living in a fairy tale.*' Aidan's words floated back to her, and the full impact of them hit her this time. Wait... Was he saying what she thought he was saying? "Why did Glenna seem so upset, earlier, when Brigid said she wanted to go home?"

Aidan held her gaze but said nothing.

"Where does Brigid think her home is?"

Aidan slowly let go of her hand.

Grace could hear the ocean in the distance, the faint pulse of it beating against the shoreline. It was always there, a constant reminder of its presence and power. Up until now, she'd thought that was a good thing.

But what if it wasn't? What if, for some people, it was a temptation they had to fight every day?

She thought of how Brigid had looked earlier—the haunted eyes, the dripping wet clothing, the shells threaded into her hair. It wasn't the first time Brigid had wandered into the ocean in her nightgown since Grace had arrived on this island.

Was the pull of it becoming harder for her to resist?

She looked down at the petals in her hand. What if Brigid knew she didn't belong here? What if this was all the time she had left? Grace lifted her gaze back to Aidan's. "Does Brigid think she's a selkie?"

Aidan was quiet for a long time  Finally, reluctantly, he nodded.

"Does anyone else think that?"

Aidan looked away again.

It wasn't just Brigid, Grace realized. Everyone on this island believed that Brigid was a selkie. Everyone, except for Aidan.

One by one, all the pieces began to click into place. *This* was what they'd been hiding from her. *This* was their big secret. It didn't have anything to do with her mother. It was about Aidan's mother.

They'd been trying to protect her.

Because if it was true—if there was an actual selkie living on this island right now—the whole world would want to know.

No wonder Glenna had tried to get rid of her yesterday.

That was why Sam had dug into her past to find something they could use against her. That was why Liam had looked so stricken when she'd told him she'd decided to stay. That was why

Tara had felt the need to lie every time Grace had inadvertently scratched too close to the truth.

Suddenly, everyone's actions made sense—everyone's except for Aidan's.

"How long have you known?" she asked, shocked by how much he'd been hiding from her.

"Brigid wrote to me about six weeks ago. She told me the story—*her* story—then."

*Six weeks ago?* "She told you in a letter? She didn't wait for you to get here first, to tell you in person?"

Aidan looked down. "It wasn't the first time she'd tried to get in touch."

Okay, Grace thought. It still seemed like a lot to put in a letter. She could sort of see where Aidan was coming from if he'd received that out of the blue. "How many times had she tried to contact you before that?"

Aidan dug the bottom of his cane into the moss.

When he continued to say nothing, any empathy she might have felt for him began to wane. "When did she *first* contact you?"

Aidan pressed down on the cane. "About seven years ago."

"Seven years?" Grace stared at him, stunned. "Why did you wait so long to come?"

He looked back up at her, his eyes pleading with her to understand. "Because I'm not related to them. I'm not who they think I am."

"If you don't believe you're related to them, then why come at all?"

"Because I accidentally replied to Brigid's letter when I was still in the hospital. I was out of my mind on painkillers. I told her I'd come, and I always keep my word." He winced. "Well, I *almost* always keep my word. I promised Tara I wouldn't tell you any of this, and here I am, telling you."

"I don't see how you could possibly keep this from me anymore, after what I just saw."

"No," he said. "Neither can I."

And that was the only reason he was telling her, Grace thought. Otherwise, he would have continued to hide it from her. "So...you don't believe them, but you decided to come anyway."

"Right."

"Because you needed a place to heal?"

Aidan didn't seem to know how to respond to that.

"Do they know that you're using them?"

"I'm not—"

"Is that why you're staying at Brennan's? As far away from the village as possible?"

"It's not like that."

"What is it like, then?" she asked as shock shifted to anger. "Why did you even bother to help me yesterday? Did you think it was funny when I told you that I thought *my* mother might be a selkie?"

"No, of course not."

"Do you think I'm crazy, too?"

"No," he said quickly.

"I would be, though, if I believed her, right?"

"Grace." Aidan closed the distance between them again. "Brigid is sick. She needs help. She needs to be medicated."

"I'm not convinced you're right about that."

"Come on. You saw her in there. She thinks she's turning back into a seal."

"Maybe she is."

Aidan put his hands on both of her arms. "This is real life. We are not living in a fairy tale."

What if he was wrong? What if this was the missing piece she'd been searching for all along—the one piece that could fit everything together? "If *your* mother is a selkie, *mine* could be, too."

"Grace." Aidan's tone turned desperate. "I don't know what happened to your mother, but she's not a selkie. And Brigid is *not* my mother."

"How can you possibly know that if you haven't taken a DNA test?" She saw heat flash in his eyes. He was as angry as she was now. But she didn't know why. Why not just get the test? Get it over with? It was a simple yes or no that could be verified in a matter of weeks.

It was almost like he didn't want to know the truth. But why? Why was it so hard for him to accept that Brigid might be his mother? Why had he rejected all her attempts to connect with him over the past seven years? What did he think was going to happen if the answer turned out to be yes? "What are you so afraid of?"

"Afraid?" Aidan let go of her arms. "You think I'm afraid?"

"You must be afraid of something. Otherwise, you'd just take the test."

Aidan dragged a hand through his hair.

"You're a journalist, Aidan. You live for the truth. Why can't you even consider that it might be true?"

"Because my real mother died when I was eight!"

Confusion flashed across her face. "What?"

"She died," he repeated. "She's gone. And so is my father."

The confusion deepened. "I don't understand."

"They were killed in an explosion in Belfast in 1991." Aidan started to pace, not an easy feat with a cane, but he couldn't seem to stand still anymore.

"An explosion?"

"From a bomb," Aidan said. "The IRA set off a series of bombs around the city that day. I take it you've heard of the IRA?"

Grace nodded slowly. He was referring to the Irish Republican Army, a paramilitary group that had fought against the British rule of Northern Ireland for over thirty years during a period known as the Troubles.

"The number of British Army troops stationed in Belfast had been growing. And the IRA wanted to push them out. My parents weren't the target, nor were any of the other civilians who died that day. They just happened to be in the wrong place at the wrong time."

She could hear the bitterness in his voice, bitterness that had built up from years of seeing the same thing happen to innocent people all over the world as a photojournalist. Parents killed. Children orphaned. Families torn apart by conflicts they had no control over and wanted nothing to do with.

"And you know what the worst part is?" he asked, still pacing.

Grace shook her head.

"My parents were Catholic. They were Republicans. They were on the same side as the IRA. Not that they condoned the violence, but they sympathized with the underlying cause. You couldn't grow up in Belfast during that time and not know where your parents stood on the conflict."

And yet, they'd been taken out anyway. Their lives deemed dispensable by whoever had ordered the placement and detonation of those bombs.

Grace understood, now, why Aidan did what he did for a living. He knew what it felt like, firsthand, to have his life torn apart by violence. And he wanted the rest of the world to know what that felt like so those people wouldn't be forgotten.

As much as she respected that, she couldn't help wondering if the past was keeping him from being able to see what was right in front of his eyes. "If all this is true, why does Brigid think you're her son?"

Aidan stopped pacing and let out a breath. "She claims I was taken from her."

"Taken?"

"Yes."

"By whom?"

"The hospital staff, after she gave birth."

"Why would they do that?"

He leaned a hand against one of the stone walls. He looked exhausted. "I don't know."

"Did she try to get you, or whoever he was, back?"

"Yes. Apparently, they told her she wasn't fit to be a mother. When she panicked, they drugged her and locked her up in an institution."

Grace's eyes widened.

"I know," Aidan said wearily. "It's insane."

Insane? That wasn't the word she would have chosen. Horrifying was more like it. "What if you *were* taken from her, Aidan? I've read articles about forced adoptions. It wouldn't be the first time a child was taken from his mother and given to someone else. Ireland has a reputation for moving babies around."

"That was a long time ago."

"Was it?"

"Yes," he said emphatically. "The adoptions you're referring to took place in the 50s and 60s. I was born in the 80s. Besides, if I *had* been adopted, my parents would have told me."

"You were only eight when they died. Maybe they hadn't gotten around to it yet."

"I have a birth certificate with both my parents' names on it—my *real* parents' names."

"Maybe it's not a real birth certificate."

Irritation flashed in his eyes. "You've got to be kidding me."

"People make forgeries of official documents all the time."

"Why would my parents want to forge my birth certificate?"

"To erase any links to your biological mother—a mother you were taken from against her will."

Aidan pushed off from the wall and started to pace again. "Unbelievable."

"It *is* possible, Aidan."

He shook his head.

"If you could just—"

"Sam put you up to this, didn't he?"

"What?" she asked, confused.

"Sam—the man who came and got you this morning."

"Uh...no."

He reached the other side of the path and turned, pacing back in the other direction. "I have a hard time believing you could have come by this theory without someone planting the seed first."

"This is Sam's theory, too?"

"Yes."

"Sam—who used to be a private investigator?"

"Yes," Aidan said tightly.

"Why does *he* think you were adopted?"

Aidan stopped walking and turned to face her. "He found my parents' names on a list at an adoption agency in Dublin. He claims they'd been on it for years, and they were next in line to receive a child when Brigid's son was transferred to the orphanage."

"Have you contacted them to verify that?"

"The agency doesn't exist anymore."

"How did Sam find the list, then?"

"You'll have to ask him that."

"Why?"

"Because I don't know."

"You didn't ask him?"

"No."

"Why not?"

"Because I don't *need* to." Aidan dug his cane into the ground again. "Even if my parents *were* on a list at an adoption agency, it doesn't mean I was adopted. My mother could have gotten pregnant after not being able to at first."

"But doesn't it make you at least wonder if—"

"There's no record of an adoption anywhere. This whole theory is based on assumptions. There's no proof."

"But there *could* be proof if you'd get a DNA test."

"I don't need a test to tell me what I already know," Aidan said, frustrated.

"You look just like them, Aidan. The resemblance is unmistakable. Can't you see that?"

Aidan's gaze shifted away.

"Don't you want to know for sure? I mean, what if you *are* related to them? You could have a second chance at having a family."

"I don't need a family."

"What?"

"I don't need a family," he repeated.

"You can't mean that."

"I do mean that."

Grace took a step back. She couldn't quite process what he'd said. "I realize that you've built your entire life around the loss of your parents—and that loss was devastating for you—but it doesn't have to be this way."

"Of course, it has to be this way. There *is* no other way."

Grace stared at him. "Are you afraid that, if you find out you're related to the O'Sullivans, you won't be able to keep doing what you do for a living?"

A muscle in Aidan's jaw began to tick. "I'm not afraid of finding out if I'm related to them."

"I think you are. I think that's exactly what you're afraid of. I think you've been holding onto this grief for so long, you don't even know who you could be without it."

"Spare me the psychoanalysis."

"Would you seriously rather keep doing what you're doing than let these people love you? Do you have any idea how selfish that is? This isn't just about you, Aidan."

"I never said that it—"

"What if losing you is what broke Brigid in the first place? What if she's breaking down again, now, because she's afraid she's going to lose you again?"

Aidan's temper snapped. "She never lost me in the first place! I was never *hers*!"

"Then tell her that." Grace's voice rose to match his. "Tell her you don't believe you're related to her. Tell her you've been lying to her—that you've been lying to all of them."

"Grace—"

"You've been lying to them. You've been lying to me. You've been lying to everyone." She turned and started to walk toward the village at a pace he couldn't possibly match. "I don't even know who you are anymore."

# CHAPTER TWENTY-ONE

She didn't know who he was, Grace thought as she walked into her cottage ten minutes later and slammed the door behind her. And she didn't know who *she* was anymore either. Too angry to do anything other than move, she stripped out of her clothes and stepped into the shower.

How could she have been so stupid? She knew better than to get involved with a man she had feelings for. Feelings clouded your judgement. Feelings made you do crazy things you would never do otherwise, like put your trust in a man you'd only met a few days ago.

She didn't know who she was more pissed off at—herself or Aidan—but it was probably herself. Because beneath the anger there was another emotion, a deeper emotion, one she'd spent most of her adult life trying to avoid. She pressed a hand to her heart. The hollow ache didn't stop there. It had spread to the pit of her stomach. She felt empty inside, like she'd lost something that had made her feel whole for the first time in her life.

She didn't want to feel this way. She didn't want to feel *anything*. What she wanted was to find a way back to the person she'd been before. The person who knew better than to let someone in. She closed her eyes and tilted her face up to the spray of water, hoping the heat might wash away some of the pain.

When it didn't, she shut the water off and grabbed a towel. There were so many emotions swirling inside her, she couldn't pinpoint what upset her the most. Was it the fact that Aidan had lied to her? No, she thought as she scrubbed the towel over her skin. As much as it pained her to admit it, she understood why he'd kept the islanders' secret. It hadn't been his secret to tell.

Was it the fact that he'd lied to the O'Sullivans by pretending to be a member of their family? That was upsetting, but it wasn't what was causing this ache inside her. No, she thought as she finished drying off. It wasn't either of those things.

It was his complete indifference to the possibility that he might be related to them.

Aidan had a second chance at having a family, at having a mother—the one thing she'd been searching for her whole life. And he didn't even care. How could she have almost fallen for someone so callous? Someone who couldn't possibly understand her at all?

Forcing the anger down, into all the empty places inside her, she changed into clean clothes and fished the petals out of the pocket of her jeans on the floor. At least a third of them had turned brown. The edges were crackly, and tiny pieces were breaking off like crumbs. Handling them as carefully as she could, she tucked them into the roomier pocket of her jacket and headed for the door.

Aidan might not believe that these petals were a warning. And he might not believe that Brigid was his mother. But Grace believed both those things. And if Brigid's time was running out, then Grace needed to act fast.

She opened the door and stepped outside. She didn't know

how she was going to get past Sam, Glenna, and Neil, but she needed to talk to Brigid, and she needed to talk to her alone. Because if Brigid was a selkie, her mother could be, too.

She headed east, toward the harbor, and followed the road leading away from the village until it forked. She remembered Brigid saying she lived north of Brennan's farm, so she turned left, away from the coast. It was one of the only roads she hadn't walked yet, and it wound up, in switchbacks, over a rocky hillside.

By the time she made it to the top, she was breathing hard. Behind her, in every direction, were some of the most beautiful views she'd seen on the island yet. She could see the full expanse of Brennan's farm, including both cottages—the large one where Brennan lived and the smaller one that Aidan rented. She could see the harbor, the village, and Glenna's studio. She could even make out Tara and Dominic's cottage in the distance, a speck of white perched on a mossy cliff.

This spot hadn't been chosen lightly, Grace realized. It had been chosen so the people who lived here could watch over everyone. She thought back to the way the islanders had reacted to Brigid that first night when she'd walked into the pub, like she was some kind of royalty. This, Grace thought, marveling at the house before her, was a house fit for a queen.

It was nothing like the rest of the homes on the island. It was sleek and modern and somehow blended perfectly with the natural surroundings. Through the glass walls, she could see four people inside: Brigid, Neil, Glenna, and Sam. She knew it was intrusive, showing up with no warning, especially after every-thing that had happened that morning. And she didn't expect any of them to be particularly happy to see her.

But it wouldn't be the first time she'd pushed into a place where she didn't belong to uncover the truth.

She was almost to the door when Glenna turned and met her

eyes through the glass. Grace expected to see a flash of irritation as Glenna prepared to prevent her from coming into the house. Instead, Glenna simply walked to the door and opened it.

Wondering where this sudden change of heart had come from, Grace waited for her to say something. But Glenna remained silent. She looked past Grace to the vast stretch of sea behind her, her expression grief-stricken. Grace took a tentative step into the house. The others turned. Neil and Sam looked as distraught as Glenna. The only one who didn't seem upset was Brigid.

Brigid's eyes had cleared. All the color had returned to her skin. And her hair had dried into soft waves that spilled over her shoulders. If it weren't for the basin of water at her feet, Grace would have thought she looked completely normal. As Grace made her way closer, though, she had a sinking feeling that the only reason Brigid didn't stand to greet her was because she couldn't bear to leave the comfort of the water. Her feet were submerged up to her ankles. And there was a thin layer of webbing between each of her toes.

How long had that been there?

Brigid held out a hand. "I'm so glad you came."

"I should have called first."

"Not at all. You're welcome anytime."

Grace took her hand. It wasn't as cold as it had been earlier, but it wasn't exactly warm either. "Are you feeling better?"

"I am." Brigid gestured for her to sit. Her gaze flickered toward the wall of glass. "Did you bring Aidan with you?"

"No."

Brigid's smile stayed in place, but some of the brightness faded from her eyes. "I'm sure he'll come later."

Grace wasn't so sure about that. But she hadn't come here to talk about Aidan. "Your house is beautiful."

"Thank you." Brigid's expression warmed as she looked at her husband. "Neil was a builder before he retired. This was his last big project."

Grace glanced at Neil as he walked over to join them. "You built this house?"

He nodded.

"Did you design it, too?"

He laid a hand on Brigid's shoulder. "We designed it together."

"I did nothing," Brigid argued. "We stopped here on a walk, once, several years ago, to take in the view. I said if I could pick anywhere on the island to live, this would be it. Neil did the rest."

Neil squeezed her hand. "You said you wanted to see everything, the whole island and the sea. That's why the walls are glass."

"I don't think that counts."

Neil's eyes never left hers. "It counts."

Brigid covered his hand with one of hers. When Neil blinked back a sudden sheen of tears, Grace looked away. She wasn't used to seeing grown men express their emotions. Her father had closed his off years ago. Her brother usually kept his to himself. And the men she dated knew better than to show her how they were feeling. But it was impossible not to feel Neil's love for Brigid when they were together.

She thought of her own parents, and of the love she thought they'd shared before her mother had left. If her father turned out to be right—that his love hadn't been enough to make his wife stay—what was going to happen to Neil when Brigid left? Would he turn cold and hard, the same way her father had?

She didn't want him, or any of the O'Sullivans, to have to go through what her family had gone through.

"How about some tea?" Brigid turned her attention back to Grace. "Irish Breakfast? Earl Gray? Peppermint?"

"No," Grace said. How could Brigid offer her tea at a time like this? "Thank you, though."

"How about a scone or a piece of soda bread? Have you had breakfast?"

"I don't need anything."

"There must be something we can offer you," Brigid said.

"Actually..." Grace glanced at Sam and Glenna, still hovering nearby, then at Neil, still struggling to control his emotions. "Would it be possible for us to have a few minutes alone?"

"Of course," Brigid said.

Neil seemed hesitant at first, then nodded. "We'll be in the garden if you need anything." He waved for Sam and Glenna to follow him outside.

As soon as the door shut behind them, Grace turned to Brigid. She couldn't believe they'd left them alone that easily. "For the past three days, your family's been trying to keep me away from you. Why are they letting me talk to you now?"

Brigid reached down, skimming the surface of the water with her fingers. A silver wedding band embedded with clusters of pearls sparkled in the morning light. "They know you're on our side."

"Your...side?"

Brigid dipped the rest of her hand into the water. "You're one of us."

Grace's brows drew together. One of them? How could she be one of them? She'd only met them a few days ago. "I don't understand."

Brigid pulled her hand out of the water and uncurled her fingers, revealing a single blue shell. "Your love for Aidan makes you one of us."

Grace looked down at the shell, then back up at Brigid. "I'm not in love with Aidan."

"Of course, you are."

Grace shook her head slowly. "No, I'm not."

Brigid seemed confused. "You're not?"

"No."

"But..." Brigid's fingers curled around the shell. "Oh."

"Oh, what?"

"You don't know."

"I don't know...what?"

"Didn't Glenna tell you what the petals meant?"

"Well, yes, but..." Grace thought of the strange way Brigid had reacted to seeing the petals earlier. It was almost as if they'd brought her hope. Grace shifted uncomfortably as a troubling thought occurred to her. "You don't think that Aidan and I are...?"

Brigid smiled.

Oh no, Grace thought. This was not good. "Wait... Is that why you made me promise not to leave earlier?"

Brigid nodded. "He needs you."

"We barely know each other," Grace protested. "How could he possibly—"

"He needs you. And you need him."

She did not *need* Aidan. She did not *need* anyone. The only thing she *needed* was to find out what had happened to her mother. "If the petals are supposed to mean that Aidan and I are soulmates, then why are they wilting?"

"They're wilting because of me." A touch of sadness edged into Brigid's voice. "Because my work here is done."

"Your work?" Grace struggled to connect the dots. "What work?"

"My work as a mother." Brigid looked away. "All three of my sons have found the person they're meant to be with. There's nothing left for me to do."

Grace frowned. First of all, Aidan had *not* found the person he was meant to be with. Second of all, did Brigid think her only role as a mother was to marry off her sons? "There are plenty of things left for you to do. Even if Aidan *had* found the person he was meant to be with—which I assure you, he has not—he would still need his mother."

Brigid looked back at Grace. Her eyes held the same touch of sadness as her voice. "Sometimes, the best thing a mother can do for a child is let go."

"Let go? But you and Aidan just reconnected. Why would you let go now?"

"It's time for me to go home." Brigid's gaze dropped back to the basin at her feet. She wiggled her toes, marveling at the way they moved in the water. "I always knew it would happen someday."

Home, Grace thought. How could one word mean so many different things to so many people? "Seal Island doesn't feel like home anymore?"

"No."

"So, by 'home,' you mean...?"

Brigid's gaze lifted to the wall of glass, and beyond it, the wild, rolling sea.

Grace's heart sank. There was no doubt in her mind anymore what Brigid meant by home. "How do you know it's time?"

"It's been calling to me," Brigid said softly.

"You can't resist it anymore?"

Brigid shook her head. "I don't need to. Like I said, my work here is done."

"So...what? You're just giving up?"

"It's not a matter of giving up. It's about accepting something I always knew would happen someday. I was never supposed to spend this much time on land. I think I've been holding on all these years for Aidan, to know that he was okay." She looked away again. "I wish...I could have gotten to know him better. But

I can settle for knowing that he's okay. And knowing that, with you, he'll find happiness."

But he wasn't going to find happiness with her, Grace thought. If this was what Brigid was basing her decision on, she was making a big mistake. "You can't leave now. It's too soon."

"I don't have a choice."

"But you stayed before. Why can't you stay again?"

"I don't belong here anymore," Brigid said quietly.

She didn't *belong* here? How could she think that? Her family was here. Her friends were here. Her life was here.

The only person on this island who wouldn't be devastated to lose her was Aidan.

Wait.

Was that why Brigid didn't think she belonged?

Because Aidan hadn't accepted her yet?

"When, exactly, did you start feeling like you didn't belong anymore?" Grace asked.

Brigid looked down at her hands.

"Was it about three weeks ago?"

Brigid nodded slowly.

If Brigid wasn't going to be angry, then Grace would be angry for her. It was just as she'd suspected; Brigid had started to feel this way three weeks ago, right after her youngest son had arrived. She was breaking down because she thought she was losing him again. How was Aidan going to feel when he realized what he'd done? That he'd missed his one chance to reconnect with his mother? To have a family?

Would he even care?

"Forget about Aidan," Grace said. "Think about Neil. Think about Dominic and Liam. Think about Tara and Caitlin, and Glenna and Sam. Think about your grandchildren, and everyone else on this island who loves you. Don't you see how much pain you're going to cause them if you leave?"

Brigid reached into the basin and pulled out another shell. "He needs them more than they need me."

"Who? Aidan?"

Brigid nodded.

Grace felt another rush of anger. Aidan didn't need them. He didn't even believe he was related to them. As soon as he was healed, he would leave this island and never look back. But Brigid didn't know that. How could she know that when Aidan had been lying to her? "If you're doing this for Aidan, he doesn't deserve it."

"I have to do something."

"Why?"

"I'm his mother. I have to fix it."

"What, exactly, do you think you're going to fix by leaving?"

"I don't expect you to understand. But one day, when you have children of your own, you will."

"If I ever have children, the *last* thing I'm going to do is leave them."

Brigid winced.

Because this wasn't the first time she'd left her children, Grace remembered. And now she felt terrible. "I'm sorry. I said that without thinking. Aidan told me what happened earlier. I know you didn't mean to leave them before."

"It's okay," Brigid said, but her voice sounded smaller.

"It's not okay. I didn't mean to say that. I just..." Grace looked down. "I'm having a hard time with this..."

"Because your own mother left you when you were a child," Brigid finished for her.

Grace nodded.

"Glenna told me that's why you came here. That you were hoping to find out what happened."

Grace nodded again. Brigid wasn't the only one who wanted to fix things for her family. There was nothing Grace wanted more than to return to Heron Island with good news. To tell her father that he'd been wrong all these years. That his wife hadn't left because she'd fallen out of love with him; she'd left because she'd had no choice.

That was what Brigid was saying, wasn't she?

That no matter what, at some point, all selkies had to return to the sea?

"Do you think it's possible," Grace asked, "that my mother could be…like you?"

"Like me?"

"That she didn't belong here. And that, when she left, she didn't leave because she wanted to, she left because she didn't have a choice."

"Grace." Brigid's expression grew sad.

"It's possible, isn't it?" Grace asked, desperate to hold onto the tiny sliver of hope that could wash away so many years of pain, not just for herself, but for her father and brother, too.

When Brigid reached for her hand, Grace felt a rock form in the pit of her stomach.

"Your mother's not a selkie."

The rock grew heavier. "How do you know?"

"Because I overheard Glenna talking to Sam this morning."

"About…my mother?"

Brigid nodded. "Glenna knows who she is."

Grace pulled her hand free. "What?"

"She knows who she is," Brigid repeated. "And she's been in touch with her recently. She can tell you where to find her."

Grace felt the air in the room grow thin. Glenna had been in touch with her mother recently? How? Why? "I don't understand."

"I don't know why your mother left you, Grace," Brigid said gently. "But it wasn't to return to the sea."

# CHAPTER TWENTY-TWO

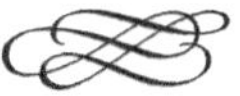

By the time Aidan made it to the village, his knee was throbbing. His head was pounding. The bandage on his shoulder had fallen off, and his flannel shirt was rubbing against the open wound. The physical pain was nothing, though, compared to the guilt he felt at what he had done.

Grace had been right. He *had* been using the O'Sullivans.

It had never occurred to him when he'd accepted Brigid's invitation that he would end up staying here for so long, or that he would actually end up liking any of these people. But he did. He liked them a lot. The O'Sullivans were good people. And they'd done nothing to deserve this.

He should have told them the truth as soon as he'd arrived. He wasn't sure why he hadn't. Maybe a part of him had wanted to remember what it felt like to belong to a family. To experience that closeness again. To feel the comfort of always having someone to talk with and laugh with, even if it was only temporary.

He'd been telling himself for years that he didn't need a family. And he'd walked away from anyone who'd gotten close, thinking he was doing them a favor so they wouldn't get attached. But maybe it was the other way around. Maybe *he* was the one who was afraid of getting attached. Maybe *he* was the one who was afraid of committing, because he couldn't bear the thought of losing someone he loved again.

How had Grace been able to see through him so quickly? Was it because they'd *both* been using work as a shield to protect themselves from ever having to experience that pain again? If so, was it possible she was the first person who'd ever truly understood him?

Before she'd arrived on this island, all he'd wanted was for his injuries to heal so he could get back to work. Now, as much as he still wanted that, it wasn't *all* he wanted. He wanted her, too. And he knew he couldn't have both.

He'd already tried that once and failed. Even if, as Grace had suggested the night before, he'd failed because he'd been with the wrong person, he didn't want to fail a second time, with Grace. He'd only met her a few days ago. How could he possibly know if *she* was the right person?

There were no guarantees. And he didn't want to hurt her if he decided, a few months from now, that he'd made a mistake. He couldn't do that to her, not after everything she'd been through. Besides, what kind of future could they have together if they were looking for two different lives? She had told him last night that she wanted to move back to Heron Island. She wanted to buy a house there and put down roots. She was even considering giving up her job for it.

He couldn't imagine staying in one place for the rest of his life. He'd been on the move for so long he'd forgotten what it felt like to have a home. Hell, he didn't even know where home was anymore. Whatever trail of breadcrumbs he might have left as a child had dried up and blown away years ago. He wouldn't even know what direction to turn if he wanted to find it.

So, where did that leave them?

He didn't know. The only thing he *did* know, at this point, was that he'd messed up, and he needed to fix it. First, he needed to come clean with Dominic and Liam. Then, he needed to find Grace and apologize. After that, he needed to go to Brigid's house to tell her what he'd told Dominic and Liam, and then he needed to apologize to her as well.

Hopefully, once she'd accepted the fact that he wasn't her son, she'd be able to relax. Neil had said that she'd been fine for years, that she'd only begun to regress *after* he'd arrived on the island. And Grace had already concluded that Brigid was breaking down because she was afraid of losing him again. If that was the case, the sooner she found out the truth, the better.

He hated to think he could be responsible for causing anyone that much pain. And he was ashamed, now, at the way he had treated her. She, like the rest of the O'Sullivans, had done nothing to deserve it. He just hoped that when all was said and done, he could persuade someone on this island to get her some help.

As a last resort, he knew a few trauma counselors he could put her in touch with. They mostly worked with survivors of violent conflicts, but one of them might make an exception in his case, as a favor. He wasn't going to leave this island until she'd agreed to speak with a professional who could help her see the truth beneath the story she'd created.

She hadn't grown up underwater. And she hadn't been next in line to be queen. He'd been wrong about a lot of things since coming here. But there was nothing anyone could say or do to convince him that Brigid was a selkie. She was having a mental breakdown. She was *not* transforming into a seal.

Grasping the cold brass handle of the door to the pub, he took a deep breath and pulled it open. It was still early, but Dominic usually came in around this time to do paperwork. Dominic wasn't the only one there, though. Liam was with him. They were standing together, at the end of the bar, their expressions devastated.

They said nothing as he made his way closer, but they moved to make room for him. As if he were one of them. As if he'd always been one of them.

When he spotted the sleek folds of brown leather in Dominic's arms, his brows drew together. "What is that?"

Dominic looked up, holding the bundle like it was the most precious thing in the world. "Our mother's pelt."

GRACE's whole body felt numb as she walked away from Brigid's house. She could hear the steady thump of her boots against the pavement and the sound of her breath moving in and out of her lungs, but she couldn't hear the ocean anymore. She couldn't hear the gulls, even when a flock of them passed by overhead. And she couldn't see the dark clouds gathering in the distance. Blindly following the switchbacks that led back to the village, all she could see was the face of the woman Sam had shown her on his phone.

Meredith Bradford.

Her mother's name was Meredith Bradford.

It hadn't been before. But it was now.

She'd changed it to become someone else. Someone who lived in Boston. Someone who owned an art gallery. Someone who wasn't married to a waterman on Heron Island.

Her father had been right. And so had Glenna. *'When a woman runs away from her husband, she doesn't want to be found.'*

Grace reached for the zipper on her jacket to close it. But she couldn't seem to figure out how it worked. Or maybe it was because her hands were shaking too hard. She clenched them into fists to get them to stop, but it only made them shake harder.

She'd waited for this moment for twenty-three years. She'd always known there was a chance that the truth would confirm her worst fears—that her mother had left them on purpose. She'd thought that she'd been ready for it.

She'd been wrong.

The wind shifted directions, and the cold air hit her like a slap in the face. How was she going to break this news to her father? How was she going to tell him that his wife was alive? That she'd been alive all this time?

How was she going to tell Ryan that whatever he'd seen in the cove that night must have been a coincidence? That there was nothing magical about their mother? That she'd left to start a new life because she hadn't wanted them?

The wind blew harder, whistling through the cracks in the stone walls. Why? Why hadn't she wanted them?

What had they done to drive her away?

When the road split, she turned right and kept walking until she came to the harbor. She kept her head down, not wanting to talk to anyone. If she could just make it back to her cottage and find a way to get the ground to stop spinning for two seconds, maybe she'd be able to breathe again.

"Whoa, there," someone said when she almost ran into them.

Grace reached out a hand to steady herself and found herself grasping the sleeve of Finn's salt-crusted jacket.

"Might want to have a look where you're going when you're walking that fast."

Had she been walking fast?

When she didn't let go right away, Finn's expression grew concerned. "Where're you off to in such a hurry, anyway?"

Grace took in the ferry captain's weathered face, the wooden pipe dangling from his cracked lips, and the pale, sun-washed eyes that reminded her so much of her own father's. "Boston."

"Boston?"

She nodded. She hadn't known where she was going until she'd said the name of the city out loud. But of course, that was where she was going.

She let go of Finn's jacket.

He stepped back and studied her for a few moments before adjusting the thick coil of rope slung over one of his shoulders. "I guess you'll be needing a ride, then."

A ride? "You can give me a ride to Boston?"

"No." Finn gave her an odd look. "But I can give you a ride to the mainland."

Right, she thought. The mainland. She needed to get to the mainland first.

"Are you feeling all right?" Finn asked.

No, Grace thought. She was not feeling all right. She was as far from all right as she'd ever been in her life. "I need to get my things."

Finn checked his watch. "We push off in ten minutes."

Grace nodded. Ten minutes would be tight, but she could make it if she rushed. "I'll be right back."

Finn gave her another odd look as she stepped around him and started up the hill to the village. She didn't have time to explain herself. She didn't need to either. There was only one person who owed anyone an explanation right now.

Flickers of anger began to burn through the shock as Grace climbed the hill. She let herself into the cottage, shoved her things into her pack, and walked back out, slamming the door behind her. There was no way she was going to let her mother get away with this. She didn't care how much it hurt to confront her. No one got to abandon their family and choose another life without having to face the damage they'd done.

"Grace?"

Without stopping, Grace glanced toward the voice that had called her name. She spotted Kelsey at the entrance to the footpath that led north to Glenna's studio.

Kelsey's gaze dropped to the pack Grace was holding. "Where are you going?"

"I'm leaving."

"What do you mean, you're leaving? You can't leave."

"I found her, Kelsey. She's not here." Grace kept walking. "There's no reason for me to stay anymore."

"Wait!" Kelsey ran after her. "You found your mother?"

"Yes."

"Where is she?"

"Boston."

"Is that where you're going?"

"Yes."

"But...what about us?"

"What about you?"

Kelsey stopped walking.

A few steps later, Grace stopped walking, too. She turned, took in the hurt expression on Kelsey's face, and let out a breath. "I'm sorry."

"You said you'd help us."

She'd said a lot of things the day before, Grace thought. Before she'd known the truth. Before she'd seen that picture on Sam's phone. Before she'd realized what a fool she'd been for thinking that her own mother could be a selkie. She'd wanted a happy ending so badly, she'd let herself get swept up in the fairy tale. But that was the problem with fairy tales. They made you believe in things that weren't real.

Aidan had been right. There was no magic. There was only reality. And holding onto false hope for a happy ending had done nothing to dull the shock of finding out the truth. If anything, it had made it worse. Real life wasn't a fairy tale. Real life was hard. Real life was going to knock you down over and over again. And the sooner you learned how to deal with those setbacks and pull yourself back up, the better.

Digging into the pocket of her jeans, Grace pulled out the handful of petals she'd been carrying with her for the past two days and handed them to Kelsey. "Take these. I don't want them."

As soon as she saw the petals, Kelsey's expression grew stricken. "They're all faded."

"They're petals," Grace said flatly. "That's what they do."

It was the same thing Aidan had said to her earlier. She hadn't been able to see the truth then, but she could see it so clearly now. The ferry horn bellowed, signaling it was time to leave. Grace turned and started to walk toward the harbor again.

"It's my grandmother, isn't it?" Kelsey asked from behind her. "I overheard my father talking to Uncle Liam on the phone earlier. He said something was wrong with her."

Something was definitely wrong with Brigid. But it wasn't what Grace had thought before. She didn't know what to think anymore. When Kelsey ran to catch up with her, Grace chose her words carefully. "Your grandmother wasn't feeling well this morning. She's doing better now."

"What happened?"

"You should ask your mother. She was there."

"I can't ask my mother." Kelsey cast a worried glance back at the village. "She thinks I'm on my way to school."

Right, Grace thought. Kelsey and Owen had planned to skip school today because they thought something terrible was going to happen to someone they loved. She didn't know how to rationalize what had happened the last three times roses had mysteriously appeared on this island. And she had no idea why it was happening again. But none of those things were her problem anymore.

The only problem she was willing to take on, right now, was making sure that Kelsey and Owen's parents knew they were safe. She'd ask Finn to give Tara and Liam a call as soon as they'd made it out of the harbor. "Where's Owen?"

"He's on his way to our grandmother's house." Kelsey stole another worried glance back toward the village. "I stayed to make sure the ferry left without us."

Grace nodded. It wouldn't hurt for the kids to skip a day of school to spend time with their grandmother. Maybe having them around would help Brigid relax "You should go before anyone sees you."

"It won't matter if anyone sees me if you leave." They were almost to the entrance to the pier, and Kelsey was still glued to her side. "We can't do this without you."

"Do what?"

"Stop whatever's about to happen." Kelsey held the petals up. "We're almost out of time!"

"Those petals don't have anything to do with me."

"Of course, they do," Kelsey protested. "They led you here— to Aidan. They wanted you to find each other."

"Oh, come on," Grace said, exasperated. "Not you, too."

"If you leave instead of following them, something bad is going to happen, just like in your friend's dream."

"What? I'll stumble across a gingerbread cottage and be eaten by a witch?"

"No," Kelsey said, frustrated. "You're not supposed to read the connection that literally."

"How *am* I supposed to read it?"

"You need to look beneath the story to the deeper meaning," Kelsey said. "The rose petals are your breadcrumbs. They're leading you home, to safety. If you don't follow them, you're going to get lost. Don't be drawn further into the forest. You're being lured there by someone who's going to hurt you—someone who's not as she seems."

Grace knew exactly who she'd been lured in by recently, and it hadn't been a 'she.' If the petals were supposed to be a warning to stay away from someone, they should have been warning her to stay away from Aidan. "My home is in Maryland."

"What if you're wrong?" Kelsey asked. "What if your home isn't a place at all? What if it's a person? What if it's Aidan?"

Grace felt another flicker of anger. "Aidan is *not* my home, and he is *not* my soulmate."

"How do you know?"

"Because I've only known him for three days!"

"So?"

"You're sixteen, Kelsey. I know it feels like love is the most important thing in the world right now, but it's not."

"What could possibly be more important than love?"

Turning, Grace shouldered her pack and stepped onto the pier. "The truth."

# CHAPTER TWENTY-THREE

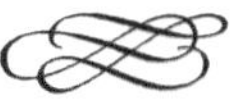

*N*o, Aidan thought. It couldn't be. But if that wasn't a pelt, what was it? "Where did you get that?"

"Sam found it," Liam answered. "About seven years ago, when he first started looking for our mother."

Aidan couldn't take his eyes off the bundle in Dominic's arms. "Where?"

"At our old house in Dublin," Liam said. "It was behind a wall, hidden beneath a few layers of insulation."

"And you're sure it's..."

Dominic held it out to him.

Aidan hesitated, then reached for it. The moment his hands grasped the leathery folds, the room began to pulse. He could hear the ocean. Like a heartbeat. Inside him. All around him. He felt a sudden urge to go down to it. To wade into it. To keep going until his body was submerged.

He pushed the bundle back toward Dominic.

Dominic took it slowly. "We're sure."

"I-I don't...understand," Aidan stammered. "H-how is this possible?"

"I know it's a lot to take in," Dominic said. "It's one thing to hear the stories. It's another to see it with your own eyes."

Aidan stared down at the pelt. Because that was what it was —a pelt. He couldn't deny it anymore. Dominic was holding Brigid's sealskin in his arms. And if that part of her story was true, what else was true?

Unable to help himself, he reached out to touch the pelt again, but stopped when he noticed there were several spots where the fur was missing. In each spot, the skin appeared rough and discolored. "What are those?"

"Scars," Dominic said.

Aidan moved closer to get a better look. The skin had been stretched and pulled together with what might have been stitches. "From what?"

Dominic brushed a protective hand over his mother's sealskin. "Cigarette burns."

"Who would...?"

"Our father," Dominic said.

Aidan looked up at Dominic, then at Liam. Remembering the way Brigid had shied away from him that morning when he'd tried to wrap his coat around her, he felt his stomach twist. In all the selkie stories he'd read the day before, there'd been a man who'd stolen the selkie's pelt, trapped her on land, and mistreated her.

Brigid had said, in the letter she'd written to him, that a man had stolen her pelt and hidden it from her. She hadn't said anything about him hurting her, but maybe that wasn't something she'd wanted to put in a letter. Maybe that was something she'd wanted to tell him face to face.

He hadn't given her a chance, though, had he? He'd hardly spent any time with her at all.

"You should have seen it when Sam first brought it to us,"

Liam said. "It wasn't just the cigarette burns. It was torn and cracked in places from years of drying out behind that wall."

Aidan looked back at the scars. "How did you...?"

"Tara," Dominic said.

Of course, Aidan thought. Tara had stitched up the wounds. She'd been taking care of Brigid the same way she'd been taking care of him and everyone else on the island. Why had he felt the need to give her such a hard time? It wasn't just guilt he felt, now. It was shame.

"She's been keeping it oiled all these years in case..." Dominic trailed off.

"In case our mother ever needed it again," Liam finished for him.

Aidan fought the urge to reach out and touch it again. "Does she know you have this?"

"She knows," Dominic said.

"How long has she known?"

"We told her the day she got here," Dominic said. "We would never have kept it from her if she'd asked for it."

"But that would have been over seven years ago," Aidan said. "Why hasn't she asked for it until now?"

Liam exchanged a look with Dominic. "I think she's been waiting."

"For what?"

"For you."

Aidan drew in a breath.

"I think she wanted to find you first," Liam went on, "to make sure you were okay."

It was only a theory, Aidan thought. But what if Liam was right? What if this *was* all about him?

Brigid had been fine before he'd gotten here. Neil had said that she'd only begun to regress three or four weeks ago. And

Kelsey had said that whenever roses appeared on this island, it meant someone's time was running out.

What if he was the one who'd set this ticking clock in motion?

"When I think about how angry I was at her for so many years..." Dominic shook his head. "I can't believe I ever thought she abandoned us. I should have known better. I should have known something must have happened."

That something, according to Brigid, was that she'd given birth to a child who'd been stolen from her, then she'd been institutionalized, where the grief of losing that child, the panic at being separated from her other two children, and the drugs she'd been forced to take had slowly eroded her sanity.

Aidan hadn't wanted to believe it before. He hadn't been *able* to believe it. Because as far-fetched as that part of her story was, it wasn't nearly as hard to accept as the idea that she might be a selkie—and that magic did, in fact, exist in this world. He'd put that wall up to keep himself from having to believe the rest of the story. But if he let that wall come down, then he had to accept the possibility that the rest of her story might be true.

Which meant...

He looked up at Dominic. Then at Liam. He'd come here to apologize, to tell them that he wasn't related to them, and that he'd been using them ever since he'd arrived. But he couldn't find the words. He couldn't seem to speak at all anymore. All he could hear was Grace's voice, over and over, in his head: *'The resemblance is unmistakable.'*

She was right. It was unmistakable. He hadn't wanted to see it, or admit it, before. But it was right there. It had been there all along. Dominic and Liam were his brothers.

And if Dominic and Liam were his brothers, then Brigid was...

"Is this really all we get?" Dominic's gaze dropped to the pelt. "Seven years?"

"I feel like we just found her," Liam said, his tone as heart-broken as his brother's.

No, Aidan thought. They hadn't just found her. They'd had her for seven years. And he could have had her, too, if he hadn't ignored every attempt the O'Sullivans had made to reach out to him.

Why couldn't he have returned one of their calls or responded to one of their emails? Why had he waited so long to come here? What was wrong with him?

He could hear Grace's voice in his head again: *'What are you so afraid of?'*

He'd shut down, earlier, when she'd asked him that. Because the question hadn't just struck a nerve. It had cut to the very core of his identity. At eight years old, he'd become a child no one had wanted. No one had ever come close to adopting him after his parents had died. And there was only one lens through which he'd been able to see the world after that—one where no one else would ever want him again.

He'd built a life around that belief. And he'd found a way to cope by burying himself in work and forcing people to see *other* children throughout the world who found themselves in the same position. So no one would forget that they were there and that they mattered.

But it wasn't just about them, was it? It was about him, too. He was the one holding the camera. And behind every single shot he took was a scared little boy crying out to be seen.

What if he could put down that lens and pick up a new one? What if, instead of working so hard to prove to the world that he mattered, he could just accept that he *did* matter? And that the only thing the people on this island had been trying to do since he arrived was show him that?

He looked back down at his mother's pelt. If *he* was the one who'd set this ticking clock in motion, then he needed to be the one to stop it. There was no way he was going to let his mother leave the island. Not now. Not until he'd done everything in his power to convince her to stay.

"Dad!" Kelsey pushed into the pub. Her cheeks were flushed, and she was breathing hard.

Dominic handed the pelt to Liam, who tucked it out of sight. "Kelsey, what are you doing here? Why aren't you on the ferry?"

As soon as she made it across the room to where they stood, she held out her hand and opened her palm. "Look."

It was the rose petals, Aidan realized. Or at least, what was left of them. They were all dried out. The edges were curling in on themselves. Some of them were beginning to crumble.

"Where did you get those?" Liam asked.

"Grace gave them to me." Kelsey looked at Aidan, her expression dismayed. "Right before she left."

"What?" Aidan asked. "What do you mean, 'she *left*?'"

"She left on the ferry. I tried to stop her…" Kelsey trailed off when Liam leaned closer to look at the petals, and she spotted the pelt on the stool beside him. "Is that…?" Her eyes widened. "Is that what I think it is?"

The phone rang. All three of them looked at Dominic. No one spoke a word as he moved to answer it.

Several moments later, Dominic hung up. "That was Tara. Neil just called. He said it's time." He walked out from behind the bar and held out a hand to Kelsey. "I told them we'd meet them there."

"Where?" Aidan asked.

"The beach."

Aidan turned as the others started towards the door. "What beach?"

"The one next to your cottage," Dominic said, then looked at his daughter. "And, yes, that's what you think it is."

THE AIR FELT thick and heavy. She tried to breathe, to draw it into her lungs. But she couldn't get enough of it. Every attempt produced a strange whistling sound at the base of her throat.

Dark clouds rolled in, blotting out the sun. Rain spat from the sky. Halfway across the beach, she stepped out of her shoes. And left them there. She wouldn't be needing them again.

Brigid gripped Neil's hand as she made her way closer to the sea. She hadn't wanted him to be here for this. She hadn't wanted anyone to be here.

She had planned to leave tonight, after everyone fell asleep. She hadn't wanted them to see her like this—to see her breaking down again. She'd broken down in front of them enough.

All she wanted was to slip away.

To relieve them of their burden.

But she hadn't been able to catch her breath since Grace had left the island. She'd felt it—the moment the ferry had pulled away from the dock. The same way she'd felt Glenna's banishment spell the night before.

Grace and Aidan belonged together. They needed each other. She had tried to help them see that. But she'd failed.

She'd failed at everything.

"They're here," Glenna said softly from beside her.

At the edge of the sea, with Neil on one side and Glenna on the other, Brigid turned. Her heart constricted at the sight of her three sons walking toward her. She wished she could run to them. To gather them up in her arms. To tell them how sorry she was for everything. But she could barely walk on her own anymore, let alone run.

"My pelt," she wheezed. "I need my pelt."

"They have it," Glenna said.

She saw it then, the dark bundle in Liam's arms. A wave of

relief rolled through her. Soon, she'd be able to breathe again. She started to reach for it. But Glenna and Neil were still holding her hands. And they wouldn't let go.

They were going to need to let go soon.

She drew in another ragged breath as she watched her sons come closer, imprinting the memory in her mind. Dominic, her eldest, her protector. Liam, her middle child, her dreamer. And Aidan, her youngest. The one who would never forgive her.

She wished...

No, it didn't matter anymore. Aidan could stay angry with her forever, as long as he had his brothers.

Except...he didn't look angry anymore. He looked...

She blinked. Her eyes felt dry and gritty, like they were filled with sand.

Was he trying to say something? His mouth was moving, but she couldn't hear what he was saying. All she could hear was the rush of the ocean in her ears.

She looked back at her pelt. Prying her hand free from Glenna's, Brigid reached for it. But instead of holding it out to her, Liam stopped walking. And so did Dominic. The only one who didn't was Aidan. He kept moving, limping toward her. Until he was right in front of her. She felt a moment of panic when she realized he was blocking her view of the pelt. Then she stopped breathing altogether.

Because his arms had come around her. And he was holding her like he couldn't bear to let her go.

Brigid stood frozen, rooted to the sand. He was hugging her. Aidan was hugging her. He'd never hugged her before. He'd never been affectionate with her at all. She'd thought...he hated her.

Neil released her hand. Unable to keep herself from touching her son any longer, Brigid lifted her arms. She braced herself, expecting him to pull away. But he didn't. He kept holding her, as if she were someone who meant a great deal to him.

Behind her, the sea crept closer. With every wave that crashed, water rushed over the tops of her feet. She could hear it calling to her. But it wasn't the only thing she could hear anymore.

Aidan's voice was breaking through. It was muffled. She could only catch a few words at a time. And none of them made any sense.

"I'm sorry. I'm so sorry. Please forgive me."

Forgive him? Forgive him for what? If anyone needed forgiveness, it was—

"I didn't believe you before. I didn't want to believe you. I wouldn't let myself see the truth."

The truth? What truth? What was he saying?

"Please, don't go."

He didn't want her to go? Until this moment, he'd wanted nothing to do with her. She pulled back and looked up at him. His eyes were desperate, as lost and vulnerable as a child's.

"I need you."

He...needed her? "Why?"

"Because you're my mother. And I didn't know that until today."

Brigid stared at him. He hadn't known that she was his mother? How could he not have known that?

They'd reached out to him over seven years ago. They'd been trying to get him to come here ever since.

*'I didn't believe you before. I didn't want to believe you. I wouldn't let myself see the truth.'*

Suddenly, all his words began to make sense. And so did all his actions over the past few weeks. He hadn't been rejecting her. He hadn't even thought they were related. "You didn't believe me."

"No," Aidan said. "I thought... It doesn't matter what I thought. All that matters now is that you stay. Please. I need you to stay. We all do."

"I don't know if I can," she said, her voice raspy and strained.

"We won't ask you to if you can't." Liam stepped forward with her pelt. "This is yours. It's always been yours." He held it out to her. "But if you *can* stay—if you *do* have a choice—Aidan's right. We need you."

They needed her? Brigid's gaze shifted from Liam to Dominic. All three of her sons were adults. They weren't children anymore. And even when they had been, they'd been on their own, without her, for years. What could they possibly need her for?

More water spilled over her feet. It was up to her ankles now. She could taste the salt on her lips, feel the spray of it on her legs. She let go of Aidan and reached for her pelt. As soon as her fingers brushed the soft fur, her heart began to pound. She remembered the feeling of weightlessness, the freedom of being able to breathe underwater, the thrill of diving into the cold, comforting depths of the sea.

All she had to do was step backwards, sink into it.

"Wait," a small voice said.

It was Freya. She was standing on the beach, clutching Maeve's hand. Brigid hugged her pelt to her chest. What were the twins doing here? They shouldn't be here for this.

Freya took a step forward. "We need you, too."

No, Brigid thought. They had their own mother. And if they ever needed anyone else, they had Tara and Glenna. They didn't need her, too.

"We need you to help us finish our fairy gardens," Freya said.

A lump formed in Brigid's throat.

"And we need more dust so we can heal Uncle Aidan," Maeve said.

Brigid squeezed her pelt. Neil could help them with that. He could manage without her, couldn't he?

"My children need their grandmother," Caitlin said softly from behind the twins. "And I need you to teach me how to be a mother."

Teach her how to be a mother? Another wave crashed, closer this time, scattering a handful of tiny shells over the sand. "You're five times the mother than I ever was," Brigid said, forcing the words past the lump in her throat.

"How can you say that?" Glenna asked from beside her.

Brigid turned to look at her niece.

Glenna's expression was incredulous. "You've been a mother to me my entire life."

Brigid shook her head. "Mothers take care of people. I never took care of you. You took care of me."

"And in return, you gave me love. Unconditional love. Something I never got from my own mother."

What was Glenna saying? That, to be a mother, all you had to do was love unconditionally? That couldn't be right.

From her spot on the sand between Kelsey and Dominic, Tara spoke up. "My mother was my best friend. But she passed away a long time ago. And I never thought anyone would ever love me like that again. Until I met you. You accepted me instantly, as if I were your own daughter by blood, not someone who'd married into your family."

Of course, she'd accepted her, Brigid thought. It didn't matter if they were bonded by blood or by vows. All that mattered was that Tara loved her son. She would have treated Grace the same way if...

Brigid closed her eyes as a rush of guilt swept through her. Grace had been so upset when she'd left the house that morning after Sam had shown her the picture of her mother. She wished, now, that she hadn't said anything. She wished that she'd kept the truth to herself.

*She* was the reason Grace had left.

How many more mistakes could she make before her family realized they were better off without her?

The sea swirled around her ankles, spitting up foam. Letting out a shaky breath, she opened her eyes. And this time, when the water began to recede, she took a step back.

Neil stepped back with her.

It was still raining, but those weren't raindrops on his face. Those were tears. She'd never seen him cry before. Not until today. When she thought of what she was about to do to him, it broke her heart.

"I need you," he said quietly.

"You don't need me. You don't need anyone."

"I've needed you from the moment I laid eyes on you. I will never stop needing you. And I will never stop loving you." He held out his hand. "Please, don't go."

"It's too late." Her fingers dug into her pelt. "I don't have a choice."

Neil kept his arm outstretched to her. "I think you do."

"I think you do, too," Aidan said. "I think you're leaving because of me. Because of the way I've been treating you since I got here, and the way I ignored all your attempts to connect with me for the past seven years. I'll never forgive myself for all the pain that I've caused you. And I promise to do everything in my power to make it up to you from now on. But to do that, you need to stay."

*Stay.*

He wanted her to stay. They all did. She had thought that leaving would be for the best. She had thought that she'd become a burden to all of them. But how could she leave if they needed her?

Wasn't that all she'd ever wanted—to be needed?

Wasn't that all anyone wanted?

She looked down at her pelt, then back up at her youngest son. She'd already left him once. The first time, she hadn't had a choice. What if, this time, she *did* have a choice? What if she chose to stay?

She could still hear the ocean pulsing in her ears. She could still feel it casting its net around her, each wave that receded like hands on a rope hauling her back. But she could hear her own thoughts again. She could hear the voices of the people around her. And her throat wasn't making that strange whistling sound anymore.

She took a breath, then another.

She had always assumed that she would have to go back one day. She had never considered the possibility that she might be able to stay on land for the rest of her life. She had thought it was a rule.

A rule of magic that couldn't be broken.

But maybe she'd been wrong. Maybe the *only* rule that couldn't be broken was that love was the strongest magic of all.

Releasing her grip on the pelt, she reached for Neil's hand.

He pulled her into his arms. Before she knew what was happening, her whole family was surrounding her. Embracing her. Crying tears of relief as they led her away from the water and onto the soft, dry sand.

She didn't know how long she held each of them. But with every embrace, her breathing came easier. Her thoughts grew clearer. Behind her, the roar of the ocean began to fade. Until all she could hear was the comforting murmur of waves washing over the shore.

When she came face to face with Glenna, she lifted her pelt. "I want you to keep this for me, somewhere safe, in case I ever need it again."

"You won't need it," Glenna said. "You belong here. With us. With your family."

She took it anyway, though. And Brigid felt another weight lift as soon as it was out of sight. Turning, she found Aidan at her side.

"I'm so sorry," he said again, "about everything."

"You don't need to apologize."

"I do," he said, then looked around at the others. "I owe all of you an apology."

That could come later, Brigid thought. She took his hand. "I need you to do something for me."

"Anything."

"You promised me earlier that if Grace left, you'd go after her."

"Yes, but—"

She squeezed his hand. "You need to go after her now."

"Now?"

Brigid nodded.

"I'm not leaving you." Aidan shook his head. "Besides, I don't know where she went, and it might take her a while to respond to my messages. She's not very happy with me at the moment."

"She's going to Boston to find her mother," Kelsey said.

"I figured as much." Glenna exchanged a tense look with Sam, then shifted her attention to Aidan. "I agree with Brigid. You need to go now. Sam will give you the name and address of the woman she's going to find. One of the fishermen can give you a ride to the mainland."

Aidan looked at Brigid.

"I'm not going anywhere." Brigid put a hand on his cheek. "Go get her and bring her back."

# CHAPTER TWENTY-FOUR

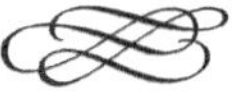

*B*oston was beautiful in every season, but autumn brought its own special kind of magic. The air was filled with falling leaves, floating down in various shades of red and gold. The sidewalks were packed with locals and tourists wrapped up in coats and scarves. In the afternoons, many of them would make their way down Newbury Street, their laughter spilling from one shop to the next as they searched for something to buy. When night fell, as it did earlier and earlier these days, the flames from the gas lamps would flicker to life, casting a warm glow over the historic brownstones that lined the residential streets of Back Bay—the neighborhood Meredith Bradford had called home for the past thirteen years.

"Another glass of Prosecco, Ms. Bradford?"

"Yes, thank you, Charles." She smiled up at the waiter, a silver-haired man who doted on her the same way every waiter in this neighborhood did. While others might have to wait hours for a table at one of the many wildly popular cafés, bakeries, and restaurants in this part of the city, Meredith never had to wait.

It was one of the many perks of being a Bradford.

"And for you?" The waiter turned toward the young woman seated across from Meredith.

"I'll have another Italian soda," Phoebe Bradford said. "Vanilla, this time."

"Right away." The waiter disappeared, leaving the two of them alone.

Phoebe looked down at her glass, a thin line forming between her brows as she tapped her straw nervously against the ice in her glass. An untouched piece of tiramisu sat in front of her. "Are you sure I picked the right dress?"

"I'm sure," Meredith said. "Here." She picked up her fork and held it out to her stepdaughter. "You need to eat something before the party tonight."

Phoebe let go of the straw and took the fork, but she couldn't seem to make herself use it yet. Meredith sat back, knowing it was only a matter of time before she took a bite. They'd been through this a thousand times before. Phoebe always lost her appetite when she was nervous. And so did her father. Whenever either of them got stressed, she brought them here, to their favorite bakery.

No matter how upset they were, they could always stomach something sweet.

Phoebe touched the fork to the dusting of cocoa powder on top of her dessert, then stopped. Her brown eyes widened, as if the worst thought had just occurred to her. "What if someone else picked the same dress?"

"They didn't," Meredith said calmly. "We went to Eden, remember? Jennifer doesn't carry anything that anyone else does. It's one of a kind. Also, that dress just arrived this morning. No one else would have had a chance to buy it yet, even if they wanted it."

"But what if—"

Meredith reached out and covered her stepdaughter's free

hand. "Jennifer put the rest of the sizes away when you were in the dressing room, after we saw how beautiful it looked on you. She said she wouldn't bring them out again until tomorrow."

"Really?"

"Of course," Meredith said. "I didn't even have to ask." As someone who spent tens of thousands of dollars in that store each month, she was used to getting preferential treatment. But Phoebe wouldn't have had anything to worry about even if Jennifer hadn't put the rest of the sizes in the back. Most college-age women didn't have $1200 to spend on a dress. And most parents weren't willing to spend that much on an outfit for a sorority rush party.

Fortunately for Phoebe, her parents were. And they both believed that she was more than worth it. Now, if they could only convince Phoebe to have that same faith in herself. "Just be yourself." Meredith squeezed her hand. "Everyone will love you."

Phoebe took a deep breath. "What if they don't invite me to join?"

"They will."

"They only pick twenty girls each year."

"And you'll be one of them."

"I've been to all the other sororities' events. I didn't like any of them as much as I liked this one."

"I know."

"It's got to be *this* one," Phoebe said. "It's the only one I want to be in."

"You'll get in."

"How can you be so sure?"

"Because you're a Bradford."

Phoebe's lips curved. The name gave her pride as well. And why shouldn't it? Her father was one of the wealthiest and most well-respected men in Boston. Phoebe touched her fork to her dessert again, slicing into it this time. "I *do* love the dress."

"It's perfect." Meredith released her hand. "It looks like it was made for you."

"And the shoes." Phoebe took a bite of the tiramisu, then glanced at the two boxes of Louboutins sitting on the chair beside her. "You didn't need to buy both colors."

"You couldn't decide," Meredith reminded her. "You can try both on later at home. It'll be easier to choose then."

Phoebe brightened. "Maybe Dad can help."

"I'm sure he'd love to help." Meredith smiled, knowing he would. "And so would your brother." Phoebe's older brother, Josh, doted on her almost as much as her father did. The two men had been out golfing together all day. They were probably at the club now, having a drink at the bar and making connections that would pave the way for a smooth transition when Josh took over his father's company one day.

Meredith loved how close they were, how involved they all were in each other's lives. That bond had formed years ago, after Phoebe and Josh's mother had died. The loss had brought the three of them together in a way that only a tragedy could.

It brought her comfort to know that her own children had likely formed a similar bond with their father after she'd left. It had helped ease the guilt she'd felt from time to time over the years. Not that she'd ever regretted her decision to leave. It hadn't been the life she'd wanted. She'd tried it on for a while, tried to make it fit. But in the end, it hadn't fit. So, she'd left.

She'd tried to do it in a way that would cause the least amount of pain to everyone. She'd never meant to hurt any of them. Her first husband had been a good man. A kind man. He'd treated her well—far better than any other man in her life up until that point, including her own father.

She had met Coop Callahan at a restaurant in Baltimore in the early '80s. She'd been working as a waitress, and he'd come in with a few friends to sit at the bar. While his friends had proceeded to get drunk, Coop had nursed the same beer all night. Every time she'd come to the bar to retrieve a drink for one of her tables, he'd asked her a question. After a while, she'd asked him a few back. They'd talked about where he was from and how much he loved working on the water. The image he'd painted of Heron Island had been charming.

Her life, back then, had been anything but charming.

When he'd asked for her number at the end of the night, she'd given it to him. When he'd called the next day and asked her to visit him the following weekend, she'd said, yes. When she'd driven out to the island for the first time, and he'd offered to take her for a ride on his boat, she'd said, yes, to that, too. She'd never been out on the water before. And it had been the closest thing she'd ever felt to freedom.

Afterwards, he'd shown her his house—a blue bungalow on a quiet, tree-lined street, only a block away from the pier where he'd kept his boat. It had needed some work. But it had seemed so much nicer than the rundown apartment she'd been sharing with three other women in the city. So, she'd told him she'd loved it. And the boat. And everything about the day they'd spent together.

He'd kissed her, then. And for the next six months, he'd been persistent in his courtship. She'd enjoyed spending time with him. She'd enjoyed the attention he gave her. And she'd even fancied herself in love for a time. When he'd asked her to marry him, though, it had caught her off guard. She hadn't expected him to propose so soon. Without really thinking, she'd said, yes.

A few weeks later, they'd been living together. Before the end of the year, they'd been married. Six weeks after their wedding night, they'd found out she was pregnant—with not one child, but two. And seven-and-a-half months later, she'd given birth to twins.

It had all happened so fast.

The day they'd brought the twins home from the hospital, the full reality of her situation had hit her. And suddenly, nothing had seemed charming anymore. The twins' needs had been endless. She hadn't been able to keep up with the messes in the house, no matter how hard she'd tried. She'd lost so much sleep those first few months, she hadn't even been able to think straight.

Coop had left the house each day before sunrise to scrape out a meager living for them on the water—a living which had barely been enough for two people, let alone four. It hadn't mattered how hard he'd worked. With each year that passed, the harvests had grown smaller. When other watermen his age had begun to move away in search of better opportunities on the mainland, she'd tried to convince him that they should leave, too. But he'd refused.

She had given up trying after a while. And had begun to consider how she might leave alone.

She'd contemplated divorce. But divorce would have been too messy. She and Coop would have had to hire lawyers. They would have had to answer questions about custody. She would have had to sign a document saying she didn't want her children. And something like that could haunt a woman for the rest of her life.

Women weren't supposed to choose themselves over their children. They were supposed to be selfless. They were supposed to sacrifice everything for their families, no matter what.

At least, that's what she'd thought.

One day, when the twins had been in school, she'd gone to the library to find a book to read. She'd told the librarian she'd wanted something with magic in it, as far from reality as possible. The librarian had given her a stack of books to try, then she'd added a thin, spiral-bound volume to the top of the stack. She'd said it was a collection of local tales she'd put together herself, and that there were a few folktales in it she might enjoy.

Enjoy had been an understatement

When she'd read the story about the selkie who'd left her husband and children to return to the sea, she'd realized—for the first time since becoming a mother—that she hadn't been alone. That there'd been other women, like her, who'd dreamed of a different life. Whoever had written that tale had given that dream a voice. And that voice had spoken to her, in a way that nothing else ever had.

All she'd been able to think about, after that, was how to escape. How could she do what the woman in that tale had done? She'd read it over and over, obsessively, searching for a clue. And when her children had crawled into her lap, she'd read it to them, too. She hadn't realized, then, what she'd been preparing them for—that her obsession with the tale, and with selkies, in general, would provide the perfect cover for her disappearance one day.

It had been genius, really.

And so much kinder than divorce.

When her son had woken her up in the middle of the night, a few years later, to tell her what he'd seen and heard in Pearl Cove, it had taken her a moment to understand what he'd been saying. He'd been talking fast, barely able to contain his excitement. Her favorite story wasn't a folktale, he'd said—it was real. He'd tried to convince her to come back to the cove with him so he could show her. And that was when it had clicked.

Her son believed in magic.

He believed that selkies were real.

What if she could make him believe that *she* was a selkie?

She would need to find a way to disappear. She would never be able to see her children again. But if she could pull it off, in time, the only conclusion they'd be able to draw was that she'd been magical, too.

Wouldn't it be better for them to think that she'd left them to return to the sea rather than know the truth? Of course, it would be. They didn't need to know that she hadn't wanted them. That she hadn't wanted to be their mother. That marrying their father had been a mistake.

She would need to act fast, though, so she'd told her son to get some rest and assured him they'd talk more in the morning. As soon as he'd fallen asleep, she'd pocketed the few hundred dollars in cash that she'd secretly stashed away over the years and walked out the door.

She'd walked for hours, slipping into the woods along the side of the road whenever she'd spotted a car in the distance, which hadn't been often. When she'd finally come to the next town, it had been close to dawn. Two food delivery trucks had been parked outside a row of restaurants. One had been a produce truck—refrigerated. The other had been filled with bread. She'd waited until the driver of the bread truck had wheeled his final load into the restaurant, then she'd climbed into the back and hid herself behind a crate. The driver had come out a few minutes later. He'd pulled the door shut and climbed behind the wheel.

By the time the sun had risen that morning, they'd been halfway to a distribution center on the outskirts of Baltimore. Getting out of the truck had been almost as easy as getting in. As soon as the driver had opened the door, a colleague had called him over to chat. While he'd been distracted, she'd climbed out and made her way to the nearest convenience store. There, she'd bought sunglasses, scissors, hair dye, and a sweatshirt. In the bathroom, she'd changed her appearance.

And when she'd walked outside again, she'd been someone else.

Her life, after that, had been a series of transformations, of shedding one identity for another until she'd found what she'd been looking for. What she'd been meant for. What she'd deserved.

She hadn't realized, when Noah Bradford had walked into

the gallery where she'd been working ten years ago, that *he* was what she'd been looking for all along. She'd never intended to marry again. She hadn't wanted to make the same mistake she'd made with Coop. And when she'd found out that Noah had children, she'd almost written him off.

She hadn't thought she'd been cut out for motherhood.

As it turned out, she'd been wrong.

It wasn't motherhood, in general, that she hadn't been cut out for. It was motherhood like *that*. Once she'd met Phoebe and Josh, she'd realized that motherhood could be different than what she'd experienced the first time around. It could actually be wonderful.

Meredith looked at Phoebe, who was still chatting happily about the upcoming rush party. She took in her stepdaughter's shiny brown hair, her flawless skin, and bright-white smile. She thought of the fancy Ivy League education she was getting, and the designer clothes she'd be wearing tonight—clothes that Meredith had paid for and helped pick out.

*This*, she thought, was exactly what motherhood was supposed to be.

~

THERE WERE moments in a person's life that changed them forever. Moments they could never come back from. For Grace, this was one of those moments.

She'd been at the bakery for the past twenty minutes, standing in line, waiting to get in. Her mother was seated on the patio, on the other side of a row of miniature boxwoods covered in twinkle lights, only a few feet away. Her back was to her, but Grace had heard every word of the conversation she'd just had with Phoebe Bradford.

Her mother had a stepdaughter. A stepdaughter she loved. A

stepdaughter she was proud of. A stepdaughter whose life she wanted to be in.

Grace hadn't just been discarded. She'd been replaced.

It wasn't like she hadn't known that before she'd arrived in Boston. She'd had a seven-hour flight to read all about her mother's new life. She'd read about her wealthy husband, her two perfect stepchildren, her beautiful home overlooking the Charles River, and her art gallery on Newbury Street. But reading about her mother's new life had been different than seeing it in person.

She thought she'd been ready to confront her when she'd walked into the art gallery, thinking she might find her there. But when one of her employees had pointed to the bakery across the street, and Grace had gotten the first glimpse of the woman who'd left her twenty-three years ago, she'd lost her nerve. She'd needed a moment to catch her breath, to think about what she was going to say.

She still didn't know.

All she knew was that she felt sick, like someone had force-fed her too much sugar. When a waitress came over and offered her a seat at the bar, Grace shook her head. The bar was too far away. She either needed a table on the patio, or she was going to have to walk out there without one.

The elderly waiter returned with Meredith and Phoebe's drinks. Grace could hear Meredith chatting with him like they were old friends. The waiter said something back, which Grace couldn't make out, but it must have been funny, because all three of them laughed.

How could she be sitting there, living her life, like nothing had happened? Like everything was fine?

Phoebe's phone lit up and she looked at the screen.

"It's Lauren," Phoebe said. "She and Gaby just got a table at Bean Rush. Can I go say, hi?"

"Of course, sweetie." Meredith picked up her glass of Prosecco and leaned back in her chair. "Take your time."

Phoebe's chair scraped against the bricks as she stood. She gave her stepmother a quick kiss on the cheek, then slipped through an opening between two elevated planters and disappeared down the street.

The wind snatched a leaf from a nearby maple tree. It spun to the ground in a blur of candy-apple red. If she was going to do this, Grace thought, she needed to do it now. Maybe the only reason it had taken her this long was because she hadn't wanted to do it in front of Phoebe.

This was a conversation that needed to happen between Grace and her mother and no one else.

Taking a deep breath, she walked to the door. The hostess was busy seating someone else, so she stepped inside unnoticed and headed for the opening to the patio. The scent of melted butter and fresh-baked chocolate coming from the kitchen should have brought her comfort. Instead, it made her feel lightheaded.

She was only inside for a few moments, but by the time she stepped onto the patio, she was having trouble breathing. The waitstaff had turned on a half a dozen heat lamps to ward off the chill in the air, but they must have turned them up too high. She felt like someone had shoved her in an oven and closed the door.

Unwinding the scarf from around her neck, she stepped into her mother's range of sight. Their eyes met for the first time. Meredith froze. All the color drained from her face. The glass of Prosecco in her hand tipped and started to fall. At the last minute, she grabbed it. And set it back on the table. Her entire expression changed, though, as she drew her arm back—from one of shock to indifference. Her gray eyes grew cold and distant; her movements measured, more controlled. Her chin lifted slightly, and her shoulders straightened, as if she were steeling herself against the recognition.

Grace remembered Kelsey's warning from earlier that day—that something bad was going to happen if she left the island, that she'd be lured in by someone who was not as she seemed. The noises on the patio began to separate, each one more grating than the last. Glasses clinking together. Silverware scraping against porcelain plates. Every time a person laughed, it seemed like they were laughing right in her ear.

Her legs grew heavier. Her boots felt like they were stuck in a pool of icing that had hardened too fast. She kept moving, though, until she came to the edge of Meredith's table.

Meredith glanced up, completely calm now. "May I help you?"

Grace's mouth went dry. After all this time, after all these years, there was only one word she could manage to get out. "Why?"

"Excuse me?" Meredith asked.

"Why?" Grace repeated.

Meredith seemed puzzled. "Why...what?"

"Why did you leave us?"

"Leave you?" Meredith let out a laugh. "I don't even know who you are."

Grace's breath came out in a rush. They had the same eyes. The same face. They would have had the same hair if her mother hadn't changed hers. "I'm Grace Callahan. I'm your daughter." She waited for Meredith to react, to say something—anything. "I thought that you'd died...or that something terrible had happened to you."

Meredith looked at her like she was crazy. "I don't know what you're talking about. I only have one daughter. And she's just down the street." When her phone rang, she glanced at the screen, then back up at Grace. "I'm sorry. I need to take this." She reached for her phone to pick up the call. "You must have mistaken me for someone else."

# CHAPTER TWENTY-FIVE

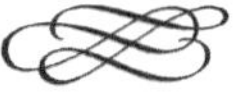

Ryan Callahan woke to the sound of his dog barking. Glancing at the clock on the bedside table, he saw that it was after midnight. The only reason Zoey ever barked like that was when someone was at the door. And if someone was at the door at this hour, it could only mean bad news.

Beside him, his girlfriend, Izzy Rivera, sat up. "What's going on?"

"I think someone's here." Ryan swung his legs over the side of the bed and pushed to his feet.

Izzy switched on the light.

Ryan pulled on a pair of jeans. If something had happened to his father...

He started to reach for his shirt, then paused at the sound of the deadbolt unlocking. The front door opened. Zoey stopped barking. He could hear his dog greeting whoever had just walked in, her toenails clicking and scraping against the wood floor as she wiggled her body in excitement.

Ryan exchanged a glance with Izzy. There was only one

person who had a key to this house and who would walk in without knocking first.

Ryan walked out of the bedroom. "Grace?" A few steps later, he turned the corner from the hallway to the living room and came face to face with his twin sister. "What are you—" He trailed off when he saw the expression on her face. "What's wrong?"

"I found her."

"I can't believe this," Ryan said, five minutes later when the two of them were seated at the kitchen table. Izzy was at the stove, boiling water for tea. Zoey was on the floor, lying on Grace's feet. Ryan was staring at the picture of their mother Grace had pulled up on her phone.

"It's her."

"I know it's her. I just can't believe it." Ryan looked up at his sister. "She looks so different."

"Different...and yet the same."

Ryan looked back at the picture. It was true. The differences were all superficial. She'd changed her hair and makeup, the way she dressed and carried herself. And she'd aged, of course. But she hadn't gotten any work done to alter her appearance structurally. There was no doubt it was her. "She acted like she had no idea who you were?"

Grace nodded.

"Is it possible she didn't recognize you?"

"No," Grace said. "I saw the shock on her face when she spotted me. Besides, I told her who I was. Even if she hadn't recognized me at first, she would have known who I was after I told her my name." She held out her hand for her phone. Ryan gave it to her. Instead of looking at the screen, she turned it over and set it face down on the table.

Ryan shook his head. "I did my doctorate research at Woods Hole. I lived in Massachusetts for six years. I went into Boston at least once a month during that time. I could have passed her on the street without even knowing it."

"You would have known it," Grace said. "You would have recognized her immediately. I did."

Ryan looked down at his hands. How would he have felt if that had happened—if he'd run into her on the street one day, and she'd pretended not to know who he was? Hearing about it was bad enough. Experiencing it firsthand would have been one of the worst moments of his life. Second only to the one he'd woken up to as a child to find that she'd vanished, and no one knew where she'd gone. "How was she able to just disappear?"

"I don't know," Grace said. "I haven't figured that out yet."

Izzy walked over and set a mug of hot tea in front of each of them. Grace lifted hers and took a sip. There were dark circles under her eyes. He could tell that she was exhausted and that she was struggling to keep it together. It was going to take more than a matter of hours for the weight of this to sink in.

They'd been searching for answers for twenty-three years, only to find that their mother had chosen to erase them from her life. If he'd had any idea that their search would end this way, he would never have told Grace what he'd seen in the cove that night. "Do you think it was a coincidence that she left the night I told her about what I'd seen?"

Grace wrapped her hands around the mug and gazed down at the steam. "No."

"No?"

She shook her head. When she looked up, her eyes were even sadder than they'd been before. "I think she used it."

"Used what?"

"I think she used the fairy tale as a way to escape. I think...she wanted us to believe that she was a selkie. That somehow it would make it easier for us, and her, if we believed that."

"That's so messed up," Izzy said.

"Yeah." Grace blew out a breath. "It is."

It wasn't just messed up, Ryan thought. It was cruel. For twenty-three years, he'd blamed himself. He'd been convinced that their mother had left because of him. Because of what he'd seen. And in a way, she had. But not in the way that he'd thought.

She hadn't left them to return to the sea.

She'd left them to start a new life. With a different husband. And different children. As if her first family had never existed.

It wasn't shock he felt anymore; it was anger. And when he looked back at Grace, he wondered why she wasn't angry, too. Sure, she'd had a few more hours to sit with this than he had, but he would have expected her to move from shock to anger as quickly as he had.

Unless...that sadness in her eyes was about something more than finding out that their mother had left them on purpose. Had something else happened while she'd been gone?

"Grace?"

She glanced up.

"How did you find her so fast?"

Grace looked back down. She said nothing for several moments. As she stared at the steam floating up from her mug, her expression grew distant, until it seemed like she wasn't with them anymore, like she was somewhere else entirely. When she finally spoke, even her words sounded like they were coming from somewhere far away. "It's a long story."

# CHAPTER TWENTY-SIX

When Grace woke up the next day, she found herself alone in her brother's house. She'd stayed up until 2AM the night before so she could tell Ryan and Izzy the story. Afterwards, she'd lain in bed for over an hour, staring at the ceiling, unable to sleep. It had been close to dawn when she'd finally closed her eyes.

Ryan and Izzy would have both left for work around that time. And Ryan would have taken Zoey with him. Walking into the kitchen, she glanced at the clock on the stove. It was almost noon. Somehow, she'd managed to sleep for seven hours.

She poured herself a cup of coffee and walked to the window overlooking the quiet, tree-lined street. Only a scattering of leaves had fallen since she'd left. She couldn't believe she was back already. Everything was the same, and yet, it felt different.

*She* felt different.

She had thought that finding her mother would bring her a sense of relief. She had thought that knowing the truth would be better than spending the rest of her life wondering what had happened. Even if the worst-case scenario had unfolded, which it had, she had expected to feel some sort of closure.

Instead, she felt empty inside, like something was still unresolved.

Last night, after she'd told Ryan the story, he'd asked her why she wasn't angry. And she hadn't known what to say. She *should* be angry. She'd lost her mother decades ago. She'd been living without her for most of her life. She'd had plenty of time to be sad. Now that she knew the truth, the only emotion she should be feeling was anger.

But she couldn't seem to get there.

What was wrong with her?

Pulling her phone from her pocket, she powered it on for the first time since leaving Boston. She'd turned it off as soon as she'd gotten to the airport the night before, not wanting to talk to anyone but her brother. She saw, now, that there were dozens of text messages waiting for her. The most recent ones were from Becca, Annie, and Will—her three best friends on the island. They'd heard she was back and wanted to know if she was okay. There were several messages from people at work. And there were three voicemails from a number with a country code she didn't recognize.

She clicked on the first one and held it up to her ear. As soon as she heard Aidan's voice, a rush of emotions swept through her. She hit the pause button, hard, and shoved the phone back in her pocket. Her heart was racing. She could hardly breathe.

Why was he calling her? She'd left. It was over. They were never going to see each other again.

She didn't *want* to see him again.

Right?

She took a few deep breaths, in and out, trying to get her bearings. How could his voice still affect her like that? How long was it going to take to get him out of her system?

She drained the rest of her coffee and set the mug down. This must be why something still felt unresolved. She still had feelings for Aidan. Even though she didn't want to. And those feelings were messing with the rest of her emotions, blocking her ability to tap into the anger she needed to deal with the truth about her mother.

She needed to find a way to turn those feelings off.

And she would...later. But first, there was something else she needed to do. She needed to talk to her father.

He would have heard that she was back by now. And he'd be wondering why. She couldn't put it off any longer. Turning away from the window, she grabbed the jacket she'd draped over the back of a chair the night before and walked out the front door.

It was a crisp autumn day. The sun was shining. A light wind was blowing in from the southeast. It was a perfect day to be out on the water, which was where her father would have been for the past several hours. He would be home now, though, taking his lunch break. As he did every day around this time.

He was on the porch when she got there, eating a sandwich he'd bought at the market and drinking a soda to fuel up for the next shift.

"Welcome back." Coop Callahan's tone was casual, but there were questions in his eyes as she climbed the steps.

"Thanks."

Coop took a sip of his soda. "I hope you didn't cut your trip short because of work."

Grace shook her head as she walked to the chair next to his and slowly lowered herself into it. "I found her, Dad."

He set his soda down. "That was fast."

She pulled up a picture on her phone and handed it to him.

He looked at the image for a long time, then nodded. "That's her, all right."

"She changed her name."

Coop handed the phone back. "I imagine she would have."

"She goes by Meredith Bradford now. She lives in Boston. She has a home there and another one on Nantucket. She..." Grace trailed off.

"What?"

Grace took a breath. "She's married."

"To?"

"A guy named Noah Bradford. He's a commercial real estate developer."

"Let me guess," Coop said. "He owns half the city?"

"Basically."

Coop shook his head.

"You don't seem surprised."

"I'm not," Coop said. "I always suspected that's why she left."

"You did?" Grace asked, relieved he was taking this so well.

Coop nodded. "She talked about wanting to leave the island a lot. And she dropped hints about wanting more than what we had. I ignored all of them. I couldn't imagine living anywhere else." He looked up and watched one of the first migrating flocks of Canada geese fly over the island. "Looking back now, maybe I should have tried. Maybe all our lives would have been easier if we'd left."

"No." Grace shook her head. "Don't say that. Don't even think it. You belong here. And so does Ryan." If there was one thing she'd learned from her trip to Seal Island, it was the importance of home. Home was its own kind of love. And maybe the greatest loves happened when the two intertwined.

She thought about Annie and Will, Colin and Becca, and Ryan and Izzy—how each of those couples had fallen in love on Heron Island, and how much a sense of place had factored into it. It had been more than just romance between them. It had been a shared life they'd wanted to build, a future they'd wanted to create on this island together.

From what she'd seen, it had been the same for Tara and Dominic, Caitlin and Liam, and Glenna and Sam on Seal Island. Their love for that place had fueled their love for each other. It was another reason why she and Aidan would never have worked. Their lives took them in too many different directions. And she had no interest in trying to tie someone down who didn't understand how important it was to belong to a place.

"I've been thinking a lot lately about how I might be able to move back here, too," Grace admitted.

"You want to move back?" Coop asked, surprised.

Grace nodded. "I haven't figured out how, yet. I still don't know if it's even a possibility."

"What do you mean?"

"I can't do my current job here."

"You could do something else," he suggested.

"Like what?"

"Like one of those podcasts or newsletter subscriptions some of the other journalists who are leaving big media companies are starting."

Grace stared at him. "How do you even know about those things?"

"From my crew." Coop lifted a shoulder. "Most of the veterans Ryan and I employ on the farm are closer to your age than mine. The two who work on the boat with me are in their late twenties. They talk about what they're reading and what they're listening to—the different places where they're getting their news. Seems like there're a lot more options for someone like you now."

Grace could hardly believe what she was hearing. For so long, her father had pushed her to make something of herself, to work hard, to keep her head down and stay in line. Anytime she'd complained about her job, or her editor, or having to cover politics, he'd said she should be grateful for what she had and how far she'd come. "You think I could go out on my own?"

"I think you could do anything you set your mind to." Coop picked up his sandwich and started to eat again. Like it was no big deal. Like it was perfectly normal for him to dole out praise.

Who was this person? What had happened to her father?

"I am curious, though..." Coop glanced back at her. "How many people are you planning to tell *our* story to?"

Grace let out a breath. "I don't know."

"What's holding you back?"

She looked down at her hands. "She has two stepchildren."

"Ah."

"Her husband was married before. Widowed."

Coop said nothing, waiting for her to go on.

"I saw one of them yesterday. The daughter." Grace thought back to the conversation she'd overheard in Boston. How trivial Phoebe's worries had been. And yet, she was a college student. Barely an adult. Maybe her worries should be trivial. "On the one hand, I can't stand the idea that she might be able to get away with this. And I feel like her new husband and stepchildren should know the truth about what kind of woman she is. On the other hand," Grace said. "I don't want to cause unnecessary pain to her stepchildren. They didn't do anything wrong. They don't deserve this. Maybe she's caused enough pain for one lifetime. Maybe it's time to end the cycle here."

Coop nodded slowly. "Not an easy decision to make."

"No," Grace said. "It's not." Keeping this story to herself would go against everything she believed in. But it wasn't just the two stepchildren she was worried about hurting. She didn't want to make her father have to relive this painful chapter of his past all over again either. Maybe the only way for any of them to find peace was to close the door on this chapter for once and for all.

"Whatever you decide, there's no rush." Coop picked up his soda and took a sip. "You don't have to make any decisions right now, about your mother or your job. You took a three-month leave of absence, right?"

"Well, yes, but..."

"Why don't you take some time off to think, to figure out what you want to do next?"

Time off? Since when did her father believe in taking time off? "You think I should take the next three months off?"

"I don't think it would kill you to give yourself a break." Coop crumpled his sandwich wrapper and tossed it in the bag. When he looked back at her, his eyes were filled with regret. "I've been talking to Ryan about things—things from the past. About the way I raised you both. I didn't always make the best decisions."

"What do you mean?"

"I pushed you too hard."

Grace opened her mouth, closed it. She couldn't argue with that.

"It was my own insecurities, my own fears, that drove the way I raised you. I was afraid that if you didn't leave this island and make something more of yourselves, you might one day experience the same thing that I'd experienced—the feeling of not being enough for someone. I realize, now, what a mistake that was. I don't want you to make the same mistake I did. I don't want you to let one person's rejection define your whole life."

Grace had never had a conversation like this with her father. She'd never seen him this vulnerable before.

"Is that why you've never brought a man home to meet me?" Coop asked. "I know you've dated. Your brother tells me things. But you've never gotten serious with anyone. Is it because of what happened between your mother and me? Is it because of how hard I pushed you? Did I make you think you weren't enough?"

Grace didn't know what to say.

"I don't want you to close yourself off just because I did all these years," Coop said. "I don't want you to think for one second that you're not worthy of the kind of love that your brother has found with Izzy."

Grace reached for her dad's hand. It was calloused and scarred from years of hard work, from pushing himself to the point of exhaustion every day so he didn't have to deal with the pain he'd felt in his personal life. "There's only one person who ever made me feel like I wasn't enough. And after seeing her yesterday, I think I'm finally ready to let that go."

Relief washed over her father's face.

"I'm only going to do it on one condition, though," she added.

Coop looked at her expectantly.

"That you do it, too."

He nodded slowly. "I'll try my best."

Releasing his hand, Grace sat back in her chair. It wasn't going to be easy for either of them. But she was willing to try if he was. And the first step, for her, would be taking his advice and not rushing back to work.

She didn't know if she'd be able to last for eleven weeks. It seemed like a long time to just think. But maybe she could ease into it.

Besides, she still had one last mystery to solve.

"Dad?"

"Hmm?"

Breathing in, she caught the faint scent of roses riding the breezes blowing in off the Chesapeake Bay. She had smelled them the moment she'd walked up to the house—the roses that bloomed every year on the anniversary of her mother's disappearance. Her mother had left in the spring. But the roses usually bloomed a second time, as most roses did, in the fall. Which meant they would be blooming now. "I know I've asked you this before, but...did you plant the roses that started growing the year after she left?"

Coop was quiet for a long time, before finally shaking his head. "No."

"Then, who did?"

# CHAPTER TWENTY-SEVEN

*H*er father had said he didn't know. But how could that be? Someone had to have planted them. They couldn't have just appeared. Every year. As if by magic. She stepped onto the pier at the end of the street. The wooden boards creaked beneath her feet. She passed a single workboat, tied to one of the pilings. She could hear the clang of a halyard against the mast of a neighbor's sailboat.

It had been easier to believe in magic on Seal Island. Magic had infused every inch of that place—from the stories the locals told, to the mists that rose out of the water and slid through the village like fish, to the ceaseless thrum of the ocean against the cliffs. By the time she had left, she had stopped believing. But for a few days, it had felt like almost anything had been possible.

She missed it, both the place and the feeling. And if she was honest with herself, she missed the man she'd met there, too.

She wondered if she would ever feel that way about anyone again. Or if the surrealness of the place had contributed in some way. Maybe the intensity of their connection had been distorted by the fact that they'd been surrounded by people who'd thought they were living in a fairy tale. Maybe it was unrealistic to expect to feel that way about someone in real life.

At the sound of footsteps behind her, she turned.

"I heard you were back," Della Dozier said, making her way to where Grace stood at the end of the pier.

"I'm back."

As soon as she closed the distance between them, Della put her arms around Grace and drew her in for a hug. "Izzy told me what happened."

Grace felt a lump form in her throat. Della had been more of a mother to her over the years than her own ever had. She wondered if she knew how much that had meant to her, how much it would always mean to her.

"Do you want to talk about it?" Della asked.

"Not really."

Della nodded and pulled back. "When and if you change your mind, I'm here."

"I know," Grace said. "Thank you."

They both turned to look out at the water. In the distance, a cluster of fishing boats bobbed on the surface, their painted hulls gleaming in the sun.

"I got you something in Ireland," Grace said, wanting to change the subject before her last shred of self-control snapped and she started to cry.

"You did?"

Grace nodded. "It should be here in a couple weeks. The person who sold it to me is shipping it here."

"You couldn't fit it in your suitcase?"

"No." Grace thought of the painting, the one of the sheep with her two lambs. She hoped Della would be able to see the same beautiful depiction of motherhood that she'd seen in it, that it hadn't been another distortion of reality influenced by the strange journey she'd gone on in search of her own mother.

"You didn't need to get me anything," Della said. "But I appreciate you thinking of me. And I'll look forward to seeing it, whatever it is, in a couple of weeks."

They fell quiet again. Beneath them, the water lapped against the pilings of the pier. On the opposite shore, a Great Blue Heron stood still as a statue on a bleached-out trunk of a fallen tree. All around them, the marsh grasses rustled.

"I have something for you, too, Grace." Della took a breath. "Something I probably should have given you a long time ago."

Grace looked at her questioningly.

Della reached into her bag and drew out a small packet, about half the size of a regular envelope. She handed it to Grace.

Grace took it from her. It weighed almost nothing. The paper was thin, the edges worn. There was at a faint sketch of something on the front and two words above it, but she couldn't make them out.

"They're seeds," Della said softly. "Your father called a little while ago. He said it was time I told you the truth."

Seeds?

Wait...

Grace's eyes widened. The faded sketch on the front of the packet was a flower. And it wasn't just any flower. It was a rose. "It was *you*?" Grace looked up at Della, stunned. "*You* planted them?"

Della nodded.

"Why?"

Della took another breath. "You were so sad back then, so lost. I just wanted you to have some beauty in your life."

"But..." Grace looked down at the packet again. "I tried to get rid of them. So many times. And they always grew back."

"That's because I replanted them."

Grace's mouth fell open. She'd replanted them? Every time? "Why?"

Della looked back out at the water. "A few weeks after your mother left, Joe and I drove to Cambridge to pick up a part for his boat. On our way home, I saw a sign for a nursery, and I asked him to stop. I knew your father wasn't going to be thinking about planting flowers anytime soon. I thought I'd get you some daisies or zinnias. Sprinkle some color around, make sure your house still felt like a home without her."

Della brushed a strand of gray hair out of her eyes. "When we walked into the first greenhouse, though, it was filled with roses. The owner had every color you could imagine. She asked us what we were looking for, and I told her why we'd come. She said the flowers I had in mind were in another greenhouse, and we started to head over there. But Joe couldn't stop staring at this one plant. And when I saw what he was looking at, I couldn't either."

A pair of diving ducks surfaced a few feet away, shook out their wings, then disappeared beneath the water again. "Neither of us had ever seen a lavender rose before. And there was only one plant that color in the entire greenhouse. The owner said that they were rare—that they were hard to come by and even harder to grow. That particular plant had already been sold to another customer, but the owner said she had some seeds if we wanted to give it a try. I asked her why lavender roses were so hard to grow, and she said she'd heard a lot of reasons over the years, but never anything scientific."

Della hesitated, as if she weren't sure if she should continue.

"Go on," Grace said.

"Well..." Della brushed a dusting of flour off the back of one of her hands. "Apparently, one of the reasons they're hard to grow is because of their meaning. Did you know that roses have different meanings depending on their color?"

Grace heard a faint rushing in her ears, the same way she had when she and Aidan had touched for the first time. After the ocean had thrown them together and scattered a dozen lavender rose petals onto the sand at their feet. "I think I might have heard that somewhere before."

"For most roses, it's just a sentiment," Della went on. "You might give red roses to a person you love, yellow to a friend, white to celebrate a new beginning. It's a way to express an emotion or to show someone how you feel about them."

"Right," Grace said slowly. "But…if lavender roses mean true love, then why would you give them to me?"

"Because, according to the woman at the nursery, they don't just mean true love. They actually have the power to help someone *find* their true love."

The rushing in Grace's ears grew louder.

"Apparently, lavender roses only grow for people who are destined to find their true love in this life. It has nothing to do with whether or not you have a green thumb. If they grow for you, it means that you'll cross paths with that person and that you'll recognize them when you meet them."

The pier seemed to sway suddenly. Grace placed a hand on one of the pilings to steady herself.

"I know." Della shook her head. "It sounds so silly when I say it out loud. But I think I knew, deep down, even then, that your mother wasn't coming back. And I wanted to do something to take away your pain. I thought, if I planted the roses, and they grew, I could tell you about them, about what they meant, and give you something to believe in again. I never meant to keep it a secret from you all these years." Della looked down at her hands. "After I bought the seeds, the owner said it would take about a year for them to bloom. When they bloomed the next year on the same exact day that your mother had left, it felt like a sign."

"Of what?"

"That maybe the two things were connected. That maybe losing your mother would somehow lead you to him. I didn't understand how at the time. But I wanted to believe it. I wanted to believe that something good could come from this loss. When you asked your father where the roses came from that first year, we decided not to tell you that I planted them. You were so young, only eleven at the time, but you seemed so much older. You were so serious. You didn't seem like a kid anymore. And we wanted you to feel like a kid again. We thought, maybe, if you could believe that the roses had just...appeared, you could believe in something again."

"What?" Grace asked. "Magic?"

Della nodded.

Grace looked down at the seed packet in her hand, and she remembered what Liam had said on their walk a few days before—that he wanted his children to believe in magic so they would have as much faith and hope in the future as possible. That those beliefs could carry them a long way in life, especially when times got tougher down the road. Was that all Della had been doing? Trying to restore her faith?

"I'm sorry," Della said softly. "It was a mistake. I realize that now. I guess there wasn't any magic in them. I thought...well, it's over now, but I thought this trip to Ireland might be good for you. I thought you might meet someone there. Someone who might distract you from what you went there to do. Because I had a feeling that finding your mother wasn't going to be your happy ending."

No, Grace thought, it hadn't been. But she *had* met someone in Ireland. Someone she might never have crossed paths with if she hadn't gone on that trip. She thought about the clue Ryan had given her, the first clue she'd gotten in over twenty years that had set everything in motion. She thought about the wind chime Taylor had given her before she'd left, and the child's dream about Grace needing to follow the petals to find her way home. She thought about how Kelsey had tried to stop her from leaving

Seal Island the day before, and what the teenager had said before Grace had boarded the ferry—that maybe the petals weren't leading her to a place.

That maybe they were leading her to a person.

What if the two things *were* connected?

Della gestured to the seed packet in Grace's hand. "That's the last of them. I went back to the nursery every year or so to get a new pack when you were still digging them up. But you stopped several years ago. There are only two left. You can decide what to do with them. Plant them, throw them away; it's up to you."

"I'm not going to throw them away." Grace tucked the envelope into her pocket. "And you have nothing to be sorry about. I wish you'd told me sooner, but I understand why you didn't."

"You do?"

Grace nodded. How could she fault Della for wanting her to find true love? For wanting her to believe in magic? For wanting her to be happy again?

She'd spent her whole life obsessing about the mother she'd lost, when there'd been someone right here, all along, who'd shown her more love than her own mother ever had.

Grace reached for her hand. "Thank you."

"For what?"

"For always being there for me."

Della squeezed her hand. "You know I'd do anything for you, right?"

Grace nodded.

"Both Joe and I would."

"I know." Grace fought to hold back the tears that had been threatening to fall since she'd arrived at Ryan's house the night before.

"I'm sure he'd love to see you. And so would Annie." Della checked her watch. "Will and Colin were at the café when I left.

And Becca should be getting off work soon. Why don't we walk back together? I'll fix us all something to eat."

"I'd like that." Grace let go of Della's hand. "But there's something I need to do first." She thought of the messages on her phone. "Can you give me about fifteen minutes?"

"Of course," Della said. "Take as much time as you need. I'm not going anywhere."

No, Grace thought. She wasn't. And it was such a comfort to know that. As she watched Della walk away, she thought of all the times Della had said those same words to her over the years. It seemed like such a simple thing to say, especially coming from someone who was as rooted to a place as Della. It would have been so easy to take those words for granted. But Grace never had. Because they were exactly what she'd needed to hear, a constant reassurance that no one was going to leave her the same way her mother had.

Della might not have taken her shopping for party dresses at trendy boutiques or bought her pairs of designer shoes, but she'd been there, time and time again, in all the ways that really mattered. And it wasn't just Della. So many people on this island had come together to fill the void after her mother had left. They had shown her endless amounts of kindness, consistency, and stability.

How many children who lost a parent were fortunate enough to live in a community like that?

What would her life have been like if she hadn't had all these people to count on? What would have happened to her if she'd lost *both* parents?

What if, like Aidan, she'd been all alone?

She turned to look out at the water again. A breeze rippled over the surface. Drops of reflected sunlight split and scattered, searching for a new place to land.

Would there have been a point in her life, after spending so many years feeling unwanted and unloved, that she would have accepted those feelings as true?

Hadn't she done something similar by walling herself off from every man who'd ever tried to get close to her? Maybe her father had been right. Maybe it wasn't just fear that had been holding her back. Maybe, deep down, she hadn't thought she'd deserved to be loved, so she'd sabotaged it every chance that she got.

If that was the case, how could she blame Aidan for doing the same thing with a family who'd tried to get close to him, when he hadn't even believed that he was related to them?

Pulling her phone from her pocket, she looked down at the screen. She wondered if he'd come clean to the O'Sullivans yet. Maybe he'd already left the island, like she had. He was probably on his way to Syria again or making his way to the front lines in Ukraine. Because those were the only types of places he felt like he belonged.

She unlocked the screen and opened the app that held the three voice messages. She was about to play the first one when she heard footsteps on the pier behind her. Figuring it was probably her brother or another friend coming to check on her, she glanced over her shoulder.

And almost dropped her phone in the water.

"Aidan?" Of all the places she'd expected him to be right now, this had been the last. "What are you doing here?"

Aidan continued to walk toward her, his cane tapping against the wooden planks with each step. "You left before I had a chance to apologize."

"Apologize?" Grace waited until he'd made it to the end of the pier. Until he'd stopped in front of her, and they were standing only a few feet apart. "For what?"

"For everything I said to you during our last conversation."

Somehow, even though her hands had started to shake, Grace

managed to slide her phone back into her pocket. Hadn't she just been thinking, moments ago, that *she* was the one who'd needed to apologize to him?

"You were right," he said quietly. "About everything."

Grace thought back to their last conversation, the one they'd had in the field at sunrise after Brigid had asked to see them both. Hadn't she spent most of that conversation trying to convince him that Brigid was his mother? And that she might actually be a selkie, too? "Wait." Her eyes widened. "*Everything?*"

Aidan nodded. "I saw it, Grace. I saw her pelt. It's real."

Grace stared at him, half-expecting him to burst out laughing at any moment and say that he was joking. But he wasn't joking. He was serious. "She's...?"

"A selkie."

Grace felt the pier begin to sway again. "And she's...?"

"My mother."

He'd said it, Grace realized. He'd actually said the words out loud. And he seemed at peace with it.

"She thought that leaving would solve all our problems," Aidan explained. "She thought that if she left, I could stay on the island and have a family—that she was the only thing preventing me from doing that. She knows, now, that she was wrong. We convinced her to stay."

Grace remembered how Brigid had seemed to be breaking down both mentally and physically only a day before, how she'd appeared to be transforming in front of their eyes. "Is she *able* to stay?"

"Yes."

Grace blew out a breath. So, she *had* had a choice. She'd had a choice all along. "And she's okay now?"

"She's fine," Aidan said. "But it was a close call. We almost lost her. And I almost lost the one chance I might have had at getting to know her."

Grace searched his face, still trying to understand what he was doing here. It seemed like a long way to come for an apology. "Shouldn't you be there, with her? Getting to know her?"

"Yes. And I'm planning to go back," Aidan said. "But only if you'll come with me."

Grace blinked. He wanted her to come back with him?

Aidan started to reach for her, then stopped, like he wasn't sure if he could anymore. "Did you listen to any of my messages?"

"No." Grace's heart began to pound. "I was just about to. Is that why you called? To ask me to come back to Seal Island?"

"I called to find out where you were. I wanted to be there for you after you talked to your mother."

He'd wanted to be there for her?

"I was in Boston yesterday," he said. "I knew that once you had a name, it wouldn't take long for you to find her. Glenna had a feeling it wasn't going to go well."

"It didn't," Grace said, too stunned by the fact that he'd been in Boston the day before to say anything else.

"When I didn't hear back from you, I figured you'd come here next. I remembered how you'd talked about this place, how you'd said it felt more like home to you than D.C." He looked around. "The pictures didn't do it justice. It's beautiful. I can see why you'd want to live here."

She *did* want to live here, Grace thought. Which only made his being here that much more confusing. Why had he come all this way to apologize, to be here for her, and to ask her to come back to Seal Island? He'd made it clear that work was his priority, that work would always be his priority. "Why do you want me to come back with you?"

"Because I want to get to know you," Aidan said simply. "I've never met anyone I wanted to get to know more."

She'd never met anyone she'd wanted to get to know more

either, Grace thought. But what was going to happen when his leg healed? When he was strong enough to return to work?

"You still have three months off, right?" Aidan asked. "I checked with Caitlin. She's holding your cottage through Christmas."

"Christmas?" Grace's brows shot up. "You want me to stay on Seal Island through Christmas?"

He nodded. "Unless you want to come back here before that. We could spend Christmas with your family instead."

*We?*

He wanted to spend Christmas together?

"But...what about your job?"

"What about it?"

"Aren't you going to have to go back to work at some point?"

"At some point, yes." Aidan shifted his weight from one foot to the other, leaning more heavily on his cane. "But I've been thinking about what you said yesterday. That my obsession with work has been a way for me to hold onto my past. I think you might be right. And I think it might be time for me to reassess what I'm doing—to consider if this is still the right path for me." He shifted his weight again. "I don't want to give it up entirely. There will always be stories, in those places, that need to be told. And there'll be times when I'll need to be the one to tell them. But I don't need to tell *all* of them."

No, Grace thought. He didn't. And she wouldn't want him to give it up entirely either. He was too good at what he did, and what he did was too important. Maybe all he needed—maybe all they *both* needed—was to find the right balance and to stop using work as an excuse to wall themselves off from anyone who tried to get close.

"I've been thinking about that veterans' center you mentioned, the one that your friends are running here," Aidan went on. "I've spent most of my life photographing wars. If they're open to it, I'd like to spend some time photographing what comes after. Maybe it could help me figure out what comes after for me."

Grace felt something begin to unfurl inside her. If he wanted to spend time at the veterans' center, that meant he wanted to spend time here, on Heron Island. With her. Could they do this? Could they find a way to make it work between these two places—these two islands filled with people they both loved?

"Come back to Seal Island with me, Grace. Let's get to know my family for a few months. Then we can come here, and I'll get to know yours."

Grace remembered that Aidan was a freelancer. He could work from anywhere. And so could she if she went out on her own. She thought about what her father had suggested earlier—that she take this time to think and explore her options. Maybe she didn't need to have all the answers right now. Maybe neither of them did. Maybe all they needed was to take the first step together and see where it led.

She thought back to the trails of rose petals that had led them to each other on Seal Island and the seeds that Della had given her earlier. She knew, now, that Della had planted the roses. But Della hadn't been able to make the flowers bloom every year on the anniversary of her mother's disappearance. And she hadn't been able to make the petals appear on Seal Island.

She didn't know why Taylor had dreamed about her being lost in the woods. She didn't know why Ryan had seen what he'd seen in the cove so many times over the years. And she didn't know why her search for her mother had led her to Seal Island at the exact same time that Aidan would be there.

Maybe she would never know. And maybe that was okay. Maybe she didn't have to have an answer for everything. Maybe that was the point. Wasn't that what magic and faith were all about? The acceptance of the mystery? The recognition that there were things in life that we couldn't explain?

Liam had told her to look for the signs. He'd said that magic was all around us, guiding us. We just had to open our eyes. Maybe there were times when our friends had to give us a nudge if we'd lost our way.

Maybe that was magic. Maybe that was faith. Maybe that was love.

Maybe the only thing that mattered was that we were open-minded. And willing to take a chance on whatever we found along the way.

"What do you say?" Aidan asked, holding out a hand.

Grace put her hand in his. "I say, yes."

## THE END

# A NOTE FROM THE AUTHOR

Dear Reader,

I hope you enjoyed *The Selkie Queen*. If you'd like to spend more time with Grace and learn more about her friends on Heron Island, I have another series of books you might be interested in.

Before writing *The Selkie Queen*, I wrote a series of books called the Wind Chime Novels. The Wind Chime Novels are set on the Chesapeake Bay in Maryland. Heron Island, the fictionalized setting of the series, is loosely based on a real-life island community near where I grew up.

If you haven't read these books, I'd recommend starting with the first book in the series, *Wind Chime Café*. I'd love to hear what you think!

Lastly, if you enjoyed *The Selkie Queen*, it would mean so much to me if you would consider leaving a brief review. Reviews are so important. They help a book stand out in the crowd, and they help other readers find authors like me.

Thank you so much for reading *The Selkie Queen*!

Sincerely,

Sophie Moss

# ACKNOWLEDGMENTS

Thank you to my neighbors for being the silver lining of the past two years. The process of writing a book can be so isolating, but it wasn't this time because of you. Thank you for constantly pulling me away from the computer to have fun, to laugh, and to build this amazing community together. I'm so grateful for every single one of you. Thank you to my editor, Martha Paley Francescato, for helping me bring this story to life. Thank you to my EnCompass colleagues for your friendship, for your encouragement, and for always giving me the space and freedom to pursue my creative career. Your faith in my writing means the world to me. Lastly, thank you, as always, to my mom and dad for your support. I'm so lucky to have you both in my life.

# ABOUT THE AUTHOR

Sophie Moss is a *USA Today* bestselling and multi-award winning author. She is known for her captivating Irish fantasy romances and heartwarming contemporary romances with realistic characters and unique island settings. As a former journalist, Sophie has been writing professionally for over fifteen years. She lives in Maryland, where she's working on her next novel. When she's not writing, she's testing out a new dessert recipe, exploring the Chesapeake Bay, or working in her garden. Sophie loves to hear from readers. Email her at sophiemossauthor@gmail.com.

# BOOKS BY SOPHIE MOSS

### *Wind Chime Novels*

Wind Chime Café

Wind Chime Wedding

Wind Chime Summer

### *Seal Island Novels*

The Selkie Spell

The Selkie Enchantress

The Selkie Sorceress

The Selkie Queen